Sydney Rewound

Kyle Hunter

ISBN 978-1-7330294-8-3

Author's Acknowledgements: My thanks to Bethany Adoption Services for their helpful information on adoptions in North Carolina.

More novels by Kyle Hunter that take you places

Circle Back Around

One December

Provence Series

Prodigals in Provence

A Promise in Provence

The Second Chance Series

Marissa Rewritten

Julia Redesigned

Sydney Rewound

Eden Redefined

Chapter One

Sydney Bennett glanced at her watch then scanned the living room. Where was her purse? Just now, when she had about two minutes to spare, she couldn't find it. She let out a sigh of frustration and jogged to the bedroom of her ranch style home, averting her eyes from the unmade bed and stack of clothes on the floor. She snatched the purse from the desk chair and dashed up the hall. "Jessie, time to go."

When she entered the kitchen, her seventeen-year-old daughter still sat at the table scrolling through her phone. "Jessie."

Her blonde daughter looked up at her with a bland expression, then rolled her eyes. "I know, Mom. Calm down."

"Your ride'll be here any second and I don't see your bookbag or anything ready. Did you brush your teeth?"

"Oh, *Mom*. I'm not ten." Jessie slid out of her chair and, with a sigh, disappeared to the back of the house. She returned with her backpack and a baseball cap, still eyeing her phone.

Sydney hoisted her own tote over her shoulder, flipping her shoulder-length straight hair out of the way, and stood near the door. Her daily background hum of tension had kicked in about thirty minutes earlier. She took a breath. "It would be nice to be ready in advance, wouldn't it? I'd like us to leave at the same time, or else you first, so I can lock up." She cocked her head at her daughter. "Make sense?"

Frowning, Jessie nodded, not meeting her mother's eyes. "I'm tired of school. I can't wait till summer."

Something inside Sydney softened. She reached out to touch Jessie's free arm. "Me too. Won't be long, though. Another month and we'll have the whole summer. We can go visit Gram at the beach. Think about that. Summer'll be here soon." Jessie responded with a shrug as she shifted her backpack higher on one shoulder. Sydney kept the perky note in her voice. "And don't forget, today's Friday."

Sydney suspected more was going on in her daughter's teenage world, but there was no time to draw it gently out of her. And lately, drawing anything but a sullen pout from her only child was rare.

Just then, a car horn sounded in front of the house. "Bye, Mom." Jessie pushed the screen door.

"Bye, have a good—" but Jessie was gone. Sydney sighed but had no time to enjoy the silence. She grabbed her keys from a hook by the door and set the alarm. Maybe they could do something special together that weekend. A buffet breakfast or a pedicure. Once Friday was done, she'd make a few suggestions to perk Jessie up, and herself at the same time.

Immediately, Sydney joined the Charlotte, North Carolina morning traffic on the way to the high school where she'd been teaching math for the last twelve years. Why did it feel like twenty? How soon till she could retire?

Sydney shook her head and let out a staccato laugh, though sadness trickled down through her chest. She was only forty-nine, so it would be a while. The career she'd enjoyed for the first fifteen of her eighteen total years had become a daily sentence harder each day to endure. Unlike some of her colleagues who planned to stay put in their jobs until age sixty-five, after which they'd receive the coveted teacher's pension for the rest of their days—she felt incapable of reaching that finish line. Could she even make it to this summer?

Sydney flipped on the radio and searched for something upbeat. Jazz or Christian rock.

One more month. She could do that, couldn't she? Never mind that the last week of that month would be an inhumane test of endurance, with conferences to prepare, a final exam to create and grade, semester grades to turn in . . . Just thinking about it made her want to turn at the next stoplight and plan a way to fake her own death.

Sure, there might be an easier way, but she'd have to find it later. She parked in the teacher's lot and sat still for a few minutes, watching her colleagues enter the building. Then she let out a sigh that was belly deep and opened the car door.

‫ಣ   ಣ   ಣ‬

Later that day, Sydney lifted her gaze to the wall clock and stifled a sigh of relief. Five more minutes to go in her last period, statistics class. She'd just handed back an exam with disappointing average grades. Collective groans still echoed around the room.

"Okay, gang," she called over the grumbling. "I'm as disappointed as you all are with the grades. As you know, this was your last test before the final, so take this seriously. See what you did wrong and make sure you do *better* on the final. It's your opportunity to turn it around, get it?" She scanned the restless seniors for any sign of confirmation. Half of the students looked like their minds were elsewhere, packing up their books, looking at the clock, pulling out phones to check for text messages.

The bell rang, and within seconds, the room emptied. Sydney turned back to her desk but noticed Rod Matheson hovering near the back of the room. Rod stood at least six feet tall. His broad shoulders and muscular arms attested to hours on the football field and in the weight room. He would have been a nice-looking kid if not for the perpetually arrogant sneer he wore like a mask. Why was he hanging around?

As she arranged her papers and books on her desk, he approached. "Ms. Bennett?"

She looked up. Instead of a sardonic grin, it surprised her to see a humbler expression. She could almost picture how he had looked as an innocent nine-year-old, before football stardom and the adulation of his peers convinced him he was a super-celebrity who owed nothing to anyone but deserved everything.

"Hey, Rod. What's going on?" She kept her tone friendly, though his grades were among the worst. And she couldn't help her undying disdain for him.

"Um, well, I wanted to ask, well, here on my test you marked this one wrong . . ." He held out the document and pointed to one of his equations.

Sydney circled the desk and took it from him. "Yes, you got that one wrong. Do you remember, we went over this last week?" She looked up at his face, seeing the furrow between his brows deepen as he likely realized his humble act was about to backfire. She returned her gaze to the paper. "This one, too. I know we went over it the day before the test. Remember?" Of course, he didn't. Sydney knew the answer. Rod had been goofing off all semester.

Rod dropped his shoulders. "Do you think—I mean, could you give me partial credit for these four? They were partly right, weren't they? That would bump my grade up a little bit."

Sydney stared at him. "You're kidding, right?" She shook her head and pointed to the equation. "I'm sorry, Rod. They *aren't* right. I can't mark them right. Even partially." She wanted to shake her head at his audacity.

"It's just that I'm still applying for colleges, and this'll mess up my average."

Anger frothed up in Sydney's chest, but she held her voice to a monotone. "I agree that your grades haven't been great this semester, Rod. I'm not sure if you didn't understand the concepts or if maybe you didn't work enough at home. I gave you a couple names of tutors, remember? I also offered to help you after class. Did you take any of those opportunities?"

He didn't answer, but she saw his jaw tighten and his nostrils flare.

She backed up a step. "I know being on the football team takes a lot of time." As do parties, doing shots and joints with friends, serial dating. "But your main job here is to study. Football is secondary."

She definitely wouldn't make headway with *that* argument, and she didn't expect to. Rod's jaw remained tight, and his eyes took on a murderous cast. Suddenly, Sydney became aware of his height over her and his muscular physique. And how close she stood to him. A slight wave of alarm grazed her mind, followed by a chill in her spine.

She kept her voice businesslike and moved another step back under the guise of reaching for something on her desk. "As I said at the end of class, you can make up points in the final. The final is worth more than this one. You have about three weeks before then. I'm sure you can bring your grade up."

Instead of the conciliatory nod she'd hoped to see, he said, "Earlier in the term and again a couple weeks ago you said if we had good averages on the tests, we could skip the final. Remember?"

"Yes, I remember. But that isn't your case, Rod."

He shifted his weight, his agitation visibly growing. "I won't be here for the final. I leave on a trip the day before. You said we could skip the final, so I made plans—"

"No, Rod. I said those who had a *good average* could skip the final. I even said the total average of all exams of the semester had to be at least ninety percent in order to skip the final. You weren't aware that you were well below that?"

When he didn't answer, Sydney threw up her hands. "I can't help you with this, Rod. I've already given you many chances to do better, but it's April. Oh, there *is* one more thing I can suggest." She'd be amazed if he took her suggestion, but she'd offer it, anyway. "I have an extra-credit assignment you could do. And it's a gift, believe me. I don't have to give extra credit, but under the circumstances." He didn't respond. Sydney turned to the desk. "Where did I put that description? Here it is, statistics in the business world research project. You may be interested in that. Didn't you tell me once you wanted to study business in college?"

He remained silent, but his expression had closed. She wished he'd just give up and leave her room. She desperately needed to begin her weekend. Maybe the local pool wouldn't be too crowded. A cool swim. That would be perfect.

She handed him the paper. "You can get a few extra points for this." He didn't take it, so she set it on the front edge of the desk. "Your best bet to raise your average is to change your trip dates and take the exam."

"I can't," he muttered so softly she almost didn't hear him. He said louder, "So, you can't change this grade? Just this once? How about I take the exam a week early?"

She stared at him. He avoided her gaze. "I've already done what I can to help you do better, but you know what? It's not my job to give you good grades so you can get into your chosen college. I do *my* job. It's *your* job to learn this stuff." She paused, knowing she was taking too much time with him. Wasting her breath. "You didn't put enough into it all semester, Rod, and now you're scrambling for favors because you realize the consequences. Face the weight of those consequences now and it'll improve the rest of your life, I promise."

A flash of what looked like utter confusion crossed his face. He grimaced. "Thanks for the lecture, Teach. You don't know anything about my life."

She crossed her arms and faced him. "No, I guess I don't. I don't know how you spend your time or how you're doing in your other classes. Maybe you think you can charm your way through high school because you're a big football star. It doesn't impress me. The numbers impress me because they prove you've made the effort to learn. Seeing if it even *matters* to you, that impresses me."

She should have said, "That'll be all, now go home." But something flickered inside, maybe a bit of sorrow over the kid's choices so far in his young life. "You have potential, Rod. Don't squander it. I mean, don't waste it."

"I know what squander means." He glowered and shot a glance toward the door.

"I assume so."

Her tone came out harder than she'd planned. As the words left her lips, Rod stepped toward her, appearing to grow larger as he did. With a guttural groan and a filthy expletive, he thrust her shoulders hard with both hands. She let out a cry and pushed back at him but hit air. She flailed her arms to catch herself. Sydney fell back against the whiteboard, bumping her head against it. She cried out when her lower back and waist hit the metal ridge which held dry erase pens. Rod stepped back, spun around, and left the room, still muttering obscenities.

Sydney dragged herself away from the whiteboard and stumbled into her chair, trembling all over. What had just happened? The lightning speed of her student's aggression was something she'd never seen in eighteen years of teaching. She'd never been afraid of any of her students, though many male seniors were much bigger than she was. She had to report it.

She winced with pain as she stood, locked up her room, and limped to the office of Wade Hannon, her principal. Pushing open the half-glass door, she saw only Pam, the secretary. The nearby offices were dark and empty. "Hey, Pam. Is Wade still here? I was just attacked by a student. I need to tell him."

Pam looked up abruptly, and her mouth dropped open. She stood and leaned forward over the counter. "Are you okay, Sydney? What happened?"

Sydney kept it brief but was glad to tell someone else, even if it wasn't Wade. "I need to tell Wade. I guess he's gone until Monday. I'll have to call him at home."

"Yes, that's the best thing to do. He'll definitely want to know about this."

"I want that kid out of my class. There's just a month left, but I don't know what else he would do." What would it be next time, a gun? A knife? Sydney shuddered.

"Wade had meetings off campus all afternoon, so he left the building a few hours ago. Give him a call, Sydney."

"I will. Thanks anyway, Pam. I'm going home, but I told you about this first. The student is Rod Matheson." She said his name slowly, clearly.

Pam's eyes widened. "Oh . . . the Mathesons won't want to hear this."

That was for sure. Sydney had forgotten the kid's parents were on the school board and prominent in the banking world as well as the community. "I don't care who his parents are, Rod isn't above the law. I may press charges."

Sydney fumed while she drove home. She touched the back of her head. A small knot had formed. Her lower back throbbed. No doubt she'd have a large bruise. She'd ask Jessie to take photos, proof of her claim. Knowing Rod's parents, they'd do everything in their power to get him off the hook, say he was worried and acted rashly, didn't mean it, or some other nonsense.

By dinnertime, Wade had not returned her phone calls. Three, to be exact, each one with mounting urgency in her tone. Where was he?

Finally, the phone rang. "Sydney, I'm sorry to be so late returning your call. I was in back-to-back meetings."

"Until six-thirty? Really, Wade? I'm just glad Rod didn't have a gun." Sydney couldn't keep frustration from coating her voice. Wade seemed unconcerned about her welfare. Was that social banter in the background, as if he were in a restaurant or bar?

"Now, Sydney, Rod isn't usually like that. I've known his family for years. He's a senior and they have a lot of pressure on them, especially now at the end of the year." His voice came out silky, unruffled.

"Are you kidding me?" Her tone became shrill. "Every kid is pressured at the end of the year. That doesn't make them physically assault their teacher. You're minimizing this, Wade, and I don't appreciate it. I was *attacked* in my *classroom* today. If you don't do something, I'm going to press charges."

"No, Sydney, don't do that. That's not the way to go. Besides, the Mathesons can to hire the best legal defense and you might go through all that for nothing." Wade cleared his throat. "I'm not saying I won't handle it. Of course, I will. I'm on your side. What Rod did is not appropriate at all. I want to make sure my teachers are safe. But don't be impulsive. We have a protocol to follow. Let me ask you, are you injured?"

Took him a while to ask. "Yes, but not badly. He pushed me, I fell against the whiteboard and hit my head. I also hit the metal railing on the bottom, so I have a bruise. But I do not want him in my class for the rest of the school year. I'm afraid of what he'll do next."

"I can try to get him transferred to Cheryl's class if you want. I'll do that on Monday, but I'll also have a conference with his parents. In the meantime, why don't you rest over the weekend? I know it's upsetting. It'll do you good to rest and recover."

After they hung up, Sydney had the lingering sense that her life dangled in mid-air, and no one cared enough to catch her. Abandoned to solve her own problems. That feeling was all too familiar.

The scene with Rod replayed in her mind multiple times. She flinched remembering the impact of the white board against her spine.

With a shiver, she crossed her arms and went to the kitchen window. And stared out at the back yard darkening under a setting sun.

Chapter Two

It had been a tense weekend. Without closure from Wade, Sydney had no choice but to endure the loose ends remaining from the incident. As she drove to school Monday morning, her stomach felt like a nest of snakes battling for supremacy. *Lord, please take this. Help me be strong.* Her quiet murmurs did little to dilute her dread of the day to come.

Maybe Wade had snapped back into reality over the weekend and realized that it was *not* okay for a teenager to assault his teacher, regardless of his end-year stress level. The weekend was over, and her boss would have to deal with the matter head-on. By the end of the day, she'd have more peace. She'd just have to get through the next few hours.

Before heading to her classroom, she stopped by Wade's office to intercept him before he got into meetings. Her spirits sank when she saw only darkness in his doorway. "Hey, Pam. Me again."

The dark-haired secretary smiled up at her. "Good morning, Sydney. Did you get through to Wade over the weekend?"

Sydney shrugged. "We talked, but he sort of put me off. I think he'll deal with it today, though. I asked him to move Rod from my class and he agreed to send him to Cheryl. I wouldn't wish Rod on anyone, but she'll only have him for a month."

She forced a slight smile, but Wade's absence increased the turmoil inside her. What if he didn't move Rod by last period? Would she have to face him? What would she do? He should be suspended, but that would be too much to hope for, right after a weekend. Wade had said he'd do it Monday. He had all day to do it, so she'd give him that time.

On her way back to her classroom, she zig-zagged through throngs of teenagers on their way to first period. Several times she imagined Rod towering over the other students, coming toward her with a hateful stare, the glint of a knife in his hand. When she finally spied her classroom, she picked up the pace and slid into safety.

Each class period of the day slogged into the next one. Felt like the longest day ever as Sydney dragged her thoughts back to her teaching tasks fifty times per hour. She checked back at the office at noon. Though Wade's office was lit, he wasn't inside. She wondered if she should call him but decided to let him do as he'd promised. When last period arrived, she was relieved that Rod's seat remained empty. Good, maybe he'd been suspended or already moved to another class. Finally, some support from Wade. Sydney's tension dropped a few degrees.

She was packing up after the last class when Wade appeared in her doorway. He wore a linen jacket, suitable for spring. He approached her desk, and she gave him a shaky smile. "Thanks for moving Rod. I appreciate it. I know it's not the end of the story, but it makes teaching a lot easier without him here." She pointed to the space to the right of her desk. "This is where I fell. Where you're standing now is where he was when he pushed me. I fell there, against that metal thing."

"Sydney, I haven't moved Rod from your class yet. He was absent today. But I did speak with his parents."

"Oh?" Should she be worried or relieved? Rod was still in her class, but his parents were aware of the situation.

"Apparently, he told them what happened, and his version varies significantly from yours." His gaze was impassive through round dark-rimmed glasses.

Sydney gaped, still gripping a textbook in one hand. "What did he say?" She could only guess. Perspiration broke out on the back of her neck. "Wade, I can prove he hurt me. I have photos of my bruises." She swallowed as her pulse began to race. "It doesn't surprise me that the little prince lied to his parents, and they gobbled up every word. That's why he thinks he can get away with everything because they let him!" She didn't care that her voice rang out through her class and probably out into the hallway.

Wade held up one hand during her tirade. "Sydney, please lower your voice. I'm just telling you what his parents told me."

"Not that you believe them. You believe *me*, right? Do you think I'm lying?"

"Of course not. But as the principal of this school, I have to listen to both sides. I've called a conference for all of us tomorrow afternoon."

"What? You mean I have to defend myself in front of them and *him*?" She stared at him. She shook her head. "I guess it's too much to expect my principal to stand up for me when I've been attacked."

Wade took her direct hit like a marble statue. "I intend to support you, like I always have. But I must hear both sides. I'd like you to be there to state your side of things to his parents. The meeting is tomorrow after school. I'll arrange for Rod's transfer to Cheryl's class prior, as disrupting as that will be to everyone at this time of year."

Sydney stared at him as something inside crumbled and fell. "Well, I'm *so* sorry to disrupt everyone's schedule." She turned away and finished packing her canvas bag. Through the edges of her vision, she saw him leave the room.

The following day crept by at an unbelievably slow rate. Finally, the last period ended, and it was time for Sydney's showdown. She was ready with all of Rod's grades for the semester, as well as her notes on every attempt she'd made to help him. As she walked to Wade's office, she felt like she was going to her sentencing. Dread filled her as she prepared herself to face her attacker. A string of pleading prayers circled through her mind. *Lord, help me to be strong, not emotional, or snarky. Help me to trust in your defense, not my own mouth.*

"Come in, Sydney." Wade ushered her into his office, his smooth politician voice doing little to reassure her as she walked into the lion's den. "Rod and his parents are already here."

His office looked cramped with five adults seated there. She entered and nodded at Rod's grim-faced parents. Rod sat in a chair beside them, eyes on the floor, knees splayed and back slouched.

"Thanks to everyone for coming," Wade said as he took his seat behind a massive wooden desk. "I hope we'll get to the bottom of this unfortunate situation quickly and go on with our lives."

Up to now, that appeared to be his goal, making it go away as fast as possible. But she'd give him the benefit of the doubt.

His gaze panned the room, and he offered a tight smile, which no one returned. "Why don't we start with you, Sydney. Tell us what happened last Friday."

Though she was the victim, her heart pounded as though she was in her first role on a theater stage. She moistened her lips. "Friday during last period, I handed back an exam. Rod hadn't done well. After class, he stayed behind, and he asked me to give him partial credit for four questions. I had to refuse because they were completely wrong. He told me that he was concerned about his average in view of college admissions. The problem is his average for the entire semester is low. I have here—" she fumbled with the papers on her lap, cursing herself for perspiring so much. "I can read you his grades for the exams during the term . . . seventy-one, eighty, sixty-nine." She lifted her eyes. "I won't go on. I have here a copy of his grades and a list of his absences for the whole semester. During the semester, I made numerous attempts to help him, giving the names of tutors and offering after-school help." She handed a copy of the test scores to Wade and another one to Rod's parents. Yes, she'd done her homework. She'd be great in a courtroom. She certainly felt like she was a defendant in one just then.

"What happened next?" Wade's psychologist voice coaxed her on.

"I told him he could pull up his grade if he really worked hard for the final exam. That's when he told me he wasn't taking the exam because he was leaving on a trip."

Rod's mother spoke up. "He told us you cancelled the final, so we made plans to go to the Virgin Islands." She was a pretty woman, appearing to be accustomed to nail and hair salons, tanning beds, and a lavish life.

"No, Mrs. Matheson." Sydney's voice was slow, calm. "I told the students that if they had a ninety percent average for *all* exams prior to the final, they didn't have to take it. I told them that from the start of the semester, in fact, to motivate them to do their best all along. I also stated it several times throughout the semester. Seeing his difficult situation, I offered him extra credit as a last resort for him. He refused."

"I didn't refuse."

"You didn't take the paper explaining the extra credit, which looked like a refusal to me. Instead, you went into a rage and attacked me."

This brought an outcry from all parties. "Sydney, just tell us in clear terms exactly what happened." Wade stared at her, and his expression hardened.

Sydney sighed. "I'm not sure what was said next—"

"You insulted me," snarled Rod.

"I did not insult you, Rod." She returned her voice to a calm, almost patronizing cadence. Her roiling emotions would be of no help in this context.

"Continue, please." Wade leaned forward on his desk.

"At some point in the conversation, Rod lunged forward and pushed me here—" Sydney pointed to her shoulders, "—and thrust me back while shouting obscenities at me." She shuffled the papers on her lap. "I have photos of my injuries."

"Then she pushed *me*. I fell, too." Rod's normally arrogant voice came out like a child's plea.

Sydney's head snapped up and she narrowed her eyes at him. "What? I did *not* push you. You pushed me, as you well know. You don't deny pushing me. My arms went out as I was falling. If I happened to touch you while I was trying not to break my head open, then it was purely accidental. And you did not fall. That is untrue." Her voice had risen. *Calm down, Sydney. This won't help your case at all.*

"What about the claim that she insulted our son?" Finally, Mr. Matheson spoke up, though his voice faltered. Could he be intimidated by his own son?

"What did I say to insult you, Rod?" Sydney stared directly at the boy. He continued staring at the floor, a surly frown molding the lower half of his face. "That your grades were low? Numbers, black and white facts, not insults. What else?" Finally, she had the upper hand. They'd listen to her now. Though Wade was saying surprisingly little.

"You said I was squandering, uh, something."

Sydney sat up straighter. "I believe you are. I said you have potential. Does that sound like an insult? No, it's a compliment. The shame of it is that you *squander* that potential by not doing enough in class." Not to mention resorting to violence.

When silence fell, Sydney's head riveted toward Wade. "Should I have changed his grade because he asked me to? Is that the way we do it around here? Someone's a football star and his parents are on the school board, so I should change his grades so that he can continue being a lazy, spoiled kid who gets no consequences for goofing off all semester?" She heard a gasp beside her from the high-maintenance Missus.

Sydney leveled a stare at Rod's parents. "Is that the kind of son you want to raise? Someone who skims by because his parents run interference for him? Keep going like that and he'll end up in a federal penitentiary." Oh, she was really losing it. Losing her calm, her resolve to let the Lord lead. Sydney's heart pounded in her chest, and she suppressed a primal urge to scream.

"That's enough, Sydney. I asked you to state facts, not opinions and emotions." Wade seemed bored with the whole thing and likely had a date for cocktails right afterward with the Mathesons.

"If I recall, Wade, we are here to discuss Rod's *aggression* against me on Friday afternoon. He asked me to change his grade. I refused. He pushed me against the white board, and I was injured." She held up a photo of the purple bruise on her lower back then returned it to her lap. "This is not acceptable, and everyone in this room knows it. Does anyone here want justice for what happened? Does everyone think this is *okay*?" She stared at Wade.

Before anyone could respond, Mr. Matheson jumped in again. "Then there's the matter of inappropriate comments to our son."

"Such as?" Sydney stared at Rod, her eyes wide, challenging him. The adrenaline had taken over. She was ready to continue this fight. If Wade wouldn't fight for her, she could dish it out. As she'd proven. One point for Sydney.

"Something about charm. Were you coming on to our son?" The man's soft voice held an accusing edge.

Sydney stilled. She stared at Rod's father, wanting to laugh. "You — you're kidding, right? You *have* to be kidding." This was too much. Really. She saw the man flinch. "He could be my *son*, though I'm thankful he is not. I told him he might charm his way through life, but his charm would not work on me. Do you call that coming on to someone?" She panned her stare from Mr. Matheson to his wife. "He seems to have quite a high opinion of himself to the point that he has the gall to ask a teacher to change a wrong grade so he can get into college." She stopped and looked around the room. "I ask you all again. Is it okay for a student to attack his teacher? Yes or no?" She stared around the room at stony faces, including Wade's.

She stood up and gathered her things. She placed the list of grades on Wade's desk but slipped photo into her purse. She waved it in the air as she added, "I'm considering pressing charges for assault. See how *that* looks on your college application."

"You don't have any proof," Rod said in a steely tone. "It's your word against mine."

She kept her face stoic, though his words caused a chill. He was right. She looked around the room. "I've had enough of this charade." She avoided Wade's eyes and made sure to slam the door on her way out.

Once in her car, Sydney held it together until she was a mile away from the school. Then tears of rage and betrayal flooded down her face. It was so unjust. She'd been attacked, and no one cared. No one had stood up for her, not the very person who should have. As usual.

And, no, she hadn't held in her emotion, her self-control. She'd let herself go like a tight rubber band. She hadn't let the Lord fight for her. She'd fought with her famous acid tongue, her defense. The one she both loved and hated.

She spoke the truth, but badly. And if Wade wasn't solidly on her side before, he sure wouldn't be now.

Chapter Three

Sydney stood after supper and cleared the table, a leaden weight pushing down inside her. She went through the motions from the table to the sink, mechanically, like she did every day, every month. Yet her insides splintered like a fragile vase. "Do you have much homework tonight?" she asked Jessie over her shoulder, pushing out a normal voice as she opened the dishwasher.

"I did a bunch of it in study hall. I'll go finish it now." Jessie pushed in the dining room chair but remained beside the table. "Mom?"

Sydney turned to her. "Hmm?" Jessie's smooth face appeared worried.

"You never said what happened today at school. You're kind of quiet. What happened with that kid who pushed you?"

Sydney sighed. "We had a conference today, and it didn't go so well. I would have told you, but I wasn't ready to talk yet. It's still heavy on my mind." She gave Jessie a lame smile.

To her surprise, Jessie closed the space between them and wrapped her arms around Sydney's waist. The gesture brought a sting to Sydney's eyes. She pulled Jessie in and rested her head on her daughter's blond waves. "Thanks, Baby. You're so sweet. I really needed that."

"I could tell." Jessie's voice muffled against Sydney's tee-shirt.

They pulled apart, and Jesse's expression was compassionate, so rare these days of adolescent angst. Sydney said, "I'm still waiting for a response from Wade, my principal. We, uh, didn't have any closure after the meeting, so I guess he'll call tonight." She sure hoped so. He'd been so dispassionate about the whole thing, as if his greatest desire was to see it magically evaporate.

"Keep me posted, Mom. Gotta finish my homework."

Jessie left the room. After her hug, Sydney felt like she'd received a blood transfusion and could go through the next few miles of her ordeal. The current status was official limbo following the debacle of the afternoon meeting. What should be her next step if things didn't go in the right direction? She could only wait for a volley from Wade. It was his serve.

She didn't have long to wait. As she finished sponging off the counters and turned out the kitchen light, her phone rang. "Hello, Wade." She flicked the light back on and returned to the kitchen table. Her voice sounded dull to her ears as she spoke. She wasn't sure what bothered her more, the injustice of it all, or her own loss of self-control during the meeting that day.

"Hi, Sydney. I want to talk about the next step for our, uh, situation."

Though she'd never been chummy with Wade, they'd always had mutual respect. His voice sounded drier, more distant than usual. Dread mounted inside her. "I want to say something, Wade. Even though I didn't feel supported today, I want to apologize for losing my cool. I didn't plan or want to come off that way. It just seemed like no one was seeing my side and we kept talking around the issue. But I shouldn't have gotten so upset."

"I understand how frustrating this must be. It's a difficult situation."

Sydney swallowed. "It's an *unpleasant* situation, but it shouldn't be a difficult one. Rod should be suspended, then removed from my class. That would provide more safety for me. There should be some consequence for him, don't you think?" Thankfully, her voice was calm, even. Her strength was depleted. Pessimism about any satisfying outcome hovered over her head.

"As there will be. But first things first. I, uh, I'm not going to suspend Rod."

"What? What will you do, then? Invite him over for cookies?" *Stop, Sydney.* She sighed. "Okay, tell me why and what you want to do. I'm listening."

"The problem is the time of year. We have less than a month until school is out. Suppose we suspend him for a week then move him to Cheryl's class—it would be a mess for all parties. I spoke to Cheryl, by the way, and she doesn't want to take on a new student a month before the end of school, and I totally understand. She has a large class already, she has her system, her exam—Rod would be more behind than he already is."

"Poor baby." Sydney bit her lip.

"If it were January, then we could do something like that. But not in April. So, I'm going to give you a couple of options and I want you to think about them. You can continue the year to the end with Rod in your class just like before, or we'll give you a leave of absence for the remainder of the school year, paid, of course, and get a sub for your classes."

Sydney drew in a breath. "So, Rod attacks me and *I'm* the one who gets suspended. Why don't you go the full route and give him straight As for the year? All subjects. Everyone would be happy."

A quiet groan emerged from his throat. "By removing you from your class, I'm protecting you from further possible harm from this student. I'm going to recommend to his parents that they get anger management counseling for him over the summer. By the time you return to school in the fall, he'll be gone. Fresh chapter. In the meantime, you get an extra month of summer vacation—fully paid." He paused. "Think on it and call me back when you decide, but if you can call sometime this evening, I'd appreciate it."

"Okay, I'll give it some thought and call you back. Soon." The fight had drained out of her, but in its place grew relief. She knew from experience that having time to think *before* making a decision was crucial in avoiding a huge mess.

When she hung up, she sank into an armchair in the living room, still seething, but at a lower intensity. It wasn't fair. She'd been assaulted and was being given leave, as though she were the guilty one. What should she do? If she returned to her classroom, would she be mocked or, worse, attacked again by Rod? If she didn't go back, would it appear she was admitting she was wrong? Accepting the blame?

Her pride was injured, for starters. In front of her aggressor and his parents, her principal hadn't stood up for her. But Wade was giving her protection in the form of paid leave from a job she was starting to dislike.

Her breathing slowed, as did her heartbeat. Wade's idea could provide a silver lining—her safety and more time off. She regretted not being able to say goodbye to her other students, though. They were the eager learners who'd made her job tolerable for the last few years. Of course, she'd still have to turn in her grades and prepare her final, but that was mostly finished. Then she'd be free all summer, a month early. It was at least seventy percent better than finishing the year with Rod in her class. She knew a deal when she saw one.

What would her colleagues and students think of her vanishing from her job a month before the end of school? Would they think she'd had a breakdown or been suspended for misconduct? How would she ever explain what had happened?

Sydney shook her head. That would be the wrong reason to stay in a potentially dangerous situation. She picked up the phone and called Wade.

"That didn't take long," he said.

"Well, I realized that you had a good idea. Staying out of school is the best way for me to assure my safety while leaving Rod in the same class to finish out his senior year. When would this start?"

"How about tomorrow? I realize that's short notice, but if we waited, you'd have to face Rod in your class for a day or two. I can get you a sub for tomorrow. Might take me a few days to get a long-term sub, but we'll start with this."

"What will you tell people about my sudden disappearance?"

"I could say it was personal leave. Would that be okay?"

"I guess so. Otherwise, it would be complex to explain." And traumatic. She couldn't see herself recounting over and over to her colleagues what had happened to her.

There was no denying she'd been thrown under the bus. But from another perspective, she was being given a gift.

The next morning, Sydney awoke as milky gray light seeped into the darkened bedroom. Lingering in her mind was the heavy residue of a dream. Rod Matheson had pushed her over a cliff. When she reached the bottom, it had awakened her, and she'd lain awake for at least an hour, perspiring in the darkness.

She turned her head to glance at the clock. Six-fifteen. It took several seconds for the previous day's events to thunder back into her mind. Still unreal. She heard water running in the bathroom down the hall as Jessie prepared for school.

And as Sydney didn't.

Normally, she'd have gotten up a half-hour earlier to start her mad daily race and join the morning traffic jam. Shower, get dressed, make coffee and breakfast, herd Jessie so she'd be on time—none of that was happening today. Or tomorrow. Or for the next four months. She blew out a breath. After twelve years, this would take getting used to.

Of course, she'd had her summers off every year, so it wasn't totally foreign to have an open weekday. The circumstances still bothered her, but she'd make the best of it.

Sydney showered and threw on a pair of capris and a tee shirt. She went to the kitchen to start the coffee and plan her day. Jessie, already seated at the kitchen table, looked up. "This is weird, Mom. You're not rushing around in a panic verbally pushing me out the door."

Sydney grinned. "Have no fear. I can still verbally push you out the door. I just don't have to push *myself* out this time." She wasn't yet sure how she felt about that. For the moment, it felt pretty good. She poured filtered water into the coffee machine and reached into the cupboard for the can of coffee.

"No fair. You get to stay home an extra month."

"I think I'll be glad, but it still seems like *I'm* the one who's being punished, not him." Rod would go to last period class that day, see a substitute teacher, and think he'd won. Conquered the evil math teacher. His ego would blow up even bigger than it already was.

Jessie tilted her cereal bowl up and slurped out the dregs. "It'll come back around to him. Isn't that what you always told me? Mean people always get it back in some way or another?"

Sydney raised her eyebrows and couldn't suppress a laugh. "You were listening all that time?" She put a hand to her chest. "I'm overcome with gratitude. My wisdom has been sinking in."

"Don't get carried away, Mom. I just think you could use your own advice sometimes."

Sydney shook her head and chuckled. She was blessed to have Jessie, who was smart and mature, well, maturing, although she often had a mouth on her. Just like her mother. Yes, she'd taught Jessie many things over almost a decade of single parenting. Both good and not so much. That reminded her. "Hey, Jessie, isn't this the weekend you go to your dad's?"

Her daughter nodded, though she was now mesmerized by her phone.

Great. So, Sydney would have her week alone, followed by a lonely weekend. "If you put your phone away while you're getting ready, you'll never again struggle to be ready when your ride comes."

Jessie sighed. "More wisdom from Mom." She stood up and took her bowl to the sink. "By the way, I *am* ready." A dash to the living room to grab her book bag coincided with the honk from the car waiting on the curb. "Bye, Mom. Enjoy your day off!"

After Jessie vanished through the front door, Sydney poured her coffee and sat at the kitchen table, cradling her steaming mug in both hands. A comforting stream of warmth poured in from the bay window on the back of the ranch house she and Cody had bought when they were first married. She barely remembered those days.

The cornflower blue sky invited her. To what, she wasn't sure. She could go for a run or do a yoga routine, activities she normally had to squeeze into a crevice of free time. Despite the quiet of the house and the absence of usual pressures, the aloneness and lack of purpose weighed on her.

Her first day of detention.

Today seemed different from the first day of summer break, which was always met with euphoria. For one thing, in summer she wasn't alone. Although Jessie had started working part-time the previous summer to save up for a car, she'd been in and out throughout the school break. Often in summer, they'd have a beach trip or two planned. Sydney would get off the school year treadmill. Catch up on house projects, lounge at the local pool, reconnect with girlfriends . . .

Girlfriends! She must be under tremendous stress to have forgotten the highlight of her year. Gratitude and anticipation flowed through her body. She had a group of close girlfriends scattered around the eastern half of the country, and she'd see them soon. None of them knew about her ordeal and that fact caused a twinge. So accustomed to handling things on her own, it didn't often occur to her to reach out to vent or ask for advice. She'd tell them during their weekend, though. They'd be a perfect sounding board and sure to have wise feedback for her.

Marissa, Julia, and Eden. She and her college friends had been inseparable back then, twenty-five years earlier. But as post-college life, marriage, and family took over, they'd gone separate ways but stayed loosely in touch through the occasional phone call and annual Christmas cards. Over two decades later, they all found themselves single, through divorce or widowhood, and most were empty nesters as well. Two years earlier, Eden had reached out to all of them with an idea. They could meet twice annually for weekends to renew the closeness they'd had in college and support each other in their new life situations. All four of the women had embraced her idea enthusiastically. Those weekends became highlights of the year for Sydney, and she knew her friends would say the same.

Their next gathering would be early next month. Sydney stood and trotted to the wall calendar near the fridge. In *two weeks*. Wonderful, so soon. For their weekends, they rotated homes or met at a beach or in a city between them. This time, it was her turn to host, so she had some catching up to do around the house. Good thing she had the time off. Okay, this forced vacation might end up being tolerable and possibly good. She had something to focus on.

Her friends were coming. Her home would be perfectly ready by then.

Sydney's gaze scoped the kitchen and into the living room. She'd start there. There was work to do, alright.

That afternoon she'd also swing by the high school at the end of the school day and clear out her desk. She'd say goodbye to the school for a few months. The sooner she turned the page on this nightmare, the better.

Several hours later, Sydney collapsed in a comfy armchair in the living room. Now, the room was tidy, looking like it rarely did these days. She'd run the vacuum and dusted, done a load of laundry, and cleaned the kitchen. Her efforts did a mediocre job of chasing away her blues.

She glanced at the vintage clock on the mantle and gasped. Two-thirty. She wanted to arrive at the high school after it was well emptied out, but not too late to get her things and sneak away. No one would see her. They'd just know that she'd had an unfortunate event—no one knew the details—and had to take the rest of the school year off. Word might get around that she'd been attacked. As much as she'd like to be vindicated, she wouldn't necessarily welcome a stream of phone calls from colleagues checking on her well-being.

Sydney dressed in an outfit she'd normally wear to teach in just in case she passed anyone in the hall on the way to or from her car. Nothing would look out of place. She slipped on a pair of sandals and rummaged in the closet, looking for a big canvas bag she stashed for beach trips. There it was, wedged in the back of the closet. It would draw less suspicion than a cardboard box filled with her personal belongings from her classroom, which would likely spell "fired" to anyone who saw her.

Thirty minutes later, she arrived at the high school, dread like metal weighing in her stomach. There were a few cars in the faculty parking lot, but the main lot was mostly empty. Shouldn't take long to do the deed. Impatience to have it finished knocked at her nerves. She braced herself, grabbed her canvas bag, and walked into the building.

She strode with purpose, trying to ignore how ridiculous a large canvas beach bag looked hanging over her shoulder. She passed one or two students she didn't know and finally spied her classroom. She turned on the lights and went to her desk, her heart pounding, hoping not to answer questions or even speak with anyone.

Sydney opened the drawers one by one and pulled out several of her own gadgets and keepsakes—favorite pens, various math tools, her letter-opener. From the desk, she grabbed framed pictures with humorous sayings, a paperweight, an English ivy vine tumbling from a handmade ceramic vase. A photo of herself with Jessie at the beach a couple of years ago.

She sighed, pushing down a thick layer of nostalgia. Her eyes rose to the wall where she'd tacked a couple of posters with quotes or math charts. Below them sat a small shelf filled with textbooks. Her books would weigh down in the bag, on top of everything else. There weren't many that were her own, just three large, heavy ones.

"Are you packing up already, Miss Bennett?" A young voice came from the doorway. Sydney looked up, sure that guilt must be written on her face in bright red.

Tessa, a ninth grader from fourth period Algebra I class, stood with a quizzical expression on her face. She must be surprised to see Sydney, since there had been a substitute teacher that day. *Think fast, Sydney.*

"Hello, Tessa. Unfortunately, I've got a, um, family emergency and won't be able to stay to the end of the school year. It was sudden, and I didn't have time to say goodbye to everyone." It was her personal emergency. A very broad definition of family.

Tessa's face clouded, making her look younger than she was. "I'm so sorry. I hope everything will be okay with your family."

Sydney smiled at her as a needle of guilt for her misleading explanation stabbed at her. At least she could say goodbye to one student. "Thank you, Tessa. I hope so, too. Have a good summer. I'll probably see you in the fall."

Tessa's face brightened. "I really liked your Algebra class, Miss Bennett. I never thought I'd understand it, but you have a good way of explaining things. I really want to take geometry with you next year. I've heard it's even harder, so I have to take it from you. If I have a choice, which I may not."

Gratitude for Tessa's words swelled inside Sydney's chest. How she needed those words. She *was* a good teacher. Her flagging self-esteem rallied just a bit. "It would be nice to have you in class again next year, Tessa. I'm glad you understood and followed everything. Algebra can be tricky."

Tessa nodded and gave Sydney an angelic smile with round, rosy cheeks. "You have a good summer too, Miss Bennett."

"Thank you." Sydney sat still for a moment after Tessa left the room. Faces of her favorite students rose to her mind's eye, Angel from fourth period, Sandra from calculus, the twins, Sean and Seamus from trig. She'd miss them. And she couldn't even say goodbye. But what would she tell them? Some lame version of what she'd told Tessa.

She glanced at the clock. Too much dilly dallying. Time to get out of there.

Sydney turned out the lights and locked her door. She'd stop by the office and leave the key with Pam, saying goodbye at the same time. The canvas tote bit into her shoulder. She should drop it at the car first, but it was out of the way from the office. It wouldn't take a minute to pop by the office.

She passed one colleague she didn't know well and returned her greeting, ignoring her quizzical look at the bag. She arrived at the office and pushed open the wooden door for the last time until the fall. "Pam, I'm glad you're here." She fished her room key from her pocket and put it on Pam's counter.

The receptionist stood. Alarm showed on her face. "Oh, Sydney. There you are. You're leaving? What happened?"

Sydney frowned and shifted her canvas bag. "I'll be brief. Wade offered me the option of staying in my class under the same circumstances, no punishment at all for Rod, or taking a leave of absence for the remainder of the year. Paid. So, I chose the latter since it would ensure my safety from that punk."

"And give you a longer summer. Good deal. I'm glad it worked in your favor." She smiled behind metal-rimmed glasses.

Sydney shrugged. Good deal? She wasn't convinced, but she would *make* it a good deal. "Have a good summer, Pam. See you in the fall."

"You have a wonderful summer and put all this behind you, okay Sydney?"

"Yes, absolutely."

Then began the walk of shame back to her car. She was unsteady under the uneven weight of the bag on one shoulder. Should have brought two. But it was over. That part, anyway.

She almost made it back to the car when she passed another math teacher, Bernie, in the parking lot as he headed to his car. "Hey, what's up, Sydney? Looks like you're leaving town for good." His white tooth smile gleamed through his reddish close-cut beard.

Sydney gave him a summary similar to the one she'd given Tessa. "Have a good summer, Bernie." She smiled then hightailed it away from the high school. As she drove, new tears thrust from her eyes and rolled down her cheeks in a warm stream. She didn't love her job anymore, but the abruptness, the finality, the circumstances that had fallen on her so fast—evoked a hollowness akin to grief.

Was this the end for good, or just for now? Was God prodding her away from her job for some reason only he knew? As she gained distance from the building, her mind groped for the bright side. She'd feel renewed by fall, wouldn't she? Would she be able to put this violent episode behind her?

Not easily.

Chapter Four

By the end of the first week of Sydney's early summer vacation, she'd cleaned the entire house, including windows, swept and hosed off the front and back porches, and rearranged the cupboards in her kitchen. All the tasks she'd been putting off for months. Her spirits lifted somewhat as she channeled her thoughts toward her upcoming gathering of girlfriends. She made a tentative menu and a list of options for activities they could enjoy over the weekend. Charlotte was a large, vibrant city with plenty they could do and see, and the May weather wasn't too hot yet. Mostly, she longed to be in the presence of women who cared about her.

She sat at the kitchen table to compose a group email to them. Their replies would give her patience to wait two more weeks until they arrived. *Hello, my wonderful ladies! The six months since we last saw each other have gone by too slowly. But we'll be together in only 2 weeks! I'm so excited to see you all. My life has had some curve balls lately, but I'll fill you in soon. Please tell me if you have requests for activities or food. Eden and Julia, send me your flight info and of course I'll pick you up at the airport. Love and hugs, Sydney.*

Normally, she'd throw in a few humorous or snarky one-liners, but just then she didn't have it in her. That place was still dry and bewildered.

Sydney's local friendships were mostly the activity-oriented kind. Women's Bible study, hiking or weekend trips with the church single-again group, dinners out. She enjoyed being with everyone, but she didn't share her pain or joy with them. She hardly saw them outside of activities or at church. With her college friends, it was easier to let her hair down, because each one of them did the same. But even with them, she sometimes found it hard to be transparent.

Her daily life working full time and raising a teenager left only a small slice of time for socializing. But her friends, the *girls*, as she thought of them, had known her for decades, even though they'd faded for a while from each other's lives. They were all busy with their homes, careers, relationships, but two weekends a year they dropped everything and focused on one another and having fun together. True, it was short term and intense. It didn't really touch the daily ups and downs that Sydney faced alone. Yet, those two weekend doses of concentrated caring, laughter, and presence helped make up for what Sydney lacked in her normal life. Or at least they helped her to forget what she didn't have.

A text came in on her phone. A fast response from one of her friends. She looked down and it was from Jessie. *Dad said he could pick me up from school, so I guess I'll see you on Sunday night. I have everything I need over at his house, so no worries. Hope you have a great weekend!*

Sydney sighed. She had looked forward to seeing Jessie that afternoon, giving her a long hug, probably admonishing her to be careful, to have a fun weekend. She'd been alone all day and, unless she planned something, would continue that way all weekend.

After a simple lunch, Sydney decided to tackle the attic. The attic, really? She must be truly desperate for useful action. It was the easiest thing in her house to ignore for decades at a time. She could easily do it for another decade, but she'd already cleaned everything else. And it *had* been on her list for about two years.

She went to the darkened hallway and pulled on the ring dangling at the end of a rope. A folded staircase dropped down. She unfolded the wooden rungs and climbed up into the shadowy space, whose only light was a vent on one end. She pulled a small chain and light spread out from a bare bulb overhead.

The first task was easy, pushing things into clumps according to categories—Christmas decorations, suitcases, old sports equipment. Next, she identified things that should have been discarded long ago and tossed them unceremoniously down the folding staircase where they thudded on the floor below. Empty boxes she'd saved "just in case", almost-new snow boots she'd used once in the last six years, a raggedy vine wreath she'd rescued from someone's trash, sure she could give it a facelift. One day.

A medium-sized cardboard box sat tucked in the corner, but Sydney couldn't remember what was inside. On her knees she crawled across the wooden planks and snagged it, but it was heavier than it looked. With both hands, she pulled it back under the light, staying crouched so as not to bump her head on the pitched ceiling with its protruding nails. Pulling the flaps of the box outward, she viewed its contents and groaned. Photos. Old ones.

She stared at the box for a moment as if it were a dead rodent. Then a force she couldn't explain led her to reach out to the small album on the top and flip open the cover. Grinning up at her from a crinkled yellow photo were her two brothers, Chet and Kevin. They must have been twelve and fourteen at the time the photo was taken. At ten, she'd have been hiding out in a book somewhere, lost in the story, but also avoiding having her photo taken. And avoiding being with her brothers.

Even as a child, they'd never been close. Unlike her ideal of an older brother, hers were never protective or affectionate. A memory flashed into her mind of a neighbor teasing her for some reason she could no longer remember. Instead of defending her, Chet and Kevin joined in the ridicule. When she'd started to cry, she heard, "Aw, Syd, don't be such a baby!" She'd run home to her room refused to come down for dinner. Her mother had admonished her. "Don't be so sensitive, Sydney. They were just kidding." She was a baby. Oversensitive. No one stood by her, not her brothers, not her parents. She'd understood then that she was alone to defend herself, to look after herself. It became a life theme. Kind of like now, in her situation with Wade.

Sydney swallowed the lump that had developed in her throat. As adults, the occasional phone calls or holiday visits with her brothers kept a loose thread dangling between them, giving the surface impression of loving sibling ties. They all likely knew it was only for show.

Over time, Sydney's childhood timidity crumbled. As a preteen, her confidence emerged on tiny, tentative feet, then grew deeper when she discovered music. But she was never able to confront her brothers in any area.

Her dad had played guitar in a hobby band. At least, that's what they'd always called it, so no one would think that was his actual profession. Their group was good, she had to admit. A mental picture of five men practicing guitars, a banjo, and a drum in the family dining room flashed into her mind like a movie reel. They'd play a song, then joke and laugh, like the best of friends. She knew Dad had enjoyed those sessions even more than the sets they played at local clubs and bars.

While they practiced, Sydney would perch on one of the dining room chairs, enthralled, thinking her Daddy was a superstar. Music gave him a creative hobby away from his busy law practice in Wilmington. Mom went along with it, saying he needed the outlet.

He was the only family member she'd felt close to. She was "his girl", he used to say, second after her mom. He encouraged her to try the guitar and she ended up catching on quickly. She'd hear the pride in his voice as he said, "You've got talent, my girl. You can work hard at this thing and go to Nashville someday."

"I will, Daddy. Watch me, I will."

And then she'd met Tyler. A light ache squeezed Sydney's throat. She wouldn't allow thoughts of a life that seemed to belong to someone else to stain her present.

She grimaced and lifted her eyes from the photo album to the vent on the far wall of the attic. Pressure built and rumbled in her chest. Despite the warning bells going off in her mind, she turned the page of the photo album and saw a picture of her dad playing guitar. She smiled, despite the ache. On the facing photo, her mom, Carolyn, was sitting on the arm of a big chair long gone, wearing a rare, relaxed smile. Sydney wasn't close to her, either, but she and Jessie were overdue for a visit. She'd plan a week over the summer. Check that box.

A filmy thought pushed for entrance into her whirl of memories. *Emma.* Sydney had shut Emma's memory up so tight, it rarely shadowed her thoughts anymore. But there it was, creating a fresh, sharp pain. She'd be almost 30 now. Sydney swallowed. What had become of her? Was she married? Did she have kids? So much about Emma, everything, really, was a mystery.

She should stop. Go back downstairs. Push away the fresh wave of memories evoked by thoughts of Emma. Stale feelings of abandonment.

She slammed the photo album shut, and the resulting cloud of dust made her cough. Old photos were not productive. They sucked you in until, before you knew it, you'd spent an hour in a painful, helpless trance.

She pushed the heavy box back to the dark corner where she'd found it. And she'd push the memories to the far corners of her mind, as well. Nothing to be gained by going back. Nothing but pain.

Sydney chose to erase the achy nostalgia by driving to the home improvement store where she bought azalea bushes for the backyard. They'd fill in some holes in her hedges and supply colorful blooms next spring.

Before she got to work, she noticed a text message from Julia and another one from Marissa. Julia had written, *Can't wait for our weekend! I've been ready for girl time for ages. Working too hard. Will you be out of school then?*

That one would require a thoughtful response. She'd wait. And from Marissa: *I'm so looking forward to this weekend! I can come early to help out with anything you need, even a day early, if you want. Sending a hug! Marissa.*

The grueling labor of hauling potted bushes and digging holes didn't stop Sydney's mind from chewing on memories. Her thoughts often landed on her mother, bringing with them a stab of guilt for how long it had been since she'd visited or even called her.

Calling Carolyn was a bit like calling a distant cousin, an exchange of life news, but devoid of the nourishing assurance she sometimes still needed from her mother, even at age forty-nine. They'd never developed that mother-daughter bond she had with her own daughter, unless, of course, Jessie was pulling one of her personal catastrophes or diva moods.

It was probably time to pay Grandma a visit. Normally, that would feel more like a chore than a vacation but niggling inside her like a burrowing insect was an additional objective. Her passing questions in the attic vibrated in her head, refusing to return to a neglected state.

As Sydney threw her weight against the shovel, hauled the root balls into the wide holes, and covered the azaleas with dirt and pine needles, long-forgotten places and events teased her mind.

When she'd finished planting the bushes, Sydney showered and changed into fresh capris and a tee shirt, which had quickly become a uniform for her. She poured a tall glass of sugar-free iced tea, then took it and her phone to the back patio. She settled at the round table under the umbrella.

Sydney let her shoulders drop as she leaned back against the woven lawn chair, breathing deeply of the balmy May breeze that stroked her face and hair. It soothed the fatigue resulting from her earlier efforts, as well as troubled thoughts stirred by her visit to the attic. With a spark of pleasure, she noted how nice the new azaleas already looked in the bed near the towering magnolia tree. Next to her on the patio sat a row of terracotta pots that spilled over with red geraniums. Sydney felt a bit happier just gazing at their perky blossoms.

She picked up her cell phone and dialed her mother's number.

"Hello, Sydney, what a surprise. Are you off work today?"

Oh, shoot. Sydney had forgotten to call later in the afternoon. She wasn't yet ready to explain her situation to her mother. She glanced at her watch and sighed with relief. "No, mom, it's four. And it's Friday." Only one week since her world had veered off course.

"Oh, I guess you've finished for the week. It's nice to hear from you." Her mother's voice lacked the usual hard edge that made her sound like a high-powered realtor. Its softness took Sydney off guard.

"How are you, Mom? I'm sorry I haven't called in a while. The end of school is so pressured, you know." And so is getting attacked by a thug student, followed by a forced leave of absence. "How are you?"

"I'm doing okay, a few health concerns, I think normal for my age. How are you and Jessie doing? When is school finished?"

"We're both getting ready for finals. School's out in about three weeks. We'll both be glad to start summer vacation." Not stretching the truth *too* much there. There *had* been a fair amount of pressure in the last two weeks. "Hey, Mom, what do you think if Jessie and I come visit you for a couple of weeks once school's out?"

Some grandmas would be overjoyed at the idea, but Sydney was never too sure about her mother's attitude. She'd always let it be known that she was a busy woman with a lot of commitments. But she'd slowed down in the last ten years since her retirement from the pharmacy. Her three children and grandchildren all lived in different cities, so Sydney wondered how her mother spent her days.

"That would be lovely, Sydney. You mentioned that last time we talked, but we hadn't followed up. Please do come."

Huh? Sydney had never heard her mother show such unmistakable openness at the idea of a visit from her wayward daughter. "We'll try not to be too much trouble. We can help out."

"Don't be silly, you're no trouble. I'd love to see both of you. You can go to the beach, read novels in the garden, whatever you want. In fact, you can stay all summer. I don't mind."

Now *that* was bewildering. "Really? I'm not sure about all summer, but we could come for a couple weeks or so. Of course, you don't have to entertain us or cook a lot. We'll be easy houseguests."

"I'm not worried about that. I'd just like to see you both. It's been a little while since you've made a visit."

A soft breeze of longing caressed Sydney's parched heart at her mother's tone. Her mother really *wanted* them to come? Sure sounded that way, and she so wanted to believe it. Her throat tightened, and she swallowed. "Okay, then, we'll come as soon as school is out. We don't want to wear out our welcome, now."

Her mother laughed. "If you say so, but I'm telling you, I don't mind. Stay the summer. It'll give me some company."

Finally, Sydney smiled. She'd take it at face value. Maybe her mother *was* lonely. She was seventy-six now and might be slowing down from her customary activities. "We'll stay a couple weeks. After that, we'll see."

After she hung up the phone, Sydney sat for a moment, unsure what to think of the new Carolyn. What might be behind her change of demeanor?

She'd find out in a few weeks.

Chapter Five

"Let's get this party started!"

Sydney almost felt like her old self as she anticipated the weekend ahead. "You didn't have to bring food, Eden." She put her hands on her hips as Eden emptied a box of specialty crackers and several kinds of imported cheeses onto the counter from a canvas bag. "I told you I had made tons of food, and since you had to fly and all—"

Eden swiped the air dismissively. "This wasn't hard to smuggle onto the plane. The cheese isn't the stinky kind." She grinned. Her petite stature and perkiness made Sydney think of a blonde elf full of mischief. "Well, it *may* be stinky, but it's well-wrapped, so I guess we're about to find out. We should probably brace ourselves."

Marissa had arrived first since she had less than a three-hour to drive from Raleigh. Eden and Julia had insisted on taking a taxi instead of accepting Sydney's offer to pick them up at the airport. They'd arrived only a few minutes earlier and for the moment, confusion reigned in the kitchen while all three women dug into their bags for the food and gifts they'd brought for the weekend.

"I can take care of these snacks if you two want to freshen up after your flight or settle into your bedrooms," Marissa said to Eden and Julia.

"I'm quite fresh, thank you, but I could use a glass of wine. It *is* almost five, after all. Cocktail hour." Eden winked at Marissa and took the glasses that Sydney handed her from the cupboard. She carried them to the living room and returned for a handful of small plates.

Julia pulled the plastic lid off a small bowl she'd brought. "This is a dip recipe I got from my relatives in Italy. Or, from their cook, I should say. That girl can do everything."

"Huh, hoity-toity relatives, eh?" Sydney lifted her brows, then peered into the bowl. "Looks delish. I'll get me some of that. I'm proud of you, sistah, for getting it all the way to Charlotte on the plane."

"I have many talents, including dip-making and dip smuggling." Julia gave Sydney a secretive smile. She carried her dip and crackers to the coffee table to join the wine bottles, stemmed glasses, and other snacks that had accumulated. When she returned, she said, "I'm so glad we flew this time. It would have taken us six hours to get here, and that's without traffic. Which basically never happens in D.C."

Julia looked peaceful and focused. Quite a contrast with the last time they'd been together, when Eden had called an emergency gathering to support her after the loss of her elderly mother. For months she'd shown the strain of juggling her interior design business with frequent visits to her mother's facility.

Elegant and beautiful as always, Sydney thought she detected an additional glow on Julia's face possibly due to the new man in her life. They'd all surely get the scoop on *that* aspect of everyone's lives over the weekend, though Sydney would have nothing to share, as usual.

"I fully agree it's better to fly than put yourself through all that." Marissa's cultured southern voice blended into the conversation. "Better to spend a few more dollars than a day of misery. I mean if it's possible."

"Oh, it's possible. We both got good deals on our flights." Eden leaned against the counter.

"You just sold your restaurant, right? That makes you a gazillionaire." Sydney turned from the cupboard and grinned at Eden. She went to the fridge and pulled out a tray of cold salami-cheese rolls, then handed them to Marissa, who quickly dispatched it to the coffee table and returned.

Eden laughed aloud. "Yeah, right. I should have just taken my private jet to get here. No, seriously, I did get a good price for it, but restaurants don't sell for as much as you'd think. And, of course, it depends on a lot of factors, if the business was profitable or not, for example. I guess you could say it was healthy when I sold it."

"I think you have a thing for business, Eden." Marissa nodded toward Eden.

Julia, who stood next to her, said, "That's for sure. You likely already know that, Eden, but you could probably run *any* business based on what you've learned running the restaurant."

Eden sighed and shook her head. "Don't know about that. I appreciate your perspective, Julia, and I respect it, since you are a business owner too. I just followed common sense. Day by day. Hired the right people. I was really flying by the seat of my pants for the first few years after Gerry died, but it worked, thank the Lord."

Sydney raised her voice over the din. "We'll have supper on the patio, but for now, we'll head to the living room where all our goodies are. I know you're tired of traveling, but I cleaned all week and I want you to admire my labors. It isn't too far, about fifteen feet." She let out a full laugh. Oh, it felt good to be with these special friends. To forget the horror of the last week of school, the confusion of her recent weeks of suspension.

Late afternoon sun streamed through the mullioned windows into the cozy living room, coordinated in colonial reds and blues, as the women settled into armchairs. They dove into the wine and snacks, chattering as they did. Once each woman had a filled plate on her lap and a glass in her hand, they took turns sharing basic news about their lives. Between their weekends, news ebbed and flowed and was sometimes downright spotty, depending on what was going on in each woman's life. Over the weekend, they'd have time to delve more deeply into details.

It was Eden's turn to summarize her status. "My kids have all flown the nest, as you know. Jordan and Claire, my twins, share an apartment in the city. They have a trip to Europe planned for later in the summer. I'm so glad they get along well enough to do that. And Brent did a work-study internship out west last semester for his senior year, but he just informed me he'll be staying there all summer. Something about a young lady, I believe." She leaned back in her chair with a conspiratorial smile. "I haven't met her yet. The kids all keep in touch, but we're in different realms." Her smile fell a few degrees. "I guess I'm fully on my own now."

"How are you feeling about that?" Marissa asked her.

Eden seemed to force a smile. "Free, I guess. It's different. Full of possibilities."

"And what have *you* been up to? Since selling your restaurant, I mean," asked Julia.

Eden blew out a puff of air and leaned back. "I feel kind of embarrassed to tell you. In the last nine months since selling my restaurant, I—I won't say I've been a bum, exactly." Everyone laughed. "But I *have* been exploring different things. Art classes, volunteer work. I've done some gardening, had my kitchen renovated. I've kept busy, but without specific direction." She let out a laugh. "You know, stuff that rich, unemployed ladies do. Not that I'm rich, of course. But I don't absolutely have to work now. I can take some time to figure things out." She shrugged. "At first, I was relieved to have all that free time, but sometimes—" she lifted her palms toward the ceiling, "I'm not sure what to do next."

Sydney understood that. A relief and a burden at the same time. "Don't worry, we'll help you plan your life before the weekend's over." They all laughed. She sobered. "But honestly, we'll be your sounding board if you want." By the look on her face, Eden probably needed one.

Petite, blond Eden, always bubbly, overflowing with compassion. She was the organizer and to some degree, the counselor of the group, but now found herself in need to *receive* inspiration and guidance.

Sitting next to her was Marissa, dark wavy hair framing her pale face. She was more reserved, but also a great listener. She was a historical fiction writer who'd been widowed three years earlier. Born and raised in Raleigh, she embodied the genteel southern lady stereotype, soft spoken and thoughtful. She'd never blurt out loud humor, like Sydney sometimes did.

And there was Julia, the interior designer, her dark Italian beauty enhanced by stunning blue eyes. Along with Marissa, she was more reserved.

Sydney considered all her friends beautiful inside and out. She sometimes felt like a misfit among them, but knew they accepted her as she was. What they knew, in any case. And though they were her best friends, there was plenty they didn't know.

Once everyone else had shared the current state of things, they all looked to Sydney. "In your email, you said you had a curve ball, Syd. What's going on?" Eden's blunt question caught Sydney off guard, though it shouldn't have, since she'd insisted that everyone else talk first. Because she was the hostess. There was that, but she also knew her update was laden with complexity.

"Well. That's a deep issue, as you're all aware." Her corny joke failed to draw laughter, as her friends apparently awaited something grave.

She leaned back against the plump cushion, trying to calm her heartbeat, which had just accelerated. "No one is dying, so relax. I had an incident about three weeks ago at my school. I was physically attacked by a student." That drew a collective gasp. "A big one, over six feet tall. Aside from a couple bruises and a bump on the head, I was okay, but instead of him being expelled, *I* was given leave for the rest of the school year."

An outcry arose from all three women at once. "How unfair. How did this happen?" Marissa leaned forward and pushed aside the cheese plate.

Sydney tensed, suddenly uncomfortable with everyone's eyes on her. "When it happened, there was only a month left of the school year. The student in question is a senior. But he'd been goofing off all year. It's true, it wasn't handled well, and it was unfair to me. Not to mention sending the wrong message to this kid. But in the end, my principal suggested I take the rest of the year as leave, I guess, as a means of protecting me from the student without having to suspend him." She shrugged. "So, I guess it was a win-win. Kind of."

"Don't know if I see it that way." Eden frowned. "You weren't defended."

"Thank you, Eden." Sydney sat up straighter. "I appreciate your saying that. I certainly felt that way from the first moment until now. But, since the principal wasn't willing to suspend the student and move him out of my class, this was the best solution for *me*. To stay safe and out of target range. At full pay.”

“Your worthless principal paid you off because it was easier for him,” Eden grumbled.

“Eden’s right. Are you okay with that, Sydney?” asked Julia.

Sydney shrugged. “No, not totally. I wasn’t defended, as Eden said. *I’m* the one who had to leave. The kid gets off scot-free. No consequences, though he’ll probably become a criminal later in life.”

“For sure.” Marissa nodded.

“But the upside for me is I get an extra month of paid leave.” Sydney forced a smile. No, it wasn’t right, but she’d adjusted and was determined to enjoy the extra vacation time. Once she stopped working so hard, that is. “You all know I was beginning to dislike my job, so it’s just as well.” It didn’t feel good letting Wade off the hook to her friends, yet she didn’t want them to spend the weekend feeling indignant on her behalf.

“So, what’s the next step? Are you going to go back in the fall? I mean, since your principal didn’t support you *and* you don’t like teaching anymore.” Eden reached for the water carafe.

Sydney swallowed and looked around the room at them. “Good question. I know I should quit on principle. That’ll show them, right? But then, what would I do for a job? I still need a job.”

“Yes, of course, you do.” Marissa’s voice was soft, soothing. “You may *have* to go back in the fall, or possibly apply for another teaching job.”

“But she doesn’t like it anymore.” Julia’s gaze turned to Sydney. “What drew you to teaching in the first place?”

Sydney frowned. “Now we’re going way back. Lemme see if I remember.” She did remember and very well. When she realized freshman year that she was completely on her own and no one, not even her family, would fend for her, she’d sought something that would always give her job security. Teachers weren’t fired. There were usually teaching jobs available somewhere. “Uh, well, I was good at math. I thought about engineering but didn’t think I’d enjoy it. Too solitary.”

"I can see that. So, being around people was one attraction for teaching."

"Yes, and being with teenagers." Sydney searched her memory. "I liked the idea of helping them grasp something that had always been pretty easy for me. Lots of people have trouble with math and are scared of it. I liked the idea of dispelling their fear by making it simpler." True, those things had also been a motivation for her. "And I liked it until—" She sighed. "Until recently, and then with this new problem."

"Is there something else you'd like to do?" Eden asked.

Sydney pressed her lips together and shook her head. "I'm starting to think *anything* would be better. I mean, teaching is— *was* a wonderful, worthy career for me and I believe I contributed a lot to young peoples' lives. But I've reached my expiration date. I've spent eighteen years teaching. But I don't know what else to do that will maintain my income level. No idea. And I have Jessie to think of."

"Yes, Jessie. Is she with her dad this weekend?" Marissa's gaze met Sydney's eyes.

Sydney nodded. "What's worse, it's May and if I wanted to look for another teaching job, I should have applied earlier."

"I have an idea." Eden reached for the bottle of red wine and tipped it toward her glass. "You could quit your job but sign up to substitute at other schools in the district. That could be a fallback plan until you figure out what to do." She glanced around the room for confirmation. "You could even go back to school to retrain in something."

Bad idea. Being a student again? No way. "I don't want to be a student again, although I'd consider it if there was something I really wanted to do." She spread out her hands. "I'm coming up blank. But subbing isn't a bad idea if I get desperate. Hey, I have an idea. Maybe I'll take out an ad for someone who'll support Jessie and me because we're decorative and entertaining." She gave them a grin she didn't feel, hoping to lighten the conversation.

"That, you certainly are." Marissa chuckled.

Sydney's friends wanted to help, but she needed to figure this out herself. Or let God show her something dramatic at the eleventh hour. He liked doing things like that, despite the anxiety it caused. To expand faith. "I have all summer to work on it, so something will come clear to me. Y'all keep praying, okay?"

"Do you have anything planned for the summer?" Julia leaned forward and swiped a cracker through the dip.

"When school's out, Jessie and I are going to see my mother. Remember that trip we all took during spring break junior year?" They'd all piled into her mom's Victorian home and spent nearly every day at the beach.

"Yes, how could we forget? The sunburns! The late-night gab fests." Julia grinned back at her. "Remind me what the town is called."

"Kennessey. It's a smallish town near Wilmington," Sydney said.

"Yes, the beach there was great. I remember well." Eden's smile broadened. "Sounds like good therapy."

"Though, I seem to remember you're not that close with your mother, right?" Trust Marissa to remember the details.

"Yeah, that's true. Maybe this visit will improve things." One could only hope, but she wouldn't bet money on that.

"How long will you and Jessie stay?" Julia asked.

"I'm planning on a couple of weeks, but, get this, my mom said we could stay the whole *summer* if we wanted to. Considering our past relationship, that's unheard of."

"Maybe she regrets the way things have been and wants to improve your relationship," Eden said.

"And see more of Jessie, too. She's her granddaughter, after all." Marissa leaned back. "Would you consider that? Staying all summer?"

Sydney let out a staccato laugh. "Let me get through the first weekend, and I'll let you know. It's not my intention to stay that long. Two weeks is usually more than enough. I'm just saying she offered, and that was a brand-new thing for her."

"It may do you good to be there where you grew up." Julia leaned her elbows on her knees. "Maybe there are good memories that'll encourage you. Jessie will appreciate that, too."

Julia's well-meaning statement was like calm water on the surface of a devastating tsunami. They really didn't know, and suddenly Sydney couldn't stop the geyser-like force that pushed up through her protective layers. The sting began in her eyes. "There's more to that story and I want to tell you," she said quietly. Every woman's eyes were on her. Sydney let out a shaky laugh. "There are things I hid from you all when we first met in college. I'll apologize for that now, but at the time, hiding it was all I could do."

Sydney had their attention. She had to go forward, yet the pain rumbled inside, clutching at her throat, even as she scrambled for her first words. She took in a deep draught of air. How many years before this didn't hurt anymore?

She looked at the floor, focused on a little rip she'd never seen before in the area rug. She'd give them some background first. Ease in.

She lifted her eyes. "Growing up, I didn't feel like I fit into my own family. I had two older brothers. They were super-boys, you know, good at everything. Academics, sports. Maybe boys were what my mom really wanted." She'd begun her life as a black sheep. Maybe if she'd been born a boy, she'd have fit in. "My mom always seemed too busy for me. But my dad and I were close for a while." She blinked. Swallowed. "One thing he gave me was music."

"Music?" Eden and Marissa said at once.

"I've never heard you talk about that. Did you play instruments?" Eden's blue eyes were wide.

Sydney nodded. "He taught me how to play the guitar and I got pretty good at it. Then I discovered I wasn't so bad at singing, either. Finally, I had something I was good at and loved that was distinct from everything my older brothers did. My dad was in a little band with some other guys, and I used to watch them practice."

"Why did you give up music? Or are you a closet rock star and *that's* your secret?" Everyone chuckled at Eden's statement, but their eyes shot back to Sydney as if expecting it to be true.

Sydney shook her head. "No, that's not the secret. Unfortunately, I gave up on music. But back then, I was active on the church worship team and in the youth group. I met a guy at the beginning of eleventh grade." Her words slowed down as she forced them out. "Tyler." The pain in her throat sharpened as she said his name. After thirty years. She swallowed. Blinked. "Later, he and I were both on the worship team at our church. We started dating. I—we fell in love. It was *crazy* first love. We were inseparable. I knew he was my destiny." Her eyes fell. "Sounds so stupid now. Anyway, we dated for a year and then—" She took a breath. "Then I got pregnant."

She was still staring at the floor, unable to look at them. Their silence was louder than their previous gasps. She lifted her eyes. And, instead of shock and judgment, their faces were etched with surprise, compassion, and pain. When she saw it, something inside broke and her tears started to flow. She couldn't stop them, and it hurt too much to try.

She pulled a tissue from the box under the coffee table. She coughed and cleared her throat. Her words came out in a rush. "It was our senior year. We had both decided on colleges. We were planning to stay in touch and see each other during school breaks. When I found out I was pregnant, I was kind of happy because I loved Tyler so much and thought that would allow us to stay together and be a family. I—I really wanted a family of my own." Her voice dropped. "But he wasn't ready to be a dad."

Sydney reached down and snatched another tissue. "His father was our pastor. Tyler didn't want to disappoint him or bring shame on him. He had a partial scholarship to Emory. Pretty much everything came before me and our baby." She looked down at her hands. "At first, I had this completely naïve vision of us getting married, putting off college for a year, and moving to Nashville and the music scene there. He told me, convinced me, I guess, that it was unrealistic."

"So, what did you do?" Julia leaned forward.

"I had to tell my mother about it. My dad had already remarried and moved away by that time, so I had to face her alone."

"Tyler bailed?" Eden shook her head. "Dirtbag."

"What did your mother do?" Marissa asked.

Sydney sniffed. Swallowed. "My mother was never one to show much emotion. At the time, I was glad for that since she didn't haul off and kick me out of the house or go into a screaming rage that could be heard all over Kennessey. We never discussed abortion since we both considered it out of the question. I didn't seriously think of keeping the baby because I was emotionally devastated. I didn't think I could raise the baby alone and my mother made it clear she didn't want to do it, either. We could have lived there together, all three of us, since her house is pretty big, but it wasn't even discussed. I often wish we'd done that. People do that all the time, and they manage." She took a breath. Now that the truth was out, the pain in her chest began to subside. "So, instead, she arranged for me to go stay with my Aunt Abby, who lived about a half-hour away."

"Just like they used to do in the old days to save the family from shame," Marissa said. "Strikes me as odd to do this in our lifetimes."

Sydney shrugged. "Mom didn't want it interfering with her life, is my guess, so she helped me give away her first grandchild. She told me it would be better for me. I could keep up with my schoolwork on my own during the pregnancy, then take my GED. She had it all planned out. She found an adoption agency and worked out all those details. Then I gave birth." Her voice broke. "To baby Emma." A sob erupted from her throat. She held up one hand as the tears flowed and she regained control. "Sorry, I really haven't been like this for the last thirty years."

"But you've held it *in* for thirty years, Sydney. I'm glad you're finally letting this out." Marissa's face was lined with compassion. "You could have told us back then. We would have understood."

"We would have given you comfort." Eden said. "Does Jessie know?"

"That's the really bad part. I've never told my own daughter. I've often thought about it, but the more time goes by, the more I think she'd hate me for not telling her." Sydney shook her head. No use trying to determine which of her failures was the worst. There were just too many.

"When was Emma born?" Julia asked.

"In July, right before my freshman year at U.N.C."

Eden gasped. "Oh, Sydney! We met you shortly after that. No wonder you seemed so despondent and shell-shocked. We thought it was because of your break-up."

"That's what I told you, and I *was* heartbroken about Tyler, the way he walked away. I couldn't talk about the rest. That's why I didn't tell you then. I wasn't so much ashamed as I was completely shattered. I wanted to die, actually. Going to school was the only thing that kept me alive."

The room went silent. Then Julia said in a choked voice, "I'm so sorry, Sydney. I'm sorry for what you went through alone. I remember you cried a lot in those days. We all thought it was because of your breakup. You never said his name, but that must have been Tyler."

Sydney nodded. "I think he wanted us to stay together long distance, even after everything, but I felt so rejected. He'd rejected our baby. That was like rejecting a future with me, I felt at the time."

"So, you cut him off?"

Sydney nodded. "A year later, I wrote to him and told him I forgave him. I didn't feel it, but thought it was what God would want me to do. I didn't hear back from him."

"You said earlier that the memories back home aren't particularly good. Now we understand why. I'm so sorry you went through that." Eden's eyes brimmed with tears. She blinked, and a few of them spilled down her cheeks. She leaned forward and laid her hand on Sydney's knee. "I hope your visit to Kennessey will be a healing refreshment for you and Jessie. In spite of everything."

Sydney smiled. She placed her hand atop Eden's and squeezed it. "I'd really love to find out what happened to Emma. I thought maybe during this trip I could do some secret investigating to find out."

"Still secret? I thought you were finished with that." Marissa gave her a chiding look.

Sydney leaned forward. "I brought a child into the world, which was bad enough, considering my situation then. But in giving her up, maybe I surrendered her to an awful life, and that's even worse. I—I want to find out that I didn't do that. I don't necessarily want to get in touch with her, but I need the closure of knowing who she became, you know?" Sydney heard her own voice pleading for understanding. "She's always been part of my history, but I just started thinking actively about her the other day when I was going through the attic. I saw some old family photos and it triggered a bunch of memories and shame. It might be positive for me to learn about her." She finished with a whisper.

"In that case, you should do it." Julia said. "I'm sure you remember my story going through old storage items. It ended up changing my life."

"Yes, it certainly did!" Eden let out a joyful chuckle. "Not that there are any Italian relatives in *your* family tree, but it may lead to healing for you."

"In any case, we support you, Sydney." Marissa sent her a solemn stare.

Though her chest still ached, and her eyes felt watery, Sydney smiled. She did feel lighter as the love and acceptance of her friends flowed into her, despite her decades of secrets. She had no excuse for not telling them, yet they didn't hold it against her.

After thoughtful silence hung in the room for a few moments, Sydney said, "Now, how about some of that stinky cheese?"

Chapter Six

Through the front windshield, Sydney saw signs they were getting close to Kennessey. Along the highway, towering oak and maple trees gave way to a pine forest. Scrubby plants grew in sandy mounds and the air that flowed through the SUV window felt salty, humid.

A year had passed since she and Jessie had visited Carolyn, who didn't want to be called *Grandma*. A bit of denial there, but they traveled there seldom enough that Sydney found it sad and humorous rather than irritating.

"What was in that bag you brought, the one by the door? Or is that personal information?" Sydney flicked a glance over at Jessie who was, naturally, swiping across her phone. Which she'd been doing for most of the three-hour drive.

Jessie slipped her phone into her knapsack on the passenger floor. "I knew we might stay for the whole summer, so I packed a few extra things. Clothes, a couple more books. Stuff like that."

"Don't get your hopes up about staying all summer, Jess. Usually, two weeks is more than enough, remember? You get bored and so do I. And Carolyn and I don't really get along too well."

"Yeah, why is that?"

Sydney frowned. "It's just always been that way. She was tied up with her pharmacy career when I was growing up. And she was really involved with Chet and Kevin's sports." Carolyn had never been very maternal, almost as if having three children was only one feature of her hectic life instead of the most important.

With a twinge, she wondered if it was too harsh an indictment. Sydney had learned acceptance over the years, but apparently not enough. Deep down, she knew that she herself had allowed the Great Barrier Reef to develop in her heart in response to Carolyn's part in giving Emma away.

She swallowed. The thought of Emma created long-forgotten turbulence in her stomach. Her discussion with her friends had finished what her moments in the attic had begun. The trauma she'd shelved decades ago now whirred in the back corners of her mind, seeking resolution. She hoped to make progress in her quest during their brief stay in Kennessey. It shouldn't take long to get the answers she needed.

Soon a colorful sign appeared on the roadside bearing the words, "Welcome to Kennessey, North Carolina. Population 10,218." More buildings sprang up, and the town's familiarity struck Sydney with both dread and comfort. The speed limit dropped, then dropped again as they entered downtown. Most of the shops that had always been fixtures in the town were still there, stirring a twinge of nostalgia. But a few new ones had emerged in the year since they'd visited. A new ice cream shop, a Mediterranean café, a few new clothing boutiques. People strolled the sidewalks, a normal day in Kennessey. Over time, the year-round population had grown with retirees, golf enthusiasts, and an increasing number of remote workers and other transfers eager to live close to the beach, a fifteen-minute drive.

During her childhood and adolescence, Sydney had loved the town. It had always been "her" town. Though she knew she'd leave for college one day, it went without question in her young mind that she'd return afterward. But her childhood security and rosy picture of the future shattered that year so long ago.

"I hope we can stay all summer." Jessie's voice broke through Sydney's faraway thoughts.

"Please don't start bugging me about this before we even get there. I assure you, two weeks will be plenty. You'll be bored out of your mind in about a week."

"I can get a job. I've only saved enough for about half a crummy car, so I have a long way to go."

"We'll see. Look, there's your grandmother's house. As the GPS would say, *you have arrived.*"

Carolyn's house was a two-story Victorian with a wooden porch across the front and down one side. The porch was Sydney's favorite feature of the old house. The light blue siding and white railing looked like they'd been freshly painted since her last visit. Really, it was gorgeous, she had to admit. Puffy blue hydrangea bushes adorned each corner, and camelia bushes filled in the rest. Below them in the beds grew clusters of Gerbera daisies and other splashes of color Sydney couldn't identify. Gardening must be one activity her mother did regularly.

Sydney had grown up in that house. For an upper middle-class family of five, it had been appropriate. For her mother all alone, way too much house. Why did Carolyn stay instead of downsizing? Must be a nightmare to clean it, although she likely still had a housekeeper. Maybe she wanted to keep it in the family or enjoy the memories rumbling around her in every room. Whatever. She had her reasons.

Her mother must have heard the car motor because she appeared on the porch, then came down to the driveway, her gait slower than Sydney remembered. Meeting them at the car was a new thing, too. Usually, she stayed on the porch until they brought in their suitcases.

When Sydney got out of the car and reached out to hug her mother, she noticed new tired creases around her eyes and mouth she hadn't seen before. Her short haircut was stylish and almost completely white. She seemed shorter and thinner, giving her a frail, birdlike appearance. Never an effusive woman, her mother still managed a warm smile of welcome. "I'm glad you're here."

Jessie circled the back of the car to hug her grandmother, who stood back and looked at her, still smiling. "Seems like forever since I've seen you, Jessie. You're so tall now. I can't remember but you seemed smaller last year."

Jessie grinned indulgently. "Yeah, funny how that happens. How are you, Gram—I mean, Carolyn. It still seems weird to me to call you that."

Carolyn laughed. "Gram is fine, Jessie. Call me whatever you want. That's what I am, your Gram." She turned to Sydney. "I have your rooms ready. The usual ones, of course." She pointed to Jessie's bike attached to a rack on the hatch of the SUV. "Looks like you have a lot of stuff, so I'll wait for you inside. I can take something light when I go, and I'll pour us all some sweet tea. Or no. I'll let you sweeten your own with that chemical stuff. I remembered to buy some."

After Carolyn went to the house, Jessie grabbed her guitar from the back seat and turned to Sydney. "Is she okay? She seems older than she did last year. I mean, a lot."

Sydney chuckled. "As you said, funny how that happens. You're not the only one who gets older. But you get taller, and she gets shorter. Here, let's take these in. I see you have a free arm." She handed Jessie a canvas tote bag.

After removing the bike and storing it on the porch, it took two more trips to get everything into the house and to their bedrooms. Sydney unzipped her suitcase and filled two drawers with her basic summer wardrobe, including two bathing suits. She and Jessie could take a few days soaking in the sun and satisfying the beach craving that had been brewing all spring. It was one passion they had in common. After that, she'd turn her attention to the pressing, urgent matters in her life. But not just yet. Was she putting it off, finding Emma and searching for a new job? Probably. But she needed the beach first.

Sydney sat for a moment in her old bedroom, which had been updated in stylish white furniture, distressed to appear older. The room bore no signs of her teenage life. Despite three decades that had come and gone, the it provoked shadowy tones of grief and negative memories. Time had diluted them and when she was home in Charlotte amidst her high school teaching rat race, she hardly remembered at all.

Until just recently. Even before her decision to learn the fate of Emma, Sydney had felt something deep and wistful calling her. Was God trying to say something? Or was she just in need of a change? The prickle of possibility mingled with dread of the unknown. She took a deep breath, stood up, and left the room.

ભ   ભ   ભ

Toasty sunshine licked Sydney's skin, and it felt heavenly. She shifted the straw hat back to lighten the shadow cast on her paperback. The constant rhythm of the waves soothed and relaxed her, unwinding the knots of the previous month. Straight ahead of her in the surf, Jessie rode the waves. She stood up, paddled back, and did it again. Her daughter was a fish, had always been.

Sydney loved the water, too, but that was one more area that had been squeezed out and suffocated by life, save their summer trips. She and Jessie both relished those beach trips because the year between was so long. Sydney had grown up there, so exchanging a sleepy coastal town for the big city had been an uncomfortable adjustment on top of all the others.

Before she got too involved in the vacation rhythm, she sent a quick text to her girlfriends. *Just arrived in Kennessey a couple days ago. Jessie finished her exams and we hit the road. Today, we're at the beach, of course. Where else would we be? Had to start the visit by fulfilling our longings for sand and sun. I'll keep you all posted and please do the same! Much love, Sydney.*

Jessie returned from an hour chasing and riding waves. Her blond hair was matted and her skin shiny with seawater. She flopped down into a beach chair.

"Tired?" Sydney smiled at her and set down the book she hadn't read at all, except the first paragraph two or three times.

Jessie nodded. "Time for a rest and maybe a nap."

"Don't forget to reapply your sunscreen." She was still a mom. "Once you're dry, that is." She leaned back against the moist beach towel draped over the chair but was suddenly restless. "I'm going for a walk, okay? Keep an eye on everything."

"Yes, the crown jewels we brought with us to the beach. They're safe with me, Mom," Jessie murmured, though her eyes were already closed under the baking sun.

Sydney laughed. "Yes, those are the ones. See you in a bit."

It was their second day at the beach. Carolyn had insisted they do as they like and not worry about entertaining her, adding that she wasn't that kind of hostess. Sydney had wanted to say, "No kidding," but was glad for her mother's hands-off attitude. Of course, they would spend time with her, but Sydney was relieved she and Jessie could also make their own decisions for part of the time. That would also give her more freedom to sneak off and do her research about Emma as well as limit chances of awkwardness with her mother. And she probably needed to look for some job postings, too. Soon. Even though the very thought of it gave her a stomach cramp.

Sydney strolled ankle-deep in waves, skirting kids digging in the sand and a dad taking pictures of a toddler delighted with the sea foam at her feet. Two older preschool children dug a hole nearby, carefully surveyed by their mother. Sydney had been in her place a long time ago, watching Jessie as a toddler play in the waves during family vacations with Cody. They'd been happy those first few years. Her craving for belonging in a family had been met. For a while. She hadn't known then that it was only a temporary state. An hourglass whose sands would trickle out at an unknown moment.

Despite the melancholy drift of her thoughts, the cool slap of water on her feet had a healing effect. The wet sand shifted under her with each step of her leisurely pace. Maybe finding out about Emma would soften the older scars that still stung from time to time. *Lord, let your will be done during this vacation. Help us get along with Mom and let me find out about Emma. Please help me figure out what to do with my life. It's hard to start from zero at my age.*

The final words of her whispered prayer brought a mirthless chuckle, followed by a tug of fear. It had been a month since the debacle at school. Despite the injustice, Sydney had provided a copy of her final exam to the substitute teacher and agreed to correct them and turn in her final grades. It seemed the right thing to do for her students, if for no one else. Wade seemed appreciative of her conscientious gestures, but otherwise offered no closure on the situation. For him, apparently, the matter was finished. She was still torn about the prospect of returning in the fall. She could always go back to the high school, as Wade certainly expected. It was secure, though she'd never feel safe again.

What a defeat it would be to return. A cowardly dash back to stability, familiarity. Did she even have a choice to do anything else? Yet, stirring inside was a thirst for more, for different. But what?

She'd enjoy a week or two of a careless summer under the sun. Then the question would likely start tormenting her. Her friends had given many suggestions, but nothing felt right. What did she want? Toward the end of their weekend, Julia had asked, "If you could do whatever you wanted and money wasn't an issue, what would you do?"

Her question had taken Sydney off guard but stoked a hunger inside at the same time. What would she do? The answer wasn't immediately clear since she'd never asked or answered it for herself. What *was* clear, if she had a choice, she wouldn't return to the same school, and maybe not even to teaching. Should she resign and sub for a year as Eden had suggested, while she mulled it over and researched options? While she discovered her passion?

Aside from music, she'd never had a passion. Even teaching had been a life raft to keep from drowning in her sorrow. She'd had to decide on a major. She was good at math and liked teenagers, so it seemed logical to teach high school math. Logic had paved the way for the next eighteen years. Though she'd enjoyed teaching for most of that time, passion had played no part in her career decision.

Eden had suggested she do a budget, so she'd know what she absolutely needed to live. This she'd done. Her house was paid off, so that was a help. Cody paid child support every month. The numbers had been a surprise and a relief. She might be able to get by on subbing for a short time, but it would be tight, with no margin for surprise expenses. And Jessie's college was coming up. Back to zero.

Sydney blew out a long sigh, aware that her thoughts had led to a clench in her stomach in the wake of her previous peace. No, she refused to ruin her day at the beach with those thoughts. Not now. Time would come when she wouldn't have a choice, but at that moment, she did.

"These mashed potatoes are great, Gram. What'd you put in them?" Jessie licked her spoon and reached for the bowl.

"Just a little half and half. Well, more than a little, actually. And butter."

"Low-cal, then." Sydney smirked.

Her mother shrugged. "It's a special occasion."

Her statement surprised Sydney. Her mother had never responded to their visits by calling them an *occasion*. Then came a guilty sting for not recognizing her mother's efforts sooner. On the screened-in porch that overlooked the back lawn, she'd set the round patio table with a floral vinyl tablecloth and matching napkins. A cluster of peach-pink camellias crowned a small porcelain vase in the center of the table. Could it be that she'd missed them? Another sting. They could have visited sooner, couldn't they? At Christmas or another holiday or even a weekend?

But the holidays were always overtaken by Chet and Kevin's families and their perfect offspring. Likely, Carolyn marveled at their wildly successful careers while they recounted their exploits and those of their children around the table. She and Jessie had joined them two Christmases ago. That had been more than enough for her, having been silently reminded of her status as the black sheep, the failure of the family. No, there were valid reasons why she and Jessie were scarce in Kennessey.

Sydney came to herself. "Thanks, Mom. It's nice to be out here on the porch before it gets too hot. Feels perfect tonight. The table's so pretty and the dinner was good, too."

"I'm glad you liked it. You both got a lot of sun today. You're rosy and starting to tan."

"I'm trying not to burn this early in the season." Sydney gave Jessie a pointed stare since her daughter was less than diligent at applying sunscreen. "Direct hint to my fair-skinned child."

Jessie rolled her eyes but smiled. She touched her red nose. "Does hurt a little bit."

"Has everyone had enough to eat? If not, I have ice cream. I didn't make a dessert."

"Mom, you don't need to go to such trouble for us." Then it took a deliberate effort to add, "It's enough just to be together." Fake it till you make it, she'd often heard. Otherwise known as a step of faith.

Jessie pushed back her chair. "I'll do the dishes, Gram. You did all the work for the dinner. It was real good."

Sydney stopped herself from staring open-mouthed at Jessie. Apparently, magic was happening in her, too. Willingly offering to do dishes?

She grinned at her mother. "You must have put a spell on her. Let's hope it continues." She winked, and Carolyn responded with a smile.

The sun had sunk, but the sky was still bright. A soft summer breeze flowed in through the screen walls of the porch, sliding a comforting caress over Sydney's arms and face. It brought a wave of contentment. Not enough to erase all the turbulence but promising a strand of hope.

A day she could honestly call pleasant and even fun ended on an up note. Text messages from Julia and Marissa had arrived during the afternoon in response to hers earlier that day. They both wished her a refreshing and healing visit, despite her memories, and assured her of their prayers.

Being far from the routine *did* seem therapeutic. Her steady background tension had dialed down to a low hum. Was that simply the beach rhythm kicking in, or was she practicing the art of denial?

Chapter Seven

A muffled drone of conversation blended with the whoosh of a milk steamer and the clang of ice cubes hitting glass. The nutty scent of coffee hung in the air over Sydney, settled at a small table in the corner of a coffee shop.

She sipped her iced latte and stared at her phone. Now or never. Why were her hands sweating? It was the beginning of a quest, nothing to be afraid of. She was also about to pry open a box that had been sealed for a long time. She probably wouldn't get answers immediately, but she had to start somewhere. It was time.

She'd dropped Jessie off at the beach before heading to the nearby coffee shop for a private place to make her calls. She had collected a few adoption agency phone numbers from an internet search and jotted them on a spiral notepad.

Sydney dialed the first number on her list. "Tri-State Child Alliance, can I help you?" The female voice was professional, but not cold.

"Hello, my name is Sydney Bennett. Uh, I'm—" she stopped, swallowed. *Pull yourself together, Sydney.* She took a breath. "Thirty years ago, I gave up a baby for adoption. I wanted to know if I can find out what happened to her. Just for my own peace of mind, I guess you could say."

"Was your adoption handled through our agency?"

"Actually, I don't know. I was eighteen at the time. My mother made the arrangements."

"I understand, Ms. Bennett. Unfortunately, in North Carolina, adoptions records are closed. That means that unless your child, who would be an adult now, or the adoptive parents gave consent in advance, we wouldn't be able to release that information to you if you had adopted through our agency."

A ball of lead seemed to drop down inside her. Why hadn't she thought of that? Of course, there would be all kinds of laws to protect the privacy of an adopted child.

At Sydney's silence the woman said, "There is one thing we could do for you."

Hope flared inside her. "Yes?"

"Well, first we need to establish if you did adopt through our agency. Thirty years ago, records were not kept in the same way, so we would have to research the archives to find your name. Then if we do find it, we can check the file for a form called the contact agreement. On this document there may be an agreement from the adoptive parents to be notified in the event that the biological mother reaches out. Another possibility is that the adopted child herself has contacted us in recent years and given her permission to be contacted."

"Those are a lot of ifs." Sydney frowned. "But I guess it's a place to start. My daughter was born on July sixteenth nineteen ninety-one. My full maiden name is Sydney Abigail Davis."

"If you'll give me your phone number as well, I'll call you once the information is available. It may take up to a few weeks."

"Thank you." Sydney gave the woman her phone number and hung up. A few weeks. That wouldn't necessarily tie her to Kennessey. In fact, she could have done all of this by phone from Charlotte, though she didn't regret coming.

For the last few days, her thoughts had been whirring around, keeping up with her emotions as she anticipated her quest. But when she hung up with the woman, everything thudded to a halt. She was hamstrung already. Since she wasn't asking for contact, only information about Emma's life, she'd believed it would be possible, even easy. What was she thinking? That someone would tell her Emma's story over the phone, and she'd thank them and go on her way? The only thing she could do was wait, possibly for weeks, to hear back from the agency. And call a few more of them, since there was no guarantee that she'd found the agency involved in Emma's adoption.

Though Sydney had made only one call, she felt emotionally spent and fragile. Unbidden, a picture flashed into her mind. Herself at seventeen, full of wonder at the life inside her. A life made from the intense love she and Tyler had for each other. *Tyler will be so excited.*

She'd always known they'd get married one day. They'd even talked about it. So, things would happen a little sooner. That was okay. Making a home with him was all she wanted. Tyler and their child. She couldn't wait to tell him. What she hadn't expected was seeing Tyler put his head in his hands and begin weeping. At that moment, her beautiful mental picture of their young family shattered like fine crystal. She'd watched it breaking and falling in shards that sliced her insides. *But we can take a year, go to Nashville. Or stay here until the baby is older. We can be a family, can't we? We can still go to college a year or so later, right?*

But when he looked up at her, misery twisting his face, tears like she'd never seen before from him, she knew the truth. He was done — with them, with her dream. Yes, it had been her dream, not his. She was on her own, like she'd always been. Alone with their child. They weren't worth fighting for or rearranging his college timetable.

When Tyler walked away from her and out of her life, she thought she'd never survive the pain. At the time, she was sure she'd never experience anything as gut-wrenching, stripping her of the will to live. But she'd been wrong. A worse agony awaited her nine months later when she held Emma in her arms after fifteen hours of labor, knowing she couldn't keep her. Sydney had stroked the tiny fingers of her newborn, fingernails the size of a dewdrop, stared at her button nose and squinty blue eyes. Her vision blurred through tears that wouldn't stop. She'd wept until she was exhausted and dried out.

A month later, she packed her suitcases. She'd hardly spoken a word to anyone since returning from the hospital. Carolyn cast worried glances and assured her several times that it was for the best. She'd be glad one day.

Sydney's father had expressed disappointment in Sydney after learning she was pregnant. But during the months of her pregnancy, he hardly spoke about it, as if it didn't exist. When it was over, he had driven her to Chapel Hill to the University of North Carolina. During the three-hour drive, he chatted to her as she sat in stony silence beside him, telling her it was natural to be nervous going to college for the first time. She didn't correct him, didn't tell him her life had no meaning anymore. Whatever came next would be filler just to avoid dying.

She'd walked through her freshman year like a zombie, half dead except for a pulse, surprised each morning that she'd awakened. She pulled herself through her classes each day. Only the distraction of studying kept her from hurting herself. One day after sleeping until noon and missing an important class, she made a decision. She couldn't continue surviving on a thread about to snap. She decided then to live, to create a new life on the ashes of her tragedy. Initially, she felt no better, but knew if she didn't want to die, that's what she had to do. And eventually, she did feel better. She did heal. Mostly.

"Excuse me, can I take this chair?" A male voice hit her ears like a blow and jerked her to the present.

Her head snapped up, and she flinched, half expecting him to push her over. A twenty-something guy in surfer shorts and curly hair pointed to a chair across from her. She gestured to the chair. "Sure, help yourself."

When she lifted her head and he looked at her, his expression changed. "Thank you. I'm so sorry for disturbing you."

After he left with the chair, she realized that her face was drenched with tears.

℘　℘　℘

The following day, Sydney entered the kitchen where her mother was drinking coffee at the kitchen table. "Hi, Mom." She eyed the coffee pot. "Do you want more coffee? I'm going to make a little more."

"I've been up for a while and I drank two cups, so I'm fine, thanks. I should have made a bigger pot. I forgot how much you like coffee."

"No problem. I'm going to sweep the porch and trim your hedges out back. That'll keep you from having to do it yourself or hire someone."

"Sydney, you don't have to do that. You're on vacation. You should relax." Carolyn waved the air with one hand, still holding the newspaper in the other.

"I don't want to go to the beach *every* day. Besides, while I'm here, I can help you out, can't I? Surely, there's something you don't feel like doing or are too weak to do."

"Are you saying I'm old?"

"Yeah, you are. Sorry, Mom. It happens." Sydney grinned at her mother, who shook her head and mustered a smile.

"Okay, then. Have a ball. The broom is in the front coat closet. There's a dustpan there, too." She looked back at Sydney, who still stood in front of her. "What?"

Sydney splayed her hands. "What else? What else do you need done? I'll do the carport while I'm at it. I like staying busy, so you can benefit from that."

While she drank her coffee and ate a bowl of granola, Sydney jotted a list with her mother's help, even though she'd had to prod her to come up with enough tasks. That would keep her occupied for a couple of days, providing service to her mother while exorcising her own thoughts of Emma.

"Hi Gram, hi Mom." Jessie came into the kitchen, sleepy crinkles around her eyes. Her skin had darkened a shade, but her nose and shoulders were pink. "I'm not going to the beach today. I think I need a break. Is there a library nearby I can get to on my bike?"

"Yes, don't you remember?" Carolyn leaned forward and cocked her head toward Jessie. "I think you've been there, but you might have forgotten. It's four or five blocks from here in that direction." She pointed to the front window. "You could walk or ride your bike."

Sydney rose and took the list from the table. She turned to Jessie. "If you're bored, you can also practice your guitar. I don't think I've heard you do that since we got here." Sydney wanted to encourage the gift her daughter clearly had, even if Sydney herself had abandoned hers decades ago in a heap of tears.

"I *have* practiced, but quietly in my room. I didn't want to disturb anyone. And I—I'm trying to write a song."

Sydney drew in a sharp breath, a gush of pride in her daughter tainted by a memory that she herself had done the same thing eons ago. She pushed out a grin. "That's wonderful, Jessie. Will you play it for us when it's finished?"

Jessie turned her head away from them. She shrugged and muttered, "I don't know. Let's see how it turns out. Don't bug me about it, I'll let you know."

"Promise. I won't bug you. It's your privilege as a musician to unveil the art when it's ready and not before." Sydney used her circus announcer's voice.

"Whatever." Jessie went to the cupboard and rummaged for a bowl.

Sydney snatched the list from the table. "I guess I'll start on the porch. See y'all in a while."

Hours later, Sydney trudged into the house and flopped into an armchair in the living room, wiping perspiration from her brow with her wrist. She'd swept the porch, front and side, continued to the front walk, the carport, and the back patio. Then she moved on to the shed in the backyard. She'd removed everything from it, swept and hosed it down, dried the walls and floors with a towel, then a leaf-blower, then replaced everything in neat rows and stacks. Her mother had always been very tidy and organized, but there were likely things she no longer had the strength to do. The hedges in the front didn't need attention, but those in the back were uneven and overgrown.

She sat depleted, her frenetic energy having spun out of her all day. The work was cathartic, therapeutic. Or at least, it had kept troubling thoughts at arm's length. The benefit was as much for her as it was for her mother. Of course, at the end of the day, nothing was resolved in Sydney's search for Emma or her decision about her career, but her fatigue felt good.

The front door opened, and Jessie came in, a canvas bag over one arm. As she passed the doorway to the living room, Sydney called to her, "Did you find some good books?"

Jessie flinched in surprise. "Oh, hi Mom. Didn't see you in there. Have you been sitting in that chair all day?"

Sydney laughed aloud and shook her head. "No, my child. I'm resting for the *first* time today."

Jessie hovered in the doorway. In the place of her normally placid or bored expression, there was something different, something secretive, sparkling. Sydney's instincts prickled. "Did you have a nice time at the library? You were there a long time." What had Jessie been up to?

Jessie grinned and let out an embarrassed laugh. "Once I got there, I kept seeing things I wanted to read, so I just read some of them right there, but brought a couple home, too. They have this little seating area that looks like someone's living room. It's nice." She shrugged, shifted her bag up on her shoulder.

Sydney nodded. Her eyes followed Jessie as she left the room.

Once Sydney rested, she decided to begin the hated process of job-hunting. She'd start with some websites where openings were posted. She hadn't looked for a job in nearly two decades. To make matters worse, she wanted to change fields and hadn't a clue what she wanted to do or even the current protocol for job seekers.

Seeing what was available that a former math teacher could do or learn to do would be her first step. Maybe she'd have some pleasant surprises or new ideas that afternoon.

She poured some iced tea and settled at the dining room table with her laptop and a blank legal pad, doing her best to ignore the rumbles of anxiety in the pit of her stomach.

An hour later, Sydney looked at her pad at the three lines she'd written. Analyst, bank loan officer, bookkeeper. She'd likely need training for all three before she could even apply. Not to mention they didn't quite register a zero on her interest scale. Despite this, she sent a resume to all three, feeling only slightly better for going through the motions.

Most of the other job openings that might fit a former math teacher required years of experience in various software and platforms she'd never heard of.

Sydney leaned back and sighed, as her exhaustion and discouragement blended together and trickled down inside her. She cast a dull gaze around the room and listened to the tomb-like silence of the big house. A ping sounded in her cell phone. Maybe one of her friends had sent her a text message. That would perk her up.

She glanced at the phone and was surprised to see a name pop up. Pam, the school receptionist. Maybe she had some news about Rod Matheson, hopefully a fair outcome.

She read, *Hi Sydney, I hope your summer is going well and you're getting needed rest. I need to tell you about something and wonder if you're available. Can you call me when you can talk for a minute? Thanks, Pam.*

Hmm. Strange. Didn't sound like the call would yield good news, but she wouldn't know until she talked to Pam. She clicked her number and Pam answered on the second ring.

"Hi, Sydney. I'm so sorry to bother you while you're on your summer break. I hope you've gotten some peace since that incident with Rod."

"Thanks, Pam. I'm with my daughter now visiting my mom near the coast. It's been a good break. I hope your summer is going well."

"It is, thanks. I need to apologize to you for something. A week or so after you left the school, I happened to overhear a couple of teachers in the lounge talking about you. I should have called to let you know, but honestly, it didn't occur to me at the time."

A chill rippled through Sydney. "What were they saying?"

"Apparently, when you disappeared without a word to anyone from the school, it was conjectured that you'd had some kind of inappropriate relationship with one of the seniors and had been suspended."

"What! I hope you're joking." Unlikely. A mixture of anxiety and anger sprang up inside Sydney. Her school disaster had morphed into something she'd never imagined.

"I wish I were. I only heard this rumor once. It came from two teachers from a different grade and subject. Language arts, I think, not math. I don't know how it started, but maybe something was said about there being an incident with a senior, but no one knew what kind and maybe they filled in the blanks themselves."

"That's terrible!" Sydney stood up and began to pace. "That means my reputation is trashed at the school, in spite of the fact that *I* was the one wronged. Could you have intervened to correct them? Not criticizing you, Pam, but wondered about the context."

"It was on the tip of my tongue to do that, but I remember Wade had asked me not to talk about the situation to faculty members. In retrospect, I could have interrupted them only to say they were not correct, but they were on their way out of the lounge. That idea didn't come to me until much later. I'm so sorry. I hope it will blow over before you come back. I wanted you to know in case it doesn't."

"Well, *I* was never asked not to talk. I can certainly do that if there's a need." Oh, yes, she could. Sydney the Mouth wasn't finished with this injustice. "Thank you, Pam, I appreciate your telling me."

"I debated whether to tell you now or wait until September. I didn't want it to spoil your summer, but thought you had the right to know. Better late than never. It probably won't be a big deal anymore by the time you come back."

After she hung up with the woman, Sydney's mind went into overdrive. How had this started? Wade had been careful to try to keep it under wraps, likely to protect Rod Matheson.

She could guess what had happened. Vanishing from school without warning would likely happen only as a disciplinary measure for something serious. If no one knew why she didn't finish the school year so close to the end, as Pam had said, people filled in the blanks.

After twelve years and a stellar reputation as a dedicated teacher, no one gave Sydney the benefit of the doubt. Even her colleagues were ready to trash her memory at the first opportunity.

She dialed Wade's number. It rang several times and went to voicemail. "Wade, this is Sydney. Are you aware there was a rumor about me having an inappropriate relationship with a student and that was the reason I was suspended? I just learned about this, a month after the fact. I hope you'll straighten this out for me. I don't know what you can do over the summer, but I need your. You can call me anytime on my cell. Thanks."

Leaving the phone on the dining room table. Sydney went out to the side porch and sat in a wicker chair. She tucked her feet up and circled them with her arms. The swaying of her mother's hanging ferns and begonias didn't calm her agitation. And there was something else twisting inside. Shame? Why would she feel shame for something she didn't do?

The shadow fell afresh. *Eighteen years old and pregnant. Let herself go. Good Christian girl ended up immoral after all.*

With all her effort, Sydney pushed away the accusation, though a trace of it lingered.

But this was a *rumor*. She thought she'd left the school turmoil behind. If she got another job and didn't return, that legacy would outlast her. If she returned, she'd have to face it herself to dispel the ugly opinions. She couldn't count on Wade to do it, despite her request.

Once again, she found herself in this familiar place. Alone to defend herself.

Chapter Eight

Sydney awoke the next morning to a band of sun streaming through the bedroom windows casting bright light across her bed. Must be late. Why had she slept so long? She shifted her head and looked at the clock on the bedside table. Eight-thirty. The previous night, she'd tumbled into bed before ten. That's what a day of physical work would do at her age. Wear her out.

Despite the late hour, she didn't hop out of bed and run for the shower. No need to do that anymore. Especially now, in her new slow-paced life. She plumped the pillow and settled her head back in the middle of it, allowing her gaze to rove around the bedroom. Matching knotty pine furniture, whitewashed for a homey country look, a puff of white Priscilla curtains moving slightly with a morning breeze from the open window.

Her mind went to the rumor circulating about her at the school and her stomach tensed. Despite her reaction, after a good night's sleep, it no longer stirred her desire to phone every faculty member in her address book to straighten them out. It still bothered her, but she'd done what she could do. She'd called Wade. But his track record for caring wasn't impressive.

Sydney quelled a desire to return to Charlotte and defend her honor. No. Not only would it not do any good, but she was tired of the fight reflex that came so naturally. Face it, in summer, her hands would be tied. She'd have to remain in peoples' minds as the sleazy teacher who preyed on students her daughter's age. Another layer on the injustice.

She should shift this burden to God. Should have been her *first* response, but sadly, it rarely was. She prayed a brief and desperate prayer. Despite the loose ends in her life, a small wave of peace stole over her as she released the matter. Or tried.

Sydney slipped down from the bed and her toes curled into the soft pile of the rug. Strangely, it felt good to be there at the Victorian house in Kennessey. She'd never had that reaction when making her perfunctory summer trips with Jessie over the years. She took a quick shower and threw on a pair of lightweight drawstring shorts and a tank. She pulled her thick, straight hair up into a ponytail. The forecast predicted higher temperatures for that day, and that trend would continue until September. It might not be Charlotte, but it was still North Carolina.

As she went down the wide staircase, she heard voices, laughter from the kitchen. When she entered the kitchen, she was surprised to see her mother and Jessie hovering together near the stove.

"You don't want the batter too thick, or it won't spread right," her mother said to Jessie, who stood watching as Carolyn poured batter into a cast iron pan with a resulting sizzle. Neither of them seemed to realize Sydney was there, so she watched them in bemusement.

"Those blueberries look like zits on the pancake," Jessie said, then laughed. Carolyn laughed, too. "Once the batter rises, they won't stick out as much. They'll get juicy and plump."

"Yum. Can't wait."

Sydney felt like an intruder but thrust out a cheery greeting. "Good morning. Looks like a cooking class in here."

"Hi Mom," Jessie said, without looking away from the spreading mound in the iron pan.

"Good morning, Sydney," her mother said. "I'm teaching Jessie my blueberry pancake recipe. She wanted me to show her how to do it."

Surprise after surprise. Sydney shook her head. Jessie had never shown interest in cooking before.

"That's always been one of my favorites, your Gram's pancakes." Sydney continued watching them. "She used to make them for us sometimes on weekends. I'm glad you're learning,

Jessie. You can become the designated pancake-maker in our house."

Jessie snorted. "Don't count on it. Maybe on Mother's Day."

Sydney and Carolyn chuckled. Felt weird to have a pleasant exchange instead of a tense one, which she hadn't had yet with her mother. Not in a week.

She poured herself some coffee as Jessie and Carolyn once again were absorbed in their project. "I guess I'll go back upstairs for a while, since you two are occupied." They didn't respond but continued murmuring together.

Sydney shrugged and took a container of yogurt from the fridge. She snagged a spoon from the strainer by the sink, took her coffee in the other hand, and headed back upstairs. A good time to make another phone call. She was ready for round two, and Jessie and her mother were distracted. Aside from that, she felt left out.

She wasn't as nervous as the first time. She made sure she still heard voices downstairs before dialing. The next adoption agency on her list was called Family Love Adoption Services. Kennessey had only one agency, and the largest nearby town was Wilmington. With a twinge, Sydney remembered her father lived there, though she hadn't called him yet. She and Jessie would have to go see him while they were in the area. But for now, she had a mission to accomplish.

"Good morning, Family Love Adoption Agency," said the female voice on the phone.

Sydney repeated her summary, which she'd polished and practiced since the last time. The woman's response was like the previous call. No surprise there. At the close of the conversation, the woman said, "We'll call you and let you know what we find, if we see your name in our records. At that point, you'll need to come into the office. Once we meet you, we'll go from there to reach out if the contact agreement allows."

Sydney thanked the woman and hung up, feeling more encouraged than she had the first time. The response was just as iffy, but now she understood it would take time. She'd begun.

She glanced through her emails from the previous day. Not much filled her inbox. Just as well. She spied a message from Wade and one from Eden. She'd get Wade's over with first. An email instead of a phone call. She'd likely need Eden's to pick her emotions back up again.

First, from Wade. "Hello, Sydney. I was surprised by your phone message yesterday. I was unaware of such a rumor, and I understand it must be distressing for you. Remember, though, it is only a rumor. Once you're back in the fall, everyone will see you there and realize you are still an employee. I neglected to inform the faculty that you were on leave for personal reasons, as we discussed. My apologies for that. I'm sure you know that no one is at the school all summer, including our support staff. I can almost guarantee you everything will be forgotten by the fall. Hope you are enjoying your summer. Wade."

He'd neglected to tell them. So, of course rumors ran wild. She wanted to scream. Again, it was up to her to straighten out the mess herself.

She filled her lungs with air. Twice. Returned her gaze to the phone. Next, Eden. "*Hi Sydney. I hope everything's going well with your visit, your mom, and your search for Emma. Let me know how I can pray for you while you're there. We're beginning a nice summer here in Indiana. I hope it holds, because my girls will be coming home for a few days before they leave for a trip to Europe. Such a life! I'd join them, but they didn't invite me! I'll figure out something fun to do this summer. Like sell my house, maybe. More on that later. I've just started mulling it over but won't rush into anything. You know me, I absolutely never rush into big decisions, so you'll probably find me here in five years, still mulling. Anyway, be sure to have fun there and don't worry about anything! Let God love you to pieces every day! Love you, Eden.*"

Sydney smiled as tenderness for Eden ribboned through her. Such a heart for others, yet her friend hadn't yet found her own happiness. Not that Eden was unhappy. Maybe just restless.

She hit 'respond' so she could tell Eden of her latest source of tension but changed her mind. She didn't want to be the high-maintenance friend with one problem after another. Even if that description currently described her life.

Eden's note triggered a wave of nostalgia for their weekend. Was it only a few weeks ago they'd been together in Charlotte? Sydney missed them all. She took a few minutes to send a group email, updating her friends on the events so far during her visit, including the attempts with adoption agencies and the lack of drama, thankfully, with her mother.

A strong thread of concern and love bound her to them, even when she got caught up in her daily routines. Currently, she didn't *have* any daily routines. Only heavy life concerns like finding a job and clearing her reputation.

With that realization, Sydney felt restless. Summers in Charlotte were never lacking in activity—errands, chores, lunch dates, afternoons at the local pool, driving Jessie places. Sydney kept busy and time passed.

That summer, she was at loose ends. How would she spend her days for the next week or so? The beach was always there, but she didn't want to go every day. She'd helped her mom and could continue to do that. She hadn't kept up with any friends from high school a century ago, if they were still living there, so she was like a stranger in Kennessey.

She and Jessie should go back to Charlotte. A week is the most they'd ever come to visit, and they'd just passed that marker. Yet, what would she do back home? Sydney shook her head, and a faint grip clutched her stomach.

As she considered returning home for any reason, it brought to her mind the school problems, her lack of close friendships, the crazy routine she had during the school year. A life she'd been content to leave behind, if only for a while.

Besides that, during her first week off from work, she'd finished the list of chores she usually caught up on over summer break. What awaited her there now? A job search? She let out a deep sigh. She'd have to continue working on that issue regardless of where she lived unless she planned on returning to her teaching job. If she were home, she'd be in a better position to combat the rumor. Maybe she'd run into a colleague somewhere and tell what really happened. Sydney snorted. Fat chance of *that* in such a huge city.

She should phone Serena and Gail, two colleagues in the math department she was friendly with, to ask if they'd heard the rumor, but stopped her hand on the phone. If they hadn't heard, she'd sound like she was guilty and trying to cover up. Her only other option was to let it fade over the summer. Then combat the lies at the start of the school year. If she returned.

Closure on Emma first. Her thoughts would be clearer after that. *Then* they could return to Charlotte. Despite Carolyn's surprise invitation, Sydney didn't want to abuse her hospitality by staying the whole summer.

Sydney trotted back downstairs to the kitchen, empty now. A plate of two large, golden pancakes sat on the counter, likely for her. Faint voices filtered inside from the backyard, her mother's fading but still commanding one blended with Jessie's softer tone. Sydney couldn't distinguish their words, but she leaned toward the kitchen window to flick the curtain to one side. The two of them stood next to a flowerbed as Carolyn explained something.

She walked to the back door and down wooden steps to the yard. The grass was cool and soft under her bare feet. "Hey, you guys. Thanks for the pancakes. Hope they were for me."

Jessie turned toward her, tenting her eyes from the sun with one hand. "Yeah, we left them on the counter for you. We ate ours already."

"That was nice. I'll warm them up and have them in a bit. I have a better idea. Um, do you two want to go to lunch today? We haven't done that yet. My treat."

Carolyn straightened and turned away from the flowerbed. "Why don't you two go? I woke up early today. I've been doing that lately, and I'm a bit tired. There's a new sandwich place downtown that has outdoor seating under umbrellas. You might like it."

Sydney caught Jessie's gaze and hitched her chin up. "Interested?"

"Yeah, but let's go early, okay? I was planning to go back to the library this afternoon."

"Okay, I can drop you off there after lunch." Sydney smiled at the two of them, but her mind was buzzing. Another trip to the library? Who or what was at the library?

An hour and a half later, Jessie and Sydney were seated under a lime green umbrella stamped with a Mexican beer trademark. Potted palms scattered around the patio lent a tropical atmosphere. The breeze was balmy, just like Sydney liked it before the furnace of summer ramped into gear. Carolyn had been right. She liked this sandwich shop. It was casual, with a vacation vibe. The sandwich descriptions on the menu made her mouth water.

They ordered their sandwiches and handed the waitress their menus. When the waitress left, Jessie said, "We don't ever go out for lunch at home. Well, not a lot. You do that sometimes with your friends."

"Well, we *should*. More often." Sydney took a sip of her iced tea. Gratitude pooled inside her at the thought that her daughter wanted them to have lunch together. They didn't always click, especially with the adolescent attitude Jessie sometimes copped, but deep inside, her daughter was a good girl. She prayed that whatever was happening at the library wouldn't change that.

"So, can I ask you, what's the fascination at the library?" Sydney propped her chin on her hand.

When Jessie's cheeks colored, Sydney's adrenalin hopped up a notch. "You can tell me. I'm a cool mom, remember?"

Jessie let out a breath and hesitated, as if she were considering whether to bring Sydney into her confidence. "Well, so, I met this guy." She flicked her hand out. "He's a good guy, so don't worry."

"Hmm. Why would I worry?" She narrowed her eyes at Jessie. "Do I have anything to worry about?"

Jessie laughed and looked embarrassed. "No, you don't. I only just met him. And I *know* you, you worry. So, I went to the library, and he was there. We started talking, and well, I liked him. Don't look at me like that, mom. I'm not pregnant, we were just talking."

Sydney gave a nervous laugh. "Okay, okay. I'm still a mama bear, is that so wrong? How old is this guy?"

"His name is Zach and he's eighteen, or almost. He'll be eighteen soon."

Sydney nodded, hoping she'd be able to maintain the go-to-lunch-together status she'd obtained just moments ago. She swallowed. She schooled her voice to a casual girlfriend level. Added a one-shouldered shrug. "So, tell me about him. What's he like?"

Jessie leaned back in her metal chair. "He's laid back and funny. We talked for a long time. His parents are divorced, so he's here spending the summer with his dad. During the school year, he stays with his mom somewhere in Georgia. He likes hanging out with his dad, though. I think they're close. Let's see, what else? His dad owns the golf course in town, the big one near here. Zach works there for the summer doing different odd jobs for his dad. He cleans the carts, things like that."

"He sounds interesting. I'm surprised he has time to go to the library, since he works."

"He doesn't go a lot. He was there that time I met him because he wanted a couple books about art. He's only going today because he's getting off early and so we can talk some more. He likes to draw, especially comics. He's into comics."

"Hmm. I hear that's a big business. If he does art and likes comics, it's a good combination."

Jessie seemed pleased with Sydney's response, as if she'd expected her to belittle Zach's interests. "Yeah, it is. He's going to college in the fall. For art or design, something like that."

Sydney's tension unwound like a chain, one link at a time. So, this Zach fellow would be gone by the fall. Couldn't get too serious, then, could it? And he wanted to go to college, so that was good.

"I see your mind working, Mom. Don't read too much into this. We're just friends."

Sydney laughed aloud. "Okay, I won't predict or worry about anything. Just friends, eh? You aren't a bit interested in him?"

Again, the embarrassed flutter of her eyelids. "Yes, I think he's cute. Mostly, I like talking to him. And I need to make a friend, don't I? I don't know how long we're gonna stay, though."

"I wanted to talk to you about that, Jess." Sydney pushed her glass away and crossed her arms over her stomach. She wasn't ready for this conversation, but it likely had to happen soon. "I'm weighing the pros and cons of staying longer, maybe the whole summer."

"Yes!" Jessie's arms shot up in the air. Just then, the waitress came with a tray laden with tall sandwiches, fries, and potato salad, enough to feed them for several days. Sydney thanked the waitress, and she left.

"I said, I'm *thinking* about it. I haven't decided. Tell me why you'd like to stay. Your input is important, of course."

Jessie grinned. Her face was animated, her blue eyes expressive, darting around as she prepared to speak. "Well, for one, I'm getting to know Gram better. That's fun. Then there's Zach. I'd like to get to know him better, too. There's the beach. We both love the beach. Home is boring. Don't you think home is boring, Mom? It's more fun here."

Sydney found herself nodding. Jessie had certainly thought about this. "Yeah, it's a little boring sometimes. But if we stay, would you be willing to get a part-time job to help pay for your car?"

Jessie was already nodding vigorously. She snatched a French fry from her plate and popped it into her mouth. "Yes, I want to work and save money. I'm seventeen, so it's about time I got my license. I can even get it here. Maybe Zach can get me a job at the golf course." She picked up a half of her sandwich and took a bite.

"You don't know anything about golf."

Jessie shrugged and wiped her mouth. "I know. Maybe I can work in the office or something. Take out trash, chase balls.

Whatever. There's an ice cream shop right next door, too. I can ride there on my bike. That would be a fun job."

Okay, this idea had potential. Sydney reached for her sandwich. "We can run by there and get you an application on the way home today."

"Great idea, Mom." She was rewarded with Jessie's full-teeth smile, activating her dimples.

The wheels in Sydney's head were already spinning. Jessie might be taken care of with a summer job, but what about her? What would *she* do all summer? Of course, it would be practical to already be in the region if and when the agencies called her to come check Emma's file. "Maybe I can get a part-time job, too." She hadn't meant to say it aloud.

Jessie clapped her hands. "That's great!"

What had she gotten herself into? Judging by the look of glee on Jessies' face, Sydney had just committed herself to staying in Kennessey for the rest of the summer.

She fervently hoped she wouldn't regret it.

Chapter Nine

The month of June crept gently into Kennessey like a southern lady drinking sweet tea. Soon after, temperatures climbed, and there was nothing gentle or ladylike about it—a typical Carolina summer. Towering pine trees around the perimeter of the Victorian kept the ground floor comfortable in the mornings. Otherwise, window unit air conditioners rumbled into the quietness of the house.

Two weeks had passed since Sydney, with Jessie's help, decided to stay in Kennessey for the rest of the summer. She'd made one overnight trip back to Charlotte to pick up mail and request temporary forwarding at the post office. She also drenched her new but neglected azaleas and packed an additional suitcase to provide more clothes for the expanded summer vacation. Almost as an afterthought, she hauled most of her pots of geraniums from the patio to the car and wedged them in the trunk next to her bags and suitcase.

She checked over the house inside and out before locking up and hitting the road. The roof would need to be replaced soon. She let out a sigh. A huge expense requiring fulltime employment. But she'd put off that thought until the fall.

Sydney had expected a twinge of longing to stay at home or return there sooner, but it didn't come. The silent house and the life she'd left there didn't beckon her. On the contrary, a shadowy oppression accompanied her brief visit but evaporated when she headed east again toward Kennessey. First time *that* had ever happened.

The day after Jessie filled out a job application at the ice cream shop, she began working there part time. She usually rode her bike round trip to work and after her shift, sometimes dropped by the neighboring golf course to see Zach. Once when Sydney stopped there to pick Jessie up after work, she met her daughter's new friend. Zach seemed like a nice guy, polite and friendly, but Sydney would still watch their relationship carefully, her mom antennas at full mast.

Jessie's life had fallen into a comfortable rhythm, working part time, hanging out with Zach, going to the beach alone or with Sydney, and practicing driving under Sydney's partially patient instruction. Though Sydney wasn't as bad a driving instructor as she'd expected to be, she normally needed a glass of wine once they got home.

Jessie's summer took a pleasant shape, but Sydney had to work harder at hers. She'd filled in her girlfriends about the decision to stay for the summer and that met with their hearty approval. She had no response from the three resumes she's sent but she did learn that several industries in Charlotte had a hiring freeze for the summer and possibly longer, stacking the scales toward the unwelcome prospect of remaining in teaching.

And apparently, she hadn't yet found the correct adoption agency. She could always ask her mother, who would be more likely to know, assuming she even remembered that far back. But Sydney didn't want to open that dusty box of pain with her mother.

Sydney filled her time jogging in the neighborhood, walking at the nearby park, or swimming at the beach. Every day or two, she checked job openings and increasingly wondered if she'd ever find something compelling enough to do. She ended up sending out two more resumes for uninspiring jobs whose titles she quickly forgot.

She also began an online course designed to assess her strengths and possible career choices. Her daily sessions with her online video mentor gave her the impression she was being proactive in her hoped-for career change. So far, it looked like another failure loomed at the end of summer.

"What are you doing every morning on your computer, Sydney? Are you writing a book?" Carolyn entered the formal dining room where Sydney had set up her laptop.

A spiral notebook and several sheets of paper were spread across the table. Through her earbuds and the perky voice of the video instructor, Sydney still heard her mother clearly. She paused the course and removed her earbuds. "I'm listening to an online course about career options. I've been thinking of getting out of teaching. Maybe soon."

Her mother's eyebrows lifted. "Oh, I thought you liked teaching."

"I used to. But for the last two or three years—" she shook her head. "I've stopped liking it. I don't know why, exactly. I think eighteen years in one career is enough."

Her mother shrugged. "That's the exact reason to stay. You've put in a lot of years and contributed to your pension. Will you lose the benefit of those years if you just quit?"

Sydney bristled. "I'm not intending to 'just quit'. I'd give proper notice, of course. And I don't *think* I'll lose the benefit of my years. I—I haven't checked into that part yet." She hadn't told her mother anything about the Rod Matheson incident, so in all fairness, she didn't know the dire state of Sydney's need to change. "My current situation at school isn't very positive. The leadership is unsupportive of teachers."

"Well, you can't have everything. I went back to work full-time once you kids were in school. I didn't necessarily love it either, but it was a big help when your father and I divorced. I had a solid career and didn't have to depend on anyone."

"So, I should stay in a job I hate until I retire? That's seventeen more years. Life's too short for that kind of sacrifice, just for financial security." She stared at her mother and blinked, frustration simmering on low heat. "It's not like I'm not planning to work at *all*. There are other jobs that could fit someone with my background." Her voice had taken on that familiar edge so difficult to rein in.

"No need to be testy. I just want you all to be secure. There's Jessie to think of."

"And I absolutely never think of Jessie, it's all about me."

"I didn't say that. I just want you to do the responsible thing."

Sydney sat back in her chair with a loud sigh and glared at her mother. It had been a peaceful month. She'd been hopeful things had changed. "Mother, I've been raising a child alone with no one's help for the last seven years. If you ask me, I've done a pretty good job, even though it's difficult at times. I've been *responsible*. I'm not sure why I have to remind you of that. I know you went through these pressures, too, but your job was your focus."

"What are you saying? That I neglected you kids?"

Guilt stabbed through Sydney. Was she being too hard on her mother? She'd certainly felt neglected, though likely Chet and Kevin would recount a different story. She sighed. "I didn't mean that. I'd just like a little support once in a while. I am unhappy in my job and have been for some time. I don't intend to become the village bum and make Jessie support me. I think you know me better than that, so stop worrying that we'll land on your doorstep."

"I'm not worried about that in the least. I'm the one who invited you for the whole summer, remember?" The lines around her mother's pinched lips deepened.

"Yes, you did. And I'm grateful, I really am." Sydney paused. No reason not to tell her, though she'd leave out the rumor. "Mom, in April one of my students *assaulted* me." At her mother's gasp, Sydney nodded. "Yes. He pushed me hard, and I was mildly injured. And he had no consequences. None. Now, that same student won't be back in the fall, but I don't want to work in that environment anymore. My principal did *nothing* about it." Except push *her* out the door before the end of the school year. "He's buddies with the kid's parents and sided with the abuser. So, you see now why I feel unsupported by my boss."

She'd intended to keep the whole incident under wraps, yet often she felt her mother understood nothing of the daily pressures of her life. Of course, she hadn't really divulged those to her, either.

"That's terrible, Sydney. Maybe it will calm down by the time you go back."

Sydney struggled for a response. She found her mother's outrage on her behalf rather diluted. "Yes, I hope so. Unless I can find something else before then."

She fixed her gaze on her mother's. It was useless to wait for compassion, for nurturing. "I'm sorry if I'm a disappointment to you, Mom. I never asked to be the black sheep of the family. I didn't follow the stellar career paths of my perfect brothers, but I didn't do too badly, either. Even if I don't teach math anymore, I can do something like be an actuary or an analyst. Something math-y." Even as she said it, her heart sank. Those careers didn't call to her, either. *Don't dream, Sydney. It's too late for affirmation.*

"I'm not disappointed in you, Sydney." Her mother's tone was crisp. "And I certainly don't see you as the black sheep. Don't know where you got that idea. You create offenses where there are none."

She paused while Sydney pushed down her roiling emotions. A primal child's cry lay suffocating in her throat, and there it would stay. She'd said more than enough. "Maybe."

"Well, I can see you're in a bad mood, so I'll leave you to your work." Carolyn turned and left the room. Something inside Sydney deflated with a whoosh and shriveled. Her mother hadn't been willing or able to read between Sydney's caustic lines.

Par for the course.

Sydney jerked in her chair. The *course*! She'd told Jessie she would pick her up from work that day so they could practice driving after her shift. Her daughter had told her, "You can pick me up at the golf course today, Mom. I get off work before Zach so I can go over and help him finish up." She'd grinned and giggled, her white teeth glistening against her suntan. "Sometimes he drives me around on the golf cart. It's fun." She had a glow and a softness when she talked about Zach. Her daughter might just be falling in love for the first time. Sydney swallowed with mixed feelings.

She glanced down at the time posted on her computer and breathed a sigh of relief. Not only was she not late to pick up Jessie, but she had time for a short walk around the lake at the park beforehand. She'd prefer the beach, but the park was closer. She had to move her legs and clear her emotions. Her exchange with her mother had left a sour taste in her throat. She was an adult. Why did she still try to extract approval from her mother?

By the time she reached the still waters of the lake, she only had twenty-five minutes. She'd go halfway around, then come back. Several walkers were scattered on the path, some with leashed dogs, some jogging, all in summer attire. She skirted around them as she stretched her legs.

Regret filled her stomach. She could have handled that interaction with her mother better. The thump of her sandaled feet hitting the packed dirt kept pace with her silent words. *Lord, why do I so often have a chip on my shoulder with my mom? It comes out so easily like my native tongue.* Finding offense where there was none, her mother had said. *I shouldn't expect any understanding or nurturing from her. Yet, I still do, then lash out like a little kid. You're my nurturer. You're my perfect parent, the one who accepts me. Help me to grasp that in my heart. Lord, soften my tongue so I have words of grace, words that love instead of cut.*

How many times had she prayed similar words? Yet she knew they emerged from the hurt she'd locked away. Maybe that's why she was here in Kennessey, to do the hard work of healing. She hoped it wasn't too late.

The golf course was a mile or so away from her mother's neighborhood, so both the course and the ice cream shop were an easy bike ride for Jessie. They'd gotten into the habit of practicing driving two or three times a week, so on those days, Sydney dropped Jessie off and later picked her up so she could practice. Only a mile, a blessed relief from the usual taxi service she provided when they were back home.

She drove down the winding driveway toward the stately club house of the golf course and parked. It was late afternoon, but the sun was still high in the sky, providing a muted blast of heat. Her gaze roved across the rolling green hills of the course. Golfers and carts dotted the smooth, green terrain, but she didn't see one of them motoring around with her daughter aboard. Sydney pushed the front door and cool air surrounded her, chilling her bare arms.

A carved wood counter extended along one end of the airy lobby and wood beams on the vaulted ceiling gave the ambiance of a fancy hunting lodge. Nearby in a cluster of low-slung leather armchairs, a few golfers sat, rehashing their game, their laughter spiraling up to the ceiling. Other golfers came and went through the doors closest to the course, pulling wheeled bags behind them.

On the opposite wall, she saw the pro shop, containing clubs, bags, and whatever else a golfer without his or her own equipment would need to buy or rent. Attached to it was a small snack bar with a matching wood counter where two customers sat and ate. The wall facing her was mostly of glass, providing a stunning view of the course, with lush green swells and a large lake. Still no sign of Jessie.

Seemed to be an upscale business. As she approached the counter, she continued observing her surroundings. A faint memory sifted back to her in filmy fragments. Tyler had worked there when he was in high school. It looked fancier now than it had back then, but time had dulled her mental picture. His uncle had owned it, though she'd forgotten his name. An unbidden memory of Tyler had less ability to create a ripple inside after all the years. Instead, a distant yet hollow ache lay in its place. She'd reconciled herself to past events and gone on, as he had long before her.

"Hello, can I help you with something?"

A male voice broke through her wash of memories. She jerked her head toward the voice of someone who had appeared behind the counter. Sydney stilled. Her mouth went dry, and her heart began thumping against her ribs.

The man froze as well, and they stared at each other for a few full seconds before he said, "Sydney?"

"Tyler." She swallowed then took a deep breath. A second deep breath. "Is it you?" Couldn't be. She was just thinking about him for the first time in a while. But ever since the day she'd begun trying to unearth the story of Emma, Tyler had entered her thoughts more often, and with a gamut of emotions. Strong feelings and faded ones. Feelings she thought had died.

And there he was. Tyler Hoffman. She'd recognize his face anywhere, even with the filling in of maturity and the addition of fine lines around his never-forgotten gray-blue eyes. She thought she might faint. She reached out her fingers to grip the rim of the counter.

He stared a second more, then a slight smile curved his lips. "I—uh, it's good to see you. How long has it been?"

She struggled to recover. Her voice came out almost in a croak. "About thirty years." She forced out a chuckle, shook her head. "Can you believe it?" This was surreal. She had to be dreaming. Seeing Tyler was the last thing she'd expected that day.

He looked good. She suppressed a desire for him to think the same about her, not because she cared. It was a female thing. He'd abandoned her and she wanted him to see she was fine, thank you very much.

She swallowed. "This is amazing, Tyler. What are you doing here? I thought you were in Atlanta or somewhere down south."

"I moved back to town two years ago to take care of Dad." His voice was relaxed, as it had always been in the past, but his gaze was focused, tense. "My dad had pancreatic cancer, and I came back to take care of him until he passed away. My mom passed a few years before."

"I'm sorry about your parents. I always liked them."

"Thanks." His eyes held hers and she couldn't interpret the expression held there. "Yeah, it was hard losing them. But I got to spend the last year of Dad's life looking after him. Those months were precious to me. During that same year, my uncle Cliff, the one who owned this place and a few other courses, decided to retire. He offered me as many as I wanted to buy."

Sydney lifted her eyebrows. "Really? So, *you* own them now?"

Tyler shook his head. "Just two of them. Two was all I could afford at the time. I go back and forth between the two, which isn't too hard since they're not far from each other. What about you?"

So far, their conversation resembled that of two old friends running into each other after a few years. Not two former lovers who'd had a child and broken apart in tragic despair. He didn't show a trace of that on his still handsome face. Of course, he didn't. It wasn't tragic for him. He'd gotten his college scholarship and gone on with his teenage life. While she'd given birth, said goodbye to their child, and had to rebuild her life from the ashes.

She realized he'd asked her a question. "I live in Charlotte with my daughter. We came to visit my mother. You remember my mother, don't you?"

"Yes, of course. The formidable Carolyn." He grinned, evoking the name she'd secretly given her mother, a name only Tyler knew.

"The very same. Jessie, my daughter, and I came for a visit but decided to stay for the summer." How much should she tell him? He didn't have the right to know. Nevertheless, she added, "I teach high school math, so I have my summers off."

"Oh, Jessie! I had no idea she was your daughter. She's my son's new best friend."

"Zach is your son?"

"Yes. He's here for the summer, working for me. He talks about Jessie a lot. There may be young love blooming."

Sydney gave him a bland smile, unsure of what to say. "Maybe."

Tyler's smile fell a little, as did his buoyant tone. "It's really good to see you, Sydney." He blinked, stared. "It's been way too long."

She didn't respond, but held his eyes for a moment, hoping he'd see her putting up a wall despite the humming inside she tried to ignore. That wall had meaning. The wall *remembered*. Yes, she'd forgiven him, but he had no right to treat her like another one of his high school friends who'd just rumbled into town. Crossed paths. He probably wanted to talk about old times, yack it up over drinks.

A clatter of voices broke the silence between them. Sydney turned and saw Jessie and Zach enter by the glass door, laughing together. "Hey, Mom," she called across the space, triggering an echo. She turned to Zach. "We're gonna go *driving* now."

"Oh, scary. I hope they clear the roads. No one's safe!" Zach laughed as Jessie swatted him on the shoulder. They approached where Tyler and Sydney stood frozen in awkward silence.

"Soon the roads will be safe, but not just yet." Sydney smiled at the pleasant young man who resembled his dad. Now she saw it.

"Hey, Ms. Bennett. I guess you met my dad," Zach said.

Tyler smiled at his son, softening his strained features. "Sydney and I have known each other since high school."

"Really? That's cool." Zach turned back to Jessie, and they resumed murmuring and snickering together.

Sydney looked at Tyler. "Well, good seeing you. We'll get going now."

"Sydney—" Tyler said, his voice laced with urgency. "I, uh. I'd like to catch up sometime soon." When she hesitated, he added, "Please. We can get a Coke or something tomorrow when I get off." He lifted his eyebrows, awaiting her response.

She should put him off, give herself that critical margin of time she always needed before making a decision. But instead, she found herself saying, "Sure. That'll be nice."

"Remember Zoey's Coffee Shop? I can get there by five. Is that good for you?"

"Sure. Five tomorrow at Zoey's." She gave him a tight-lipped smile and turned to Jessie, her stomach churning like the early winds of an approaching hurricane. "Ready?"

Jessie nodded. "Bye, guys." She waved at Zach and Tyler as she and Sydney turned to leave.

So normal from an outsider's perspective, Sydney and Tyler, two old friends catching up. On the inside, the storm picked up violence, uprooting old memories from forgotten places, hurling them into the sky. The bizarre scene at the golf club reception might have been from a movie. Couldn't be her life. Couldn't be Tyler she'd just seen after three decades.

When they were in the car, Jessie said, "So, you knew Zach's dad in high school, huh?" Her voice was laid back but didn't hide her eager curiosity.

"Yup." Sydney stared straight ahead. Started the car and put it in reverse.

"Were you guys friends?"

Sydney sighed. She had to change the subject, and fast. "Yes, we were."

"You dated?"

She turned her head to Jessie. "Yes, we did. Happy?" She forced out a grin. "It was a long time ago, Jessie. Let it go."

"It's funny to think of you being my age and dating someone."

"Hard to believe I was once seventeen? Thanks a lot. It's not like I'm a hundred."

"I know. So, you're going to see Mr. Hoffman tomorrow? I thought I heard him say that."

"Yes. At a coffee shop, just to catch up on old times." She sent Jessie a smile, hoping her interrogation was over. "Ready to drive? I think you're almost ready for your test, after a few more practice runs."

"I feel like I'm almost ready."

Jessie was ready to take on the highways, to operate a two-ton machine by herself. Was Sydney ready to meet Tyler for coffee after thirty years? The very thought caused her throat to go dry and her heart to thump against her ribs. She stared ahead at the pavement in front of her and took a deep breath.

Would she ever be ready?

Chapter Ten

All Sydney's life, the sound of the waves provided calming comfort, like a heartbeat, steady and reliable, giving life and renewal. She breathed deeply, savoring her aloneness amidst clusters of bathing-suit clad families. She'd been walking for an hour, ankle-deep in the surf.

When she'd arrived at the beach that day, her thoughts, and the muscles in her shoulders felt like a wad of tangled rubber bands. With each step on the soft, wet sand, the knots loosened as the peace of the coast did its healing magic.

Still, the setting didn't entirely erase the shock of seeing Tyler Hoffman after thirty years. How could she reconcile the young man she'd known so well, loved so deeply, with the stranger standing before her yesterday afternoon? A stranger with an entire adult life she knew nothing about. She hadn't played even a small part in the majority of his life. Would they now make up for that colossal gap?

She wanted to feel indignant. He thought he could just invite her for a drink, and they'd catch up, just like that, after turning away from her so long ago. Another part of her hungered to know what those years had been like for him, who he'd become, what influences had shaped him while he'd been absent from her life.

Had she really forgiven him? Her hesitation made her swallow. Yes, she had. She'd even written him a letter to let him know, though she'd been unsure of his address. Just in case he was wracked with guilt over his actions. As he ought to have been. She'd wanted to release him but also knew forgiving him would be the key to *her* recovery and healing. He hadn't responded, and she hadn't contacted him again.

About seven years earlier, she'd gotten curious and looked him up on Facebook. His page wasn't very active and showed an older photo with a dark-haired woman, presumably his wife. With them were two children, a preteen girl and a younger boy, Zach. Of course, he'd gotten married. But the other day, Jessie had said Zach's dad was divorced and his mom lived in Georgia.

Sydney pulled her phone from her shorts pocket. Four o'clock. Her stomach tightened. In an hour, she'd meet Tyler face to face over coffee. She could only imagine, after the scene at the golf course the day before, how awkward it would be. What would they talk about after thirty years? After all the stale hurt of the past?

At five o'clock, Sydney pushed the glass door of Zoey's Coffee Shop, relieved to see only a few clusters of patrons or individuals in front of laptops. She scanned the room in case Tyler had gotten there earlier. As she met his direct blue-gray gaze across the space between them, she drew in a sharp breath and her pulse pounded. Just like she remembered. He occupied a small table close to the back wall. He'd sought privacy in choosing his seat.

She approached the table and pulled out a chair opposite him, still fighting the sensation of walking through a dream. "Hi." Feeling shy, she sat down, breaking eye-contact.

When she looked up and met his gaze, he responded with a half-smiled. His teeth were straight, his jaw strong, square. She caught her eyes roving over his face. She saw confidence, determination. His wavy dark brown hair was styled shorter than in high school and was laced with gray near his temples.

"I still can't believe I'm sitting across from Sydney Davis. You look great. Thanks for coming today. I know it must have been a shock when you saw me."

"Huh. You got that right. I'm not sure I've recovered yet." Sydney forced out a friendly smile. She still didn't know how to act with him. Cool and distant? Happy to see him and eager to fill in all the gaps? She fell silent.

Tyler chuckled and leaned back. "I had a little shock, too. But a good one. Hey, do you want something to drink? A Coke, an iced latte?"

"Iced latte sounds really good on a hot day like this."

"Be right back." He rose and went to the counter to order. Her eyes roamed around the shop while she waited and tamped down her nerves. The drinks would take a few minutes, and she'd use the time to practice deep breathing.

He returned to the table too quickly. "They'll bring us the drinks when they're ready."

She nodded and scrambled for something to say. "Do you still drink loads of sweet tea?"

He laughed. "No, not anymore." His voice softened. "You remembered that. I remember you used to like butter pecan ice cream. Like, all the time."

"I think we're both more health-conscious than that now."

"I'm sure of that." Tyler said no more but looked across the table at her. "Sydney." He shook his head. "Still can't believe it. I know I just said that, but I guess I'm feeling awkward."

"You, awkward?" Sydney smiled, thankful that she wasn't the only one. "That would be a first. You were always the most confident person I knew."

Tyler chuckled. "It's easy to be confident when you're eighteen and you don't know anything about life. I hope I'm much wiser now." Silence dropped between them. He cleared his throat and leaned back. "Do you want me to start? I could always interrogate you first."

"Yes, please, you first."

"After that, I want to hear about you. Deal?"

Her story might be more difficult than his, but she shouldn't judge him. She still pictured him as a carefree eighteen-year-old sailing off to freshman year, having unloaded his burdens and responsibilities.

Maybe she *hadn't* fully forgiven him.

"So, I'll start with college. I majored in business, as you could probably guess. After graduating, I got a job working for a management company in Atlanta. It was a good position, and I learned a lot. I was there thirteen years." He stopped, glanced up at the counter, and back to her. The drinks were taking a long time.

Sydney didn't say anything but mentally drew a picture of his life and career progression. So far, his path had been predictable.

Tyler leaned forward on one elbow. "When I was twenty-nine, I married Daphne. She was a widow with a five-year-old daughter. A year later, we had Zach. Fast forward a few years. I got a different job, where I worked another ten years until I moved up here."

"That was two years ago?"

He nodded. "I was ready to stop working for big companies and tired of big cities. We were outside Atlanta most of that time, but it was getting hectic, even in the suburbs. I missed Kennessey—the slower pace, the beach, old friends. Daphne and I divorced around ten years into our marriage. Zach was nine at the time." He took a breath as his face sobered. "So, when my dad got cancer, I knew I wanted to be with him. It wasn't hard to make the decision to come back. I was able to work with Uncle Cliff part time at Silver Lake during the year I took care of Dad." He stopped and pressed his lips together, as if to say he was finished with his school public speaking assignment.

"That's the quick summary version, I take it." What else could she expect? "What's your stepdaughter's name?" He'd parented a daughter. Did she ever make him think about Emma?

"Megan. She was always a sweet kid, but when Daphne and I split up, it was obvious where Megan would put her loyalties. She's twenty-four now and lives in California, but we have a good relationship. I see her when she visits the area."

"That's good, I'm glad. And you seem close to Zach, according to Jessie."

"Yes, I'm thankful for that. I'm so glad to have him here this summer. It'll be my last chance to spend large amounts of time with him before he goes to college."

Sydney gave him a muted smile. The impression of making the acquaintance of a total stranger competed with the familiar set of his jaw and his habit of leaning on one elbow as he talked. "Jessie says he's interested in studying art and comics or animation."

Tyler nodded. "Zach showed an aptitude in art from the age of two. I'm happy he's continued in a straight line, which is so rare. Do you remember? I wanted to be several things when I was his age. For a while I thought of being a pastor like my dad, but business was always my thing. It's been a good career for me."

"And now you're applying what you learned to your own business."

He tilted his head forward and shot her a pointed look. "Your turn."

Okay, she'd give him the surface version, too. Post Emma. "When I went to college, I didn't know what I wanted to do with my life. I was always good at math and liked teens, so I majored in math and got into the teaching program. I moved to Charlotte for my student teaching and later got a job there, so I stayed. A couple of years after that, I met my ex-husband, Cody. We dated a couple of years then got married. I taught math until Jessie was born, then took a few years off until she started school. My marriage ended when Jessie was almost eleven. I've been raising her myself since that time. She spends every other weekend at her dad's. He's remarried and lives in Monroe, which is a town close to Charlotte." She stopped and turned out both hands, palms upward. "So, you see, my story is rather dull. I've been teaching high school math in Charlotte for a total of eighteen years." The surface summary supplied information yet said nothing of the tissues and sinews of her life between the dry facts. Not to mention her doubts, longings, and dreams for the future, which had all but died.

"You never remarried." His blue-gray gaze didn't waver.

"No. You?" Her voice came out clipped.

He shook his head and silence fell for a moment. Then softly, he added, "I let the girl of my dreams get away and it was never the same after that."

"Daphne?" She'd play dumb, just to be sure.

He leveled a stare at her. "No, not Daphne."

Sydney didn't know what to say, but a low rumble began inside her.

A college age girl with green streaks in her hair set their drinks down on the table. Perfect timing. "I'm sorry these took so long, you guys. Here you go, two lattes."

When she left, Sydney grinned. "You ordered a latte, too. You must have good taste."

Tyler took a sip. "I developed a taste for them cold. It's like iced coffee, which hasn't caught on yet in this town."

Sydney tasted her drink, holding it in her mouth for a moment before swallowing. Refreshing as well as a distraction from the conversation.

Silence stretched out between them. Now that they'd finished their speedy and superficial life summaries, would the air become heavy with awkward silence? They never had that problem in the past, but under the shell of civility lay a history of pain and complexity.

Tyler took a deep sip then pushed the glass aside. "Sydney, I want to say something to you." Sydney braced herself. "I never thought I'd get this opportunity, to be honest. I didn't think I'd ever see you again." His eyes seemed to darken with intensity.

He glanced down for a moment and shook his head. "I don't even know where to start, but I regret how things ended back then. When you told me about the baby, I was terrified. I wanted to be the man you thought I was, but I didn't think I could do it. I was eighteen and over my head."

She stared at him and lifted her brows. "And I wasn't?" Her voice lowered to a hiss. "I was carrying your child in my *body*. I wasn't over my head?"

"Yes, of course you were. And I've thought of that so many times, how you went through all of it alone then gave her up by yourself. At the time, I didn't *think* I had any other option. But that decision has haunted me ever since. I want you to know I didn't just walk away and enjoy my college life unburdened. I was plenty burdened. I thought about you all the time and wasn't sure how I'd ever live with myself."

Sydney's shoulders relaxed. She realized she'd been stiff as a reinforced wall. She shrugged. "I understand. Kind of." She did, intellectually. And it was finished a long time ago, after all. "I did forgive you, you know. Did you ever get my letter? I sent you a letter sophomore year and told you I'd forgiven you."

He shook his head. "No, I never got it. I wish I had. I would have loved knowing you'd forgiven me, but it wouldn't have helped me forgive myself for not doing the right thing. For allowing it to happen in the first place, then for walking away."

Was she glad he'd suffered for how he'd handled it? Only to the degree that it showed his integrity, belated as it was. A half-dozen snarky responses popped into her mind. Instead, she looked up and said, "Thanks for telling me this, Tyler."

The pain etched on his face softened, and he looked away from her. "It's the least I can do, Sydney. I wished that I'd been willing to trust God with our lives back then. I wished we'd gotten married and started our little family. We loved each other and would have made it work. We would have struggled for a little while, but it could have worked out and God would have helped us."

She watched his handsome profile as he spoke. His jaw tightened.

He turned his head back to her, and Sydney was surprised to see tears gathered in his eyes. Something unlocked inside her with an imagined clang and grace flowed in, almost causing her to gasp at its power and purity. Her eyes stung, too. She blinked and swallowed. "Yes, he would have. But—and I'm telling this to myself at the same time—God is big enough to work good things into our lives in spite of our mistakes."

Tyler swallowed. "Thank you for that. I just wanted you to know I wasn't the heel who walked away and never looked back. Not in my heart."

The tears that moistened his cheeks made Sydney want to grab his hand, but she refrained. That could be misinterpreted. But the barricades she didn't know she still had fell then.

Softly, he asked, "Do you mind telling me what happened after the last time we saw each other?"

She didn't want to, longed to change the subject, but his face beseeched her. Maybe after this, the circle would close, and the past would return to its shelf. "I'll tell you. Then we won't talk about that part again." She took a breath and lowered her voice. "I, uh, I told my mom I was pregnant. She took charge of the situation, although we told my dad a couple weeks later." She swallowed. Blinked twice. "My mom assumed that I'd want to give the baby up instead of keeping her. I didn't think I could do it alone, so I agreed." Sydney's heart pounded as she spoke, even though she'd recently dug the trauma out from the past when she told her friends. Tyler was different. "She arranged everything. She sent me to live with my Aunt Abby in Leland for the rest of the spring semester, which you probably know, since I disappeared from school for the rest of the year. Aunt Abby had a big house and was willing to take me in. I finished my senior year coursework while I was there then took my GED. In July, I gave birth to Emma—"

"Emma?"

She nodded. "Some birth mothers don't name their babies before giving them up, but I wanted her to have the dignity of a name. Not just for my sake, but in case she ever looked up her original birth certificate. I don't know if that's possible, but I wanted her to know that even though I couldn't keep her, she was loved and that she was important to me. So, I named her."

Tyler didn't stop tears that flowed down his tanned cheeks. He smiled. "That's a nice name. Emma." His voice broke. He swiped at his tears with one wrist.

Sydney sniffed and rummaged in her purse for a tissue. She handed one to Tyler and took one for herself. They exchanged sad smiles. "It was really *hard* to give her up. At the last minute when I held her in my arms, I—I really thought about keeping her." She swallowed. Sniffed. "Afterward, I went to college. I didn't cope very well at first. Then I met these three women who became my lifeline, along with God, of course. I went back and forth with *him* for a while, but in the end, I let him help me and get me back on track. My friends knew I'd had a painful breakup, but they didn't know about the baby." Not until a month ago. Her eyes rose to meet Tyler's. "Did you ever think about the baby, wonder about her?"

He nodded. "At first, I did. It was kind of amazing to me that I was a dad to someone I'd never meet. I knew you'd given her up. Most of the time when I thought of her, I regretted not manning up to be her dad and your husband."

Sydney leaned back. Yeah, she'd been through that thought about eight million times the first year. By the time she'd moved on and let the burden go, she'd been more than ready. "I assume she was adopted by a lovely family and given a great life. And her birth parents went on with theirs." She smiled. "We didn't do all that badly, did we?"

He shrugged. "Aside from not staying together and later having failed marriages? It could have been better, but I guess we did the best we could."

"Yes, we did."

Their conversation had provided closure that they both needed. "Could we stop talking about this now?" Her eyes searched his.

Tyler nodded and smiled, though the rims of his eyes were pink. Sydney was relieved to end the conversation about Emma, but a puddle of sadness remained. Having gotten his guilt off his chest, Tyler likely wouldn't feel the need to see her anymore. She was better than a priest in a confessional.

"So, what do you think we should talk about now?" She leaned forward on her crossed arms.

"I could explain to you the finer points of owning a golf course." Tyler grinned.

Sydney wrinkled her nose, but was glad the conversation had shifted. "I'm low on golf knowledge and interest, I'm afraid. But I'm glad you enjoy running the courses. I'm sure you do a great job."

"That's kind of you. I do enjoy it. Tell me a little more about your life in Charlotte."

Having faced the dreaded cavern of past hurt, there was a new lightness in their conversation. Another hour passed as they filled in some of the missing years. Sydney felt more comfortable speaking to him as an old friend, letting her personality through, sharing memories and some laughter. She told him about the years of teaching, what it was like to raise Jessie alone, and even about her altercation with Rod Matheson and her early dismissal.

Tyler whistled and shook his head. "No, that's not right. You could have been killed or at least really hurt. Your principal handled that badly."

"I agree. I'd say he *didn't* handle it. But once I had the chance to think it over, I realized that getting an additional month off was actually a gift to me. It's true, my principal took the coward's way out and I didn't get justice. But I knew the result wasn't so bad for me either."

"So, you decided to come here for the summer."

"We usually come for about a week, maybe two. And that's always been plenty. You remember my mother and the relationship we had when I was a kid."

He nodded. "Yeah, I remember. Feeling like the outsider in your own family was hard for you."

"Well, over the years, especially with her involvement in giving Emma away, my mom and I stayed at arm's length. I'm hoping we'll get over some of that during this summer. She's the one who suggested we stay the whole summer."

"When do you start your new school year?"

Sydney drained her cup and set it back down. "It starts in mid-August, which is coming up. But honestly, I'd love to do something else. I just have to figure out what."

"You'll figure it out. In the meantime, it'll do you good to be here for the summer."

Sydney wondered if he might be right. She hoped it would be therapeutic for her and Jessie on many levels.

Tyler leaned forward, resting both elbows on the table. "Here's a thought. Since our kids hang around together, we ought to have each other's phone numbers. Wouldn't that be a good idea? Be on the safe side?"

He'd taken her by surprise, just as she was wondering what was next. "Um . . . yes, it would, I guess." She told him her number, and he texted her back. A ping sounded in her purse.

"Now you have mine, too. That way, we can keep tabs on the kids and maybe their parents can hang around together sometimes, too."

A grudging smile spread across her lips. Her eyes connected with his. She swallowed. "Maybe they can."

Chapter Eleven

Sydney's feet pounded rhythmically on concrete sidewalks. Sweat poured down her back as she rounded the corner to a street parallel to her mother's Victorian. Since arriving in Kennessey, she'd developed a two-mile circuit and ran it about three times a week. That day, her brain kept pace with her sneakers as she rewound her appointment with Tyler. It still seemed unbelievable that, after so many years, she'd seen him again, had sat across from him and had a conversation.

She hadn't known what to expect, whether his goal was to catch up on three decades and connect for old time's sake or address the issue that had torn them apart so long ago. At least he hadn't shied away the trauma. She hadn't been the only one to slog through the emotional aftermath of it. He, too, had suffered from his decision. *Their* decision.

His tears touched her in a way that she could only describe as healing. It was as though the cloud that had hovered in the background of her life for years suddenly blew away and, in its place, a lightness remained. In that moment, she was sure she'd fully forgiven him. It felt good, different. Free.

Instead of two miles, maybe she'd run three. Her energy abounded.

Sydney had almost forgotten how she used to feel as a teenager when she was with Tyler. Fully herself. Of course, he was still a stranger to her, but there'd been a flicker of that easy feeling during their conversation. Surprisingly, once they'd gotten past their biographies and Emma, she'd been more at ease than she'd expected.

Her mind's eye kept conjuring Tyler's still handsome face, enhanced by age, maturity, and life experience. *Admit it, he looked good, even better than before.* He'd kept himself in shape. Sydney shook her head. She would *not* think of him that way. He likely wanted only to seize his opportunity to have closure with her and absolve his own guilt over the matter. She wouldn't expect anything more. At any rate, she lived in Charlotte; he lived in Kennessey. Three hours apart. And being a man, he'd likely hurt her. Again. *Drop it, Sydney.*

After her third mile, Sydney slowed to a jog, then a walk. The June morning was just starting to heat up at nine-thirty and she was drenched. As she rounded the corner to head for the house, her phone rang. She pulled it from the zippered pocket of her shorts and scanned the face. She drew in a breath. Tri-State Adoption Agency.

"Hello?"

"Hello, Ms. Bennett. This is Angela from Tri-State Adoption Agency. I wanted to reach out to you because our inquiry came back. I apologize that it took so long. We can't find any record of your adoption in our files. They searched the older records that were stored off-site, and we can't find anything. You must have done your adoption somewhere else."

Her heart sank, but she wasn't surprised. She'd grabbed blindly for information about Emma's whereabouts. "Thank you for your call. I'll check elsewhere." She still had two more agencies who had yet to call her back. One of them might be a match with the past.

She walked back to the house as her body cooled from perspiration. The foyer was quiet. Sydney showered and slipped on cotton shorts and a tank. She snatched her straw hat and a paperback before returning downstairs. She'd get a snack and read a while in the yard, hopefully settling her thoughts in the process.

As she cut up an apple and some cheese, her mother came into the kitchen from the backyard. "Hello, Sydney. Did you go running today?"

Sydney nodded. "Early this morning, it was perfect, but it's hot now. Do you garden when it's hot out?"

Carolyn pulled off her gardening gloves and set them on the edge of a small table by the back door. "I do it in the early morning or after five. I don't have the stamina I used to."

"I'm sure the heat would be bad for you. Do you want me to pour you a cool drink? Tea or flavored water?" Sydney pulled a pitcher of iced tea from the fridge door, then placed a paper plate laden with apple slices and a chunk of cheese on the kitchen table.

"No, thank you. I have a cold drink in the fridge."

They were civil, cordial, but not loving. Not warm. Was it the best Sydney could hope for? She'd taught her heart not to long for more than that from her mother. She was who she was. Sydney had always interpreted that as disapproval or disinterest. It could have been simply her mother's disillusionment with something unrelated to her.

"Are you tired of us yet?" She grinned at her mother, though her question was serious, and sat down at the table. Doubtful she'd get an honest answer, but her mother's face might tell the truth.

Carolyn looked surprised. "No, of course not. I enjoy the company. I'm not as busy outside the house as I used to be so it can get lonely." She gave Sydney a wistful smile with a little shrug of her frail-looking shoulders.

Sydney leaned her elbows on the table beside her plate. "You used to have a lot of relationships in town from the committees and stuff you used to do. Garden club, Bible study, different things. You don't see those people anymore?"

"I see a few of them, but we all get old." She chuckled, but it didn't reach her eyes. "Remember Sarah Longnecker? She died a couple of years ago from heart problems."

"Oh, I'm sorry. She was your best friend for years."

Carolyn nodded. "And the Johnsons, who you may remember, they moved to Florida. Seems like one by one, people either die or move away or just lose touch. Sometimes at the store I run into people I know. I've been less active in church this last year. A lot of the activities stop in the summer, anyway."

"That's too bad. There must be something you could get involved in with other people. I'm sure it's harder as you get older, but there are senior groups, aren't there?" The idea that her mother could be lonely had never crossed her mind. Guilt stabbed at Sydney. She could have kept in touch better, visited more often.

"I suppose. The seniors at church sometimes go on little day trips, but I'm not that interested, nor do I have the energy anymore."

Silence followed. Sydney bit her lip. "I—I'm sorry we haven't visited more." True, it was difficult during the school year, but unlike other professions, she had regular breaks during the year and in the summer.

Carolyn tilted her head and looked away without response. Sydney had hoped for a "that's okay, I know you're busy", to lighten her remorse, but it didn't come. At least she'd acknowledged it to her mother, even if she alone knew the reasons behind her neglect. And some of them were legitimate.

"Mom, did you know that Tyler Hoffman moved back to Kennessey? He owns the Silver Lake Golf Course."

She thought she saw her mother stiffen at the mention of Tyler's name.

"Yes, I knew he'd come back, but didn't think to mention it to you. I haven't spoken to him, though I did see him once at the hardware store. I don't think he saw me that day." Her mother looked uncomfortable, trudged to the dishwasher, and started pulling out clean dishes. She stacked a few plates on the counter. Maybe she felt guilty for saying nothing to Sydney about Tyler's return. They hadn't spoken of him in years and never referred to the trauma they'd all endured. Like it was forgotten. Like it never happened.

"I'd heard that Silver Lake had a new owner." Carolyn spoke over one shoulder as she placed a stack of plates into the cupboard. "I knew Cliff, of course. He was a friend of your father's. But I'd heard he'd retired and sold them all, then moved out of state. I don't know where."

"He did. But Tyler was able to buy two of the courses. He came back before that to take care of his dad. Did you know his dad died of cancer about a year ago?"

"Yes, I knew that. It was a shame. After he retired from the church, I lost touch with them. He was a good pastor for years. I left the church a year later to go where I attend now. I didn't care much for the pastor who replaced Pastor Hoffman."

Sydney hesitated. How much should she say to her mother? In the past, when she'd tried to share things, her mother had either minimized her feelings or been too busy to hear her heart. Or else, she tried to tell her what to do, as she had the other day over the teaching decision. If Sydney wanted a better relationship with her mother, she should try again. "I saw Tyler the other day. It was a shock, after thirty years."

Carolyn turned and wiped her hands on her apron. Her eyes showed nothing, but tightness pinched her mouth. "Where did you see him?"

"Remember when Jessie met a guy at the library? Well, his name is Zach, and he's Tyler's son. He works for Tyler at the golf course. Jessie's ice cream shop is right next door, so she goes over there sometimes after her shift to see him. The other day, I picked her up there so she could practice driving and Tyler was there." She paused, remembering her shock. "It was quite the surprise for both of us."

"Yes, I imagine it was. You hadn't seen him at all since—since you lived here? Were you in touch during that time?"

Sydney shook her head, a wave of sadness blowing through her like a cold breeze. So many years had passed. So many regrets. She should have reached out to him at some point after the hurt began to fade. But she hadn't. "No, we didn't have any contact for all those years. He wrote me a couple of letters in the beginning, but I didn't answer him." Following her words, an ache awakened in her stomach. She stared down at her plate of apples, then pulled it toward her. She reached for the knife and cut up a few more slices of cheese. "We met for coffee yesterday and caught up on the last lifetime." She avoided her mother's eyes while she bit into the apple. Whether her mother approved, disapproved, or wished it had stayed hidden, Sydney didn't know or even care. She was still enjoying the effects of freedom that forgiveness brought. And she didn't mind seeing Tyler again.

"You did? Do you think that's a good idea, Sydney?"

Sydney stopped the next bite midway to her mouth and frowned. "Why not? I mean, we're not kids anymore."

"I don't know. It was such a hard chapter of your life. I don't even want to talk about it."

"It *was* a hard chapter, but it happened. Avoiding it doesn't change that." She heard the edge in her own voice. "It happened, and it mattered. To me, at least."

"What do you mean by that? I helped you through it. I didn't create the problem."

"Do you still blame me for that?"

"Oh, Sydney, let's not talk about this. You've gone on with your life, Tyler has, everyone has." She turned and pulled the top shelf of the dishwasher out too abruptly. A glass fell over and clanged against another one.

"I didn't mean to rattle you, Mom. I don't think there's any harm talking about life as it happened."

"I just don't see the point, as I've said. Just don't get hurt again, Sydney."

Sydney sighed. She wasn't eighteen anymore. She could handle herself. "Thanks for your concern." She knew her words could be taken two ways, sincere or sarcastic. With a stab inside, she realized she'd meant it both ways.

"I wonder if he continued playing the guitar."

Sydney blinked. The elephant in the room had deftly been ushered out the back door. For the best, of course. They'd said as much as could be said without things tumbling downhill fast. She still had a few weeks before leaving, so best not to push too much in the wrong direction. "I don't know if he kept up with music. We didn't talk about that."

"It's a shame you gave up *your* music." Carolyn pulled the silverware basket from the dishwasher. "This last thing to do . . . I don't like putting away silverware. I have to examine it so closely to make sure it goes into the right slot." When she was finished, she replaced the basket and closed the machine. She turned to Sydney. "Since you have free time this summer, you could pick up the guitar again, if you feel like it. I think your guitar is still in the attic, but I don't know what shape it's in. That might be fun for you. Doesn't Jessie play?"

"Yes, she does." Her mother must have forgotten. Every time they'd visited, Jessie had brought her guitar, including that visit. Sydney wondered how her mother's mind was working. She'd successfully steered them away from Tyler.

Sydney forced a chuckle, hoping to lighten the tension that still snapped between them. "I passed it to her, like a baton. I don't have it anymore, but now she does." The pressure that had built up inside her began to seep away, but not fast enough for her. She needed her book outside. Under a tree. Alone.

Sydney paused then. "Why did you say it's a shame I gave up on music?" Was anything behind her statement?

Carolyn shrugged and sent Sydney a cool stare. "Do you take *any* statement at face value, Sydney? Seems you're always trying to start something. You don't have to fight everyone all the time." She paused. "I sometimes wonder if that contributed to things going downhill in your marriage to Cody. Not blaming you, but I'm sure it didn't help."

Sydney flinched. That had come out of nowhere. Cody was another mark on her bad record, even if he was the one who'd left. She wouldn't admit her mother was right. Sydney's feisty verbal habits hadn't helped her drowning marriage at the time.

Just then, she would choose not to fight back. She'd ignore the retort that hovered in her throat. "You may be right, but Cody is another discussion. I'm sure I have my share of blame. No, Mom. I was just curious about your thoughts on my music. That's all. Just curious."

Her mother sighed. "It's just that you loved music, I remember. You were good at it. You got that from your father. It was the one thing that lit up your eyes. I know you talked about Nashville, and I thought *that* was unrealistic, but I still encouraged you in your music."

Sydney didn't remember being encouraged by her mother in very many areas. Had she simply forgotten? "I didn't know you felt that way. It was a teenage hobby, I guess."

"No, it was more than that. But we move on. Once you left the church and the area, you had other things going on. But you never seemed to find that spark again." She looked pointedly at Sydney, catching her eyes. "Don't let the difficulties of life take you away from yourself."

"Back then, I had a lot of reasons to get away from myself," Sydney said quietly, then stood. She'd eat the rest of her snack outside. She forced cheer into her voice. "The yard is beckoning me, and pretty soon it'll even be hot in the shade." She pushed in the chair and sent her mother a bland smile. "Don't work too hard, Mom."

Though it was steamy outside, being out of the house instantly lifted some of Sydney's tension. She dragged a lawn chair under a sprawling magnolia tree and settled into it, her book propped on her lap. She'd escape through the novel she'd been trying to dig into for at least a month. Lately, her thoughts raced around inside her skull so fast that she found herself rereading the first chapter numerous times.

That day was no exception, as her mother's words flowed back to her. Was she always trying to start something? Was her harsh tongue always at the ready, prepared to defend or wound like a cornered animal? Had it contributed to the demise of her marriage?

Unbidden, harsh words emerged from the past, arguments with Cody that became more and more frequent. Yes, she'd contributed. How many times had she defended, with her mouth as a weapon, instead of listening? If she had, would it have preserved their family, kept her husband from wandering to another woman? It had been too easy to put all the blame on him.

Sydney squeezed her eyes shut as conviction washed over her like an unwelcome shower. For years, she'd been fighting through her efforts and her words, as though she were completely alone and the only defenses she had were her wit and her tongue. Indeed, she'd felt alone after losing Tyler and Emma. And she'd carried that solitude like a suit of armor ever since.

Despite the years of toxic misunderstanding that had accumulated between Sydney and her mother, Carolyn's words cycled back into her mind. *Don't let the difficulties of life take you away from yourself.* Sydney was strangely touched by those words. Her mother wasn't a good example of that philosophy at all, but her statement still rang true.

In that moment, Sydney knew that, to some degree, she'd done just that, almost by decision in her freshman year of college. She'd developed tools of self-protection that almost seemed a part of her. Humor. Blunt words. How many relationships had been damaged in their wake? And how much of herself had she lost through the tragedy of the past? Would she have developed into a different woman, softer and more approachable, if her transition to womanhood hadn't been so brutal?

Her mother's comments about music had surprised her, too. Sydney's loss of her music was proof that she'd lost parts of herself. She'd always thought her mother had been too absorbed in her own activities and her two sons to notice what music had meant to Sydney back in the day. *It lit up your eyes.* She'd noticed that?

Sydney had found music even before she'd found Tyler. She lost Tyler but had walked away from music voluntarily. After all, it wasn't a neutral hobby, but would always remind her of him, of Emma. Of her failures in life.

Before she could stop herself or even understand what she was doing, Sydney rose from the lawn chair and walked into the house.

She passed the living room where her mother was seated reading on an iPad. A glass of iced tea sat near her on the end table.

Upstairs, Sydney walked to the end of the hall where a narrow ladder was tucked into the ceiling. With a pull of the string, the stairs unfolded, and Sydney climbed up.

The attic at her Charlotte home was intolerably hot this time of year, but the Victorian had a window on either end that her father had installed. It was still hot but bearable for Sydney's objective.

She pulled the metallic string hanging from the ceiling. Light filled the space, blending with the daylight streaming through the windows. Her eyes roved over the stacks of suitcases, boxes of Christmas decorations, and other cartons whose contents were unknown. In a darkened back corner, she saw the outline of a guitar. With a deep breath, Sydney scrambled beneath the area where the roof narrowed down toward the floor and pulled the guitar case out toward the center of the small room.

Surprising that it was still there. It could very well be ruined, but Sydney wanted to look at it. Touch it. A layer of dust coated the case. Perspiration trickled down her neck as the heat from the attic intensified every moment she sat there.

She grasped the guitar in both hands and carried it down the ladder while her bare feet groped each rung. She tucked the staircase back into the ceiling and returned to her bedroom. After wiping the dust from the case, she opened the lid. At first, she felt nothing. No emotional reaction at all.

Then fragments of memories began to trickle back. Practice sessions at the church and the warm camaraderie the team had together. The feeling of belonging she'd experienced in a diverse group that shared a passion. Tyler catching her eye across the stage as they warmed up for the worship set.

They'd practiced together at his house or hers or in the park nearby. She was more of a natural than he was, but his technique had been honed with diligent practice. She learned new chords and practiced them. The worship songs weren't suitable for some of the funky new jazz chords she'd discovered, and that's when she began composing. At first, it was only melodies. Tyler had encouraged her to add words to the songs. "Start with strong feelings you have about something," he'd suggested.

"About you?" She'd sent him a loving smile.

He laughed and leaned forward to kiss her. "No, there are plenty of love songs out there. Besides, you'll write me a song one day and it'll be just for me to hear."

"Yes, I will. So, this morning God showed me something in Psalms that I liked. Psalm twenty-five. I could write it out in my own words and see if it fits with the music."

"Good, that's the idea. You can also look at the praise songs we do at church or listen to some of the artists you like. Study the lyrics to see how they're structured."

He'd given wise advice. She'd followed it and begun to write songs. It took her a few months to be willing to play them for him, then for others. Finally, at Tyler's urging, she played one of them for the worship pastor and he asked her to play it in church.

"Only if no one knows I wrote it," she'd insisted. "I can do it then, and they won't know. That way, if no one likes it, I won't be embarrassed."

The congregation loved the song and requested it often. When they learned she'd written it, she was showered with praise and encouragement. This spurred her to write even more as her confidence took wings.

Sydney had no idea where those songs were. The notebook containing her sheet music was probably up there in one of the unlabeled boxes if she'd even kept them. At least her mother hadn't gotten rid of anything of hers.

A deep sigh escaped her chest. She'd woven a magnanimous dream that she could actually go to Nashville and make something of her music. In reality, that wouldn't have been the best first step, but a kid could dream, couldn't she? Especially with Tyler at her side, everything seemed possible.

She reached down and fingered one of the metal strings that lay loose on the fingerboard. It thudded. She plucked another one which sounded like a tin can hitting the floor. Parts of the neck were coming unglued. Sydney chuckled at the awful noise and wondered if the old guitar was salvageable. A solid wood guitar would gain value with years, as the wood fibers broke down and a resonance matured in its hollowness. But sitting in a hot attic for three decades wouldn't pamper an instrument in the least.

"You found it." Her mother's voice from the hallway startled her.

Sydney looked up at her, feeling none of the tightness or resentment she had a while ago. "Yes, I'm surprised it was still there. I'm glad." She looked down at the smooth wood, then back at her mother. "See, you inspired me."

A soft smile spread on Carolyn's face. "I'm glad I can still do that."

Sydney grinned back at her. "Yes, Mom, you can. Thank you."

Her mother looked away, seeming uncomfortable. "I'm glad to see you with that guitar. Maybe the light will come back to your eyes again."

Then she disappeared down the hall.

Chapter Twelve

"Mom, Zach's dad is going to call you today about Zach's birthday."

Sydney looked up from where she sat at the dining room table in front of her laptop. She'd almost completed her online course and still had no clue what rational career choice might exist for her. "Is he having a party for Zach?"

Jessie settled with her bowl of cereal into a soft wingback chair near the table. She'd been working a lot of hours at the ice cream shop but had that day off. "Not a party. Zach doesn't know anyone here since he doesn't live here, but I think Mr. Hoffman is planning something for the four of us."

Warmth stirred inside Sydney, though she tried to keep a poker face in front of her daughter. "That sounds nice. Zach'll be eighteen?"

"Yup. The big one eight. And I'm right behind him."

"Uh-oh. Get ready, world." Sydney grinned at Jessie. "Hey, Jess. I miss you. You're working a lot."

Jessie stuck a spoonful of cereal in her mouth, then mumbled, "You miss me? Aww. That's nice, Mom. I *have* been working a lot. I take all the shifts they give me, since I *need* my car."

"Well, you don't technically need one here. I'd rather see you drive here than Charlotte, though. It's nice and calm here, with a fraction of the cars on the roads."

"Do you think I'll be ready to take my test by the end of summer? Maybe even sooner?" A hopeful gleam lit Jessie's blue eyes. Her hair was still moist from her shower and hung in blond corkscrews framing her face.

"Maybe. So, how are things going with Zach? Are you two dating?" Sydney still wasn't sure, and so far, Jessie hadn't divulged any details.

Jessie made a face. "If you must know, we're really good friends. Like, best friends. That's all for now. It's nice for both of us, since we're only here for the summer and we don't know anyone else."

"Would you like it to be more?"

"I'm not sure yet. I'd like to have a boyfriend, since I've only had one in my life. He hasn't asked me to be his girlfriend, and he hasn't kissed me or anything. We have fun together all the time. I wonder if we're supposed to just be friends, since he's going to college, and I won't see him anymore."

Sydney pursed her lips. "That's possible. Doesn't sound romantic to me, if you're not sure you like him except as a friend. And that's okay, friendships are important. If something else is supposed to happen either now or later, it will." A light breeze of relief coursed through Sydney. Yes, friendship was good.

Jessie finished her cereal and sipped the milk from the edge of the bowl. "As always, your mother wisdom is astounding."

Sydney spread her hands as if to say, *but of course*. "Since you're off today, do you want to go to the beach?" Sydney hadn't been there in almost a week. Once they'd returned to Charlotte, she'll wish she'd spent the maximum time soaking in the waves and sun.

"That's a yes!"

"Let's go right after lunch. By the way, you've been calling your dad regularly, haven't you? I don't want him blaming me for taking you away for the whole summer and him not hearing from you, either."

"Yes, I have. I called him just last night. He's glad I'm having a good summer here. I thought he'd really miss our weekends, but he seems cool with it. He's glad I'm working, like a responsible teen." Jessie gave her a funny grin, along with an eyeroll.

"That's good." Sydney stifled a laugh. Wonderful. She hadn't taken Cody's weekends with Jessie into consideration when she decided to stay the summer in Kennessey. Talking about phone calls reminded her she still needed to text her friends the huge news about running into Tyler again, as well as the lack of progress regarding Emma and job hunting.

Just then, the phone rang. Sydney looked down. It was Tyler. Her tummy did a little flip inside. It still seemed unreal to her. And why was she responding that way? "Hello, Tyler." She exchanged a glance with Jessie.

"Hi, Sydney. How have you been since we last spoke?" He had a nice-sounding voice. Warm, strong.

Sydney laughed. "Two days instead of thirty years? That'll take some getting used to. I'm fine. And you?"

"Good. It's our busy season, so it's crazy here, but good. Listen, Zach's birthday is tomorrow, so I thought it would be nice if we all went to his favorite restaurant on Saturday. There's this Italian place he likes near the water. So, I'm inviting you and Jessie to join us. Sorry for the late notice."

She smiled. "No worries. Yes, I think I can speak for both of us." She glanced over at Jessie, who was nodding vigorously, her eyes wide. "That'll be nice." While she spoke, a call buzzed in at the same time. From the Family Love Adoption Center. Her pulse jumped for the second time.

"Great. The place is called Casa Luisa, and it's casual. Good food, I think you'll like it. Can we pick you ladies up at six-thirty? I'll make us a reservation for seven."

"I'm sure we can be ready by then. Thanks, Tyler. It'll be nice to help Zach celebrate his big birthday."

Tyler paused. "Your mom won't shoo me away, will she?" There was humor in his words, but a realistic threat as well, given Carolyn's comments the other day. And given their history.

Sydney laughed "No, I'll ask her not to."

"Yes, stand your ground. We'll see you Saturday at six-thirty."

Sydney smiled despite his reference. The dinner would give her another chance to get to know him. She'd been afraid of not seeing him again, though she didn't even know yet how she felt about all this. But Zach's birthday dinner would be a safe date, since the kids would be there. She was intrigued to see how everyone would relate in that setting.

She'd phone Family Love as soon as Jessie left the room. Guilt stabbed at her. She had to hide it from Jessie because she'd never told her only child the truth, that she had a half-sibling somewhere. Back then, she'd wanted to put it behind her, and by the time Jessie was old enough to understand, it seemed too late.

"Wish I'd known about the beach before I took a shower," Jessie mumbled as she stood up.

"We don't have to go." Sydney gave her wide-eyed expression.

Jessie shot her a frown. "That's okay, I can take another one."

When she left the room, Sydney waited until she heard the back door open and shut. She'd check their message first. There might be no need to call back. She punched in her pin code at the prompt and listened to the message. "Hello, Ms. Bennett. This is Chelsea Gray from the Family Love Adoption Agency. We were not able to find your name in our records. We used the name you gave us, Sydney Abigail Davis, but we don't have any records with that name. Just wanted to let you know. Good luck in your search."

Sydney fell back against the chair and let out a sigh. Strike two. And no need to call back.

☙　☙　☙

Sydney slipped onto the side porch, which had become her favorite place to be alone when the heat permitted and sank into the cushion of the white wicker chair. She closed her eyes for a moment as a gentle breeze stroked her face and hair. Spending the afternoon with Jessie at the beach was as relaxing as she expected, despite threads of turmoil that still simmered on the back shelf of her mind.

Her phone sat on her lap. First up, call Dad. She sighed. Their current relationship was without ripples, but it was a pale version of the closeness they'd had when she was a child. After her brothers, he'd been the next man to emotionally abandon her. When her parents divorced, he'd moved to Wilmington closer to his law practice. Later, he remarried and their bond weakened further. But still, he was her dad. She owed him a few visits that summer, even if each one was an aching reminder of what she'd lost.

Had he been irreparably disappointed in her when she'd gotten pregnant at seventeen? They no longer had the ability to talk about deeper things, including hurts of the past.

She called his number and hit his voicemail. "Hi Dad, it's Sydney. I wanted to tell you some great news. Jessie and I are here in Kennessey for the whole summer. I hope to see you and Melody while we're here. Call me when you can, and we'll set a date. Love you."

Felt like an obligation call. She'd reached out, done her part. Now it was up to him to respond.

Next, an email to her friends. Sydney typed out a summary then skimmed her paragraph prior to sending it. Certain phrases caught her eye. *Still slumming and sunning in Kennessey. You'll never guess, ran into Tyler, my old beau. Aaawk-ward!!!*

She stilled. A thread of discomfort began inside. She'd been bland and breezy. Surface. Information without soul. Revealing nothing of her heart.

It hit her then and she breathed deeply at the impact. Most of her communication with her friends, written and even verbal, was similar. She'd joked, she'd summarized. How they'd tolerated her in their group up to then, she didn't know. *They* were real. Rarely had she gone beneath the surface and invited them in. Not until the last time, when she'd revealed her secret.

She'd protected, feared. After telling them about Emma, she'd felt emotionally exhausted, but clean. They knew yet still accepted and loved her. Did she really want to return to humorous, well-guarded Sydney? It was starting to feel like an itchy sweater she wanted to fling off.

She deleted her message and started again. *Hello Eden, Julia, and Marissa, my sisters. I was thinking of our last time together and am so grateful for all of you. Makes me miss you so much! Thank you for hearing me and loving me instead of judging me. I shouldn't have hidden the story of Emma from you all these years, and I hope you'll forgive me.*

Sydney blew out a deep breath. Her heart was exposed, but she'd keep going. *I'm realizing that a lot of my problems, even in my family, come from my stupid mouth, either hiding or attacking. I'm working on that, too. I'd appreciate your prayers! It's hard for me to be "real", but I'm gonna work on it.*

So, I do have some news. I ran into Tyler the other day. Yes, shocking. I hadn't seen him in thirty years. It was awkward at first. We met for coffee the next day and were able to talk about the past. That felt good, like it took away my bitterness. He lives here now and owns a golf course. Two, actually. His son is a friend of Jessie's so we'll celebrate his birthday Saturday. The thought is scary, weird, and a bit wonderful. I'll keep you posted.

I love you all. Thank you for putting up with me all these years. My secrets, my hiding. Feel free to confront me when I'm doing it. Please, I need accountability! Love Sydney.

ʘ   ʘ   ʘ

At six-thirty sharp on Saturday evening, the doorbell rang. "You ready, Jessie?" Sydney called down the hall. She heard a

123

muffled response from the bathroom. "They're at the door now, so hurry."

Sydney's casual knee-length summer dress swished around her legs as she descended the staircase. The dress was one of her favorites, so comfortable, and the aqua colored fabric lightened her dark blue eyes a shade. At least it appeared that way to her. Leather sandals with narrow cork wedges kept her from being too dressy, which she definitely didn't want. Tyler had said the restaurant was casual, but it was still a special occasion.

Anxiety simmered inside. Sydney hadn't seen Tyler since their truth session at the coffee shop. This evening would be different. Lighter, at least. Sydney took some deep breaths and strove to relax, to let go. *Please take over this evening, Lord.*

When she opened the door, Tyler and Zach both stood on the porch, looking fixed-up and quite handsome. She smiled at them, suddenly feeling shy. "Hi. Come in."

"Requesting the honor of your presence," Tyler said with a mock bow of his head. Sydney didn't miss the way his eyes quickly roved over her. "You look very nice, Sydney."

"Thanks. You guys aren't too tacky yourselves. Jessie's almost ready." They stood in the wide foyer. She turned to Zach, whose straight dark hair had been neatly combed, even though he was dressed in his usual jeans but a decent-looking polo. "Happy birthday, Zach."

"It was yesterday, but thanks."

"But we're celebrating today in your honor." Tyler grinned down at him. "Eighteen years, can you believe it? It's a big day." Zach shrugged, as if it was like any other day. The family resemblance was obvious, with the square jaw, slight dimple, and blue-gray eyes.

"Hello, Tyler." Carolyn's voice sounded from the kitchen doorway. With small steps, she approached him. Her face looked tight, but to her credit, she forced a cordial smile.

"Mrs. Davis, it's nice to see you. It's been a long time." Tyler had turned his full attention to her mother. The air snapped with tension. Sydney held her breath for a second, fervently hoping her mother would be polite, at least to Tyler's face. Her mother herself had said it was a long time ago, and they'd all moved on. Had she?

"Yes, it has. And now you're all grown up, and this is your son." She turned to Zach, and her smile softened. "Hello, Zach. I'm Carolyn, Jessie's grandma. I hear you have a birthday today."

"Yes, ma'am. Well, it was yesterday, but we're celebrating today at a restaurant."

Her eyes widened. "Oh, my. That sounds lovely. Well, I hope you all have a wonderful time. What restaurant? Maybe I've heard of it."

Sydney let her breath out. *Thanks, Mom.* She was being appropriate and over the top sweet with Zach, who wouldn't know that wasn't her normal style.

"Casa Luisa," Tyler said. "That's Zach's favorite place here in Kennessey. He has other favorites back in Atlanta, but since this is my home now, I figured we could find a couple favorites here, too." He looked down at Zach with a grin. "Since you'll be visiting me frequently, right Pal?"

Zach shrugged again, but his gaze had been averted to the staircase. Jessie was coming down, looking fresh and feminine in a short, flared skirt and shimmery tank top. Maybe she'd wanted to make a grand entrance down the long stairway. She looked so pretty. Emotion tightened Sydney's throat. Her little woman, growing up fast.

Jessie carried a wrapped gift in the bend of her arm. Zach's gaze was riveted to her as she reached the bottom stair. He seemed more attracted to Jessie than the other way around.

"Hi Zach. Happy birthday. Hi Mr. Hoffman." She handed Zach the gift, big and square. "This is for you."

"Thanks, Jess. I'll open it at the restaurant."

The Casa Luisa was a dimly lit, cozy restaurant on two floors. The hostess seated them on the second floor at a reserved table with a view of the ocean. Once they settled in at their table, Sydney pushed down the anxious flutters in her stomach. At least things had gone well with her mother, though she'd hear the truth later.

"So, Zach, my man, you're eighteen, but sorry to say, *only* eighteen, so you can't have any alcohol tonight. As much as you might like that." Tyler turned to Sydney. "You're over eighteen, so would you like anything?"

Sydney laughed. "Yes, I'm a bit over eighteen. I'll take a Merlot."

They ordered drinks, then food. Their banter and conversation felt so light and normal, despite the bizarre circumstances, covering a variety of topics, none of them too deep. For that evening, Sydney was thankful for surface talk that hopped from one subject to another—the beach, the golf course, the ice cream store, art, college. She relaxed her shoulders. Tension seeped away.

"The food here is great. I'll remember this place." Sydney pushed her empty plate toward the waitress, who cleared the away their dishes.

"Open your present, Zach." Jessie gestured toward the colorfully wrapped square.

"Looks like a book." Zach ripped into the paper. "Oh, wow. Thanks, guys." He held up the book, a hardback volume of cartooning techniques. "This looks great."

"That's from Jessie." Sydney leaned back. She finished her last sip of wine, which she'd nursed throughout the meal. She'd wanted to keep her head clear on this remarkable occasion.

"What did you get from your dad?" asked Jessie. Sydney glared at her.

"He got me a used car for college. I mean, it's a nice car, but not brand-new."

"Has pretty low miles on it." Tyler reached for his water glass and took a sip. "I got it a few months ago from a good friend of mine and he garaged it for me until now to keep the secret." He and Zach exchanged a grin.

The sound of singing broke through their conversation as four of the wait staff approached their table. "Happy birthday, happy,

happy birthday to Zach, Zach, Zach," they chanted a non-traditional birthday tune. One of them carried a small ice cream cake with a sputtering sparkler on top. Zach slid further down in his seat, apparently not enjoying the attention or the singing of his name, which sounded more like ducks quacking. Sydney and Tyler laughed aloud, to the point that Sydney's eyes watered. It felt so good to laugh.

The wait staff finished singing, placed dessert plates and forks on the table, and all but one of them left the table. The remaining server said, "Would you like me to take a family picture?"

Sydney exchanged a glance with Tyler. He turned to the server and responded, "Sure. Zach is eighteen, so it's a big day." Sydney found herself wondering what it would be like if they *had* been a family. If they'd stayed together, had had other children. Tyler handed the woman his phone and showed her how to use the camera.

"So, I'll need you kids to crowd next to Mom and Dad so I can get you all in."

Zach and Jessie played along. Tyler pulled his chair close to Sydney and slid one arm around her bare shoulder. Awareness of the closeness of his face to hers and the weight of his arm over her shoulder caused prickles all over her. She breathed in the light, woodsy scent of his aftershave.

"One, two, three—smile!" They all grinned, and the flash lit up the table.

After she left, Zach grinned and said, "Hey, Mom and Dad, do you want some cake?"

Sydney laughed. "One offspring is enough for me, thanks, though I'm sure you're a nice kid, Zach."

"True, I'm a very nice kid. So, since it's my birthday and I'm *such* a nice kid," he said, looking from Tyler to Sydney, "you have to answer a question. Tell me how you two met. I mean, a long time ago."

Sydney's breath fled out of her. It had to happen sooner or later. What would Tyler say?

They looked at each other. A smile hovered at the corners of his lips. He didn't seem uncomfortable at his son's question. "Well, correct me if I've forgotten anything, Sydney." He looked back at Zach. "We were in a class together. Math or something. Eleventh grade."

"Biology," she corrected.

"Yes, biology. I noticed her right away. I sat behind her in class, and she had this long, silky hair, kind of like now, but even longer back then. I couldn't stop looking at it. And of course, she was even cuter from the front. Then I found out we attended the same church, so I tried to get to know her."

Sydney stared at him. "You did? You planned that?"

He grinned back at her like the cat who ate the canary. "Yup. I'm very goal oriented when I want to be, and I wanted to get to know *you*. What made it a lot easier, is that we were on the worship team at church together."

"You were?" Jessie's eyes grew round. "You never told me that, Mom. Did you sing?"

Everything tightened up inside Sydney. She desperately wanted to steer the conversation in another direction but couldn't without looking suspicious. All her years of hiding the truth were about to come crashing down on her. "I think I told you I played guitar some when I was a teenager. I'm fairly sure I did. And I did sing a little." She kept her voice light, nonchalant, hoping Jessie would question her own memory.

"Yeah, but the worship team. I didn't know about that." Jessie frowned.

"So, we got to know each other in church and in school." Tyler finished, as if he'd say no more, and signaled the waitress. "Can we have more water, please?" Good chance he had the same desire to avoid the past as Sydney, though he seemed to enjoy telling the story.

"So, how long did you guys go out?"

Sydney needed to jump in just to make sure Tyler wouldn't say too much. "About a year. Something like that." Her tone indicated she'd half forgotten, though of course, she hadn't. She knew very well how long it was. A year and three months. They'd met in September of their junior year. They were crazy in love and exclusive by November. They got pregnant in October of the following year, their senior year, and in December, everything fell to shreds.

"Why'd you break up?"

Sydney knew that was coming. She and Tyler both let out an uncomfortable chuckle. Again, she jumped in. "We went to different colleges. Different states, different schools. We lost touch." Entirely reasonable.

"Then you met my dad." Jessie licked her fork and pushed her dessert plate aside.

"A few years after college, yes."

Maybe that would be enough to satisfy their curiosity. But no.

Zach asked, "Do you have a picture of you guys back then? Back when you were dating?"

"That was thirty years ago, Zach. Almost twice as long as you've been alive." Sydney had lost her appetite for dessert. And the ice cream cake was the non-descript birthday standard. It was always better to pay for one.

"As a matter of fact," Tyler said, as he leaned forward to pull his wallet out of his back pocket. "I *do* have a photo from that time."

Sydney's head whipped toward him. "You've *got* to be kidding."

Tyler smiled smugly. "Nope. Here it is." In his hand was a dog-eared photo, which he passed across the table to Zach before she could get a glimpse.

"That's cool." Zach stared at the photo and snickered. "You guys look so young." He showed it to Jessie, who appeared to be in shock. She looked at the photo and back at Sydney, not once but twice.

The rumbling was louder and more painful in Sydney's stomach. Where would this conversation end? *When* would it end? No time could be soon enough for her. She'd likely tell Jessie the truth one day, but not then. Not like this.

"Can I see it?" Sydney waited for Jessie to hand it back across the table. She stared down at their youthful faces, hers and Tyler's. A different kind of pain emerged. Innocence and joy gleamed from the faded photo. Their love for each other blazoned clearly, unhidden by curling, cracking paper. Tyler's arms surrounded her from behind, and his cheek connected with hers. They both were grinning broadly. Had she smiled so widely since then?

So young. So sad that a love so intense was only a stale memory which, to date, nothing had equaled or surpassed.

Sydney's eyes stung. She blinked. It wasn't the moment to give in to the pain. And he'd kept the photo all those years.

"You're crying, Mom?" Jessie's voice sounded like a child's, full of surprise and wonder.

Sydney pushed out a chuckle but blinked again. "No, I'm just touched, I guess. You know, old memories. All that."

Tyler took the photo from her hand and held her gaze for a long moment.

"Have you carried that around for thirty years?" she asked him.

"No. I did for a couple years, then I put it away somewhere. I dug it out just the other day when I ran into you."

She nodded and turned back toward the kids. "Anyone want to walk on the beach? The sun is setting now. Should be beautiful."

They all agreed and made their way down the wooden steps leading from the dining room to the sandy expanse below. Sydney was spared more probing questions, though the raw place the photo evoked still ached as they walked. As their conversation tumbled out and mixed with the roar of waves, orange sun slipped down into the sea.

Chapter Thirteen

Jessie was up early. She entered the kitchen fully dressed as Sydney finished her coffee and devotional reading at the table. Sydney looked up. "What time is the service?"

"Ten-thirty. Zach's picking me up in —" she looked up at the wall clock. "Twenty minutes. I have just enough time to eat and go."

During the ride home from the restaurant the previous evening, Zach asked Jessie if she wanted to go with him to his church. She eagerly agreed and looked at Sydney. "Mom, why don't you come with us? Gram won't mind if you don't go with her this time."

True, her mother probably thought it strange that Sydney had never returned to the Bible church where she'd been raised. She might have guessed that for Sydney, too many memories would be evoked and, worse, the chance that someone would recognize her and bring up the past. *Aren't you the girl who got knocked up senior year? Was that guy Tyler the father?*

But how many people would recognize her thirty years later? Really, there was little risk except in Sydney's own head. Jessie already knew she'd been in the worship band. No one at church knew about the baby, unless they'd guessed when, at age eighteen, she disappeared for seven months before the end of the school year. Wouldn't take too much to figure *that* out.

So, she chickened out once again. "Maybe I'll go with you all sometime, but not just yet. I'd like to go with your gram. Carolyn, or whatever you're calling her these days." She laughed.

Jessie huffed. She wasn't buying it. "Whatever. I don't know why you like that place better. It's boring." That was true. When Pastor Hoffman retired and was replaced by a younger man, apparently, he was too edgy for Carolyn. She and several of her friends moved over to the local Baptist church, where the sermons were encouraging, but the traditional style suited them better.

Jessie sat down with her cereal bowl across from Sydney. "I'm gonna get hungry if I don't eat more than this, but I'm lazy in the morning."

"How about a piece of fruit?" Sydney looked up from her e-reader, which contained her Bible and about sixty other books. Relief coursed through her at the mundane nature of Jessie's conversation.

"The dinner was fun last night, but it was weird to see that photo."

Sydney's relief was short-lived. "Weird to see your mom as a seventeen-year-old?" A strand of discomfort dangled inside her.

"Yeah. And to see you with Mr. Hoffman when both of you were my age. Seems like you really loved each other." Something soft and wistful laced Jessie's voice.

"We did. Maybe that's why I never talked about it because it hurt when it ended." At least she didn't need to make a clumsy attempt at hiding that truth. "It's kind of rare, though, for people to stay with the people they dated in high school. It's healthy to meet other people and have more maturity before marriage, you know?"

"I guess so. But you guys seem to get along well now. I think he likes you, Mom."

"Tyler?" Sydney blinked.

Jessie grinned. "Yeah, did you notice the way he looks at you?"

"I, uh. No, I didn't." Did she? Maybe a little, but she thought it was in her imagination. Last night, there seemed to be a subtle shift in his attitude toward her. She hadn't wanted to notice, to run too fast. To be hurt again.

"If you came to church with us today, you'd see him again."

Sydney's eyes narrowed. "Are you playing matchmaker, Miss Bennett?"

Jessie laughed. "I probably don't have to, Mom. Anyway, as you wisely told me only a few days ago, if it's supposed to happen, it will."

Sydney had to laugh. She reached out and squeezed Jessie's forearm. "You're pretty smart, you know that? 'Course, I taught you."

"Come with us, Mom."

"I will soon. Not today." Once Jessie returned, Sydney would learn if anyone had asked about her and what they'd said. She'd be on pins and needles until then.

Or maybe she was putting too much stock in her own fame. Thirty years go by and, really, no one cares. Not even two months later would anyone care. That was just human nature. One day, she'd tell Jessie everything that was appropriate to tell, and she wouldn't hide anymore.

ಜ   ಜ   ಜ

Dearest Sydney, I can't tell you how I felt when I read your last email. It really touched me and even brought tears to my eyes.

Sydney blinked and her throat tightened at Julia's words. *I love that you're growing and stretching, even though I'm sure it's uncomfortable sometimes. I know it was hard to share about Emma with us last month, but I feel so much closer to you now. It was such a big event that shaped you. Now I understand you much more.*

How interesting that you ran into Tyler, and you'll be seeing him again! That's juicy news and I want to hear more as it develops.

Sending you a big hug. I stand and pray with you, my sister! Much love, Julia.

Sydney couldn't stop a few tears from trickling down her cheeks. Dear Julia. Soft and reserved, she also had trouble revealing too much about herself. But she, too, had moved forward. Sydney hadn't made a brave decision when she'd told them about Emma. She'd never been brave in any circumstance involving Emma. That day in May with her friends, her words had simply gushed out on their own.

From now on, she'd learn to make those choices by will, even the hard ones. Her thoughts went to Jessie. Yes, even the terrifying ones.

C8   C8   C8

On Tuesday afternoon, Sydney parallel-parked in front of a row of shops in Kennessey's downtown. She ought to come to town more often. The colorful block of buildings had been upgraded to attract shoppers, with the addition of hanging flower baskets, potted palm trees, and outdoor seating at the cafés.

Late June meant no more mercy in temperature until the tail-end of August or September. At least Kennessey was cooler than Charlotte, thanks to the nearby ocean. She left the cool car and stepped into the sticky day, opened the trunk, and hauled out her old guitar. She'd learn within the next few minutes if it had any chance of survival after its long entombment in the attic. The worst thing for an instrument, she'd recently read somewhere.

The guitar shop had been a fixture of downtown Kennessey for at least fifty years. It wasn't her first visit. She'd been there thirty-some years earlier.

She entered the shop and saw a large variety of instruments filling walls and floor space. Two customers browsed. "Can I help you?" A voice from the front counter called to her. The voice belonged to a salesman, about thirty, with a ponytail down his back and wearing a black rocker tee-shirt.

"Hello." Sydney approached the counter and set the guitar case on it. "This was my guitar when I was a teenager and it's been in my mother's attic since then." She cringed when she saw the man's brow furrow.

"Let's have a look. Normally, guitars don't do well at all in attics, unless they have climate control. Which most don't."

Sydney opened the case, and the man gingerly took the guitar out. He examined it from one end to the other in silence, save for disapproving grunts. Now and then he shook his head. It wasn't reassuring.

"Can it be repaired?" Sydney met the man's gaze.

He shrugged. "Maybe, but it would be a long process. First, look here. The neck joint has come apart. High temperatures soften glue, as you can imagine. Many years of it—" He shook his head again. "I'll have to reattach this, remove some frets, and reinstall them. You're looking at an expensive job. In your place, I'd buy a new one."

Sydney sighed. "I expected that. But this one has sentimental value."

"You can still keep it, hang it on a wall or whatever, but I have some used guitars that are a great value that you can play. There are new guitars, too, if you prefer."

She paused, the gears of her mind spinning. Should she spend money on one? Was her interest in just preserving her legacy, as spotty as it was? No, she wanted to find the light her mother talked about. Maybe it was still there. She had to find out. "Okay, I'll look at the used ones."

They left the guitar on the counter and the man showed her a corner of the shop where five guitars hung. "These have all been refurbished. Look, here's a nice Fender for one-seventy-five. It's a great basic guitar. Then, if you want to spend a little more, I have a Gibson here and an Ibanez. They've all come to the store within the last month. You can try them all if you want."

Sydney nodded. The truth was about to come out. Did she still know how to play anything? She who'd been bound for Nashville and a music career? She swallowed. "Okay, I'll do that for a few minutes while you wait on customers. I'll let you know when I've made a decision." She didn't want him hovering around to learn at the same time she did if her mind had been scrubbed of anything musical over the last three decades.

She let out a long breath. Looking at the instruments before her, intimidation gripped her stomach, but soon loosened and was replaced by something else, ever so light, like a butterfly fluttering. She took the Gibson down from the wall. It was pricey, but a good place to start. She remembered basic chords, C, D, E, G, and strummed softly. It sounded rich and melodic. Felt unbelievably good to hold a guitar again. She tried barre chords but remembered only two of them. Maybe with practice. She and Jessie could play together. She grinned, and a small giggle escaped her throat.

Her girlfriends and students would never recognize her just then, holding an instrument and feeling a sweep of joy. She hardly recognized herself.

Sydney tried all the guitars on the wall and chose the Fender. It still cost nearly two hundred dollars, and she'd need a case, too. Her future employment was uncertain. A crazy idea to buy anything at all. But the price was good for a quality brand. After her purchase, she left the store and put both guitars and a bagful of finger picks in the trunk of her car. When she settled into the driver's seat, she let out a long sigh. She'd begun.

The golf course parking lot overflowed with cars, and it took Sydney several minutes to find a spot. She could have asked Jessie to wait for her in front but didn't want to miss the chance of seeing Tyler. Was it true what Jessie had said that morning, that he was attracted to her? She couldn't deny the chemistry emerging like a spring seedling, despite being sealed away for three decades. Maturity and years of hard knocks added a new layer, but the hum of attraction she'd had in eleventh grade was back for a new iteration.

Jessie had returned from church two days earlier with nothing to report except how much she loved the service. She announced she'd never go back to Carolyn's church.

Another day at her mother's church had been enough to convince Sydney, too. Yes, she'd join them soon, face the past however it looked today. Tyler and Zach attended there, another plus.

The two guitars in her trunk, she decided not to say anything to Jessie just yet. She had to get used to the idea herself. Jessie and her mother would likely be pleased.

Sydney entered the lobby of the golf course, again marveling at how elegant and upscale it looked. Tyler must be financially comfortable to buy not one but two, not to mention the proceeds. But she knew little about running a business. He could be mortgaged up to his eyeballs.

A noisy group of preteen kids entered from the course. Probably a group lesson of some kind. Tyler stood behind the counter talking to some customers, looking sure of himself yet attentive to them. As she hovered near the door, he looked up, and a smile spread across his face. He gestured to her.

Sydney approached the counter just as the customers left with their clubs and the kids left the building through the other door.

"Hello, Sydney."

A light tan enhanced his good looks and clear gaze. Inside her, agitation banged around. Tyler gestured with his head toward the kids. "That's one of our summer golf camps for local kids. It's hard to hear yourself think when they're here, but they seem to be having fun."

Sydney smiled and turned to watch the last one slip through the front door. "What a great idea to teach golf to kids."

"Yeah, it's fun to have them around. They come in from every neighborhood. We have scholarships for a lot of them." He came around the counter to stand beside her. "I wanted to tell you how much fun Zach and I had the other night with you both."

"We had a great evening, too. Thanks for inviting us." She wouldn't mention the content of their conversation. It wasn't the time or place, though it likely hovered in their unspoken thoughts.

"We'll have to do it again soon. In fact, I have a couple of ideas on that subject."

"Oh?" She waited as the flutters built up momentum. Just like in eleventh grade.

"I assume you're here because you're taking Jessie driving, right?"

She nodded. "You are correct."

"When you're finished—"

"Assuming we both survive."

He laughed. "When you're finished, why don't we meet you both down at the beach and we can walk together, say, five-thirty? We can meet behind the Go Fish Restaurant. It'll be cooler and less crowded at that time. The other night when we walked after dinner, it reminded me how much I love to walk on the beach before sunset. I don't make enough time for it. Are you game?"

"Sure, if Jessie's up for it. I'd bet money she will be. Especially if Zach comes." She smiled. As a business owner, did he *really* have free time to walk on the beach? Or was this an exceptional effort for her sake? "What's the other idea?"

"Ah." He held up one finger, then pointed to the front door. "Did you happen to notice the flyer on the door when you came in? The annual Summerfest is this Saturday and Sunday downtown over the July Fourth weekend. We could all go to that together. They have food, booths, and music. It's usually a fun time."

"Another good idea. Sounds fun." Sydney grinned at him. Two dates in five minutes with the same man. "I think we're making up for lost time here."

His eyes locked with hers as he smiled. "Yes, I'm trying."

Sydney's neck grew warm as he gazed at her. Maybe Jessie was right.

It had been a mistake to tell Jessie they'd be practicing parallel parking that afternoon. It was nearly rush hour. Not that rush hour in Kennessey was as congested as Charlotte. Sydney scrapped the plan and went instead to the parking lot of an office building outside of downtown and they practiced parking between the lines. Turned out that Jessie wasn't very gifted at that skill, and it took many repetitions. Sydney was proud of the patience she'd developed since the beginning of their driving efforts.

"Ready to walk on the beach? It's about quarter past."

Jessie merely sighed, her face flushed from frustration. "I think I've had enough for today. Let's go meet the guys."

"Yes, let's. It's so nice to be able to just drive to the beach in about fifteen minutes. It's also nice to have guys to meet there." They both got out of the car and switched places. Sydney pulled out into the afternoon traffic and, like many other people, headed toward the waterfront.

"*Sure* you don't want to move here, Mom?"

Sydney didn't answer at first but chuckled. Move there? Where did that come from? In fact, it did appeal to her. And she'd like to travel around the world one day, too. "You'd want to leave all your friends in Charlotte? Your youth group, your school?"

Jessie snorted. "My fair-weather friends, you mean? I haven't heard from anyone since I've been here. I wrote to Janice and Beverly a couple times."

"They didn't respond? That's weird. You're good friends with both of them."

"Since they got boyfriends, I guess I'm off their radar."

"That's terrible. I'm sorry, Jessie."

"No big deal. They're losers. I'll make new friends."

"Yes, you will. Look, there's Zach over there with his dad. He's a good friend, at least."

Sydney parked behind the restaurant. She spotted Zach and Tyler near the trail, which began at a row of rental houses, their stilts reminding her of birds' legs. Each time she saw Tyler, she felt a bit less awkward, though she still had to pinch herself, so crazy it still seemed to her that he was part of her present instead of her past. She and Jessie joined them, and they all walked toward the beach single file along the narrow sand path through the reeds. "How was the driving lesson?" Tyler asked.

"I'd rather not talk about it." Jessie grimaced and exchanged glances with Zach, who gave her a sympathetic look.

"She's getting it. It's just a matter of time." Sydney tried to catch Jessie's sulking gaze.

Tyler led the way. Tall grasses stroked Sydney's bare legs and cool sand slid between her feet and her flip flops. Heavenly. They crossed the expanse of soft sand and arrived at the edge of the water. The tide was rolling out, leaving behind darkened packed sand. Only a few sun-bathers remained scattered on the beige landscape.

"See you later, guys." Zach and Jessie turned to leave them.

"Hey, Jessie. Do you have your phone?"

"Yeah, Mom."

"Meet us back here in—" She looked at Tyler.

"Doesn't matter. You're on vacation." He grinned as a gentle breeze ruffled his hair.

"Right." She was so used to the mom thing. Always keeping track. "Okay, see ya in a while," she called to Jessie, who'd already started edging toward freedom.

She and Zach took off running the other way, laughing as they went.

Tyler and Sydney looked at each other and grinned. He said, "Guess it's just us this time. Want to go that way?" Tyler gestured his head toward the setting sun, which spilled brilliant light across the sculpted waves.

Sydney nodded. "It's beautiful. I could look at the setting sun for hours, but it only lasts for minutes."

Tyler and Sydney walked in silence. She'd taken off her wide-band flip flops and carried them in one hand. The tepid water swirled around her feet in soothing swells. Still seemed strange to be walking beside Tyler on the beach. They'd spent many hours in the ancient past doing the same thing.

"Do you usually work long hours during high season?" Sydney sought to break the quiet that stretched between them, fighting a momentary fear that, without the kids, they'd have nothing to talk about after all the years that had elapsed. They were, after all, different people now. Three decades had shaped them, and maybe they wouldn't even get along anymore. She knew almost nothing of Tyler Hoffman.

"Some days I do, but I try not to. I have good employees and don't feel like I always need to be there."

Sydney smiled. "Now *that's* a good work ethic. Knowing when to quit and have a life. Good for you."

Muted pinks and blues began their journey across the sky, dimming the swath of sunlight. The setting sun bathed Tyler's profile with an orange glow, but she saw his jaw tighten. "I had to learn the hard way. My work ethic contributed to the demise of my marriage. I won't say more about that now. When I first bought the golf courses, I did put in a lot of time. I was divorced by then and didn't have Zach living with me. I wanted to front-load the time investment so it could run smoothly after that without tons of my hours." He grinned. "I'm willing to employ people."

"You're contributing to the economy by supplying jobs." She took a breath and watched a seagull take flight with a shriek over the waves. "It's a shame we so often have to lose something in order to learn." A wave of sadness at the harsh reality flowed through Sydney's mind as a thought of Cody.

After a few moments of silent strolling through the surf, Sydney said, "I assume Zach doesn't know about Emma." She'd hesitated to bring it up, but the question had weighed on her mind since the previous Saturday, when they'd gone out for dinner.

Tyler didn't appear taken off guard by her statement. "No, I— I've never told him. I don't think my reasons were entirely valid or pure, either. I didn't want him to see me as that kind of example. Getting my girlfriend pregnant, even though I was a practicing Christian, then hightailing it to college and abandoning her." He didn't look at her, but his face looked tight. So, *that's* the way he'd seen himself for the last thirty years.

"Hey." Sydney stopped walking and touched his arm. He stopped and looked down at her. "I understand what you're saying.

But you don't think Zach would give you grace with your teenage failings, if he knew your regret?"

"Hopefully, he would. But during his formative years, I chose not to tell him. When you're in that situation, you make the best decision you can, as I'm sure you've experienced yourself. You haven't told Jessie either, right?"

"No, I haven't. And I'm not standing here judging you. I went through the same questions. What do you tell, what do you keep hidden in the past? It's a difficult question when you're raising children, especially when they're too young to understand a lot of it." They started walking again. "I do plan to tell her at some point."

"I'm sure I will, too. I just don't know when. It was easy to hide it all before. Now, seeing you again, the question is there in my head, when's the right time to say the truth." He laid one hand on her shoulder. "Don't get me wrong, Sydney. I'm really happy we ran into each other. Seems ordained, to me."

Sydney didn't have an answer for that. A smile tugged at her lips. "Maybe it's God saying, 'Let go of the past mistakes and regret. Grace and forgiveness are there for you, so go forward.' What do you think?" That sounded wise and mature, though she still needed to take her own advice.

Tyler only nodded and squeezed his eyes shut for an instant. "Yeah. I think you're right. He knows how long I beat myself up."

"You could have knocked me over with a feather, excuse the cliché, when you brought out that photo. Tyler, you kept that photo for *thirty* years! And Zach asked about it, as if he knew you had it."

"I don't know if he knew about it or not. I never showed it to him, or even my ex-wife, though it might have been fine to show her. It was kind of fun to have the kids see it."

"You think? I was terrified of the questions that would come next. We got off easy."

"For now, anyway. One day, I want you to tell me more about that chapter of your life. Your time with your aunt and everything that came after. I want you to fill in the gaps for me."

Sydney paused and looked down at a tiny crab scuttling across the sand near her feet. She took a breath. "We have a lot of gaps to fill, but I'm not sure it's a good idea to revisit the past." She lifted her head. "But, hey, what am I saying, I'm the one trying to find Emma."

"You are?" Tyler stopped walking and stared at her.

She hadn't meant to tell him abruptly like that. "I don't mean I'm trying to find her so I can have a relationship with her. Not necessarily. I just want to find out what happened to her. I want to find out if she's happy and has had a good life. I'll feel peaceful about her if I know." She'd like to know she hadn't ruined Emma's life, as she had her own at the time.

"If it's good news, that is."

"I believe it is. She was adopted by a family who, theoretically, cared about her and gave her a nice life. Now she's almost thirty so she may have a family of her own." Sydney swallowed. "I could be a grandmother." Her eyes found his. "We could be grandparents." Laughter escaped her throat. "That's such a weird thought. Haven't you ever wondered what happened to her?"

He shrugged, still looking at her. "Once in a while. But I'll admit, I've put it behind me. All except for you. I never fully put you behind me, Sydney. I want you to know that."

They stood for a moment, inches apart as silence stretched between them. She blinked. Let out a breath. "I guess I let go because I felt I had to. I'm sorry I never answered your letters, those couple you wrote during freshman year. I was hurting and didn't know how to respond. So, I didn't." She averted her eyes. "But I should have. Maybe—" She shook her head. Better not go there into the land of what ifs.

He lifted a hand and moved a strand of hair away from her face then let his fingers trail down her cheek. "Sydney Davis, I've never forgotten you. When I didn't hear back from you, I was sad, but I understood and knew it was my fault."

A pause hovered between them. The intensity of the moment weighed on her and she suddenly wanted to flee the past. "Let's not be sad anymore, Tyler." Her voice was soft, so unlike her. Maybe she was learning. "Let's enjoy the sunset."

He returned a solemn smile and stepped back. "Okay. Sorry to be maudlin. I didn't mean to let it go there. You have to know that usually I'm a pretty cheerful guy." He began walking again. "I enjoy my work and have lots of relationships in town." The uplift in his voice seemed forced, but at least they'd moved on.

"You'd have to. You probably know everyone in Kennessey."

"Seems that way. Golfing brings people together."

"Hmm. That makes sense. It's a social sport. I did try it a few times in college, I want you to know. It didn't stick. I was more interested in volleyball. Then later, running, swimming, yoga."

"That's how you stay in good shape. I'll give you a few golf lessons if you want. I bet you'll enjoy it if you learn the nuances of the game."

"If you're willing to take the challenge, okay. If anyone can make me like golf, I'm sure you can. It'll give me something to do with my time until I go back to Charlotte. Or maybe even *after* I go back since I may be unemployed." She'd said it lightly, but underneath, the subject felt like a rock in her stomach.

Tyler's brows furrowed. "When do you go back?"

She blinked. She didn't want to talk about leaving, but it was a fair question. "Mid-August."

"You'd go back to the same teaching context, after what happened?"

Sydney turned her gaze out toward the approaching tide as the foam swirled around her ankles. "I don't know. I spend a lot of time thinking about what else I could do, sent out a few resumes. A couple analyst jobs, a bank job. Yawn. But I have a teenager to support. If it were just me, I'd be freer to take risks or try something completely different."

"One of our high schools here in Kennessey must need a teacher, or at least a substitute teacher."

"I'd actually love to quit teaching. My enthusiasm for the classroom started to flag two or three years ago."

"Stay here, then. You can find something here that's different."

She saw the yearning on his face and felt an overpowering urge to agree to stay. It felt like freedom and a second chance. But she knew it was unrealistic. "You sound like Jessie now. She told me the other day she wanted to move here. But what does a mathematician do in a tourist town? I could count tourists on the beach and report it to the local paper." She chuckled, but a thread of despair laced her thoughts.

"God'll provide. You know that. Anyway, we can think outside the box and come up with something for you."

"There's something else." She swallowed a sudden lump in her throat at the thought. "After I left school, my principal was going to let the faculty know that I had had a family emergency and wouldn't be finishing the school year. That would have answered a lot of questions, but he forgot to do that. So, a rumor has sprung up that the reason I didn't go back is that I'd had an inappropriate relationship with a student."

Tyler's mouth dropped open. "What? That's terrible, Sydney. Does your principal know?"

She nodded. "Yes, and he's taken the same blasé attitude about it as he did with the attack. He says it's just a rumor and will blow over by the fall. He's not going to do anything. I feel I need to go back to defend myself and my reputation."

"Is that a strong enough reason by itself to go back?"

Sydney shrugged. "It bothers me. I've had a good career for twelve years in that school. I'm very respected by students *and* colleagues. Those who know me may realize it's out of character for me, but I don't know how far the rumor will go." She sighed in frustration. "I'm still thinking about the best way to handle it. Should I contact people I know and have them spread truth instead of rumor? That may work, but it's summer. No one's there."

Tyler fell silent, as if searching for something encouraging to say. There was nothing to say, and Sydney knew it. "Okay, let's change the subject now," she said. "I was peaceful a minute ago and now the anxiety is kicking in."

He laid a hand on her shoulder. "I still think a new job is the best thing, even with this other problem. My opinion, of course. You have two months. Things may come together between now and then."

She smiled at him. "Thanks for the reminder. I have time. I'll try not to poison my summer worrying about it." It didn't solve anything, but she did have over a month to figure things out. To see God work. Yes, she should remember him.

"And—" Tyler's voice changed tone, laced with uncertainty. First time she'd heard that in him. "I'd love to see you once in a while until you leave. Is that okay?"

A wave of warmth pooled inside. Warmth with a trace of fear. She hadn't misinterpreted his words, his look. She smiled and nodded. "Yes, that's quite okay."

Chapter Fourteen

Two days later, Sydney got the last call she'd been waiting for, this time, from the Cape Fear Christian Adoption Agency. Again, there was no trace of her in their archives. She let out a sigh as she deleted the message and hung up. What now? Maybe she wasn't supposed to learn about Emma. She could continue with all the adoption agencies on the east coast, or she could do what she'd been putting off since her arrival. She could ask her mother.

A groan of frustration escaped her throat, not only because of the disappointing response, but her dread of bringing it up. Clearly, she couldn't keep her quest private anymore.

It was early Thursday afternoon, and Jessie was at work. Carolyn was reading in the living room after Sydney had served the two of them a light lunch on the patio. The ceiling fan overhead made the June heat tolerable, and the meal had been surprisingly enjoyable. No tension, no coolness. Carolyn shared news about residents Sydney remembered from her youth. They talked about events in the town, including the upcoming festival. When Sydney told her she and Jessie would be going with Tyler and Zach, Carolyn raised her brows but said nothing. It wasn't the time to probe into her mother's attitude regarding Tyler.

Now, she'd throw a wrench into it all that pleasantness by plowing head-on into the past. Sydney went to the living room and sat in a wing chair opposite her mother, who was on the verge of dozing off. Her eyes opened, and she blinked a few times. "Hello, Sydney. Have you been sitting there long? I got drowsy."

"No, I just sat down. What are you reading?"

Carolyn waved the air with one hand. "Oh, I got a new eBook that was on sale, so I'm giving it a try. One of those summer beach reads for women. Not usually my cup of tea."

"I'm guessing the book isn't riveting." Sydney chuckled.

"No, not yet. I usually get a bit tired in the afternoons, anyway. I've started napping occasionally."

Sydney frowned. Her mother was only seventy-six. Since they'd arrived in Kennessey, she'd noticed more fatigue and a slower pace then she'd expected. "Is everything okay, Mom? I mean, health-wise?"

Her mother looked taken off guard, then recovered. "Oh, you know, the usual things for someone my age. I don't have the energy I did."

A decline in energy was normal. Her mom's slow pace made a stark contrast with her past energy and full docket of activities. Startling, but perhaps typical.

"Mom, I have to ask you something."

Carolyn suddenly looked alert, apprehensive.

A hot churning had begun in Sydney's stomach. She forced herself to push out her first words. "Lately, I've been thinking about Emma." She paused to take a breath. Her mother's face was impossible to read. "I—I don't necessarily want to start a relationship with her, but I'd really like to know what happened to her, just for my own peace of mind." Now that she'd started, it was easier to keep going, but her hands had become slick with sweat. "I've phoned a few adoption agencies in the area, and no one has a record of me. I hope you remember the name of the agency you used." She waited.

Her mother didn't answer for a moment, but her frown deepened. "What if you find out this girl's been looking for *you*, Sydney? Have you thought of that? You know how adopted children sometimes want to find their birth parents once they're older. Are you ready for that?"

Sydney shifted in her chair. Yes, she'd thought of it, but not for long. "Well, if that happens, then I can make a decision then, can't I? My goal is simply to find out what *happened* to her, so she's not some black hole forever in my mind."

"I understand. If you must do it for your own peace of mind, I'll try to help you. I don't remember the name off the top of my head, but I have some old papers somewhere upstairs that will jog my memory." She paused. "I don't recommend it. Leaving the past where it lay and moving forward is the best thing, in my opinion. Has seeing Tyler again made you think of this?"

"No, he didn't even know until I told him the other day."

"What does he think?"

Sydney shrugged. "He understood my desire to know. I'm not sure if he's thought of it as much as I have in recent days."

"And Jessie doesn't know?"

"No, not yet." Sydney shook her head. A heaviness weighed down inside her. Maybe she should have left well enough alone and not started all this. "I'll tell her one day, but finding the right time is—it's hard. You can imagine."

"Yes."

Jessie's voice sounded from the doorway. "Tell me what? Sydney and her mother both flinched in surprise. "I heard you talking about an adoption or something. What's going on, Mom?"

Sydney's mouth went dry. She turned her head toward the doorway and groped for words as she and Jessie stared at each other. Now was the time her secrets would tumble out. She took a breath and moistened her lips. "Come in and sit down, Jessie."

Jessie entered the living room and sat down on the edge of the other wing chair facing Sydney. Her lips were pinched and her eyes wide. She gripped the arms of the chair, waiting.

"I thought you were at work today."

"They let me off early because we had too many employees. I was upstairs. I guess you didn't hear me."

"There's something about my past that I've never told you. I—I intended to tell you, but I wanted to wait for the right time. Since you heard part of our conversation, I want to tell you now." Sydney let out a breath and glanced over at her mother, who sat still, an impassive mask on her face. No support there.

Sydney's heart thudded in her chest. She, who had addressed unruly teenagers for years in her math classes, perspired under the cool gaze of her daughter. It was time to tell her the truth. *Help me, Lord.*

She took a breath. Better to just spit it out, which was her style anyway. "When I was your age, I got pregnant." There, it was out.

Jessie's eyes widened, and her mouth dropped open. "With Mr. Hoffman?"

Sydney nodded. "We—we messed up. As Christians, we knew it was wrong, but we were intimate and got pregnant. We were seniors in high school. So, um, we decided to give the baby up for adoption. We felt too young to be parents. It was a very hard decision. I never wanted to talk about it because of that, but also, you were young."

Jessie's brows bunched together. "Mom, I'm seventeen! You never told me *all my life* that you had another baby? Somewhere in the world, I have a half brother or sister?"

"A sister," Sydney said quietly. "You have a sister." Her pulse thudded. The look on Jessie's face ripped her apart. This was the moment she'd long dreaded. "I named her Emma."

Jessie stared at the floor, an incredulous look still on her face. "Emma. A half-sister. I have a sister named Emma I never knew about." Her head whipped up. "How could you hide this from me, Mom? I'm not a baby anymore." She turned to Carolyn. "You knew, too. Am I the only one who didn't know? Does Zach know?"

Sydney's breath hitched. "No, Jessie. Not yet. His dad is going to tell him, too, but you can't say anything to Zach. It's Tyler's place to do that when he's ready."

Jessie shook her head. "How—how did you *never* say anything? Am I even a part of this family?" She leaped up and ran out of the room. Sydney heard her steps thumping on the staircase and the door slam overhead.

A long, deep sigh flowed out of Sydney's lungs like a punctured balloon. Despair and relief mixed inside her, but tears stung her eyes. The burden of the secret was gone. But in its place, a wound she needed somehow to heal with her daughter.

"You can't blame her, really." Carolyn's voice was quiet, dry. Dullness filled her eyes, but tears had gathered there. She blinked. "This thing has long put a shadow on our family. I hope this is the end of it and we can finally go on."

Sydney pressed her lips together, frustration stirring inside. "I'm sorry I ruined your life, Mother." She couldn't keep the acid from her tone. "You dealt with it in the way that suited you, and I'm so sorry that it didn't completely disappear."

Carolyn lifted her head and stared back at Sydney. "What do you mean by that? I dealt with it because you were practically a child. I made the best decision I could on your behalf."

"You sent me *away* to go through it alone so you wouldn't be embarrassed." Sydney's voice had risen.

Her mother's mouth dropped open and she sat up straighter. "I did no such thing. I did what I did because I wanted to save *you* embarrassment. I encouraged you to give her up because I thought it would be better for your future. You'd have a chance to go to college, get married, have children under the right circumstances. Didn't you know, Sydney, that I did it for *you?*"

"Did you?" Sydney and her mother stared at each other. The air crackled with tension.

"Yes, I did." Carolyn's voice dropped, but there was still an edge. "I wasn't worried about my reputation, as you insinuate. If you don't believe that, then you'll have to live with those feelings of bitterness and believe the worst about me. Like you always have, in fact."

Something broke and tumbled down inside Sydney. Had she misjudged her mother all these years? She swallowed. "You did it for me?" Her voice sounded small but sullen.

"I didn't want you ridiculed at school and talked about by the people who knew you. Nowadays, no one thinks a thing about a young girl who gets pregnant, it's so commonplace. But back then, I was afraid you'd end up with a very different future than the one I had envisioned for you."

Sydney stared at the floor, as a flash of understanding of her mother's perspective flooded her mind. Her mother, who'd handled the situation alone for her. Sydney had been an emotional wreck. At the time, she'd been relieved that her mother had intervened to make the arrangements, since she herself hadn't the strength or knowledge. Her father had been silently distant for the most part, likely disillusioned and ashamed of his daughter.

Had her mother not wanted to be bothered with raising her daughter and granddaughter at the same time? Sydney would never know whether that had played a part. And if it had, could she forgive her mother for that?

She'd forgiven Tyler for his much larger role in abandoning her. Had she ever forgiven her mother for her perceived abandonment? Hot tears spilled down Sydney's cheeks. Her gaze found her mother's. "I'm sorry if I've misjudged you all these years, Mom. I know I let it put up a barrier between us."

Her mother blinked. Her eyes brimmed again with tears and her chin was taut. "I'm sorry about that. I'm sure I've contributed to that barrier, too. And I can see how you felt abandoned by everyone to go through it alone. Now—" she shrugged helplessly, her hands outstretched, "now I can see how you might have felt alone. I'm sorry, Sydney. I hope you believe me when I tell you I did everything for your good. I didn't think it was healthy for you at your age to raise a baby alone. Of course, I would have helped you if you'd really wanted to keep her. I wouldn't have put you on the streets with your child. But I wanted you to have the best shot at a happy life."

Sydney nodded slowly and bit her lip. "Yeah, I can see . . ." Maybe her mother cared about her after all. "I guess—" There was too much to say and her energy to talk about it had drained away.

She shrugged. "I wasn't the favorite to begin with, and then I messed up. I understood why I was sent away. But it still hurt."

"Is that what you think? No, Sydney, I didn't have favorites. I loved my children equally. And I certainly didn't send you away as a punishment for your predicament. Not at all, as I've told you." Her mother's voice softened. "In hindsight, when you were young, I probably didn't tell you I loved you often enough or do enough special things for you as the only girl. I'm sorry about that. It wasn't natural for me to think that way." She fell silent.

Sydney sat motionless and blinked away more tears that had gathered. Special things . . . yes, she would have loved being treated as special, being the only girl. She wouldn't have needed the approval of her brothers because she'd have been important in her own unique way.

She swiped her cheeks with the back of her hand. "Okay, what do you think if we focus on the present?" She offered a tight smile that she didn't feel.

"I think that's a good idea. I hope you understand better what happened all those years ago. And now, it seems things are somehow circling back around, but in a better way, I hope."

Sydney nodded and wondered if her mother was referring to Tyler. She flicked away a few new tears. "Thanks, Mom. Let me know what you find out about the name of the agency. I—I have to go talk to Jessie now."

Usually, Sydney bounded up or down the stairs, taking them two at a time. This time she took one step at a time, praying as she went. Praying for Jessie, but also overcome with gratitude that the impasse with her mother that had endured for decades had splintered that day. She prayed it would happen again with her daughter.

Sydney reached Jessie's bedroom door and tapped lightly. No answer. She tapped again and heard a muffled, "Come in."

She turned the knob and saw Jessie lying on her bed, arms crossed in front of her. Her red eyes showed she'd been crying, but just then, she looked furious.

Sydney pulled a wicker chair alongside the bed and sat down. She leaned forward and propped her arms on her knees. "I understand your anger, Jessie. I never meant to lock you out of my private life. That was never my intention." She took a breath. Blinked. "It was so hard to talk about, and I just didn't know how or when. But, by the time you were old enough to understand, so many years had gone by, I'd mostly put it in the past. Once in a while, I thought about it and it seemed like it had happened to another person, another lifetime ago."

Jessie didn't respond or look at Sydney but appeared to be listening. "I know it sounds like I'm making excuses. I—I wanted to explain. I made a lot of mistakes in my life. I regretted bringing a child into the world and not being able to take care of her. But it still hurt *really* badly to give her up. It tore me up inside. But you know what?"

Sydney shifted her elbows to the edge of the bed, bringing her closer to Jessie. She was gratified when Jessie turned and looked at her, her beautiful blue eyes glossy with new tears. "When I held you in my arms for the first time—" her voice broke then. Her eyes filled, and tears tumbled down her cheeks. "I felt whole again. I wasn't broken anymore. God had given me a beautiful daughter—not a son, a *daughter*. He gave me an amazing, precious gift, despite the fact that I'd messed up. That was his grace, Jessie. *You* were his grace to me."

She swallowed, willing Jessie to understand, to somehow perceive the flood of love and longing that poured from her across the bed to her sulking daughter. "I love you so much, Jessie. I wouldn't hurt you for anything. I hope you'll forgive me for not telling you about Emma."

Though Jessie still frowned, tears slid out of her eyes. Her frown twisted as she fought emotion. She squeezed her eyes shut. When she opened them, her face was wet, but her eyes linked with

Sydney's. "I forgive you, Mom." She leaned forward and Sydney pulled her in, arms encircling her shoulders. She held Jessie for several minutes, silently weeping, thankful though undeserving. She rocked her gently, like she did when Jessie was a small child, and stroked her blond curls.

When they pulled apart, Jessie gave Sydney a half-smile. "I love you, Mom. I understand, a little bit."

"I'm glad. You're my girl, you know. My treasure. A treasure I don't deserve."

Jessie leaned back against the pillow. "Mom, can I help you find Emma?"

Sydney nodded. "Yes, you can. We'll find her together. My intention was to find out about her, just so I'd know what happened in her life. But if she wants to get in touch with us, well, we'll see when the time comes, okay?"

Jessie nodded. "We'll do it together."

༒ ༒ ༒

Sydney turned off her phone and settled under a crisp sheet on her bed. It had been an intense day, and she felt like a limp rag.

A mental image floated into her mind, of Tyler walking beside her on the beach, bathed in orange sunlight. And his words, *I've never forgotten you.* Warmth stirred inside. She'd been surprised, struck by the depth of his regret about Emma, having beaten himself up over it for years. And speechless at the thoughts of her he'd kept all those years.

A reflection came unbidden, and her scalp prickled. Could Tyler be trying to make up for his failure of the past, or at least be influenced by his guilt feelings? They weren't starting with a blank slate. There was muddy water they couldn't ignore under that bridge. With so much time elapsed, it almost seemed like a new relationship. But were either of them forcing it because of the past?

Sydney sighed. Why was she asking herself these questions? She'd been peaceful and happy a moment ago. Tyler hadn't shown anything but genuine interest in her, hadn't he? Now, a nest of questions and doubts had formed, just a few, but still. Only time would tell Tyler's true motivation. That and close observation.

Chapter Fifteen

After breakfast the next day, Jessie sat across from Sydney at the kitchen table while Carolyn pruned petunias in clay pots in the shade of the front porch. "You ready?" Sydney held the cell phone in one hand.

"Yup. Ready as I'll ever be. I'm glad Gram remembered the right adoption agency." Jessie looked at the phone with an expectant grin. "This is exciting."

"Or nerve wracking, depending on your perspective." Sydney shot Jessie a fake scared expression and Jessie laughed. "I'm ready, too." It had taken a few hours and all three of them pouring through old files before they found information about the adoption. Finally, Sydney wasn't groping in the dark but had a viable lead.

Her need to ask her mother for the phone number had led to tangible changes in their relationship she could never have orchestrated herself. And she'd been too bruised and embittered by the past to have sought them. They'd likely still bump heads once in a while, but a change had begun like a fresh, healing breeze.

Sydney dialed the number her mother had given her and put the phone on speaker mode so Jessie could hear. She'd make her daughter a full partner in her research from now on. "Hanover Adoptions, Betty Gibson speaking."

She exchanged a smile and a wide-eyed glance with Jessie. "Good morning, Ms. Gibson. My name is Sydney Bennett. In nineteen ninety-one when I was a teenager, I gave up a baby for adoption. I'm trying to learn what happened to her, for my own peace of mind. Would you be able to locate the record for me to see what kind of contact agreement there might be?" At least she now knew the process and the vocabulary.

"Yes, of course. I'll put in a request. What is your maiden name and the exact date of the birth, Ms. Bennett?"

"My full maiden name is Sydney Abigail Davis. My daughter was born Emma Rose Davis and her date of birth was July sixteenth, nineteen ninety-one."

"Thank you. Our records have been digitized, even the older ones, so we should be able to locate the record within a few days. If we find it, we'll have you come to our office when we open the record."

"A few days? That's wonderful, Ms. Gibson. Thank you so much."

"Are you in the area? Our office is in Wilmington."

"Yes, we'll be coming from Kennessey."

"Oh, good. That's not far, about forty minutes or so."

Sydney gave the woman her phone number and hung up. Jessie already had her palm out. Sydney hi-fived her. "We're not there yet, but at least we know this is probably the right agency. Did I tell you I called three of them before asking your Gram?"

"No, three? Wow. I'm glad we have the right one now. I looked at Facebook last night to see if I could find Emma by her birthdate, but I couldn't find it."

Sydney leaned back in her chair. "I'm not surprised. She may be on Facebook, but you'd need more than her birthdate, I'm afraid. Her adoptive parents might have changed her name, too. She'd almost thirty, so she might have gotten married and had kids already."

"Really?" Jessie's eyes widened. "I guess she's old enough to have kids, since that was a long time ago. I might be an aunt." She grinned. "Hey, what if she lives here in Kennessey? Wouldn't that be cool? We can go meet her."

"Whoa, slow down." Sydney laid a hand on Jessie's arm. "We have to take one step at a time. Like I told you, my original intention was to just find out what happened to her. I wasn't planning to connect with her. But the more I think of it, I might be open to it, if she is. But it would be kind of weird, don't you think?"

Jessie cocked her head. "Might be at first. She might be mad at you because you gave her up."

"Yeah, I've thought of that." Sydney slid the chair back and stood up. "There's nothing we can do about it until they call us. What time are you working today?"

"I go in at twelve. I took tomorrow off so we can go to the festival with Zach and his dad."

Sydney paused. "You're not mad at Zach's dad because he didn't want to raise the baby, are you?"

Jessie shook her head. "No, I understand. Sometimes I think about what it would be like to be my age and suddenly have this baby to take care of. It would freak me out. I think I'd do what you guys did."

She smiled, relieved by Jessie's statement. In this case, understanding certainly went a long way.

When Jessie left for work, pedaling her bike down the street, Sydney slipped out to the front porch with her phone to call Tyler. She'd never called him before and felt awkward, but the need weighed on her. Her call went to voicemail, as she'd expected. He'd be busy renting clubs to customers or whatever golf course owners did.

On her phone screen, she saw a call had come in earlier that morning from The Triangle Investment Corporation, one of the five companies where she'd sent her resume. "Hello, this is Shenay Brewster from the Triangle Investment Corporation. Sydney, we received your resume, and we'd like to arrange an initial phone interview for you for this coming Monday at ten a.m. I apologize for the late notice. Please call our office before five o'clock today to confirm whether you'll be available at that time."

Sydney stared at the phone. Finally, a prospect for her future employment. She said aloud to the breeze, "Let me check my calendar. Hmm. Perfectly available for an interview." She called the number and confirmed the appointment for Monday. When she and Jessie returned Charlotte, would she have a new career, instead of dreading the potentially messy return to her old one? She couldn't block a thread of hope. Maybe her life was about to turn a corner.

Five minutes later, her phone rang. "Sydney, what a nice surprise." Tyler's voice filled her with warmth. "I just saw your name on my phone. Is everything okay?"

"Yes, everything's good. Great, in fact." Sydney steered her thoughts from her interview to her reason for phoning Tyler. "So much has happened. Yesterday, I told Jessie about Emma."

"Oh? How did she take it?" His voice held an edge of vigilance, possibly as he thought about Zach.

"Well, at first, she was furious that I'd kept it from her. She'd overheard me talking to my mom about it. But after that, we had a good talk, and she forgave me. She wants to help me find Emma."

"That's a relief. I'm glad she's not still angry at you. And I'm sure it's a load off your mind."

"You've got that right. I told her not to say anything to Zach about Emma. I said it was your place to tell him whenever you're ready."

"Thank you for that. I kept it buried for a long time, but now it's out on the surface. I'm glad. I think it's healthy."

Sydney paused. "I'm glad you think so. I know it was a shock to see me then maybe uncomfortable to talk about Emma. I wasn't sure how you'd react."

"Of course, I'm on board with you. It's important to you."

Sydney bit her lip. Finding out about Emma might be *her* project, but she was part of Tyler's past, too.

Tyler added, "I don't think I would have gone looking for her, but I support your efforts, Sydney."

"Thanks." She was glad for his support, but wished he had more enthusiasm about his daughter. More like a supportive bystander.

"We're still on for the festival tomorrow, right?" he asked.

"Yes, we are. I'm looking forward to it." And she was. It would be fun to get out of the house around others in a festive atmosphere, but she looked forward to being with Tyler and Zach again, too. And no secrets would come out that day.

"We may see a few people from the past. Will that be okay for you?"

"I've decided it's time to be brave and stop avoiding things. Anyway, it's not like people knew what happened, remember it, or even care."

"I think you're right about that. Most people are wrapped up in their own lives. They won't think about something that happened thirty years ago." He let out an audible breath. "I'll tell Zach about Emma after the festival."

"Just think, once he knows, everyone who matters will be in the loop. We won't have to worry about one of the kids asking awkward questions." Sydney chuckled, remembering the photo.

"Absolutely. I'm looking forward to seeing you tomorrow, Sydney."

When they hung up, Sydney rocked in the wicker chair as she rewound their conversation. It was okay if Tyler wasn't fully engaged in finding Emma. He'd taken ownership of his failings, which was essential. But he wasn't embracing her in the present, except as a spectator. Was Emma Sydney's project alone, just as she had been *her* problem in the past?

℃ ℃ ℃

The festival extended over several streets, parking lots, a park, and a grassy field in front of the town hall. Every area had its theme, games, food, town history skits and other local entertainment. Craft booths lined each side of one street, blocked off to traffic for the occasion. Food trucks and crowds choked another one nearby. Colorful banners hung from every light post, and the sounds of the current band filled the air. Red, white, and blue banners adorned the fronts of booths to commemorate the July fourth holiday, and fireworks were scheduled after nightfall.

Eleven-thirty and the crowds were already thick. At their meeting place by the flagpole in front of the town hall, Sydney scoped for Tyler and Zach, certain that everyone in Kennessey was meeting at the flagpole. Then she heard her name. She lifted her head and saw them as they wove through the crowd. Tyler had raised his hand up so she could spot him easily. Jessie said, "There they are."

Sydney hadn't seen Tyler in four days, and it seemed long. Amazing how quickly she'd gotten used to him. Yet she was still getting acquainted with him. Again. She'd worn a floral cotton sundress, loose at the waist, wide-band leather flip flops, and her straw hat. Not only was a dress more comfortable on a scorching July weekend, but she'd been driven by a need to look pretty that day, for reasons she still had trouble admitting.

Jessie and Zach zoomed together like two magnets and were already murmuring and snickering together. That morning, Sydney had reminded her not to say anything about Emma to Zach. She solemnly promised she wouldn't, even if she admitted it would be difficult to keep the secret for a few more days.

"Hi, Sydney." Tyler grinned as he reached her. "Sorry we're a bit late. I got held up by a few people on my way over here."

"Ah, I knew you were still the popular guy you were in high school. Probably more so since you're Mr. Golf now. Feel free to show us around the place, since we're lost sheep in this crowd."

"Gladly. You look beautiful, by the way." His gaze lighted on her with appreciation. "I like the straw hat." He reached up and touched the rim.

Pleasure flushed through her at his visual assessment. "It's my signature accessory. Especially anytime it's over eighty degrees." She tipped it toward him and smiled back. Was she flirting? Maybe just a tad.

After a brief consultation with Jessie and Zach, they agreed to split up for an hour, then meet back at the first food truck in the row to have lunch. Sydney enjoyed when the four of them were together, but savored the chance to walk alongside Tyler without kids. Yes, it was nice to be with another adult. But truthfully, he'd often occupied the back of her thoughts, which resembled a bird flitting around, looking for its nest.

"A bunch of great things happened this week." Tyler looked neat in khaki pants with sandals and a turquoise polo. Sydney was still trying to get used to the adult Tyler, a version of the boy she'd loved, but with broader shoulders and the face of a grown man.

Tyler led them toward the craft sector, and they fell into step with other browsers. "Well, I did get a call for the analyst job I'd applied for, and I have a phone interview Monday. Although between you and me, I have no idea what an analyst does." She laughed. "I hope to overcome my ignorance in the next two days. But the real news involves my mom. I only gave you the short version on the phone yesterday." They entered the shade of a sprawling oak tree, a canopy over the canvas-roof booths. The temperature seemed to drop by ten degrees.

Sydney explained having to ask her mother for the name of the adoption agency and that Jessie had overheard them. "I'd never realized that I hadn't ever forgiven my mother for her actions during that whole episode. Not that she'd done anything wrong, but I'd always assumed she'd sent me away because she was ashamed."

Tyler's brows gathered as she spoke. "Did she tell you otherwise?"

"She had me go live with Aunt Abigail to save *me* from shame. I don't know why, but I never thought of that at the time."

"You probably felt banished."

"At the time, I did. But the conversation opened my eyes to *her* perspective. She didn't cause the problem, but she took charge of it. I was grateful for that at the time, even though I misjudged her." Her voice dropped. "For the next thirty years I misjudged her." She shook her head. "We—had a really good talk. It kind of changed our relationship. "

"Oh, that's so great, Sydney. After all these years." Emotion laced his words. Of all people, Tyler would know the significance. "And everything seems okay with Jessie, too. She acts normal. She's cute and energetic and sticking to Zach like Velcro."

Sydney laughed. "Yes, she is all of that. She's my helper in trying to locate Emma. In fact, she's jazzed about it. We're waiting now to hear back from the agency we called yesterday."

She stopped, cocked her head, and looked up at him. "I bet you're tired of hearing about Emma, aren't you? I don't mean to talk about her so much." If her suspicions about his attitude were right, he might be getting annoyed at frequent references to Emma. Not that she was testing him. She really didn't want to beat the same drum with him if he'd moved on.

Tyler put a hand on her bare arm. "No, that's fine, Sydney. It's on your mind."

"But we haven't seen each other in so long. I *can* talk about other things, you know."

He laughed. "Don't worry. It's not just your life you're talking about." His tone sobered. "It's mine, too. We'll have time to talk about a lot of other things, and I'm looking forward to that. But you've helped me be motivated to talk to Zach about the adoption."

"It's like little by little we're clearing away old weeds of misunderstandings and secrets. It feels good, doesn't it?"

"It does. I hope you still feel that way if Emma writes back and says she wants to meet you."

Sydney pressed her lips together. "I haven't let my mind go there yet. Jessie seems more motivated for a meeting than I am. I've always said I just wanted to know, that's all. I'm not sure if I want more than that."

"Makes sense. And that's okay. You're not a bad person if that's all you want. I've never had a strong desire to learn more, though I've often been curious. I'll benefit from your findings." He grinned, and they started walking again, slowing at a booth of watercolor paintings.

"Hey, guess what? I bought a guitar the other day."

"You did?" Tyler chuckled. "You keep surprising me. Are you going to be wearing your high school jersey next time I see you?" They both laughed. "Just kidding. I think it's great. Tell me what brought that about."

"Mom and I were talking about it. I went to the attic and found my old guitar up there. Of course, it was falling apart, after thirty years. I took it to that instrument shop on the main drag downtown to see if it could be repaired. I ended up buying a used Fender. I've been quietly practicing in my room."

"Why quietly?"

She paused. "I don't really know. I'm pulling out parts of my old life a little at a time, so maybe I didn't want to overdo it. Jessie plays. She knows I used to play, but she doesn't know how important it was for me."

"Or how *good* you were at it. And that you composed, too."

"I regret letting it go for so long." Her voice dropped as she expressed the wonder she still felt. "My mom told me that it used to light up my eyes."

"It did." Tyler's voice softened. "You were gifted, and you loved it. It's good to reconnect with that part of you after all this time."

She smiled and nodded. "Yeah, I'm glad. Do you still play?"

"Yes, I've kept it up over the years. I play at church once in a while and I play at home just for the fun of it to relieve stress from work. Once you get up to speed, we can play together again."

A smile crept up her lips and their eyes locked together. Amazing, all the full circles. Warmth tingled inside her as their shared gaze recognized both the past and the present.

"Excuse me," a woman said. She was grasping the hands of two children.

"Oh, we're sorry." Tyler stepped back and let her pass. He and Sydney laughed. "We're blocking traffic with all our reminiscing."

They wandered into the next booth, which featured a different style of artwork, and allowed their conversation to drift to what they were seeing and what paintings they liked. Sydney was relieved they were on mundane ground. Since seeing Tyler again, they'd delved into all the hard topics of the past. She wanted more than that from him now. She wanted to learn whatever he was willing to share with her about the man he'd become.

The hour flew by. "We should have told them an hour and a half." Sydney puffed after rushing across the field. They arrived at the meeting place, but Zach and Jessie weren't there yet. "Figures we'd hurry up and then wait."

While they stood together, three different people greeted Tyler. He'd been gone from Kennessey almost as long as she had, save the last two years, but he seemed to know everyone in town. "Maybe you should run for mayor one day. You know everyone, and they all seem to love you."

Tyler grinned and nodded at someone who'd waved at him. "Just goes with the territory, I guess."

"Probably true, but you must also have continued being a pretty nice guy."

He slid her a sly look and a wink. "I'll let you decide that."

Zach and Jessie arrived a few minutes later, panting from their dash across the temporary fairgrounds. "We were at the arcades and Jessie beat me the last time. Can you believe that?" Zach's tan had darkened and complemented his dark hair and blue eyes. He was a good-looking kid, though Jessie didn't seem smitten just yet. More the other way around, Sydney guessed. But she was glad her daughter had a good friend to brighten up what could have been a dull summer, except for all the drama Sydney herself had brought.

She reveled in the fact that, despite their age, Zach and Jessie were willing to talk to their parents openly and hang out with them. And together, they were able to joke around, laugh, and be young. So many of the teens Sydney saw day to day and year after year had a hardened armor of surliness. They seemed unreachable, unimpressible, locked down. The young adults in front of her were different, and she was grateful.

After they stood in line at the food trucks and received their meals, Tyler led the way to nearby picnic tables. A family vacated a

"Ha. Nice of you say that, even though I'm a master of none."

They finished the dance and were met by the light applause of a row of onlookers. As they returned to their seat, a couple around seventy years old stood close by. "It was a pleasure to watch you two," the woman said. "We're the Fredericks if you don't remember us. I always knew you two would get together. You were so cute in high school."

Sydney and Tyler exchanged a glance. She thought that would end the conversation, but the woman said, "How long have you been married?"

Sydney hoped Tyler would answer something ambiguous since she was lost for words, but Jessie piped up loudly from her seat. "Thirty years." She flashed a smile at them.

"Oh, my. Such a long time," the woman said. "That's wonderful. Good to see you, Tyler and Sydney. See, I remembered your names."

"Sharp as always, Mrs. Fredericks." Tyler nodded to her as the couple ambled off.

Sydney put her hands on her hips and turned to Jessie, who was laughing. "What are you doing, daughter? You'll totally confuse the poor couple."

"If you guys get married one day, they'll *really* be confused!"

Now, where did that come from? Better to let it go. Sydney tried to avoid Tyler's eyes but couldn't resist. He was grinning at her but held out his hand again. "Another dance, Mrs. Hoffman?"

Chapter Sixteen

After the final words of the sermon, Pastor Anthony prayed a blessing over the congregation as gentle guitar notes began. He opened his eyes and left the stage as the worship band increased the volume. The singers approached the front, signaling the congregation to stand for a rousing last song.

Sydney sat in a row toward the middle of the auditorium which had been renovated a few years earlier. More modern and much larger than in had been in her youth, it hardly resembled the same place. Jessie and Zach sat on one side of her and Tyler on the other. She felt at ease, despite all the water under their bridge. Seeing a few vaguely familiar faces didn't cause any tension that day.

As the song ended, everyone stood up and gathered their belongings and their children or greeted those around them.

"Did you like the service, Mom?" Jessie's blue eyes searched Sydney's.

"Yes, very much. I should have come here all along. It's more my style."

"And you grew up here, so you probably know some people, too."

"I probably do." She could finally say it might be nice to see people from her past.

For the first few years after losing Tyler and Emma, she refused to go to the church when she returned home for visits from college. Despite her efforts, she'd still occasionally crossed paths in town with old neighbors, schoolmates, or teachers.

Gradually, the tsunami of memories lessened, but after her professional life started, the visits to Kennessey lessened as well. Most of the current church members were strangers to her, likely newcomers to the area or those who'd migrated from other churches. Many of her high school friends and classmates had moved away.

And some had returned, like Tyler.

His eyes caught hers, and they exchanged a smile as they maneuvered out of their row. The four of them joined the flow of church attendees that filled the aisle and herded from the sanctuary to the front door.

"See, you survived a visit to the past." Tyler's voice, laced with humor, was low near her ear. "Though nothing looks the same as it did back then."

"Got that right. And that helps. The service was great. I like the new pastor. His style's different from your dad, who was irreplaceable." She dropped her voice and looked up at him. "I'm sure you still miss him. And your mom, too."

"Yeah, I do. Some days more than others." His eyes lifted to pan the crowd. "But he left a good legacy."

"And we're looking at it now."

Apart from waving at a few people she knew and had seen in recent years, there were no awkward comments or knowing looks from anyone, no reason at all for Sydney to have dreaded her visit there. Most of her discomfort had to do with *her* memories, not what people knew about her. True, some had undoubtedly guessed, but thirty years later, no one would remember or care.

"I'm hungry. How about some lunch?" Zach asked. "Can we get pizza?"

"Good idea." Tyler turned to Sydney as he opened his passenger door for her. "Are you two able to join us?"

She looked at Jessie, who'd already settled into the back seat. "Do you have to work today, Jessie?" She only worked occasionally on Sunday afternoons.

"No, not today. Let's go for pizza with the guys."

Fortunately, they were just ahead of the after-church crowd. The hostess seated them without delay on the patio of the pizzeria. Umbrellas overhead cut the heat only slightly, but Sydney didn't mind. She'd worn a cool linen sundress and was enjoying the company and the meal. Far less stressful than Zach's birthday dinner.

Following their meal as they left the restaurant, Tyler let Zach and Jessie go ahead of them. Sydney hesitated, sensing he wanted to say something to her.

"I need to grab my chance without kids around to ask if you'd have dinner with me this week. A real date if you're open to that." He grinned and raised his eyebrows. "I know a seafood place by the water you'll love."

She shouldn't have been startled, but she was. Startled and happy. "A date? I'd love to. What day did you have in mind?"

"How's Wednesday? I can leave the course early that day. The weather is supposed to be cooler for a few days, too. I'll make us a reservation and call you about the time."

"I'll look forward to it." The flutter started and didn't stop until he dropped them off at the Victorian.

છ　છ　છ

Dear Marissa, Eden, and Julia, my wonderful friends,
Thank you all for your sweet words in response to my email. I'm working on the vulnerability thing, so I'm grateful for my cheerleaders!
Here's an update. None of the three adoption agencies I called were the right ones, so I had to ask my mom.

Sydney summarized the conversations with her mother and Jessie as fresh gratitude bubbled up inside her.

I can't express how relieved I am that Jessie finally knows about Emma. My secret weighed on me for so long!

I have an online interview tomorrow for an analyst job in Charlotte. Going thru the motions since I don't know didly about analyzing! If I analyzed more often, I'd get into far less trouble!

And no news from my slothful, worthless principal, except that he forgot to tell the faculty I'd left for a family emergency, and now people think I was dismissed for inappropriate conduct. This whole incident has trashed my good reputation. Very mad about that. I'm scared of having the same job and I'm scared of not having one. Deep down, I don't feel marketable except as a teacher. I've dug myself into a one-career hole.

On a happier note, I'm gradually getting to know Tyler again, which is strange, fun, and a little scary. We'll have our first real date this week. (Yikes!) His son and Jessie are friends. Tyler moved back here two years ago. My mom never told me. (Wonder why...)

She was rambling. Really, it would take an in-person weekend to fully describe all that had happened.

So, that's my news. Please tell me yours! Oh, and I bought a second-hand guitar. I think I'm connecting with my inner teenager! Love, Sydney

ରେ　ରେ　ରେ

Tuesday morning after breakfast, Sydney poured herself a second cup of coffee and returned to the kitchen table. Outside, the rumpled white sky signaled summer rain. A perfect day to take her time.

Her interview the previous day hadn't raised her hopes in anything but a possible acting career. She deserved an Oscar for how she'd muddled through, pretending to know anything about what an analyst did. The memory brought up a chuckle.

Sydney sipped the hot coffee as her humor seeped away. The next interview would be better if there was a next time.

The ring of the phone cut through her despondency. She glanced at the screen and her breath hitched. "Hello?"

"Good morning, Ms. Bennett. This is Betty Gibson from the Hanover Adoption Agency. I have good news for you. We found your adoption record and are ready for you to come to the office. Looks like there are some positive provisions in the contact agreement, so we can look at these together. Can you come Thursday morning at around ten?"

"Yes, of course. Can I bring my daughter?"

"No problem. Please bring some identification with you, something with your maiden name on it. A birth certificate if you can."

"I have that." Good thing she'd thought about that when she left Charlotte. She'd anticipated their asking her, considering all the privacy regulations adoptions had around them like a protective fence. "We'll see you Thursday. Thank you, Ms. Gibson."

Jessie was reading her Bible on the back porch. Sydney stuck her head through the doorway. "Are you free Thursday morning at ten?"

Jessie lifted her head with a quizzical expression. "Thursday? I think I work in the afternoon, like usual."

Sydney grinned at her daughter. "We have an appointment at the Hanover Adoption Agency to read the file."

Jessie let out a whoop and a broad smile spread across her face. "They found you."

"Yes, they found me, and the lady said there was a provision for contact. Not sure yet what that means, but she said we should come. We'll find out everything then."

One step closer to learning what happened to Emma.

ʘʘʘ   ʘʘʘ   ʘʘʘ

The following evening, Sydney sat in the passenger seat of Tyler's Toyota, a pleasant tingle vibrating in her stomach. She'd worn a lavender cotton dress, purple-tinted shell necklace around her neck, and wedge sandals. She'd wanted to be dressy without overdoing it. Tyler's verbal compliment had seemed sincere, but his eyes had confirmed his assessment. It had been *so* long since a man had looked at her that way. It bolstered her feminine soul, but since it was Tyler, it did far more, as the acrobatics in her stomach proved.

"I wanted to wait to see you to tell you that Jessie and I have an appointment tomorrow at the Hanover Adoption Agency in Wilmington."

Tyler glanced over at her and raised his eyebrows. "That's great news. They found your file."

"Yes, and it seems there's some provision for contact. I don't know how much. Even if I only wanted information about Emma without contact, I'd still have to write to the adoptive parents to learn about her. The agency wouldn't have that information unless at some point, Emma herself had given it in hopes of finding *me*."

"This time tomorrow, you'll have those answers, at least some of them." Tyler put on his turn signal, then pulled out onto a highway that led to the beach.

Sydney couldn't read his profile or the tone in his voice. "It's a patience game all the way. I'll probably have to contact them by letter, then it's up to them to respond. Could take months if they respond at all. We can't get our hopes up too high."

"Is that what led you to spend the summer here in Kennessey?"

"Not totally. I could have done the phone calls from Charlotte, but we needed to come see my mom. I hadn't been here in a year. She's the one who invited us for the whole summer, believe it or not."

"I didn't know that. That's a first, isn't it?"

"It *is* a first. Maybe with age, she started realizing how little she saw us, along with the fact that I don't work in the summer." Sydney allowed the warm breeze through the window to caress her face. "Tell you the truth, having summers off kept me teaching for the last three or four years."

"The promise of having a chunk of time off isn't a great reason to stay in a job you don't like." Tyler looked over at her, his eyes hidden by his sunglasses. "By the way, how did your interview go on Monday? I forgot to ask."

Sydney sighed. "Quite honestly, they'd be desperate to hire me. Unless they don't mind completely retraining someone. They asked me about my ability to analyze data and present it in simplified terms, to interpret a data base I've never seen before. Yada, yada." She laughed. "My best response, and my most frequent was, 'given the opportunity for training and understanding the company culture, I'm sure I can handle the job.'"

"Don't sell yourself short. I'm sure you can. But it's only mid-July. You're sending resumes, so something's bound to come together."

She shot him a grateful smile for the reminder. "Some days I block job hunting from of my mind, though I can't afford to do that. It's easy when I'm enjoying the summer here. I don't want to think about the fall. I'm so afraid I won't have a choice but to go back to school."

"Not necessarily, Sydney. There are other things you could do. You have a lot of skills, whether you believe it or not. Math skills can sometimes translate to computer skills. Do you have computer skills? Marketing? Anything like that?"

"I can find my way around a computer, but not marketing. I suppose I could learn, but how much time can I invest in retraining at this point?" She let out a long sigh. Tyler could offer moral support, but he couldn't solve the dilemma for her. "Thanks for your encouragement. There's always unemployment benefits."

"Don't give up yet. I'll have some more ideas to throw at you. But here we are, so our next task is to have a wonderful meal. Ready?" He pulled into a parking spot behind a two-story restaurant that faced the ocean.

They got out of the car, and Sydney was struck by the salty smell and the moist feel of the ocean air. She crossed her arms, as if pulling it into her. "Ah, how can I waste time talking about work when *this* awaits us?" She extended one arm toward an elegant stucco building and the early evening sun spreading a peach-stained light blue glow behind it.

A hostess seated them on the second floor of the restaurant in a shadowy alcove with a flickering candle on the table. The facing glass wall afforded a spectacular view of the ocean below. The rhythmic shush shush of the waves was music itself.

After they'd ordered drinks and their meals, Tyler leaned forward on his elbows. The candle cast a shifting glow over his features. His blue-gray gaze caught hers. "Here we are."

"Here we are." Nerves bounced in her stomach.

"I never thought I'd have this opportunity again, Sydney."

Words left her, clever words, any words. "Me either," she managed. "We came to a restaurant similar to this one when we'd been dating for a year, didn't we? It was our anniversary." It was probably unwise to bring up the past, but how could they not?

Tyler seemed unruffled by her reference. A slow smile widened his lips. "We did. That place closed, but a bunch more have sprung up along the coast and all over town. In other words, we have many more to visit together." He leaned back. "This one is my favorite for special occasions."

She swallowed, blinked back at him across the dimly lit space. He'd considered her a special occasion.

The server brought their wine and glasses of water. After she left, Tyler lifted his glass. "To Sydney part two."

Sydney let out a soft laugh, embarrassed. "I'm sure we can toast something better than that. I'm not necessarily any better than I was thirty years ago. I've surely developed some bad habits which you don't know about yet. Just give me time." She cocked her head and batted her eyes, hoping for a laugh.

"You're not the only one." He chuckled then paused. "You're afraid you'll disappoint me?" He reached across the table and grasped her hand. "We're both hobbling through life by the grace of God. I guess we've both learned that by now. You'll be disappointed with me sometimes, too. I guarantee that."

Sounded like he was planning for a future relationship. Could it really be that easy to step back into the life of Tyler Hoffman?

Sydney drew in a deep, conscious breath, aware of her hand still nestled in his. Her eyes dropped to their clasped hands. "So, how about we come up with another toast? To no more secrets, to old friends reunited, things like that."

He released her hand and lifted his glass. "To *now*. How about that? To whatever now means to us."

Yes, she'd lived far too long in the shadow of the past, newly flooded with light. Now was what counted. Now with Tyler in their adult chapter. She clinked his glass. "To now. Right now. I can almost smell the shrimp." She grinned, and he didn't.

"I wasn't talking about the food."

"I know. I'm just—" she gave him a one-shouldered shrug, "not good at saying pretty things."

"You don't have to say anything in particular. Just be yourself." He took a sip of wine. "I like your humor, even though I know sometimes it's a cover-up for your deeper feelings. Sorry if I'm playing amateur psychologist."

She swallowed. Blinked. Her eyes lifted to his. "You're not fooled by my clever disguise?"

Tyler smiled. "Not fooled. Intrigued sometimes. That's okay, I understand. One of my good qualities, you'll find, is patience and persistence. I'll get below that protective surface, if you'll let me." He paused and swallowed. "I want to, Sydney."

She sighed deeply. "I had fewer barriers at seventeen, but you got through those. I'm trying to be more . . ." She searched for the word. "Authentic, I guess. But don't be shocked by what you hear. You asked for it."

He laughed. "No worries. I can't wait to hear, in fact." He paused, and his face was solemn. "I keep saying it, but this is a chance I never thought I'd have again. I know it doesn't guarantee anything, but I won't let it pass by."

Sydney reached for her wine glass and met his eyes as she let his words sink in. Words that answered the thirst building inside her. Muted laughter, the whisper of retreating waves, and the aroma of grilled seafood completed the painting surrounding her. If only she could stop time. This moment forever, Tyler Hoffman across from her. No school pressures, no mistakes or secrets, nothing but now.

Tyler didn't mind intense conversations, upfront declarations. He'd always been that way. Though she'd sometimes squirmed, she'd loved that quality in him, back when her walls were much shorter. She could do it again.

The meals arrived and the conversation lightened as they enjoyed grilled shrimp, scallops, seasoned rice, and fresh roasted vegetables. Tyler wiped his mouth on a napkin. "I've waited to tell you that I talked to Zach about Emma."

She stopped her water glass halfway to her mouth. "You did? When?"

"Yesterday after work. I told him after dinner."

"Really? Tell me. What did you say?"

"I sat him down and told him I needed to tell him something about my past he didn't know."

Sydney nodded. "I said a similar phrase to Jessie."

"I tried not to sugar-coat it and make myself look innocent, so he'd understand that what I'd done wasn't acceptable."

"How did he respond? Was he angry you'd hidden it?"

Tyler shook his head. "No, he wasn't angry. Might be different for boys or could be influenced by the fact that from the age of nine, he hasn't lived with me, except for summers and some vacations. He was surprised, of course. He heard me out. He just said, 'Wow, Dad, that's wild. Thanks for telling me.' That's it. I asked him if he had any questions. He asked where Emma lives. I told him we didn't know, but you were trying to find out. He had no other questions and his behavior since then has been normal."

"That's such a relief, Tyler. I'm happy he took it in stride. You were worried about that."

"A little. So, now there are no more secrets." He lifted his hands, palms upward.

"There's no one else who needs to know anything. Aside from me, I'd like to know about Emma, but that's another matter."

"I'd like to know, too. If for nothing else, so it'll ease your mind."

He reached out again and squeezed her hand for the second time that evening. It felt so good. She didn't want him to let go. Especially when his thumb gently rubbed her knuckles.

"Do you want any dessert?"

She shook her head. "I'm stuffed. That was exquisite. You chose well."

"Would you like to walk on the beach? The sun isn't quite gone yet."

Sydney had been so distracted by their conversation and by Tyler's nearness that she'd forgotten to enjoy the view. She turned her head toward the wall of windows. Pastel colors bled across the sky, lighting the tips of the now-darkened waves. "Oh, that's so beautiful." She turned back to him. "Yes, I'd love to."

The beach was becoming a familiar and coveted spot. It had already been, but now even more, walking there with Tyler. She slipped off her sandals and dug her toes in the cool sand. Tyler did the same, and they strolled toward the bright layer of sun that melted into the sky, as seagulls called, flying further and further toward the horizon.

As they walked, Sydney asked him about the golf courses, how he established them, and what he loved most about it. She enjoyed hearing him describe the different facets and how they tied into his interests. Her understanding of adult Tyler was growing.

"Sounds like a huge financial investment for just one golf course, let alone two. None of my business, of course."

"Nothing's off limits, Sydney." He held a small smile as his eyes searched her face. "You're right, it was a load of cash. But my uncle Cliff worked out an arrangement with me. I've actually only paid him half so far, and that with what I'd saved plus some loans. He's letting me pay the other half whenever I can. That's the only way it's been possible. I'd love to expand one day, add a nicer restaurant and other amenities, more programs for youth, things like that. But for now, I'm just getting solid."

"Seems like you're off to a great start. Thanks for your transparency. I'll—I'll tell you anything you want to know, too." Sydney couldn't think of anything she'd want to hide from Tyler. Not a thing, despite a mental warning to be careful, to not trust too much. They hadn't yet talked about their failed marriages, but that would likely come up if they continued in their relationship. She'd be ready to talk about that, too.

Tyler returned her question about her career, but she was less motivated to talk about it. "I had some students from tough neighborhoods, and some from privileged backgrounds. Ironically, it was a rich, pampered kid who attacked me. I almost prefer the kids from sketchy backgrounds. They're dealing with more baggage, have fewer opportunities. I always tried to bolster their self-esteem and confidence in their ability to get math."

"I'm sure you gave them something they'll always keep. Did you teach all kinds of math? Geometry, calculus, trig, all that hard stuff?"

She nodded and smiled. "And, algebra, and business math. A bit of accounting."

"See, Sydney, you have an enormous number of skills. Think of how many professions you just described. How about accounting? I may have mentioned that before. You wouldn't be starting from zero."

Sydney shrugged. "I'm not sure I'd like it. If I didn't, I'd be back where I am now. At zero."

"You could always change if you found it wasn't your thing. You're need something for the immediate future, right? Nothing has to be forever. Take time to find your niche."

She stopped walking and looked up at him as his words fell into place in her mind. "You're right." The tension that had begun to accumulate during their discussion unwound slightly. "I wanted to have a plan for the fall so I can close the teaching chapter and know I'll still be able to pay my bills."

"You can bounce ideas off me anytime." The planes of his face were darker now as the evening glow mellowed to dark blue. Softly, he added, "I'm here for you, Sydney. I've spent years *not* being there for you, but I want to be now."

Sydney breathed deeply, drinking in his words as they touched a bruised place inside. She'd done everything alone for so long. Even when she was married, she did the lion's share herself, running the household, raising Jessie. She'd been alone for as long as she could remember, except when she'd been with Tyler. "Thank you, Tyler. It means more than you can know."

They stood close together on the sand, facing each other. Despite the cooling of the evening, warmth mounted in Sydney's chest and crept up her neck. A gentle breeze rustled her hair over her shoulders like a caress.

Tyler reached up and lightly stroked her bare upper arm. "I want even more than that for us, Sydney." He stared at her. "I need to tell you that I've been restless since we ended so many years ago. It took me a while to get married, and I thought that was it, but found I was still restless. I missed *you*. All along, I missed you. A big piece of my heart was gone."

His jaw tightened, and his throat pulsed when he swallowed. Moisture glinted in his eyes. "When I saw you walk into the clubhouse that day, aside from being surprised, I was so grateful God brought you back to me." He stopped and a short laugh escaped his throat. "I shouldn't tell you this yet. I'm probably going to send you running. I want to tell you what I feel, but I don't want to scare you away."

"No, you won't." Her voice was soft. Running away was the last thing she wanted to do. A stray lock of hair danced over her cheek in the breeze.

"I want to kiss you, Sydney. Is it too soon?" His voice was soft, his gaze intent.

"It's been thirty years, Tyler, so no, it's not too soon."

Tyler joined her soft laughter and gently tipped up her chin to kiss her. His lips were unhurried at first, as if he were tasting her.

He drew her closer and tightened his arms around her. She melted against him, leaning into his kiss as it deepened, as she surrendered. In his kiss were memories, but also promises. It was nothing like their first awkward teenage kiss, this adult male declaration that said so much, and held nothing back. His kiss expressed regrets and hopes, hunger and thirst. It left her breathless.

They drew apart, but their arms stayed locked around one another. For a moment, Sydney couldn't speak. Then, "Oh, Tyler." She blinked, then let out an awkward chuckle. "See, I told you I wasn't good with words." He laughed. She added, "Could we do that again?"

His second kiss was deeper, more intense than the first. Sydney didn't want it to end. When it finally did, she leaned against him as his arms encircled her. She murmured, "Does this mean you like me and we're going out?"

He laughed softly. "I like you—*so* much. Ever since eleventh grade. If you want to be my girlfriend, I'd be honored, Sydney Davis. I'll even hang out with you in study hall."

"Tyler and Sydney version 2.0." Her whisper was mixed with the sound of waves.

"Yes, that's it."

She pressed into his chest as he tightened his arms around her shoulders. When she lifted her face to his, he kissed her again.

Chapter Seventeen

Sydney glanced over at Jessie, who was slouched in the passenger seat of the SUV as they drove to Wilmington that morning. It was already after nine, but Jessie had been up late the night before, watching a movie on TV with Zach. They'd still been absorbed in the program when Sydney came home from her date with Tyler.

She was relieved for a silent drive as thoughts of Emma and Tyler wrestled for priority in her mind. The coming appointment would give her the next step in her search for Emma.

And yet, the memory of her evening with Tyler brought a warm flutter, pushing through her thoughts of her coming appointment. The look in his eyes, the feel of his lips on hers, and his strong arms around her circled back in her mind. She could hardly take it in, this renewal of the bond that had indelibly stamped her youth. Right before it blew up, leaving a smoking crater behind.

And here he was again. The undeniable pull he'd always had on her seemed just as powerful. Could it fill some of the emptiness of recent years, or would it end up destroying her once again? Had she agreed too quickly to "going out" with him?

Despite her fears, she knew she was helpless against her attraction to him. If she weren't careful, that force would absorb her too fast. Despite their turbulent history and the warning bells it triggered, her thoughts circled repeatedly to his honest admission: he'd thought about her over the years and had missed her all along.

He'd even carried their photo for the first several years after they'd broken up.

She'd have missed him more, if she hadn't locked his memory in an ironclad box in the back of her mind, sure that thoughts of him would block her healing.

And now maybe they were being given a second chance. The wonder and grace of it overwhelmed her. How could they, Tyler and Sydney, have a second chance thirty years later, after making some first-rate mistakes? She shook her head, a smile emerging, followed by surprising tears that stung her eyes. *God, you are amazing. Your heart for us overwhelms me.*

A glance sideways reassured her that Jessie was still napping, or else she'd be asking questions about the sudden smile and tears, or about her date with Mr. Hoffman.

Sydney hadn't yet entertained questions around the fact that she and Tyler didn't live in the same city. That was the only barrier she could identify, aside from her fear of being hurt again. He himself had said there were no guarantees. They weren't kids anymore. As adults, they were in a different place and might eventually conclude that life had drawn them too far apart to make it work again. Either one of them could decide that. She'd be wise to keep a small fence around her heart. Just in case.

Nine-forty am. They weren't far from the adoption office. Time to turn her reflections toward Emma. Just then, as if sensing her thoughts, Jessie stirred. Her eyes opened, and she yawned and stretched as far as the inside of the car allowed. "Wow, I fell asleep. When do we get there?"

"In about ten minutes. You were really out of it, Jess." Sydney grinned at her daughter.

"Yeah." Jessie blinked a few times. "I was really sleepy. The movie last night was good, then we kept talking after it ended. Finally, I had to tell him to go home. It was, like, midnight or something."

"I think he likes you. More than a friend. Don't you think?"

Jessie nodded. "Yeah, he told me he did. I told him I still wasn't sure, but really liked hanging around with him."

"What did he say to that?"

"He said we could be friends either way."

"That sounds mature of him." Probably got that from his dad. Sydney felt warm again, as her thoughts went back to Tyler. Oh, boy. She was like a teenager again herself, even as she talked to *her* teenager about attraction.

"So, what about you, Mom? You went out with Mr. Hoffman last night. Did you guys have a good time?"

She'd been certain it would come up within the hour. "Yes, we did. We had dinner at a really nice restaurant on the beach. The food and the view were wonderful. You'd like this place."

"And? C'mon, Mom, don't leave me in suspense."

Sydney laughed. "We talked a lot. What else do you want to know?"

Jessie rolled her eyes. "I know he *really* likes you. I can tell. And Zach can tell, too. Of course, he lives with his dad and knows it. So, do you like him?"

The conversation was reminiscent of those from high school. 'Do you like Sean? He really likes you. Maybe he'll ask you to the fall dance.' She sighed. "Yes, I like him. A lot."

"So, are you two, like, dating?"

"I guess you could say we are now. We talked about it." She didn't want to give too many details. Didn't seem appropriate since Jessie wasn't her girlfriend. She wasn't like Eden, Marissa, or Julia. Which reminded her she'd have to text them. This news would make their mouths drop open.

"Did he kiss you goodnight at the door?" A sly look crept across Jessie's face. Her daughter's morning nap hadn't spared Sydney the full interrogation.

"Yes, he did." She didn't need to tell Jessie about the mind-blowing kisses on the beach beforehand. Those would stay etched on her mind for a long time and keep her longing for more.

"Look, we're here. Now you've heard about my date. We'll have to move onto other things, like finding Emma." Saved from further questions, just in time. Jessie narrowed her eyes as if to say, "I'm not finished yet."

The Hanover Adoption Agency resided in a neat red brick building near downtown Wilmington. Several vibrant green cycas palms spread across a small green lawn enclosed by a wrought-iron fence. Sydney and Jessie walked up the brick path and mounted a wide brick staircase. The building fit right into the nineteenth century historical landscape of old Wilmington.

"This place is pretty." Jessie looked around at the palms in the yard and flowering plants spilling from baskets on the porch.

They entered the building and approached a receptionist. "Good morning." Sydney noticed the woman's name plaque. "I spoke with you on the phone a couple of times, Ms. Gibson. It's nice to finally meet you. We have a ten o'clock appointment."

"Good morning, Ms. Bennett. Is this your daughter?" Betty Gibson gave a friendly smile to Jessie.

"Yes, this is Jessie."

"Glad you could come today, Jessie." She turned her attention to Sydney. "Our social worker, Morgan Clarke, is expecting you. I'll tell her you're here."

A few minutes later, a thirty-something woman with dark-rimmed glasses and curly black hair came to the waiting room. "Good morning, Ms. Bennett. I'm Morgan. Can I call you Sydney?"

Sydney and Jessie stood. "Yes, absolutely. This is my daughter, Jessie." She smiled at Jessie. "My partner in discovery."

Morgan grinned. "Perfect! Come with me, and we'll see what your file says."

A few minutes later, they were seated around a conference room table with a file folder between them. "As Betty told you, our files are all digital, so I printed these off. I need your identification first. Just protocol, to make sure we're giving access to the right person."

"Of course, that's completely normal." Sydney pulled the folded birth certificate from her purse and handed it to Morgan. She examined it for a moment then pushed her chair back. "I'll just make a photocopy to keep in the file."

When she returned to the room, she handed the birth certificate back to Sydney and opened the folder. "Emma Rose Davis, July sixteenth, nineteen ninety-one," she murmured as she scanned the papers. "I have here her original birth certificate, which gives your name, Sydney Abigail Davis. And here is what I'm looking for—" She snatched up one page from the stack. "The contact agreement."

Sydney tensed. Had Emma been looking for her all these years? She was about to find out.

Following a brief scan of the document in her hand, Morgan said, "Emma was adopted right away by a couple who had been on our waitlist for over a year. Steve and Monica Treadwell, formerly of Wilmington."

Morgan continued skimming through the paper. Sydney and Jessie exchanged a glance. Formerly? Where were they now?

"They adopted Emma, as I said, right after her birth." Her eyes met Sydney's. "They came to the hospital to get her before you were even released, so rest assured, she had a home from day one."

A wave of emotion knocked Sydney from inside, almost taking her breath away. Even while she lay desolate in her hospital bed after holding Emma for the last time, Emma's new parents were there to whisk her away forever. She swallowed and blinked several times, breathing deeply to stem the tide of tears that threatened to break loose. Morgan's face softened, and she gave Sydney an understanding smile before returning her attention to the file.

"Sometimes, adoptive parents change the baby's name, but Emma's didn't. They must have liked her name and found it fitting."

"Oh, that's nice." Sydney's voice cracked and she cleared her throat. "All these years, I've thought of her as Emma, and she was. Morgan, you said that the Treadwells were formerly from Wilmington. Where are they now?"

"They moved to Michigan a few years after the adoption. Fortunately, they were conscientious enough to update their address with us each time they moved. Not everyone thinks of doing that."

Sydney let out a breath. They'd raised Emma in Michigan, so little chance that they'd meet her. A tiny thread of disappointment and a larger wave of relief welled up inside her. Jessie might drop the idea of having a reunion with her half-sister. That would make life easier for everyone. But the fact that the Treadwells had left their addresses meant that they were still open to contact and hadn't changed their minds. She could learn about Emma's childhood and progress to adulthood.

"Here's the contact agreement. It allows for written contact by the birth mother to the adoptive parents."

"Not to Emma herself? Is there any effort by Emma to contact me?"

Morgan shook her head. "I don't see any requests here by Emma." Her eyes met Sydney's then shifted to include Jessie. "Not all adopted children have a desire to learn about or contact their birth parents. Sometimes they do and contact us, and they can also find websites designed to reunite people who are looking for each other. It may even happen years later. But it doesn't work if it's just one direction."

"Seems the parents were open to contact, if they updated their address."

"Maybe that's the reason. But occasionally, adoptive parents give us their address in case there arises a genetic issue later on and they need to get information from the birth parents. In the Treadwells' case, we don't know their motivation."

Sydney nodded, though a weight settled inside. "What is the date of their last address change?"

Morgan scrutinized the file up and down. "Looks like it was around two thousand six."

Fourteen years ago. They might have changed addresses since that time and the forwarding order would have expired by now. And

Emma was an adult. "Well, it's all we have, even if the address isn't recent, so we'll contact them and see what happens." She looked at Jessie. "Right, partner?"

Jessie nodded. "Right." Her voice was small, as if she, too, saw the fading likelihood of contact. Yet, Sydney could almost see the wheels of her daughter's mind turning. Emma Treadwell in Michigan might be easier to find on Facebook.

Morgan closed the file and crossed her arms on the table. "If you want to contact the Treadwells, you can write a letter to them and bring it here to our office. We'll add a cover letter and send it for you. You can include photos if you like. I'll send it to the only address we have on file. It's possible they've moved, as I'm sure you're aware. It's best to allow for that possibility, so you aren't too disappointed.

"Can we include a letter for Emma?" Jessie asked.

"Yes, of course. But it is the parents' choice to give it to her or not. They may choose to give it to her since she's no longer a child." Morgan looked back at Sydney. "If the Treadwells respond to you, we'll notify you and you can come get their response or we'll fax or mail it to you, if you prefer. Then, you'll know what to do next."

Sydney pressed her lips together and nodded. "We'll work on the letters over the weekend and bring them back next week." She looked at Jessie. "Ready for this?"

Jessie's wide-eyed expression was joined by a solemn nod. "I'm ready."

Sydney took Jessie to lunch in downtown Wilmington before they headed home. With a pang, she thought about her father. She'd contacted him and they'd talked but hadn't set a date for a visit. It was her turn to call back. She'd been negligent of him, too, in her decades of flight from the past. True, he'd been less available, less of a dad to her after his remarriage to Melody. She sighed as she pulled the SUV onto the highway in the direction of Kennessey.

She'd have to add him to her list as one more person she needed to forgive and let off her hook.

As soon as they got home, Jessie wanted to get started on the letters.

"I need to call Tyler first. He wanted me to tell him what happened," Sydney told her. "Want some iced tea?" She pulled two glasses from the cupboard and grabbed a bin of ice from the freezer.

Jessie sighed and crossed her arms as she leaned against the kitchen counter. "You're acting like his girlfriend already."

"I am not." Sydney laughed then and tousled Jessie's hair. "He asked about it because he knows it's important to me. To us. And don't forget, he's Emma's father."

"I keep forgetting that. I think of Emma as *our* project."

"Jessie?" Sydney waited for her daughter to raise her eyes from picking polish off her nails. "Does it bother you if I'm dating Mr. Hoffman? Tyler?"

"No—I don't know." She shrugged. "Seems weird to me. You've never gone out with anyone since you and Dad split up, except for that guy, Michael, or whatever his name was."

"Jessie, look at me." Jessie's blue eyes lifted to Sydney's. She thought she saw uncertainty there. "I love you, and I love the close relationship we have. If I get close to Tyler or any other man, it won't change what you and I have together. Do you believe me? You're my precious girl." At Sydney's words, tears pooled in Jessie's eyes. Sydney drew her close and held her tightly for a few moments. "I wouldn't let any relationship come before you. I hope you know that. I'm sure Tyler wouldn't want that, anyway. He's a good guy."

"I know. You seem pretty happy around him, so I'm glad. I just—" Jessie's voice was muffled against Sydney's shoulder.

She kissed the crown of Jessie's head, then pulled back to look her in the eyes. "No one will replace you, Jessie. Not ever. Even when you go to college and one day meet someone you want to marry. Even then, we'll always have a special bond, like we always have."

"Okay." Jessie pulled back and drew her wrist across her moist face. "I love you, too. And I'm glad you and Mr. Hoffman—Tyler like each other, especially after what happened before when you were my age."

Sydney hugged her again, then stepped away. "We've only gone on one date. We might decide we don't like the adult version of each other." She grinned with a one-shouldered shrug.

"I guess that's possible." Jessie smiled, seeming peaceful. Then her body jolted. "Oh, I forgot, I have to work at four today." She pulled away and sprinted out of the kitchen and up the stairs.

Sydney watched her disappear through the doorway, her throat tight with the gratitude that welled up inside her. After a silent prayer of thanks, she reached for her phone.

ભ ભ ભ

Later that day, Sydney received jubilant responses from Julia and Marissa regarding her adoption news and budding romance with Tyler. She grinned, feeling as though they were right there with her. *Your summer has been so much more exciting than mine.* This from Marissa.

Sydney had responded. *Maybe you can base a future fiction character on my life. We'll see what happens next. Might end up being a thriller. Or a tragedy.*

Eden had texted. *Exciting news about Emma and Tyler. When did you find out about this rumor circulating at school?*

Too bad Eden reminded her about that situation, just when she was feeling victorious about Emma. *About a month and a half ago I got a call from the school receptionist who'd overheard it in the teacher's lounge.*

After ten minutes, Eden responded, *I'll call you soon, day after tomorrow probably. I want to talk about this with you.* Maybe Eden had a great idea to save Sydney's honor in the face of vicious lies. She hoped so.

192

Sydney scanned her inbox again just in case. No new message apart from a thank you note following her online interview with the Triangle Investment Corporation. No surprise there. She'd been able to schedule another interview for two weeks later with a Charlotte-based finance company, again as an analyst. Maybe it would yield better results, though her previous hope had slipped away along with most of her motivation.

↊ ↊ ↊

Friday morning after breakfast, Sydney and Jessie surveyed their workmanship at the dining room table. They'd agreed that Sydney would draft the letter to the Treadwells, and Jessie would give her input. Then they'd each write their own letter to Emma.

The previous evening, Sydney had labored for over an hour composing her letter to the Treadwells on a legal pad. She'd written a first draft then read it, finding it too much like a business letter. All dry facts. As she'd told Tyler, she wasn't good with words.

She crumpled the paper, then started over. Following her second draft, she edited and word-smithed for another half hour until her hand-written page looked like a diagram from the circuitry of a computer. Earlier that morning she'd recopied it to present to Jessie.

In the dining room window, the air-conditioning unit whirred causing the curtains to flutter. Mid-July in Kennessey no longer permitted open windows or doors. Some days, the ocean breeze reached the Victorian house, giving enough of a reprieve to spend time on the porch or in the yard.

Sydney had to admit, she enjoyed the old house and felt at home there. They'd settled into a routine, and it would be hard to return to Charlotte in another month. Sydney winced at the thought. She'd gotten into the habit of pushing Charlotte and her job far out of her mind. Unwise, but easy to do, with the compelling quest around Emma and frequent thoughts of Tyler.

193

Sydney took a long swig of her iced tea and picked up the sheet of paper on the table in front of her. "Okay, Jess. Tell me how this sounds to you. Take notes or interrupt me where you think something should change or you have a question."

"Okay." Jessie sat up in her chair, pen poised in her hand, an attentive look of her face.

"Here goes." Sydney would have grinned, but her heart was thumping too hard.

"Dear Mr. and Mrs. Treadwell,
My name is Sydney Bennett. Thirty years ago, I gave birth to your adoptive daughter, Emma. Currently, I have another daughter, Jessie, who is with me as I write to you now. The reason for this letter is our desire to learn about Emma's life and what it was like, to satisfy what has felt like a hole in my life for many years.

First, allow me to give you some background so you can know more about me and the circumstances of giving up Emma. I became pregnant with Emma at age seventeen (the age of my daughter Jessie.) I was deeply in love with the baby's father, and we'd planned to marry one day, but we were young. We felt we were too young to be parents, and we were overwhelmed. I'm sure this is a common story with adoptions. It was a difficult decision, but I thought it would be best for Emma to be raised by a family that was able to give her what she needed.

In subsequent years, I finished college and became a high-school teacher. Eventually, I got married and had my other daughter. We live in Charlotte, North Carolina. I healed from the trauma of giving up Emma, but in recent months have begun to wonder about her. I felt the need to learn what her life had been like, if she had siblings, what she was interested in, what was her career choice, things like that. As I shared these desires with my daughter Jessie, she became interested, too.

We would be grateful if you would be willing to supply this missing background on her life. If you decide to tell Emma about us and she wants to reach out, we are open to that. Thank you for reading this letter and for understanding our desire and request. We hope you'll write back to us.

We have also enclosed photos of us and two short letters for Emma, one from me and one from her half-sister Jessie if you are not opposed to giving them to her.

Thank you in advance.

Sincerely yours, Sydney and Jessie Bennett"

Sydney looked up at Jessie and waited. She hadn't spoken at all during the reading of the letter.

"I think it's good, Mom. We might go through it one more time so I can see if I'd want to change anything. Doesn't sound like you want to meet Emma, though."

Sydney sighed. "Well, Jessie, I'll be honest. I'm not really sure if it's a good idea for us to meet her. First, she lives in Michigan and has her own life. She might not have ever thought about her birth mother. We can't force our way in. This letter opens a door, but the next step will be hers, if she chooses."

Jessie nodded. "Yeah. I guess you're right. If the Treadwells give this letter and our other letters to Emma to read, *she* can decide."

"Right. Might just end up being a correspondence or, at most, a phone call. Which would be an okay first step. If it's meant to go further, it will."

Jessie pursed her lips, a despondent expression on her face.

"I think this is a good start, don't you? Then we'll trust God with the outcome."

"Yeah, I forgot about God's will," Jessie murmured. "Let's read the other letter. The one to Emma."

"You go first."

Jessie pulled her letter from the table.

"Hello, Emma.
My name is Jessie and I'm your half-sister. I'm almost eighteen years old. You are the only sister I have. I'm happy to have a half-sister. This fall I'll be a senior in high school. I like playing the guitar, going to my church youth group, and going to the beach, and lots of other things. I'm good at music, math (my mom is a math teacher) and soft ball. I usually play on our neighborhood team. I'm not good at creative writing or art. We live in Charlotte, North Carolina but are spending the summer at my grandma's near the beach. I'll be happy if you're willing to write to me and tell me about yourself. I hope you will. Sincerely, Jessie Bennett."

Jessie looked up at Sydney, who nodded and smiled in approval. "That's great, Jessie. I don't think I'd add anything to that. Sounds very friendly and open."

"Now yours."

Sydney had struggled even more with Emma's letter than with the Treadwells'. How to reach out to someone she'd abandoned as an infant?

"Dear Emma,
My name is Sydney, and I'm your biological mother. I don't know if you have wondered about me over the years or wondered why I gave you up for adoption. As you might have imagined, I was a teenager when I was pregnant with you. Even though I felt I was too young for motherhood at that time, I was amazed by the wonder of your life inside me. I wanted to keep you and was very sad that I couldn't."

She swallowed, wincing as if knives were lodged in her throat. Her eyes stung, but she continued.

"I believed you would have a better life if you were adopted by a couple who was in the position to raise a child. I don't

want you to think you weren't wanted. You were wanted, but the circumstances weren't easy.

I hope you've had a happy and good life with your adoptive parents. I have often thought of you over the years and hope and prayed that you did.

I went to college and eventually got married. I had my daughter, Jessie, who is your half-sister. We live in Charlotte, North Carolina. I hope that answers some questions you may have about me and why you were adopted. Please know that I've never forgotten about you and always prayed for you, Emma. Your bio mother, Sydney."

When she finished, she felt like she'd just finished a round in a boxing ring. She blew out a breath of air and dabbed her eyes with a tissue. Her gaze found Jessie's. Two tears had traced a path down her daughter's smooth cheeks. She offered a half-smile. With a broken voice, she said, "That sounds nice, Mom. Makes me want to cry."

Sydney pressed her lips together and bowed her head as more tears flowed. "Me too."

"Mom? Maybe you should just add a phrase that if she wants to reach out, we're open. What do you think?"

"Yes, okay. I will." And if Emma did respond, she'd open herself to that. It was a new door she was willing to face.

Chapter Eighteen

Sydney's father, Richard Davis, wrapped her in a hug, then turned to give one to Jessie. Sydney and Jessie had just finished lunch with Sydney's dad and his wife in a downtown Wilmington restaurant after giving their letters to the Morgan at the Hanover Adoption Agency. "I hope I'll see you a time or two again before you go back to Charlotte."

"Absolutely, Dad. Sorry it took so long for us to connect." He'd have good reason to be hurt that they were in Kennessey several weeks before contacting him, but he didn't show it.

His wife, Melody, waved the air dismissively. "That's okay. At least we had a chance to get together. I'm glad you're enjoying the summer." Her father's wife had always been pleasant in a bland, nonspecific way that left Sydney feeling it might be fine with her if she never saw them again. She'd try to believe the best, though it was against her nature.

As Sydney and Jessie approached the parking deck, Jessie said, "I wish we never had to go back to Charlotte."

Sydney shot Jessie a grimace as they entered the darkened building. She scanned the space for her SUV. She spied the car and rummaged in her purse for her keys. "Really? I know you're happy we spent the summer here, but what about your friends? And your youth group? And what about your senior year at your school?" They got into the car, and Sydney stared at Jessie, awaiting her answer.

Jessie shrugged. "I could do it here." Her eyes reached Sydney's then darted away as she crossed her arms and looked out the front windshield. "I like it here. It's smaller and there's Gram and the beach. And don't you want to live closer to Mr. Hoffman?"

Yes, she did. But it was a leap to think about uprooting her life for Tyler's sake. She'd lost everything for him once before.

"It's way too early for me to think that way, Jessie. We went on one date." And a few walks on the beach and phone calls since then.

"And he kissed you. That means something, right?"

"Well, yes. It's a beginning. But only a beginning. You know it may not lead to anything permanent."

Jessie grunted. Sydney couldn't help but chuckle. "I'll pray about possibly moving. Maybe after your senior year, okay? You do that, too. We'll both pray and God will show us what to do. Deal?" That should close off the discussion for a while. She'd add that question to her Charlotte-based prayer needs.

A weight pressed into her stomach each time she thought about the fall teaching decision, which still left her completely stumped. She could, as she'd suggested, finish out the school year at her old job for Jessie's sake so she could graduate. Then they'd seriously reevaluate. That might not be so unreasonable, if she could handle just one more year of teaching. In any case, no alternatives had shown up yet. And time was passing fast. Her phone interview for the second analyst job with Emerson-Carroll Finance would be Wednesday. She was no better equipped than she'd been for the first analyst interview.

One thing was for sure. She couldn't sponge off her mother for the indefinite future. Sydney tried regularly to contribute to the food budget and utilities, but her mother had always waved away her offer, saying, "I'm just glad you two are here." That admission, while it didn't solve anything, still brought warmth, since such sentiments had been rare during Sydney's past visits. So, Sydney often came home with unsolicited bags of groceries.

But her problem remained. A conscientious adult raising a teenager needed steady employment.

Sydney pulled out onto the highway in the direction of Kennessey, and an unrelated thought struck her. "Hey, Jessie. When I was pregnant with Emma, I went to live with my Aunt Abigail. Well, she was my great-aunt, but I called her Aunt. Would you want to go by her house? She died and someone else lives there now, but it's on the way."

"Sure, Mom, if it's on the way."

Sydney didn't remember the address anymore, but knew it was in Leland, a town about a half hour from the beach. She'd be able to find the house once she was in the city limits. She wanted to go one last time before closing that chapter. Of course, if Emma responded to them, it would be reopened in a new way, but she wouldn't think of that just yet. After giving the letters to Morgan at the agency, she'd reminded them not to get their hopes up. If the Treadwells responded at all, it would likely take several weeks minimum.

A lot had changed in Leland since Aunt Abigail's death twenty years earlier. During the six months that Sydney had lived with her, she'd spent most of her time doing schoolwork or at medical appointments. She never learned her way around town, except for the route to the beach. But from the time she left for college, each time she returned to Kennessey, she'd gone to see Aunt Abigail, who'd become like a second mother to her.

Sydney drove down the main avenue, her eyes panning the stores and side roads for signs of familiarity. "Honeysuckle Lane," she said aloud. "I just remembered the name of the street. Thank goodness." At the stoplight, she typed the name of the street into her GPS and within several minutes, they were on the street. From there, it was easy to find the house.

She pulled up in front of the house and idled the car at the curb. "This is it." The flood of emotions Sydney had expected was only a trickle. The beige two-story house etched in her memory had been painted light blue and white shutters had been added. What had been average sized trees now towered over the lawn and sidewalks. The long front porch was the same, with rocking chairs and a bench swing extending an invitation, feathery potted ferns hanging from the overhang. Sydney had spent many hours on the porch, finding solace there. When she'd first arrived, she'd been like a wounded bird, crying frequently and seeking solitude. In time, Aunt Abigail's motherly kindness had seeped into her pain and allowed her to unfurl like a tight flower bud.

In the spring of her senior year before her pregnancy was too far along, she'd persuaded her aunt to take her to the beach or let her drive herself there. By that time, she'd reconciled herself to her fate. But the beach allowed her space to weep until she was dry and mourn the life she wouldn't have with Tyler and his child.

"How long did you live here, Mom?" Jessie's voice broke into Sydney's memories.

"Six months. I missed the last half of my senior year in high school."

"Did your friends know you were pregnant?"

"My best friends knew. And of course, everyone else probably guessed." Didn't matter anymore.

"Bummer to miss senior year. I can't wait for my senior year."

Sydney turned to her. "Exactly. That's why you're *never* going to do what I did."

Jessie rolled her eyes. "Okay, can we go home now?"

Absolutely. The past was gone and the present awaited.

"Can I drive us home?" Jessie offered an angelic smile.

Sydney feigned an exaggerated expression of fear, then grinned. "Okay. I think you might be ready for the highway. Just stay in the right lane, okay?"

Yes, she did have to step fully back into the present.

ର ର ର

The following day, Sydney was again in the passenger seat as Jessie drove herself to work. "I'll call you when I'm ready for a ride home." Jessie got out of the car and Sydney circled the front to take the driver's seat. Jessie looked cute in her uniform, a pink and blue striped smock over denim shorts, her blond curls stuffed under a bright pink baseball cap with the words, "Berti's Best Ice Cream" embroidered across the front.

"See ya later."

"Good luck on the golf course, Mom. I think you'll need it." Jessie grinned and disappeared through the glass doors of the ice cream shop.

Sydney had reluctantly agreed to let Tyler give her a beginner golf lesson. After that, he would realize how ungifted and disinterested she was in golf and let it rest. But she'd do her part and give it a try just to say she had.

But there was a deeper reason. This was Tyler's world, and she wanted to see it through his eyes. Yes, she'd bumble around the golf course and embarrass herself, that was certain. But she'd see a new facet of *him* along with the surface aspects of the sport.

She locked her car and heard a ping on her phone. A text from Eden. *Hi Sydney, I'm sorry it took me so long to get back with you. My girls were here all weekend and just left on their Europe trip. Can you chat tomorrow morning?*

Sydney responded. *Hi Eden, sure, how about eleven?*

Perfect, I'll call you then. Looking forward to it! Love, Eden.

Sydney entered the clubhouse. Within two minutes, Tyler emerged from the office behind the counter, a smile spread across his face. "I'm glad you didn't stand me up. Golf isn't that bad, you'll see." He rounded the counter to where she stood.

She grinned and met his eyes. "It's not the golf I'm worried about. Once we're done, I hope you don't have to close for lawn repairs."

He laughed, then his face sobered. He reached up to trail one hand down her bare arm. A chill to rippled down. "I missed you, Sydney. It's been two days."

Heat puddled inside her. It had seemed long for her, too. She'd adapted quickly to Tyler and Sydney 2.0

"Here, let's get you some clubs." A brisk tone entered his voice as he became the expert.

He led her to the pro shop, currently empty of customers, though a young man typed into a computer near the cash register. He looked up and nodded at them. Dozens of golf clubs and bags of all types and colors filled an entire wall. Clothing, visors, water bottles, and other golf-related merchandise adorned displays in the center of the store.

They entered a small room. "Here's where we keep the rental clubs. You'll get a set of fourteen clubs. Each club has a name for each type of shot you may make for example, close-up, far away, in the sand, and so on." Of course, he was dumbing down his terms for her sake, and she was grateful. Sydney panned her eyes across the collection of clubs, suddenly intimidated. She blew out a breath.

He grinned at her. "You'll see, it's fun. I promise I'll be a patient teacher."

And so he was. Though hitting a ball into a hole hadn't yet seized her with passion, she savored the tranquility of the emerald green slopes spreading out in all directions, allowing her to slide her pressures to the back burner. The humidity was lower than usual, and a gentle breeze stroked her bare arms and neck beneath her ponytail. Of course, it didn't hurt to have Tyler guiding her, his close presence teaching, demonstrating, and encouraging her. Once he explained the big picture of the sport, her mathematical mind began to appreciate the game.

As they rode in the cart to the next hole, Tyler said, "You're doing really well, Sydney. I think you might be a natural."

"And I think you say that to every student."

"I'm serious. First, you've quickly picked up the logic of the game. Second, you have an athletic physique. You seem *made* for golf." They slipped down from the cart.

"Oh, you're laying it on a little thick." She laughed and reached for the club he handed her. "I guess athletic is far better than flabby. Unlikely that I'm made for golf, though."

She tried to remember the points he'd previously explained as she gripped the club, carefully got into position, then swung, but there were too many to retain at once. Instead of digging a hole in the turf, the ball flew out of view. It might be a good swing, or it might have gone into the nearby shopping center.

"Excellent!"

"Really?"

"I told you, you're a natural."

"It'll take me a while to be sure you're not just building me up me with lies."

As the rest of the lesson unfolded, Sydney had to admit she was enjoying the sport, not only because of Tyler. As awkward and ignorant as she still felt, she could understand how people became addicted to it. She didn't picture herself doing likewise, mostly because she'd need lots of time and money for that, but she could enjoy it. She and Tyler could golf together. She stopped her mind from imagining golfing regularly with him, walking the green, talking about their days. *Slow down, Sydney.*

After the lesson, they hopped onto the cart and headed back to the building. "What time does Jessie get off work?" The cart made a quiet hum as Tyler drove.

"Not until around eight. She'll call me when she's ready."

"Sounds like we have time for a walk on the beach *and* a simple bite." He lifted his eyebrows as if to ask if she agreed.

She did.

Was it moving too fast? That could be dangerous if the past was any indicator. She felt as powerless to slow down with Tyler Hoffman as she had the first time around.

℃ ℃ ℃

Fortunately, the following day was open for Sydney. Life had gotten far busier than she'd anticipated at the start of the summer. After eating breakfast and doing a few chores for her mother, Sydney went to her bedroom with her phone and settled into the pillow shams propped against the headboard of her bed. It would be nice to have a conversation with Eden rather than an email or a text.

At eleven sharp her phone rang. "Eden! It's *divine* to hear your voice."

Eden laughed. "And likewise, my suntanned friend! I'm sure you are by now."

They chatted about Eden's visit with her daughters and Sydney updated her on Tyler, the adoption letters, and her coming job interview. Finally, Eden said, "I wanted to talk to you more about this rumor you mentioned last week in your email. It bothered me, Sydney. I wanted to ask how *you're* feeling about it."

"Awful and helpless." Sydney had been able to tuck it away amidst her other pressing preoccupations. Namely, Tyler. But Eden had dragged it front and center.

"Have you been able to do anything about it?"

"Since it's summer, there's not much I can do. I told my principal. Of course, he minimized it. In fact, that's when I learned he hadn't said anything about my leave of absence to the faculty. Even if I go back in the fall, I'll only be able to verbally defend myself, but that probably won't clear me in peoples' minds."

She heard Eden let out a sigh of frustration. "Your principal has failed you in so many ways. But I guess you know that already. You said you heard about it over a month ago. Why didn't you let us know, Sydney?"

"Um . . ." Sydney paused. Good question. "I don't know. I wish I had."

"You could have asked for advice. You need to do that more and let us help."

"I know. It hit me the other day that if only I'd let a couple of colleagues know about the attack right after it happened, they'd know the truth, and the rumor wouldn't have started. I didn't want to make a big deal of it, so I didn't say anything. And now it's too late."

"You didn't want to make a big deal?" Eden's voice had risen. "You were assaulted! Help me understand this, Sydney. Aren't you important enough?"

At her words, a fissure opened inside and started to throb. Sydney's throat tightened and her eyes burned. "No, I guess I didn't think I was. I didn't want everyone worrying about me, so I didn't say anything. Except during that meeting with the kid and his parents. *That* was a disaster. I really lost it then."

Eden's voice softened. "As you should have. And what's wrong with people worrying about you? That means they care. They love you. Not saying anything has denied you a lot of TLC over the years."

Sydney found herself nodding as her eyes began to sting. "Yeah." Her voice was soft as Eden's words hit dead center. "Like with Jessie, though she was gracious with me. I either don't say anything or I say too much and in the wrong way. Maybe that's why I often feel alone, despite Jessie and you all."

"Sydney, there's no reason to feel alone. People love you and are there for you. You assume you're alone to solve things, but you're not. But if you hide problems and hide yourself behind jokes, no one knows, and they can't help. You see?"

"I . . . I do. I started feeling alone after my pregnancy. No, actually before that, in my family. But when I got pregnant, I was shipped off to wait it out, as if I were being punished. When it was over, I wanted to close the door, so I said nothing. It wasn't a part of me anymore."

"But it was. And it's colored everything you've done since then. Events like that don't just fade away. You interpreted that you're alone, and that isn't true. You don't have to believe that anymore, Sydney. What's done is done. Getting pregnant at seventeen isn't the unpardonable sin."

"I failed everyone." Sydney's voice came out small. She could still see her dad's clouded face, his pinched lips when he heard about his disgraced daughter in whom he'd had such hopes. Nashville, really? She'd failed herself, too. And God. Is that when her distance began with him?

"No, you didn't. You were seventeen. And you weren't alone, Tyler is responsible, too. He's even more responsible, in my view."

Sydney swallowed. Her throat ached. "I guess that's why it feels so dirty now to have rumors circulating about me. It reminds me that I was *that* girl. Morally sketchy."

"No, you were *not*." Eden's voice was forceful. "You *are* not. That's why it bothered you because you were not ever *that* girl. So, you fell into temptation with a boy you adored. So. Don't punish yourself anymore, Sydney. Now, this rumor is that—a rumor. You know good and well what kind of woman you are and what kind of teacher you have always been."

Sydney sniffed. "You're right. But I can't prove it. If I don't go back to school, I can't defend myself."

"Maybe it's time to stop defending yourself. With your words and your choices. Let God defend you. 'Don't be afraid, for *I* am with you. Don't be discouraged, for *I* am your God. *I* will strengthen you and help you. *I* will hold you up with *my* victorious right hand.' Remember that? He keeps saying 'I'. Not you."

Sydney smiled as tears pricked her eyes. "Yes. I love that verse. I often forget."

"You're not alone. You have friends, but we're just peons compared to the God who loves you and has promised to fight for your honor, fight against whatever disturbs you and makes you cry. He'll fight for you because you're *worth* it to him. Try him and see if he won't."

Sydney pressed her lips together as warm tears tumbled down her cheeks. "Thank you, Eden. I love those words you just said." She did. And she'd forgotten them too frequently. "There are lots of passages that tell me the truth."

"Those teachers whose opinions you esteem—you'll probably never even *see* them again, if you don't go back."

Eden was right. But Sydney's reality was still there in her face. "At this point, I have every likelihood of going back to that school."

"If you do, remember who's gone there ahead of you. And remember who you are. And I might add, who you're not."

☓ ☓ ☓

Sydney watched the road from where she sat inside the small brick building with an austere, nondescript interior. The DMV of Kennessey. No sign of Jessie and the driving inspector. Sydney almost wanted to bite her nails but sat on her hands instead.

"You look scared to death. Your kid must be taking the test." A female employee spoke to her from behind the counter.

"It's pretty scary to let your baby out on the highway in a lethal machine."

The woman laughed. "I know *that's* right. Had to do it twice myself already. I needed a stiff drink the first couple of times they went out alone. And lots of prayers, of course."

Sydney returned the woman's smile. The anxiety she'd grown accustomed to had calmed and nearly vanished as Eden's words still tumbled through her mind like lyrics to a well-loved song. She'd begun praying, *Lord please fight my battles.*

When she turned back to the plate-glass window, Jessie was parking in front of the building. Her face hadn't crumpled in tears, nor was it joyful. Yet, when she entered the building, she shot both arms into the air. "I passed!"

The atmosphere in the car was jubilant as they drove back home, Jessie at the wheel. She drove carefully, as if she knew this was for real.

"Gram'll be so proud of you," Sydney said. "Now we have to figure out what you're going to drive."

"I've saved up almost three hundred dollars this summer and have about four hundred from my last job. Dad said he'd pitch in some, too."

"That's a great start, Jess. I'll do what I can, of course. I have to see first if I'll have a job this fall."

"Really?" To her credit, Jessie kept her eyes on the road, but her voice seemed to convey worry.

"Well, I'll do something, of course. I'm trying to find another job, so I don't have to go back to teaching." Which she likely would have to do, since nothing else had come through. She'd rather think of the present. She'd try hard to let God fight that battle in her mind, too. "What do you think if we celebrate your success? I'll ask your Gram if we can do a barbeque and invite Zach and his dad."

"Great idea. I can't wait to tell Zach I passed."

Carolyn had been polite enough to Tyler when he'd come with Zach to pick Sydney and Jessie up for Zach's birthday dinner. Seemed like ages ago. How would she act for an entire evening with the source of Sydney's teenage disgrace? Had *she* forgiven Tyler?

She'd find out very soon.

℘   ℘   ℘

Friday evening, the smell of smoking burgers and bratwurst filled the backyard, stirring nostalgia in Sydney for many barbeques of the past. This one was decidedly different, with Tyler and Zach present and Carolyn appearing to enjoy herself in a nearby lawn chair. Tyler supervised the grill while Zach and Jessie threw a frisbee in the lush green grass of the back yard.

When Sydney told her mother she wanted to invite Tyler and Zach, her mother's eyes had widened and for a moment she didn't respond. But she recovered herself quickly and said, "They're your friends, so you should have them here. And Jessie's license is a cause for celebration."

Another miracle. Or else an exquisite display of diplomacy and southern grace, despite what might be stirring in her mother's memory. Maybe all was forgiven and nearly forgotten. When Sydney added the fact that she and Tyler were seeing each other, her mother had simply nodded and left the room. That one might take more time, though her mother might have expected it sooner or later.

Once they were settled on the screened-in porch, plates of meat and rolls, macaroni salad, quinoa salad, and condiments spread before them, Tyler prayed a blessing over the meal. The evening was warm but tolerable, and the ceiling fan overhead added a cooling breeze. A wave of contentment stole over Sydney as her eyes panned the table and her favorite people. Yes, she could now include her mother in that category. Things had certainly changed.

"Here's to Jessie." Tyler lifted a glass of iced tea.

"Here, here." Sydney said as everyone at the table raised their glasses toward Jessie.

"Can't believe I finally got it, after hundreds of practice hours. Well, seemed like hundreds." Jessie beamed.

"Hey, that's what I can do for a career. Driving instructor." Sydney chuckled and reached for the macaroni salad. "I mean, I get results, don't I?"

Jessie rolled her eyes. "I'm the one who passed the test, Mom. But you were a good teacher."

"You've always been a good teacher, Sydney." Carolyn straightened up in her chair. "It's a shame you don't like it anymore. You've put in so many years already."

Sydney frowned, unwilling to let go of the festive atmosphere. "Exactly why I need a change. Too many years. Maybe I'd enjoy being an analyst or an accountant or something. But honestly, after this summer, it would be hard to go back inside, especially to a cubicle in an office building." With no summers off.

"You could caddy for the club. That would keep you outside," Tyler offered with a grin.

"Yeah, you could take Zach's job when he goes off to college." Jessie laughed, and Zach joined her.

"Very funny." She sent Jessie a fake scowl, but inside a hollowness formed, a little voice that told her there was no place for her. She hadn't heard that voice in a long time. She'd almost forgotten it had been a part of the Victorian house for years and had followed her into adulthood. Despite Eden's words of encouragement, she still had stale wounds that tried to push through her resolve.

Sydney's humor and contentment drained out of her, replaced by that stubborn conviction that she was alone to figure out her future. Wasn't she? Hadn't she always been alone every step of the way? Had Eden been correct in saying Sydney had chosen to be alone because of her beliefs?

As if sensing the change in her mood, Tyler sent her a concerned glance and reached to squeeze her wrist. "We'll figure it out, don't worry."

She returned a lame smile and stabbed a bratwurst with her fork. "No, *I'll* figure it out. It's my responsibility." Her voice had dropped, but instantly she regretted her words. Hadn't she learned anything since her conversation with Eden?

She didn't dare look at Tyler's face. Here he was, expressing his desire to help, to stand with her, and as much as she wanted that, she'd pulled away. Flung it back at him. *Way to go with that mouth, Sydney.*

She tried to backpedal with fake cheer and one-liners for the remainder of the meal, probably fooling Jessie, who was still enthralled with her success. But she sensed she hadn't fooled Tyler. After the meal, she encouraged her mother to relax in the living room. Meanwhile, she and Tyler cleaned up after the meal, mostly in silence. When they were finished, he said, "Want to go sit on the front porch? It's a nice night out there."

The sky had darkened to deep blue with a few stars piercing the velvet expanse. Sydney and Tyler settled onto the swinging bench as fireflies glinted in the semi-darkness. The heat of the day had mellowed to a gentle caress on Sydney's bare shoulders. Tyler slipped one arm around her and pulled her close to him. He kissed the top of her head, letting his lips rest a moment longer on her forehead. His gesture warmed her in a deep, barren place. At that moment she longed only for that, his arm around her and the comfort and warmth from his body next to hers. At the same time, she braced for what he might say.

After a lengthy silence, he said, "You're not alone to figure this out, Sydney. And I'm sorry you sometimes feel that way. I wish I could take the weight away from you."

She turned her head toward him. "The other day I talked to Eden on the phone, and she told me the same thing. Sometimes I feel alone and afraid, but don't show it. Fake bravado, you know." Her eyes fell away from his as shame unfurled inside her, spreading the pain of discovery. "That's my defense mechanism. That's who

I've become, sorry to say. It's such a part of me I don't know how to stop."

Tyler gently tilted her chin back up until he met her eyes. "You don't need to change, Sydney. I love your sense of humor. You make me laugh and smile. But let it be real, not just a defense. I know both are there inside you. Are you able to tell the difference?"

Sydney leaned against him and let out a deep sigh. "Often, yes." He saw her self-protection, but seemed to like her, anyway. She didn't deserve it. "Sometimes I know exactly what I'm doing but can't stop myself. I'm working on it. I asked my friends to hold me accountable. You can, too, Tyler."

He kissed her temple. She couldn't see his eyes anymore but heard him sigh. "I see your self-protection and know I contributed at least in part to putting it there. That's the truth. I wasn't a man for you when you needed one."

"But you are now." She turned to face him. "You *too* were molded through that experience, even if you regret how you handled it. It's not just through success that we grow and learn to be godly." She needed to have that same talk with herself.

He gazed at her, and his eyes roved around her face. "Thanks for saying that. And I like that you're speaking from your heart instead of joking around." His smile was patient, understanding. "I was beginning to think it might take a long time to really get to know you."

His word caused a chill. The price of hiding was too high. She'd never noticed it before. Too high and too exhausting.

Tyler's arm tightened around her shoulder. He slid the other one across to form a ring around her. She laid her head on his chest, feeling his heartbeat beneath her head.

She loved him. She'd never stopped loving him.

She'd gone and fallen for Tyler Hoffman a second time. Though she couldn't help it, she wasn't sure it was a good idea.

Chapter Nineteen

After Tyler left and Sydney went to bed, her thoughts continued to rumble in her mind. Tyler's words. Eden's words. God speaking through them both. She didn't fall asleep until hours later.

The next morning, she woke up later than usual. The sun streamed into her bedroom, creating a starburst off the smooth edge of her guitar. She needed alone time that day, and she knew exactly where she'd go.

After dressing, she went downstairs and poured coffee, but didn't see her mother in the kitchen or living room. Through the window over the sink, she spied Carolyn reading in a lawn chair on the screened-in porch. She took her coffee mug and slipped out.

"Hi, Mom." She remained standing. "I don't want to disturb your reading but wanted to say good morning." She also wanted to find out if her mother had any commentary about their barbeque dinner the previous evening.

Her mother lifted her chin and managed a reserved smile. "Good morning, Sydney. I went to bed early, so I didn't say goodnight. Did the guys stay very long?"

"Not too long. Tyler and I were on the front porch. Not sure what Jessie and Zach were up to. Video games, maybe." After a pause, Sydney added, "It was a nice evening, don't you think?"

"Yes, very. It's nice to get to know Tyler as an adult. It still seems a bit strange to me, but I'm glad you two are reconnecting."

"I'm glad you feel that way, Mom. I guess we all figured it was no use hanging onto the past. It kind of blocks things . . ." She finished with a shrug.

"Is Jessie working today?"

"Yeah, she goes in at noon. I'm going to check my email, then drive to the beach to take a walk. Do you need anything before I go or while I'm out?"

"No, thank you. I have a meeting at church this afternoon, so I might be gone when you come home."

"I'll see you in a little while, then."

Sydney went to the dining room and opened her laptop. This wouldn't take long. She'd rather head directly to the surf but felt duty-bound to check her inbox for responses her resumes and her one interview, as a responsible adult with shaky employment. Her fingers worked quickly on the keyboard. Her online interview for the second analyst job was Wednesday. She had to admit, her hopes and enthusiasm for the position were at an all-time low, but she had nothing else.

Suddenly, the air in the room seemed stifling. Sydney bolted from the dining room, snatched her purse, sunglasses, and straw hat, and headed out the front door.

Watching the waves curling and foaming in unhurried rhythm would lower her blood pressure, she was certain. She left her flip flops in the tall grasses alongside the walkway between rental houses. Gritty, warm sand shifted under the pads of her bare feet as she headed to the edge of the water. Soon, cool waves swelled around her ankles, soothing her feet and her soul at the same time. Her plan was to walk. And walk. As long as it took to sort through the tangles in her mind.

Lord, I'm a mess. Maybe you brought me here so I could learn things I'm doing wrong. What I keep seeing is your kindness. You let me run into Tyler again, and you're pointing out things I need to change. I didn't know I was still carrying it around until I got here. I thought I'd healed and gone on with life.

In some ways, she had. She'd gone on with her life, made a career, a family. She'd raised a sweet, wonderful daughter. Taught a lot of kids math. Sydney shook her head. That was fine on the surface, but what had she done with her heart? The heart that had broken thirty years earlier?

Sydney's steps were regular, yet her thoughts were far from the beach. What Eden had told her and what Tyler had clearly seen, probably ever since the day they'd met again, was a protected heart. Somewhere along the line, when she'd felt deserted by her true love and her family, she'd assumed God had deserted her as well. True, she'd maintained a polite acquaintance with him. She prayed when she had difficulties, sang songs in church. Her faith habits were theologically sound. But she didn't truly thirst for him, depend on him. Act like she needed him or had joy in him. And she didn't let him fight her battles for her. She'd lost the burgeoning love she felt for him when she'd composed worship songs back in the day.

Instead, she developed a protective callous of self-reliance and verbal wit to shield her. She frequently spotted it in herself in the superficial nature of her relationships, even with other women. Even with her best friends, Julia, Marissa, and Eden. She longed to have the transparency and acceptance they had with each other. There was a reason she felt ever so slightly on the outside. She loved them like sisters, but even with them, she'd sometimes felt like the black sheep.

Lord, I'm tired of being a black sheep. I'm tired of being the clown and hiding my heart. Her eyes stung. She kept walking. *I felt like a black sheep in my family, even before getting pregnant. I was vulnerable back then. Vulnerability led to brokenness, and that didn't feel very good. So, I buried my heart. I—I want it back, Lord. I'm not sure how, but the first thing I need is you taking a bigger place inside me.*

Sydney skirted three small children digging in the sand with neon-colored buckets and shovels. They squealed in delight and scrambled as a wave nearly reached them. The beach was getting crowded already. The scent of coconut smacked in the air. She swiped at more tears that fell. And kept walking.

I lost the best parts of myself. It's like a bone that healed wrong. She blinked. Maybe he'd brought her there to break that bone and reset it. To revisit the past head-on. *I'm sorry I didn't let you be life to me back when I wanted to die. Reinventing myself seemed the only way, but I did it myself my way. I don't want to be that person anymore. Help me stop hiding. Help me to be real. Help me to open my heart fully to you first, and other people, too.*

Eden and Tyler's words had thrust through a fabric that had already begun to weaken. She'd already seen it, already been sick of it. To have depth and authenticity, even if it meant hurting sometimes—seemed worth it.

When Sydney arrived home, she felt lighter, cleaner inside, even if it was only a beginning. The house was empty, silent. She went upstairs to her bedroom, closed the door, and took her guitar from where it leaned against the wall. She climbed onto the bed and leaned against the wooden headboard.

She plucked and strummed, and soon the sounds filled the room as well as the raw cavity inside her, one that had waited empty for a long time. A chord slipped into her mind. She tried a few combinations and discovered it, an E major seventh. Then the A major seventh followed, and others as well tumbled back into her memory and through her fingers. Maybe one day she could compose again.

She'd been practicing when Jessie was at work, gradually rebuilding callouses on her fingers. Sydney should tell her she'd gotten a guitar and had no idea why she hid this from her daughter. Would her musical gift return? Even if she had a gift, she'd still have a long way to go after thirty years of neglect. And that wasn't the point, anyway. Rediscovering herself and the joy she'd had. The light in her eyes, as her mother had pointed out. That was what she sought.

A piece of her real self.

ॐ   ॐ   ॐ

Sydney's mother entered the dining room where Sydney sat at the table, having just finished her interview with Emerson-Carroll Finance. "You're dressed up." Her eyes roved over Sydney's bottom half, clad in drawstring shorts and flip flops. "Well, your top half is dressed up. I tried not to make noise in the kitchen during your interview. How did it go?"

Closing her laptop, Sydney sighed. "Oh, I don't know. Depends on how desperate they are, I guess. I think I can learn it, but that's just me."

"No question you can learn it, Sydney. Think of all the math you know. That's a good foundation for many jobs."

Sydney shrugged. "I don't know how many other people are vying for this job. They'd probably rather have someone with experience, though they did say that several of their employees came from other disciplines."

"That's a good sign, and it's true, too. A former teacher might be in demand because he or she would be accustomed to leadership, organization, discipline, those kinds of qualities."

Sydney leaned back in the chair. "Wow, Mom. Thanks. You just made me feel like I have a chance." She grinned. "And it's true. All those qualities are required of teachers, and I think I've developed them over the years. And the numbers thing has always been natural for me." She pulled her iced tea toward her for a deep gulp.

Her mother's comment had left a warm spot inside. As though Carolyn had seen some professional success in Sydney's life, possibly on par with Chet and Kevin. She wasn't the family screw-up after all. She might not be a doctor or engineer, but she knew numbers and had dozens of career options at her fingertips, according to Tyler. Almost imperceptibly, her desperation lightened, taking on another hue. One that tasted like hope with a pinch of confidence.

"The man who interviewed me described the job in more detail and it actually sounds like something I might like. I was surprised but it was kind of appealing."

But what was less appealing? The job was in Charlotte. Jessie's request to move had begun to take root inside her, speaking with soft voices into her objections. Yet, she had to do the responsible thing. If they offered her a full-time job, she'd take it.

ର ର ର

A few days later, Sydney sat next to Jessie in a row of padded chairs at the church. It was just the two of them that day, since Tyler had taken Zach to the University of Georgia for a freshman visit scheduled for the following day. It had been an especially moving service. Or maybe the shift inside Sydney since her day on the beach had done what she'd prayed and opened her heart a tad wider.

The service ended on a celebratory note, with everyone on their feet clapping and swaying. Sydney and Jessie stood up and a low rumble of conversation began.

"Do you think they got to the college yet?" Jessie asked as she snagged her backpack purse from under her chair.

"Probably not yet. They had to go all the way to Athens."

"Athens? That's in Greece, isn't it? That's pretty far." Jessie grinned.

"They'd be gone longer than a couple days, in that case. The

University of Georgia is about five or six hours from here, I think, but don't quote me."

"When will they be home?"

"They'll drive back on Wednesday." Three more days. Such a long time. Something sagged inside Sydney. "When does Zach have to move there to start his freshman year?"

"I think he said mid-August. That's coming soon. I'm gonna miss him."

"No doubt about that."

They filed into the aisle. Sydney already felt at home in the church and regretted staying away for so long. Its updated appearance helped keep her mind in the present while she was there.

"Sydney Davis! Is that you?"

Sydney's head shot up, and she scanned the surrounding crowd. They funneled with the other church members through the double doors and spilled out into the lobby. Her eyes lighted on the source of the voice, a vaguely familiar face that was thirty years older. The woman must be around sixty now. Gray streaked her dark waves, and she wore wire-rimmed glasses. Suddenly, the woman's identity snapped into place in Sydney's mind. "Tonya Canfield? Is that you?" Tonya had been one of Sydney's youth group leaders. Tension stirred in Sydney's stomach.

"The very same. I haven't seen you in—how long has it been, Sydney?"

"I guess thirty years. I've visited here and there over the years to see my mom, but never ran into you. Tonya, this is my daughter, Jessie." Sydney turned to Jessie. "This is Tonya Canfield. She was one of my youth group leaders way back when."

"Hello, Jessie." Tonya grinned. "Are you in high school?"

Jessie gave the woman a shy smile. "Yes ma'am. I'll be a senior this fall."

They stepped to the side of the double doors to clear the throng leaving the building. She turned to Sydney. "Did you move back to Kennessey?"

"No, we live in Charlotte, but we're here for the summer. I teach school, so I have summers off."

"Oh, how nice. Is your husband here?"

"Uh, I'm divorced."

"Oh, I'm sorry. Did you and Tyler ever get married?"

Sydney's heartbeat increased its tempo. It was a fair question, but she wished it hadn't been asked. "No, we drifted apart after high school, and both ended up marrying other people."

"I guess you've seen him, since he lives here now."

"Yes, we're friends. We've reconnected." Now if Tonya would kindly move on without asking more probing questions. "And what about you?" Though Sydney didn't want to prolong the conversation, returning the question would not only be polite, but it might divert the focus from her.

"Dan's still working at the same company, and the kids are grown with their own families. Amy and her husband live here. They have two kids."

Sydney gave the woman a bland smile. "That's nice. Well, it was good seeing you, Tonya."

"Very good to see you, too! Oh, I've always wondered if you ever got to Nashville. Remember you planned to go there with your music?"

Now Sydney's heartbeat was nearly a tympani drum. She glanced over at Jessie and saw her eyes wide with confusion. Sydney forced out a laugh. "Oh, no. I didn't. It was a teenage dream, you know. I'm sure lots of kids want to go to Nashville or Hollywood one day."

"But you were good enough for Nashville, in my opinion. And those songs you wrote, they were great. I remember we used to sing them in church."

"Thanks, that's sweet. I haven't really kept up with music. Too many responsibilities in life."

"Oh, that's a shame. Well, so nice to see you." She turned to Jessie. "And good to meet you, too, Jessie. Bye, now."

She waved to someone across the crowded room and left them. Sydney and Jessie walked to the car in silence. Sydney was certain she wouldn't escape questions from Jessie. She sighed. Might as well come clean.

Once they were in the car, Jessie said, "Mom, what was *that*? Nashville?"

Sydney started the car but didn't change gears. "Well, you knew that I played the guitar when I was a teenager. Remember I told you?"

Jessie nodded but continued to stare.

Sydney's mouth was dry. Why had she hidden everything for so long? "I practiced a lot back then and wrote a few songs."

"But that lady said you were good enough for Nashville. You always made it sound like you were just fiddling around. Were you really good at it? Did you write songs they sang in church?"

"Um, yeah." Sydney forced a conversational tone into her voice. "I got pretty good at the guitar. I wrote some songs, but with the baby and college and everything, I just . . . stopped." She looked over at Jessie, who still looked stunned.

Jessie turned her face to stare out of the windshield, arms crossed. "I don't even *know* you. There's like, tons I don't know about you, Mom. What else are you going to tell me? You were married before you married Dad? Do you have more kids somewhere?"

"No, of course not." Sydney sighed. "Jessie, it's not a big deal. So, I was a good musician when I was your age. Lots of people let that go when they move on in life. I did. I shouldn't have let it go, but I did and forgot a lot of things."

"But you never even *said* anything about it, even when I started playing. It seems weird to me. There's no reason not to talk about stuff like that." She shook her head, still scowling.

"I'm sorry, Jessie. Lots of things happen in a person's life that they don't necessarily talk about."

"But this was a big thing for you." Her face closed like a rock. "Anyway, it doesn't matter."

Sydney sighed again and began driving. Jessie was silent all the way home. When they entered the house, she stomped upstairs without a word and slammed her door.

"What have you done now?" Her mother's voice met her from behind as she stared up the staircase after Jessie.

Sydney turned, bristling. "What do you mean by that?" The fight instinct crumbled then, and her eyes stung. "Jessie found out about my, uh, early musical talents, which I never told her about. Someone at church remembered me from back then."

"You never told her about that? Did she know you used to play guitar?"

"Yes, but all her life she thought I only *dabbled.* She didn't know—" Tears of frustration and regret spilled out and she snatched at them with one hand. "I don't know why I never told her. I simply didn't want to talk about it because it was a big dream for me that got destroyed." Her voice had risen. "I associated that with everything else that happened and—" The tears returned, and she swiped at the air in frustration. "It hurt too much."

Her mother was silent, but when Sydney raised her eyes to her mother's, she saw compassion there. "Jessie will understand if you tell her that."

Sydney nodded. Of course, her mother was right. Or at least, she hoped so. Here she was again, needing to reconcile with Jessie for a deliberate deception. Hopefully, it was the last time.

That evening, Jessie chose to eat by herself on the side porch. Sydney slid out and sat near to her on a wicker chair. "Seems I'm apologizing to you a lot these days." She offered the hint of a smile. "Jessie, what happened years ago was so devastating for me that I quit music altogether. I shouldn't have, but I did. It was easier to become a new person that way, or so I thought. That's why I never talked about it, though I should have told you. I was avoiding the past in every way I could. That's all I can say, Jessie. It was so painful, I needed to run away.

Jessie turned her head, a frown still on her face. "Because of Emma?"

Sydney nodded. "It was so hard, and I was young, so I closed off emotionally from my former life." She cocked her head and reached out to stroke Jessie's arm. "But I think I'm coming back. The other day I bought a guitar."

"You did?" A light glimmered in Jessie's eyes.

Sydney smiled. "I wanted to try to recapture the joy I had when I played it before. I'll show it to you later."

"Okay. Um—It's okay, Mom. But is there anything else you haven't told me?"

"No, nothing. Nothing big, anyway. If anything comes to mind, I'll tell you right away."

Jessie offered a soft smile. "Okay, that works." She paused. "Would you sing one of your songs for me someday, one you wrote?"

Sydney swallowed. "If I can remember, I will. I don't know where the sheet music and lyrics are. Maybe in the attic. I'll have to look for it." Not that she'd remember how to play them, but other chords had come back to her. Maybe her compositions would too.

An hour after dinner, Sydney brought her guitar to the living room where her mother and Jessie were reading. "So, here's my guitar. I bought it used at that little music store that's been downtown forever."

Jessie reached out and slid her hand down the curve of the smooth wood. "It's nice. Have you been practicing?"

"I've fiddled around, no pun intended. Just trying to remember some chords. Do you know the B minor barre chord?" When Jessie nodded, Sydney added, "Can you show me?"

Jessie took the guitar and strummed a few chords. "You stick out your index finger like that, put it across all of these strings, then your other fingers create the rest of the chord. See?" She demonstrated the position as she spoke, then strummed.

"Sounds good. Let me try. I vaguely remember that one." Sydney tried the position Jessie had shown her. It felt strange at first. She strummed and a buzzing twang resulted. She tried it again, pushing harder on the barre. It was better the second time. How long before these chords became familiar again? She tried a few more times, and it got better each time.

"That's good, Mom. But you're not really ready for Nashville."

Sydney laughed aloud, and Jessie joined her. That was music in itself.

Chapter Twenty

Sydney got out of the shower on Monday morning and toweled dry, then ran a comb through her thick, shoulder-length hair. The mirror reflected a darker tan, highlights that weren't there before, and the serious need of a haircut.

Summer was passing like a lightning bolt and would speed even faster as the end of summer approached. Her stomach tightened with thoughts of the fall. Of her lack of prospects and her dread of going back to her job. Of course, she'd felt that for the last few years, but this year worse, not only because of the assault and the rumor, but because of Tyler and her mother.

When Tyler came back from Georgia, she'd talk to him about it. She needed a sounding board and some feasible ideas. Aside from that, she was craving his arms around her. They'd talked briefly the previous evening, when he and Zach had arrived in Athens. He said Zach seemed excited about his new school and college life. Time would tell if he and Jessie became more committed.

Maybe Tyler had called while she was in the shower. Sydney reached for her phone and there was no message from Tyler, but a message from—Wade? What did he want? Time was long past for an apology, so it couldn't be that. She listened to his message, and he asked that she call him. Nothing more.

Anger burned in her stomach at the memory, clear as a summer day, of the way he abandoned her in favor of cronyism. Then forgot to assure the faculty that she'd left for a legitimate reason. Her mind replayed in living color that awful meeting last spring in Wade's office with Rod and his parents. Wade had failed her in every possible way. It would feel so good to say to him, '*You're an embarrassment to your profession!*' No, she was working on her mouth and her faith, as she tried to abandon old strategies. *Lord, help me represent you when I talk to Wade. I don't want to be Sydney the Mouth.*

She stared at the phone for a few seconds, steeling herself against a new flood of fury, but stopped herself. *I need your wisdom, Lord. What should I do? Go back to teaching? Or do you have something else for me?*

Of course, it would be lovely to stay in Kennessey. Jessie would be thrilled. For a while, that is. Then she'd start missing her school, her friends, her youth group. She'd be bored without Zach. And what would Sydney do if they stayed? She'd already launched that argument to Tyler. It simply wasn't realistic. She had a home in Charlotte. Roots, relationships, routines. She'd been there for years.

Before she called Wade back, she'd check her laptop and see if there was a response from her interview. It might have gone better than she thought, and if it were positive, she'd be able to cut a clean break with Wade. They said they'd contact her within the week. Maybe today was the day.

She opened the email app on her phone and sat on the bed, scanning the messages. There was one from Eden, bless her. Eden was a faithful friend, one who would hold Sydney's feet to the fire in helping her grow. Her other friends were likely waiting for news of Sydney's revived romance with Tyler. Her mouth stretched into a small smile. She'd write a group email after she called Wade or that evening.

The smile was short-lived when she saw an email from the Emerson-Carroll Finance Company, her most recent interview. She clicked open and scanned the message, spotting the words "thank you" and "however". They'd passed her over. Rejected, despite her masterful performance when her verbal skills had been firing on all cylinders. They thanked her for her time. Assured her there had been many qualified applicants and it had been a difficult decision, blah, blah, blah.

Sydney hit 'delete' and closed the app. She ought to be more deeply disappointed since the job had been her only true lead. Again, she was at zero, after two months. The likelihood of returning to school had just risen by at least forty percent.

She blew out a puff of pressure that had built up inside her and considered her call to Wade. Not the best time, since she now had nothing to fall back on. But she needed to return his call.

Wade answered on the second ring. "Sydney, thanks for calling me back. How is your summer going?"

Conciliatory, friendly, as if nothing had happened.

"Fine, thanks. I hope yours has been good." She kept her tone cool and distant and hoped he noticed.

"I think you'll be interested in this piece of news. Rod Matheson, the student who assaulted you, recently assaulted someone else. He was drunk at a party and got into a fight. That person has decided to press charges."

She bit her lip. "I can't say I'm surprised."

"When this happened, I realized you really had a legitimate case last spring."

Boiling began deep in Sydney's stomach. *Easy, girl.* She took a deep breath. "So, you decided I wasn't lying or exaggerating after all because it happened to someone *else*?"

Wade let out an uncomfortable laugh. "No, of course I didn't think you were lying, Sydney. I never said that to you. But now, with this second case, we realize it's a pattern, and he needs help. I've spoken to his parents and made some recommendations." Which he said he'd do last spring.

Sydney blinked and drew in another calming breath. "Well, I'm glad that other victim was important enough to you to realize it was a problem. I apparently was not."

"Sydney, you're still angry after all these months." Wade must be clairvoyant or extremely observant.

"After the way you dealt with the aggression last spring *and* the way you refused to protect my reputation with the faculty, I realized that I was nothing to you. Rod could have seriously hurt me for all you cared. That was a bald fact that I had to swallow, but I did. And if any other student assaulted me or worse, it was simply too bad for me."

"Now, that's going a bit far. I wouldn't have let anything happen to you or any of my teachers."

"You could have fooled me."

Silence filled the line. Then, "I'm sorry you feel that way. I thought you'd be relieved that you were sort of, I guess, vindicated. Don't know if that's the best word."

He didn't say, "I'm sorry I let you down," or "I'm sorry I didn't stand up for you." *Her* feelings were the problem, not his failure.

"If I had been suspected of doing something wrong, the word would be just fine. But since I wasn't, I had nothing to be vindicated *for*. You should have stood behind *me*, not Rod, when he assaulted me. And you should have notified the faculty that I was not dismissed for conduct but had been attacked. Well, that's on you, Wade. You can feel bad about that if you want to, and you should. But I don't want to work under a principal who doesn't give a flip about the safety of his teachers."

"What—what are you saying?"

"I'm saying I quit." Don't know where that came from, but it felt so good. Powerful and energized.

"Sydney, you realize it's early August. You'd have had to turn in your resignation much earlier."

"Oh, I'm sorry I didn't respect your calendar. I didn't decide to quit until just now, so I couldn't have resigned any sooner. My apologies for the inconvenience." She hadn't raised her voice at all, yet Sydney the Mouth was still in evidence. But it didn't seem like such a bad thing this time. "I'll send my resignation to you today."

Another uncomfortable chuckle. "It's late in the summer. It's going to be hard to find a new teacher by September. And the students love you. You're one of our most popular teachers."

"I'm glad I left a good legacy, then. I'm sure you'll find someone else. Find a young lady fresh out of student teaching. She'll be naïve enough not to realize the proper role of her principal."

Wade ignored her jab. "She'd never be able to handle high school students in math. They're a tough crowd."

"Yes, I saw that. They even attack their teachers with impunity."

Gently, he said, "Sydney, please. Think it over. I'll hold your position for you for another few days or even till the end of the week."

"No need. I'm done. You've cured me from wanting to teach in public school." That wasn't quite accurate. She'd been cured for at least three years. "Good luck, Wade."

When they hung up, Sydney stood still in her bedroom. She looked down at the screen of her phone. Yes, it felt good in that moment to retaliate by quitting her job. But now, she was unemployed. Officially jobless.

She grabbed her phone again and sent a group text to her friends. *Just quit my job. Wanted to let you know. More later! Love Sydney*

She'd have to let God handle her reputation, since she wouldn't be there to do it. After letting her new status sink in and feeling little aside from relief, she went downstairs and found her mother trimming potted ferns and geraniums on the front porch. Before getting her attention, Sydney took a moment to breathe in the breeze carried by the shade and the splash of color from the flowerpots.

She said, "Mom, news flash. Want to hear?" Her mother turned, and Sydney recounted her conversation with Wade. "I quit, Mom."

Carolyn stood still with her pruning shears in one hand and blinked a few times. Sydney braced for her mother's criticism for her irresponsible behavior. Instead, the tiniest of smiles stretched the corners of her mother's mouth. "Good. I'm glad you quit, Sydney."

"You are?"

"Yes. You weren't happy anymore. And that young man who pushed you—" She shook her head and her lips tightened to a grimace. "You did the right thing. And I hope you told your principal off, too."

Sydney laughed. "In a way. I used my best snarky but cold voice. I think he got the picture. But now—" she shrugged, "Now I'm unemployed. The other day you said you thought I should stay there because I've put in so many years."

Her mother waved the air and shook her head. "No, I've changed my mind. There's no rule that says you should stay in a job because you've been there a long time and you've built up a pension. Pensions are good, but not if you're unhappy. You're young enough to do something else that you'll like better. My word, how many people who work in all kinds of jobs are former teachers?"

Sydney couldn't suppress a grin then. "You're right, Mom." She stepped forward and threw her arms around her surprised mother for a stiff hug. "Thank you."

଼ଥ   ଼ଥ   ଼ଥ

With a casserole heating in the oven and Jessie making a salad for them, Sydney had time to check her phone and hopefully talk to

231

Tyler. She'd texted him earlier but had said nothing about her job situation. He'd texted back to say he'd call later and included a few heart emojis, which made her smile.

She closed her bedroom door and texted him. *Is this a good time to talk for a minute? Not long, just touch base.*

The phone rang immediately, and the warmth of his voice flooded through the phone to her waiting ears. "I miss you."

She laughed. "The feeling is mutual. Tell me how it's going down there." She'd wait patiently to give her news. She sat down on the bed and leaned back against the pillow shams.

"We had some meet and greet type things this morning and tomorrow he'll get a tour of the campus, the dorms and all that. We're staying in a dorm now, but they'll show him the other buildings. Kids who live further away have the option to do the tour when they arrive for the fall semester, but Zach jumped at the chance to come early. He has one other school in mind and wanted to see this campus so he could compare them."

"Understandable. Why did he choose U of G?"

"It's good for graphic arts and not too far from his mother or me. Georgia is his home, I guess, so that counts, too. I'm glad his mother and I will be paying in-state tuition."

"Yeah, for sure. I forgot he was raised down there. I'm glad you have that time together as father and son. It's a kind of rite of passage."

"True. It's a thrill for me to do this with him, like my father did for me."

Silence fell for a moment. Sydney's mind went to the college visit Tyler had made with his father, the one where he crossed that bridge, leaving her behind with their child. Suddenly, she didn't know what to say. "That sounds nice."

"It should have been." His voice became quiet. "I'll be honest with you, Sydney. It was torture. I second-guessed myself all the way through freshman year, but couldn't share any of it with my dad, since he didn't know about Emma. I kept wondering if I'd lost you forever or if I still had time to be her dad. To marry you. I thought about it almost every day. I wondered what that would have been like, but knew it was too late."

Sydney blinked, and for an instant, felt his pain instead of her own. "So, you acted excited for your dad's sake even though you were in turmoil."

"Yeah, I did. I remember feeling like a fake, a liar, a terrible Christian, and a generally despicable person."

She swallowed, and heaviness formed in her stomach. Would they ever get past the shadow of that event? "I'm sorry you felt that way. It should have been a fun time for you, like it is for Zach." Their conversation had taken an unintended turn. "Here we are again. So, how about if I change the subject? I quit my job today."

"You what?" Surprise rang in his voice, and then he laughed a hearty rumble.

"You're laughing. I'm two steps from being destitute in the street with my child and you're finding humor." She had to chuckle, joining his jubilation.

"I'm laughing because I'm glad you did it. But please tell me what happened. I'm dying to know."

"Bet you are! Well, my principal, Wade, called me this morning for the first time since last April. *April*! The man hasn't given me a second thought in four months, except when he emailed me back about the rumor. He informed me that Rod, my aggressor, assaulted someone else, so my case has more legitimacy, since it's now a pattern."

"What a weasel."

Sydney grinned, enjoying Tyler's support. "The reason for his call was to inform me of that and vindicate me, as he said—"

"Vindicate you? For *what*?"

"Exactly. He didn't apologize for what happened or not standing up for me. He wanted to let me know that Rod was in big trouble now. As he should have been to begin with. So, I told him I didn't want to work in a place where I'm not supported or protected."

"Excellent. You did well."

"Thank you, though I am still unemployed."

"I told you I'd help you come up with a plan. Don't worry, Sydney."

"You know, I'm not as worried as I probably should be. I keep having to remind myself I'm not a teacher anymore."

"Are you relieved?"

"Yes."

"That's answer enough, in my mind. How did your mom respond?"

She heard Zach saying something in the background. "Believe it or not, she was supportive. Imagine that!"

"I'm so glad. We'll be back by three or so on Wednesday. When can I see you?"

"Won't you be tired after driving for six hours?"

"Not too tired to see you. I'm sure Zach and Jessie will want to catch up, too."

"We could come over and bring you supper. Where do you guys live?"

"In my parents' old house. You remember where that is?"

"Yes, I remember." Her voice was soft. She reached out in the air with one hand, wishing she could touch his face. Soon he'd be back. She had to savor his presence while she could before she left Kennessey and faced job hunting in Charlotte.

When she hung up, Sydney looked at her watch, still smiling at Tyler's response to her new dilemma. She'd have to compose a fast resignation letter before the day was out. The thought made her grin. She'd also send a farewell email to her colleagues in the math department and explain the events behind her transition. That was all she could do. It would have to be enough.

Sydney had made lasagna for dinner. It was heavy for a summer meal, but her mother loved it. She had fifteen minutes before the casserole would finish cooking, so she'd sneak up to the attic and see if she could locate her notebook of compositions. She hoped the paper was still intact, that is, if she even found the notebook.

For the second time that summer, Sydney pulled down the folding attic staircase and ventured up into the dark space. It would be fun to surprise her mother and Jessie.

Fortunately, the attic was neatly arranged. Sydney's first impulse was to look for the notebook in the same area where she'd found the guitar. Her mother was an orderly woman and might have kept them in the same place. She scrambled toward the wall where the roof narrowed and saw only cardboard boxes. Several had her name on them. She should look through these anyway, but for now, she needed to find one in particular.

Not seeing any other way, Sydney opened each box. Some had packing tape, which she pulled away like a dusty zipper. In the fourth box, she saw something familiar, an orange three-ring binder where she'd kept her compositions. She opened the binder and on the inside cover, there was a heart drawn in magic marker, *Sydney loves Tyler*. She touched the inscription tenderly, as if it were a delicate flower. The pages inside were wavy and faded with age, but maybe there'd be enough to decipher and recall.

She descended the staircase, her notebook under one arm, and folded the ladder up into the ceiling. She left the notebook on her bed and went downstairs to finish preparing the meal. When Sydney entered the kitchen, Jessie was at the counter fixing the salad. "Hello, my dear child. How was work today?" She gave Jessie a hug, then opened the drawer to search for an oven mitt.

Jessie shrugged. "Kind of slow. I miss Zach. When did you say they're coming back?"

"Wednesday. I talked to Tyler this afternoon and told him we'd come over when they got home. We can take dinner to them since they'll be tired from the trip. Sound good?" She opened the oven and pulled out the steaming casserole dish of lasagna.

"Yes, definitely. Mmm. That smells good. It's Gram's favorite."

"That's why I made it. Jessie, I quit my job today."

Jessie turned away from her bowl of raw spinach. Her eyes and mouth went round with surprise. "You did?"

Sydney told her a brief version of her conversation with Wade.

"So, what are you gonna do? We'll still be able to, like, eat and stuff, won't we?"

Sydney laughed. "Of course, we will. God will provide. And don't worry, things will come together. It's not like I don't have skills."

Jessie looked doubtful. "You seemed more worried before, like, ever since we got here. Now, suddenly, you're not."

"Yeah, that's true. I've learned a lot about faith since I got here. And it just seemed so wrong to me to go back. I couldn't do it."

"I'm glad, then. It's wrong for kids to push you around."

"Thank you. I agree. So, you really missed Zach. Are you getting some mushy feelings about him?"

Jessie's face colored, answering Sydney's question. "I guess a little bit."

"So, are you two going out now?"

"We haven't talked about that, since I told him I didn't know how I felt. I'll tell him before he goes to school. Won't that be weird, Mom, since you're going out with Tyler?"

Sydney shook her head. "I don't think so. It's more of a fun coincidence, don't you think? Really, we don't know what will happen in either relationship. But you two can stay in touch while he's in college and things will either go forward or not. No pressure."

Jessie nodded. "Yeah. I guess so."

"Are you ready with that salad?"

Later, Jessie and Carolyn were reading in the living room, which had become a new and peaceful nightly habit. Sydney came in with her guitar and the orange notebook and sat down. They looked up at her.

"What's that?" Her mother lowered her glasses on her nose and peered over them.

"I found my old compositions in the attic."

"Oh, that's wonderful. I hope they're legible. It's been so long." Carolyn pulled off her glasses and folded them, as if preparing for a concert.

"Play a song, Mom. I want to hear one of your compositions." Jessie set her book face-down on the end table.

Sydney shot her a glance. "Don't expect too much. I haven't seen these in decades. And I barely remember how to even play. Here's one I remember. It has easy chords, so hopefully I won't make an idiot of myself in front of my loved ones."

"Oh, Sydney." Her mother waved the air, but there was a smile on her face.

"*Every day—* is that how it goes? *All day long I look for You, I see Your love in all you do for us, how I love Your love for me.* Something like that." Suddenly, Sydney felt embarrassed. "Anyway, I'll practice these and do a proper concert when I'm ready."

"No, keep playing, Mom." Jessie leaned forward. "Play another one. Just one."

Sydney took a deep breath. What had she started? "Okay, just one more." She tried the chords first, recalling the melody. She remembered this one, because she'd sung it by herself from time to time over the years. "*You never said it would be smooth and easy, but You promised You'd be there and never leave. Each step of the way, You've held my hand faithfully, without You, Lord, how empty life would be.*"

"I remember that one," Carolyn said softly. "It was my favorite."

"You sing pretty, Mom. You should sing more. Which ones did you sing in church?"

"I don't remember." Sydney's gaze went from Jessie to her mother. "I've got some catching up to do."

"I'll get my guitar and we can play some songs we both know." Jessie left the room.

"I must have a cassette tape somewhere of the ones you did with your band, you know, all the church people with their instruments. You used to practice here in the dining room, like your father did." Her mother paused, as if trying to recall. "I don't know where I put it. Maybe in my closet. I would have wanted to protect it from the heat of the attic. If I find it, we'll have to find something to play it on."

"It would be fun to hear it." And it would be strange to hear. Was she ready to go back there?

Maybe now she was ready.

Chapter Twenty-One

Streams of perspiration dripped down Sydney's neck and into her eyes. She pulled a bandana from her pocket and mopped her face. Enough weeding for one sweltering August morning. Though she'd started before seven, once she was into it, she wanted to finish and now the sun burned without mercy.

She collapsed into a patio chair she'd set up under the carport and reached for her thermos of iced herbal tea. Several icy gulps later, her breathing returned to normal.

The looming tension of her teaching job was blessedly absent, though a new one threatened to sprout in its place. Her August deadline was more fluid now or would be except for Jessie's school year around the corner. It was time to dive into a completely new career, one Sydney would need to identify on her own and quickly. Maybe Tyler was right, and she had enough skills to find something easily. Yet her two failed interviews told a different story.

Sydney rose and went inside to shower. Afterward, she checked her phone, out of habit rather than expectation. A text from Jessie saying she'd be at to the golf course after her shift, and a phone message from the Triangle Investment Corporation.

She sank down on the bed, curious. She'd had no news from the company since the automated thank you letter a full month earlier. Sydney had written them off. She dialed into her voicemail and listened to the message. "Hello, this call is for Sydney Bennett. This is Shenay Brewster from the Triangle Investment Corporation. I'm calling to offer you a level one analyst position with our company. Normally we'd arrange a second in-person interview, but due to some staffing changes, we have a greater need to fill this position quickly and we think you'd fit perfectly. Please give me a call, Sydney, at your earliest convenience. I look forward to hearing from you."

For several seconds, Sydney stared at the phone as the news sank in. Her life was about to turn a corner, just as she'd hoped. Tyler had been right. Things were coming together. And in the nick of time. Thinking of Tyler caused a swell of pain in her belly. She swallowed the lump that throbbed in her throat. Charlotte wasn't that far. Three hours. They could still see each other.

Sydney called the number for Triangle. "Hello, Ms. Brewster? This is Sydney Bennett. I was pleased and surprised by your phone message."

"Hello, Sydney. Thanks for returning my call so quickly. I apologize that there wasn't any further contact for a few weeks. As I mentioned, we're doing some reorganizing, and weren't in a position to make the offer before now. I'll discuss with you the particulars of the position, the salary and benefits, and the starting date. I realize you may have other offers on the table, so I'd request that you get back to us by next Wednesday to let us know your final decision."

For the next few minutes, Ms. Brewster talked about the position. Sydney would work in downtown Charlotte on the fifth floor of a high-rise office building. Her salary would be over a third more than she earned after eighteen years teaching high school. Benefits were generous, and the initial three weeks' vacation per year would increase with time. Starting date, in two weeks.

Two weeks. When Sydney thanked the woman and hung up, she remained seated on the edge of the bed, her thoughts whirling like a fall storm. She would have returned to Charlotte in two weeks anyway if she hadn't quit her teaching job. Almost as an afterthought, she said aloud, "*Thank you*, Lord, for this new job. You're never late, you're just in time." She tried to smile. She'd have a new challenge, new colleagues, new friends on the job. No more papers to grade. When work was over, it was over. She could spend her evenings doing other things besides preparing for the next day and grading homework.

And the salary was huge compared to what she was used to. She could pay for Jessie's college, put a new roof on the house. She'd have money to take Jessie on a senior trip, visit Tyler and her mom regularly. Financial stress would be a distant memory. Job stress too. Probably.

She was glad. Yes, she was. Thankful. Really. But she knew two people who wouldn't be.

ʘ ʘ ʘ

Sydney's gaze roved to the people seated left and right of her. Anxiety and contentment surged through her, an incompatible mixture leading to more anxiety. On the one hand, all five of them were in church that day, including her mother, and they took up nearly half a row. Like a family.

On the other hand, she'd hadn't told Jessie or her mother about her job offer, trying to decide the least damaging way to disappoint them. She'd mentioned it to Tyler at dinner the previous evening, then minimized it and quickly changed the subject. His expression had changed, but he hadn't said much.

How would she go back to Charlotte for an undetermined period? Her hand lay in Tyler's, and it felt so good. She'd missed him while he was in Georgia. They'd talk more later about the job, and he'd give her the courage to tell Jessie.

Apparently, the three-day absence and the prospect of Zach soon leaving had made Jessie's heart grow fonder. She confessed to

241

being about thirty percent less platonic toward Zach than before. Sydney had to laugh. "I can tell your mother's a math teacher."

After the service, Sydney turned to Tyler. "Can you guys come over for lunch? Nothing fancy, but we'd love to have you."

"We'll have to miss this time, hate to say." Regret infused his smile. "We have a lunch appointment with Daniel Swanson. He wanted to be able to see Zach before he left for school, so he invited us over for lunch. Remember him?"

"No, but that's okay."

"He's a good friend of mine and has enjoyed getting to know Zach too. He's leaving on vacation soon so it's his last chance to say goodbye."

"Sounds nice."

Tyler slid one arm around Sydney's shoulders and squeezed. He leaned toward her ear and whispered, "I'd much rather be with you."

It was Sydney's idea to pick up a box of fried chicken at a local place. The crusty, fried aroma filled the car on the way back to the house.

"Want to eat on the porch? Jessie and I will get it set up."

The chicken hit the spot and hadn't taken half the afternoon to cook. Sydney licked her fingers and wiped them on a napkin. Throughout the meal, Jessie was jovial, chattering about Zach. Carolyn was quieter than usual.

"Did you enjoy the service, Mom?" Maybe that was the problem. Her mother had stepped out of her routine. "I'm glad you came with us today." Sydney reached for one more spoonful of macaroni salad.

"Yes, I liked it very much. I do like your preacher. I didn't when he first came, but he was good today. And the worship, too. It's livelier than my church and I kind of miss that."

"Maybe you can come with us from now on, Gram."

Carolyn gave Jessie a muted smile. "You'll be leaving soon, and I have friends at my church. But I did like yours."

Jessie shot a pointed stare at Sydney.

"What?"

"Have you been praying about whether we should move here?"

"Yes. Have you?" She had, but her untold news fell like ten pounds of rocks in her stomach.

"I sure have. What's the Lord telling *you*?"

"He's waiting to tell me anything about anything. He likes doing that because it builds our faith."

Jessie harrumphed. Sydney's mother looked uncomfortable.

"Mom, regarding this discussion, don't worry that we're going to land on your doorstep and invade your home permanently. We'd . . ." Sydney moistened her lips. Another secret from Jessie and it was killing her. But she wasn't ready. "We'd get our own place if we end up moving here." She turned a stare back at Jessie. "Which isn't by any means certain." She leaned back and noticed again how tired her mother looked. Something wasn't right. "Mom, you can go relax if you want. Jessie and I can clean all this up."

Carolyn shifted in her chair but didn't rise. "I will, but first I need to tell you both something. I've been waiting all summer because I didn't think it was a good time. Also, I didn't *want* to tell you, since everything's been, well, so nice since you both got here."

Though her mother's words warmed Sydney, her scalp prickled with dread. She and Jessie stilled and gave Carolyn their attention. "What's going on, Mom?"

Her mother's mouth tightened, and the small creases deepened. A wave of tension rippled through Sydney, and her pulse pounded. "What is it?"

"I have cancer."

Sydney's mouth dropped open as she and Jessie stared at her. "You what? What?" Sydney's voice rose and her hand shot out to grab her mother's arm. "Did you just find out about this?"

Carolyn shook her head. "No, I got the diagnosis late spring, shortly before you got here. I didn't want to tell you until it was further along."

"And you didn't tell me? Why, Mom? Why didn't you tell me? What kind of cancer? What is your prognosis? Tell us."

Her mother held up one hand. "I'll tell you everything I can. Let's go to the living room. I'm not feeling well but I wanted to tell you before I went up to rest."

As they moved to the living room, a voice inside Sydney cried out, *Oh God, no, why now?* Tears pounded against her eyelids and pain throbbed in her throat. She blinked and kept blinking. She ought to hear the facts first. Many cancers were curable. Maybe her mother's was. She looked over at Jessie, whose face contorted as tears began to flow.

Carolyn sank down on the couch, and Jessie took the opposite armchair. Sydney slid next to her mother. Her mother gave a deep sigh and said, "It's breast cancer. They didn't catch it very early. They said it was stage three when they detected it."

"Can you get chemo or a mastectomy, or anything that will save your life?"

Her mother shook her head. "Chemotherapy isn't often recommended for people my age. It can do more damage than good. They recommended surgery and oral medications to control the spread. I don't want surgery, so I'm taking the medicine and I go back for frequent visits."

"Are you going to get better, Gram?" Jessie's voice was small.

"No, I'm afraid not, Jessie. But at least it's a slow thing. Well, we don't know how slow. I might have six months or a year left."

Sydney caught her breath, and a sob erupted. "No! Six months? Mom!"

Carolyn waved at the air. "It could be more. Could also be less. It's not an exact science because once the cancer cells multiply, they can go fast. Or the medication could help."

"I feel like we just started a new relationship, Mom." Sydney made no effort to stem the tears rolling down her cheeks. She grabbed her mother's hand, cool and bony. "You can't leave us now! Should you get a second opinion? Maybe there are other treatments you can try."

Her mother shrugged. "I've checked into some of them. Sometimes the treatments are worse than the disease. I'm sure you've heard that, and it's true. I'm seventy-six years old and I've had a good life. I have beautiful children and grandchildren and above all, the Lord Jesus. I'm ready if he wants to take me."

Sydney wasn't ready. She'd never be ready because she'd wasted her whole lifetime being angry and bitter at her mother. Maybe God brought them back to Kennessey to forgive and be forgiven before her mother went to her heavenly home. Only it was too late.

Carolyn slowly eased up to standing. "I'm going to go rest. I'm sorry I've made you both cry. God will take me when he's ready, but let's not be sad with the time we have left." She leveled a stare from Sydney to Jessie and back to Sydney. "I'm *very* happy that we've had this summer together. Please excuse me now." She trudged across the room and painstakingly up the stairs.

After a moment of paralysis, Sydney and Jessie stood at the same time. Sydney opened her arms, and Jessie fell into her embrace. For a moment, they wept together. "She didn't tell us." Jessie mumbled against Sydney's blouse. "We've been here all summer, and she never told us."

"I know. Gram's like that. She doesn't want to bother anyone, I guess. And she's an introvert."

"But we're her family. She's dying, and she never told us." Jessie pulled back. Her face was tragic.

"No, she didn't. She probably didn't want to spoil our summer."

Jessie seemed to consider that for a moment, then said, "Let's go to the beach. I feel like I gotta get out of the house."

"Good idea." She was Sydney's daughter, after all.

They walked to a stretch of beach frequented by locals and the occasional renter. Toward the end of it lay a lonely strand with a rocky outcrop and a jetty people used for fishing or picnics. Sydney and Jessie walked there together, either silent or crying softly.

Sydney gestured to a rock that jutted out a dozen or so yards into the ocean. They climbed on the top and found flat grooves where they could sit. The ocean breeze was stronger there, and the steady, cool pressure of it was soothing, healing. Sydney allowed the reality of her mother's illness to tumble through her mind as she prayed and strove for acceptance. After a while, Jessie said, "We should move here so we can take care of Gram."

Sydney pressed her lips together. Her mother's news gave fresh weight to her dilemma. She needed to spill the truth to Jessie, but instead she said, "Tyler did that for his dad when he had cancer."

"His dad had cancer too? Zach didn't tell me."

"Yeah, he did. Sadly. That's why Tyler moved back to Kennessey two years ago. Then when his dad died, he decided to stay. His uncle offered to sell him the golf courses, so here he is."

"I think we should help Gram until she goes to heaven. She'll be weaker as she gets sicker. She's gonna need our help."

"It's a big decision, Jessie, moving here. You'd regret missing your senior year in high school, wouldn't you?"

"I'll do my senior year here."

Sydney hesitated. "I need to tell you, Jessie. On Friday I got a job offer. I haven't given a response yet. I wanted to pray about it before telling you."

Jessie froze with a stare as the news sank in. Her tears returned in a fresh gush. She bowed her head and wept until she began to sob. Sydney couldn't bear it and turned away, her insides feeling ripped to shreds. Tears stung her eyes. After several agonizing moments she said, "Jessie, I've lived in Charlotte for twenty-six years. I have history there. So do you." She spoke without conviction, though her words were true.

Jessie drew a tissue from her shorts and blew her nose. "But you grew up here, so you have history here, too. Don't you like it here, Mom?" Her voice croaked.

"Yes, you know I do. I didn't think I did, because of my bad memories. But this summer has changed that and brought me back to things I like. But I like Charlotte, too. The bottom line is I have a job there waiting for me. I *don't* have one here."

Wind whipped her hair into her face. She moved it behind her ear. Before Jessie had a chance to retort, Sydney added, "I need more time to think and pray, Jessie. Everything is so sudden, Gram's illness. This job. I could turn it down if I had anything else. And my relationship with Tyler is new. You can't count on our past together. We're different people now, so it's like a brand-new relationship. There's just too much to think about." Her final words, mostly to herself, disappeared in the wind.

As she thought about her mother, the job, Tyler, the weigh was crushing.

As they left the beach and headed back to the car, Sydney said, "Jessie, I need to spend some time with Tyler. Do you want to come with me and hang out with Zach?"

Jessie shook her head. "I need to be alone tonight. I'll talk to him later."

"Okay. You don't mind if I go if Tyler's available?"

"No, go ahead."

Before starting the car, Sydney texted Tyler. *Are you free for me to pop over for a little while? I need to talk.*

By the time they reached home, he had responded. *Yes, absolutely. Come on over whenever you can.* "He's free, so I'll drop you here and go, okay?" Sydney pulled into the driveway and let Jessie out.

Tyler's house was an attractive ranch on a peaceful, roomy lot with clusters of towering pine trees. It looked different from the house he'd grown up in, since he'd done some painting and a couple of renovations and had brought his own furniture.

She poised her hand to knock, and he opened the door. Seeing his face brought her strength, though a fist of grief followed. He gathered her in his arms and held her for several minutes. The previous evening, they'd dined together on a romantic terrace. Since that time, her world had shifted on its axis.

He loosened his arms and leaned in to kiss her. She responded with hunger and despair. When they pulled apart, he smiled until he saw tears puddled in her eyes. "Hey. What's going on?" His voice was gentle like silk. He drew her into the house. "Let's sit on the deck in back. I'll get us some cold drinks."

Sydney nodded mutely and followed him through the house to the deck. When they were seated, she said, "My mom has cancer."

Tyler's brow furrowed. "Oh, no. "That's terrible news." He grasped both her hands. "Did she just tell you this today?"

"Just after lunch. Did you know?"

"No, I didn't. I don't see her a lot or haven't until I started seeing you. I'm so sorry." He reached up and stroked her cheek, wiping a tear away with his thumb, then pulled her in for a hug.

She let his warmth steal over her for a moment, then pulled back. "I know you've been through this. I haven't been close to my mom for most of my life, but this summer, everything changed. And now, I'm going to lose her." Her voice broke. A sob and a wave of new tears escaped. "There's never good timing for cancer, but now we won't be able to enjoy our new relationship."

"You have the present, Sydney." He cocked his head and met her eyes. "And you came this summer. As you said, everything changed."

"Yeah." She lowered her eyes. Little was better than nothing. The hardest was yet to come, but at least they were more connected now. She met his eyes and swallowed. "I—I told Jessie today about the job offer. She took it hard."

At her words Tyler's lips tightened. "Have you decided to take the job?"

Sydney buried her face in her hands for a moment, unable to look at him. She lifted her head. "I don't think I have a choice, Tyler. It's the only offer I've got."

"I don't want to influence you, Sydney. If you feel that's what you have to do, we'll find a way to see each other. But keep in mind, there are jobs in Kennessey too. And even more in Wilmington, which is close."

She sighed. "All summer Jessie's bugged me to move here, which surprised me, because she'll be a senior and has her friends in Charlotte. And now, there's my mom." Hastily, she added, "And you, of course. You're a compelling reason, but we're kind of new."

Tyler didn't respond for a moment. "You have to be comfortable with the decision. You know your mom will need help later on. Unless one of your brothers could help."

Her head jerked toward him. "No, not them. It would be *my* place. They have their families and careers, but now I might have one too. Oh, Tyler, it's a terrible decision to have to make. Anyway, I didn't come here to talk about a possible move. I have so much on me now, it's hard to think clearly about anything."

He reached out to caress her arm. "I know it's a lot. Selfishly speaking, *I'd* like you to move here. I missed you when I was in Georgia, and that was only a few days. But I don't want to pressure you."

She leaned toward him. "I missed you, too, Tyler. But I don't know how I can give up a job offer when it's all I have." She paused. Yes, there was something else. "Along with that, I, um, I don't want to be impulsive."

He reached for her hands. "Are you concerned about us?"

"I feel like—" How could she say it? *I feel like I'm falling in love with you, but I don't want to get devastated again.*

"Yes?"

"Sometimes I feel like, well, I'm falling fast and I'm afraid."

"Sydney," he drew her hands to his lips for a feather-light kiss. "We're both taking a chance here. But so far, so good, right? I'm falling fast for you, too. I feel God has blessed us in spite of our mistakes by giving us a second chance. Don't you see it that way?"

Sydney nodded. "I do, absolutely. But I sometimes wonder—" *if it's too good to be true.* The thought hit her broadside. Is that what was holding her back? With or without the job?

He smiled. "We'll take it one day at a time, but we have to trust God at some level. I guess I've learned that through all the years of guilt I carried. Then when you walked into the clubhouse that day, I felt like he was smiling at us."

"I hope you're right about that, even though the past doesn't vanish. Sometimes I wonder about your guilt. Could any of this possibly be—" she hesitated, "some kind of penance?"

Tyler's eyes widened, and his body jerked slightly backward. "Penance? What do you mean?"

"Well, this summer the subject of Emma kept coming up in one way or another, like a phantom. Sometimes I sense that you still feel a lot of guilt, but maybe you'd feel less guilty if we can make it work now. That might not be in your mind, but it might be subconscious. I just wanted to be sure—" Her words came out in a rush. She shrugged and spread her hands.

Tyler's face had closed, and his brows furrowed. "Is that what you think?"

"No! Tyler, it's just a question." What had she done? "We have an open relationship and I wanted to bring it up, just in case. I'm a mathematician. I think of all the angles." A wave of heat filled her face. If only she could take back her words. But as she considered the job, she had to know.

"Well, stop thinking of all the angles. That'll make you miserable, Sydney. I'd never thought of the idea of doing penance. I feel a lot for you. It's not coming from guilt over my past actions." A hard edge had entered his voice.

"For which I forgave you, don't forget."

"Yes, I know. Or so you've said. But have you, really?"

Her brows knit. "Yes, of course, Tyler. I just want to make sure you forgave yourself to the point that it doesn't ever stand between us."

"We can't guarantee it will never come up in our conversation. It exists. Emma exists. And soon, you may hear from her. We can't erase the past."

She sighed in frustration and fell back against the couch. "I'm not trying to erase it. I just don't want it to shadow what we're developing *now*. It's hard to have water under the bridge like we do. We aren't starting from zero."

"Like I said, we'll take it one day at a time." His voice grew softer. "We won't bring up the past if it makes you feel better."

She wasn't getting anywhere. "Tyler, just forget what I said to you. I wasn't trying to create a problem. I've got a lot on my mind, and that thought of penance came to me the other day. I wanted to bring it up but didn't mean to offend you."

"I'm not offended. You *are* under a lot of stress and have big decisions to make. I'd like to walk with you through it. I hope you'll trust me one day." His voice dropped. "Though sometimes I wonder if it's too late. Maybe you'll never trust me."

Something in his voice chilled her. They hadn't had any conflict since finding each other again, even though she knew it would happen sooner or later. This wasn't really a conflict but didn't feel good, either. They couldn't change the events of thirty years earlier. Was it possible to find a happy, stable relationship with such a shaky foundation? Had God indeed made all things new for them?

Or were they trying to force things because they both still stumbled under guilt and regret from the past?

An hour later, Sydney drove home. Her parting with Tyler wasn't as warm as it had been just hours ago. Had she just ruined everything once again with her mouth? She shook her head. Wouldn't surprise her at all. She had a history of doing that and hadn't learned much from the pain it caused. "Oh, Tyler." Tears slipped out of her eyes as she drove, blurring the stoplights. Thoughts of her mother's illness, on hold during her tense conversation with Tyler, flooded back and tears poured down her cheeks.

She wouldn't even think of Jessie's anguish at returning to Charlotte. Despite Tyler's assurance of wanting to help, she felt utterly alone.

Chapter Twenty-Two

Sydney tossed in bed for most of the night, rewinding her conversation with Tyler, the news from her mother, the load of her decisions. Finally, she gave up trying to sleep and slipped from her bed. She tip-toed past Jessie's room and down the stairs, then out to the back porch. The night air was cooler than inside the house. A swath of moonlight painted the wood planks with a soft glow. Sydney breathed deeply of the sweet scent of gardenia blooms lacing the air.

She settled into a lawn chair and tucked her knees up under her linked arms. They'd been in Kennessey almost three months and during that time, life had turned upside down. She'd come to search for Emma, but while she awaited a response from the Treadwells, she'd shoved those thoughts far away, as weightier matters filled her mind. She'd quit her job and a new one dangled before her, a gift she would have grabbed a month earlier. She was about to lose her mother and might have unwittingly pushed Tyler away. She'd closed him out of her life many years ago. *She'd* been the one. Would she never stop making a mess of her life, or else finding herself in the middle of one despite her best intentions?

Tears should have come, but instead, gathered in her throat in a painful heap that refused to flow. There seemed no answer, but she needed one soon. She bowed her head and squeezed her eyes shut.

Let it go, I'll take it. Sydney stilled. She didn't dare believe she'd heard God's voice in her heart. It was likely wishful thinking. She'd love for him to tell her what to do, since she had three reasons to stay in Kennessey and one to return to Charlotte. Was he telling her, to let the security of the job go or do the responsible thing?

She wanted to be able to help her mother, as Tyler had done when his father was dying. God could provide in either case, whether she moved or didn't. Was she simply being stubborn? Or terrified?

Take a risk and let me handle the outcome. Just keep moving forward. I'll go before you.

Was he saying she should move? No, he was telling her first to rest in his strength. To listen to her heart and not allow fear to stop her from hearing. What was her heart saying? What did she *want*? Was his answer there in plain sight evidenced by her desires? A door had opened in Charlotte while a different one beckoned in Kennessey.

But she was afraid. Afraid of giving her heart again to Tyler. Afraid to refuse the only job opportunity she had. Afraid of losing her mother, of disappointing Jessie. Life in Charlotte had been pressured, sometimes dull, often lonely. But predictable.

Her mind followed the same cycle at least two more times— *Take a risk. I'm there. Don't be afraid.*

Lord, I'm afraid.

I'm here, just keep moving toward your heart. I'm there too.

Finally, something inside seemed to break, and her resistance tumbled like rusty chains. *I'm not alone. I never was. You can catch me, whatever happens. Even if I follow my heart against what's rational.*

It was too hard handling everything alone, so why did she choose it when she didn't have to? Tension in her muscles fell away, and she felt gloriously small in the presence of a loving Father who knew exactly what to do.

Then the tears came. Tears of relief, of renewal. And a lightness she couldn't define and wouldn't refuse anymore.

ଊ   ଊ   ଊ

The following morning, Sydney awoke after eight. She stretched, letting the late morning sun ripple over her in a warm wave. Thoughts of her encounter—her *conversation* with God— flooded back to her, and she couldn't stifle a grin. The peaceful lightness she'd received in the tiny hours of the night still seeped through her joints, her heart, her whole body that morning. Along with the certainty of what she must do.

She showered and threw on a tank and her favorite surfer shorts. She loved dressing like that all summer, like a true beach bum, though she didn't go so far as to wear her straw hat inside.

Sydney stopped herself from heading downstairs and instead grabbed her phone. The girls would want to know. Everything.

Hi, sweet friends, I have crazy news to tell you. First, thanks for praying for me this summer. I felt your prayers and needed them so much. I'll keep this short, but please pray for my mom. She has stage 3 breast cancer. That has us all torn up. Then the other day I got a job offer in Charlotte and the thing I wanted so much, well I'm not sure I want it anymore. Can you really SEE me working downtown in a high-rise wearing heels and a pencil skirt while I sit in front of a computer all day? Yes, the salary's great, but really.

So, as irresponsible as this may seem to you, I've decided to MOVE to Kennessey for a while (or longer) to help my mom. Jessie's on board to finish high school here. And of course, Tyler. Will keep you posted. Love Sydney.

Sydney pressed "send" and breathed a deep sigh. She needed them in the loop with her.

Before she reached the kitchen, the voices of her mother and Jessie reached her ears. Good thing they were together because she had news for them. Sydney entered the kitchen and greeted them with a kiss on their cheeks, something she'd never in her life done with her mother. Her mother's eyebrows lifted, but she turned back to watching Jessie mix something in a glass bowl. "Another cooking lesson? Y'all haven't done that in a few weeks." Sydney spied over their shoulders.

"It's Jessie's turn to show me what she can do," Carolyn said. "She's been in training, and now it's time for her exam."

Jessie chortled. "My own recipe. Gram's pancakes with Jessie's awesome sauce. Not sauce, really, just some nuts, chocolate chips, and strawberry chunks."

"Mmm. Can't wait." Sydney sat down and quietly enjoyed watching them together, almost bursting with the desire to inform them they'd benefit for months to come with cooking opportunities.

Finally, the pancakes were finished, as was Sydney's first cup of coffee. They sat around the kitchen table, prayed, then dug in. As they were finishing the first round of pancakes, Sydney told them, "Hey, stay here a minute at the table. I have some news for you girls."

She looked pointedly at Jessie. "You asked me yesterday if I'd heard from God about moving here. I want to let you know that I have. Just last night. He told me, yes, we should move here."

"Yaaay!" Jessie screeched, raising her arms in the air. "Gram, you better dig out all your recipes. We have some work to do."

Her mother didn't respond right away. Sydney tossed her a direct gaze. "Mom? We can get a place nearby and hang out, then when you start to get sicker, we'll take care of you. How 'bout it?"

"No."

Sydney's smile fell. "No? You don't want us here or you don't want our help? What will you do, go into a hospice facility all by yourself?"

Her mother straightened in her chair. "No, you won't get a place nearby. You'll stay here in the house." Another throaty *yay* from Jessie. "It would be ridiculous for you to rent an apartment when there are plenty of rooms here standing empty. Besides that, last I knew, you were unemployed."

"Between jobs," Sydney corrected. "It sounds a little less 'loser' to say it like that." No need to tell her mother of the job she let go.

Carolyn waved the air. "Oh, Sydney. You're not a loser because you quit your job. It was overdue. Lots of fine people are unemployed for whatever reason."

"Yes, of course. Thanks for the support. So, I've thought about this." The previous night at about three a.m., Sydney had worked the angles. Now she was on a roll. "My house is paid off, so I can put the furniture in storage and rent it out. That'll give me around fifteen hundred or more cash per month. That'll help us pitch in for food, which I'll insist on doing, buy gas and other essentials. Like suntan lotion. I'll check into unemployment, though I'm not sure if I'll qualify."

"You're rent free here. Don't think you'll be paying me rent. I won't accept it." Her mother's lips were set in a firm line.

Sydney laughed and squeezed her arm. "Okay, thanks, Mom. I'll get something part-time or whatever. Wilmington isn't that far. I may find something there, since it's a bigger town. Or even some remote position I can do from here would be even better." Maybe the analyst position? Or a different one?

"You can substitute teach," offered Jessie.

"Yes, I can do that. If I get desperate." The toddler department at Macy's would be a better fit.

"You may qualify for unemployment if you tell them you were in physical danger. Your student attacked you and your principal didn't protect you. You might have a case."

Sydney nodded appreciatively toward her mother. "Maybe you should have been a lawyer instead of a pharmacist, Mom."

"Tyler will give you some more ideas." Jessie leaned forward on her elbows. "He knows everybody in this town. He'll know of an opening somewhere."

At the mention of Tyler's name, some of Sydney's jubilation seeped out like a leaking balloon. She'd felt a distance when she left his house the night before. She wanted to see him and hoped the feeling was mutual. To set things right, to reassure herself. "Good point." Her head bobbed a nod.

"Once you get up to speed with your guitar, you could make an album or sing at a bar." Jessie's impish grin was so cute, Sydney didn't know if she should hug her or smack her blond curls.

"I think that could be categorized as stand-up comedy more than musical entertainment, but thanks for the idea. Don't think I'll pray about that one, though."

The three of them brainstormed for a few more minutes, then Sydney felt she had to get real. "Okay, daughter. If you're changing schools, you'll need to register. I assume you'll attend the same high school I did if it still exists centuries later. We'll have to go back to Charlotte for a bit and hire a mover, find storage, find a renter—" Sydney fell back against her chair. "I'm exhausted already."

"No need to be in a hurry, Sydney," her mother said, a soothing calm in her voice. "Just get Jessie enrolled in school and take the rest a bit at a time." Yes, good idea. Jessie could stay in Kennessey while Sydney made trips back to Charlotte to set the plan into motion.

Sydney stared for a moment at her mother. "Mom. Look into my eyes. Are you absolutely *sure* that you want two new roommates?"

Carolyn's smile broadened, and it lit up her tired face. "Very sure. Now, we have more pancakes to eat. Then you two have some work to do."

Sydney took the stairs two at a time after she had finished the breakfast dishes. She'd bring her laptop back down and check the internet for Kennessey information and phone numbers.

Her phone sat on the bedside table, its rapidly flashing light signaling a phone message. Might be a fast response from one of her girlfriends, shocked by the upheaval in her life. She opened it and with a wave of relief that stung her eyes, saw three missed calls from Tyler. He'd left one message but called back two more times. After typing in her code, she listened to his message. "Sydney, it's Tyler. Hey, I need to see you today. I felt weird after our time yesterday and I want to try to make it right. Please call me when you get this."

Sydney's fingers fumbled with the phone keys. He answered right away. "Sydney, I'm so glad to hear from you. I'm not doing penance, really, I'm not. Your statement caught me by surprise, but when I thought about it, I could see why you'd want to make sure. And now that we've done that, we can move on, can't we?"

"Yes! Let's move on. Together, I mean." Joy must be flooding out of her pores if that were possible.

"Good, I'm so relieved. Are you free for lunch? I want to see you."

"Yes! Me too."

He laughed. "You sound pretty happy. Is there good news about your mother?"

"Uh, no, but there is news I'll share with you when we meet."

"Okay. Want to meet at twelve-thirty? The beach is hot and crowded then, but we can go to the Island Café on Rupert Street. Do you know it?"

"I'll find it."

Sydney parallel parked a few blocks from the waterfront. The café sat nestled on a side street, with its terrace in full shade. From a block away, she saw Tyler waiting for her at the door. A smile curled her lips. As she approached, he met her at the curb. She went into his arms, and they stood still for several moments, wrapped tightly together. He pulled his head away. His expression was solemn as his eyes searched her face. "I'm sorry, Sydney."

"Don't be. I'm the one who opened the can of stinky worms with my legendary mouth. Hey, maybe I could buy a muzzle for myself."

He chuckled then leaned to cover her lips with his. Neither of them cared about their public display nor the noon heat that beat directly down on them. A trickle of perspiration dripped between Sydney's shoulder blades, but she was far more aware of Tyler's warmth permeating her body as it pressed into hers.

"Let's sit over there. I put our names on the list. They said it'll be about ten minutes."

"Just enough time." Sydney and Tyler sat on a wooden bench near the café.

Tyler took her hands. "Sydney, I'll say what I said last night. I'm falling fast for you. In fact, I'm falling in love with you, with the adult Sydney. I'm not imagining some carry-over from our teenage years. And I'm not trying to redo what I did so wrong before. This is now, and—and you're a unique grown woman who I'm getting to know and love all over again." He reached up and moved a tangle of hair from her cheek.

Surprising tears stung Sydney's eyes. "Me, too. I love you, Tyler. It just feels so—risky, I guess. But God is working with me on my ability to risk. I was scared, gun-shy for so long."

"I understand. It's not like I've never hurt you before."

She blinked and caught his eyes in hers. "We're done with that, okay? It's a new era. And I have some news for you."

At that moment, she heard, "Tyler, party of two" on the speaker from the café. They stood. "Can you tell me inside, or is it super-personal?"

"I can tell you inside. I'm pretty sure you'll be happy."

Once they'd settled at a table on the terrace and ordered lunch, Sydney recounted her evening wrestling match with faith, and how God had spoken to her.

"That's why you seem so happy. He lifted your fears."

"It seems so. But then I realized he was asking me to move to Kennessey."

Tyler's eyes widened with his grin. "And give up your job opportunity?" When she nodded, he said, "Sydney, that's great. I prayed for wisdom and direction for you, but of course, wanted you to come for my sake. For our sake." He reached across the table and took one of her hands in his.

"So, I told Jessie and my mom this morning. Of course, Jessie was overjoyed. I said we'd get a place nearby, but my mom wants us to stay with her in the house."

"That sounds logical."

"Well, I didn't want to assume anything. Having a summer guest is one thing. Having those guests move in for good is another. But she was glad, and of course, it's helpful since I'm unemployed."

"For the moment. If you want to work full or part-time, you can find something easily. In fact, I may need a part-time accountant at Pine Hollow this fall. That's the name of my other golf course. You did say you knew some accounting, right?"

"I would think so. I taught it for years. Thanks, Tyler. Maybe I'll try it. We can talk more when the dust settles and see whether my accounting skills are anything like my golf skills." She grinned.

"And of course, you'll get free green time as an employee. But you'd have gotten that anyway, since you have friends in the right places."

Sydney shook her head and laughed, fanning her face with splayed fingers. "Oh my, you're overwhelming me, Tyler. Free green access? I'll need to take care of the priority stuff first. Like enrolling Jessie, emptying my house and renting it. That'll help financially. Wow." She took a breath. "So much change at once. I can't believe we're talking about this. We haven't even talked about Emma at all today. Imagine that."

They laughed together, then Sydney took a sigh. "On one hand, I'm *so* happy I don't have to say goodbye to you." She watched his face soften as they locked eyes. She reached her other hand across the table to weave her fingers into his. "And on another hand, I'll be here to help my mom as her health deteriorates." Her buoyancy seeped out as her tone softened. She swallowed. "That day is coming, and I want to be here with her."

"Okay, lovebirds, here's your lunch." A cheerful voice interrupted their extended gaze as she placed sandwiches and sweet potato fries in front of them.

After lunch, Tyler decided to play hooky from work. He drove them to Southport, a quaint coastal town about thirty minutes south of Kennessey. For nearly two hours, they walked down historic streets and sat by the water. Sydney felt she'd fallen into a dream. Peace about the job or rather, absence of one, invaded her. And Tyler loved her. Still and anew. Ditto for her. She'd never expected such a blessing in a million years.

Tyler drove her back to the restaurant where they'd eaten lunch to pick up her car. "I guess we need to go get our respective kids, huh?" Sydney moved to get out of the car.

"That would be the responsible thing." He grinned at her. "C'mere." He pulled her close for a lingering kiss. "Thanks for spending the day with me." They locked eyes for a moment.

"Anytime." Her voice came out in a whisper.

"By the way, did you remember that Zach's leaving next week? He's going to his mom's for a few days, then will head out to freshman orientation. Daphne said she'd take him. I said okay, since he'd been with me the whole summer."

"That sounds fair if it's what Zach wants. I almost forgot he was leaving already. Jessie hasn't talked about it, but she gets a sad look when she mentions him." Sydney swallowed, imagining her daughter without her summer best friend. "We should plan a farewell for him."

"I was thinking the same thing."

Before driving to pick Jessie up from her shift at the ice cream store, Sydney checked her phone just in case she'd texted. She had, saying Zach was picking her up from work. They'd probably want to spend a lot of time together until he left. How would Jessie adapt to Kennessey this fall in a new school without Zach's friendship?

And how would Sydney feel back in Kennessey, without the familiar routines worn over so many years? Moving was a big deal. And Kennessey wasn't just a town, but the place her whole future had been upended. She'd only looked at the advantages of moving there. True, she'd lose a well-paying job. She'd still face random painful memories. But she could handle that now.

She'd lifted Jessie's heartache about leaving. And even if her mother didn't have cancer, there was Tyler. It was serious now. They loved each other. And if none of *that* were true, she knew she shouldn't be afraid. God himself had told her so.

Chapter Twenty-Three

Sydney raised her eyes from her book as the front door opened. It was eleven-thirty. Jessie looked startled when she saw the lamp lit in the living room and Sydney waiting up for her.

"Hi, Mom."

Sydney closed her book. "You're a little late, aren't you?" It was at least thirty minutes past her curfew.

Jessie nodded. "Sorry. We were talking about how it's gonna be when Zach's at college."

"Come on in and chat with your old mom." Sydney gave what she hoped was an inviting smile and gestured toward the wing chair facing her. "Are you doing okay with Zach leaving next week?"

Jessie shrugged and slid into the wing chair, letting her woven purse slide to the floor. "I'm sad. He really helped me have a great summer."

"He really did. And I'm so happy you met him, though you knew all along he'd be leaving at the end of the summer."

Jessie nodded. "Yeah. It came up so fast. Well, not really. It seems that way now."

"Have you decided to date long distance or just stay friends?" She hoped Jessie was still willing to share such things with her. Sydney had always tried to give her daughter a safe place where she could be honest about her own life and the stages of her growing up. This was the testing ground to reveal the fruit of those efforts.

Jessie sighed. "I'm still not a hundred percent sure how *much* he's more than a friend, but he kissed me and—and I liked it. So, I think that says something."

Sydney smiled and nodded. "It might. But you don't have to know right now. You'll both meet other people in the coming year. You'll make new friends. You'll see how much you miss him. He'll be back to see his dad, and you, of course. And you'll keep in touch."

"Yeah, we will. Did you have a good afternoon with Tyler?"

"Yes, really nice. We had lunch, then drove down to Southport for a little while. I really like him." She wanted to be transparent as Jessie had been with her. "I think I love him."

"I know." Jessie gave her a sly smile. "I knew, like, that first day we went to that festival. I knew before you did."

Sydney laughed. "You did, eh? Smart girl. I think I never really forgot about him."

"Maybe you'll marry him. That would be weird with Zach, wouldn't it?"

"You've mentioned that before and I don't want that to stop you from dating Zach if that's what you want. It's not like you'll become brother and sister. You don't have blood in common. Anyway, don't worry in advance." She'd try her best to take her own advice. As Jessie reached down for her purse, Sydney said, "Jess?"

Jessie looked up expectantly. Sydney took a breath. "I want you to think about something for me, okay? We've had a great summer and now Zach is going to college. You've told me you're ready to leave your Charlotte friends and your youth group and do your senior year here as the new girl. I know we've told Gram and Tyler that we're moving here, but if you're not sure or if you change your mind, that's okay. I want you to be happy with your senior year and with your decision. I can always come here a couple of weekends a month while you're at your dad's and take care of your Gram until you finish your senior year. We can make that work. Just think about it."

Jessie was silent for a moment. "That would be hard for you and Tyler, right?"

"Doesn't matter. We'll see each other when I visit. He would understand. I just want you to be happy, Jessie."

"Thanks, Mom. I've thought about it. A lot. I knew Zach was going to leave. I really like it here and I still want to move. I met some girls at church, and I have a couple friends from the ice cream store.”

“But you’ll let me know soon if you change your mind. I’m going to enroll you in school before the end of the week.”

“I will.” She leaned over Sydney to hug her. “Thanks, Mom.”

“Thanks for what?”

“For wanting me to be happy, even if it makes you less happy, because of Tyler. But if we move here, we’ll both be happy.”

After Jessie left the room to go to bed, Sydney prayed for her daughter, for her bruised heart in saying goodbye to Zach, and for her coming year in a new place. While she was at it, she included her mother’s health and her future with Tyler, and a few other details such as packing up her life in one city to begin almost from scratch in another.

Now that the pain of losing Zach had come full term, Sydney needed to make sure one last time with Jessie. She’d be disappointed if Jessie changed her mind but was willing to wait a year if she had to.

Her temptation to wonder what the coming year would bring for both of them was tempered by her prayer and her assurance that the control and burden was no longer hers.

മ മ മ

The following morning, Sydney greeted her mother in the kitchen as she was preparing her coffee and setting out her substantial pile of medications. She was more open about it now that Sydney and Jessie knew about the cancer.

“Last night I got a call from Chet.” Her mother looked up as Sydney headed for the coffee pot. “He and Kevin and their families have been down at Ocean Isle for a week, and they wanted to come up and see us after lunch tomorrow. Just the boys, not their whole families. The older kids didn’t go, and the younger ones have friends who came.”

Sydney stiffened. “How good of them to consecrate a couple hours of their vacation to visit their mother and sister.” Over the years, her brothers had vacationed and socialized together regularly with their families but had rarely invited her and Jessie, or Carolyn.

At that, Carolyn just shrugged. "At least there's that. I'm sorry you all aren't closer, but I'm glad at least the two of them have managed to be. They have a lot in common and their children get along."

Jessie would have gotten along, too, if she'd been invited. Sydney and Jessie would have felt less isolated, less alone, if they'd been more included in the family. At least that was starting to happen with her mother, even though she'd eventually lose her. A sharp pain shot through her at the thought.

"Do they know about your cancer?"

"Yes. I—I consulted with Kevin about it, you know, since he's a doctor."

"Of course." Still, it hurt more than a little that her mother had told her two brothers months ago, but only told her about the cancer two weeks earlier. Whatever her mother's reasons, there was no point in nursing a wound. Her mother was dying and she, not her brothers, would have the privilege of accompanying her in her final months. She should be—and was—immensely thankful that they'd overcome their differences that summer.

"They're coming after lunch, so I don't have to go to any trouble making a meal."

Less time away from the beach for her magnanimous brothers. Well, good. She wouldn't have to pretend for too long and they could assuage their consciences. A win-win. "How long has it been since you've seen them, Mom?"

"Chet and Emily came up at Easter and Kevin and his family came at Christmas. They call regularly, more often now to check on my health."

Sydney frowned but knew she hadn't done any better. "It'll be nice to see them." She plastered on a smile she didn't feel and was certain her mother wasn't fooled.

Sydney sat at the dining room table, which had become her office, to research her next steps for the move. Before digging into that task, she paused to read emails from Marissa, Julia, and Eden.

They were brief, but still filled up her heart with their support and promises to pray for her move and her mother's health.

When asked, Jessie hadn't seemed close to changing her mind about moving. A relief. Another relief was her reminder that she'd made other friends that summer and wouldn't be alone without Zach. She wouldn't start school without knowing anyone. The church youth group hadn't been as active over the summer but would start up the fall schedule soon. Yes, things were falling into place.

So, what was nagging on the inside ever since her conversation with her mother? Her brothers. During her normal routine in Charlotte, she could neatly block them out of her mind. They weren't close, and she didn't feel welcomed or loved by them, aside from random perfunctory phone calls in both directions.

But there was more. She'd always wanted to be accepted by them but, as a child, had been teased and ignored. As they all grew older, they'd conveniently left her out of their lives and social activities. Even before learning about her teenage pregnancy, they'd never cherished her as their little sister. True, Chet currently lived over three hours away from her in Savanah, but Kevin was only an hour and a half away in Columbia, South Carolina. In all fairness, he and Katy had raised four children, and he'd maintained a busy medical practice for years. She ought to cut him some slack.

Sydney sighed. Maybe they'd held onto their shame of her all these years, even when she'd managed to shed it. There was that black sheep feeling again, leaving an oily, rancid taste in its wake. She wouldn't feel it for months at a time, but then unbidden, it would spring up, then quietly slither away. Would she ever be rid of it for good?

Didn't matter anymore. In God's view, she wasn't a black sheep. Her mother didn't think so either. She probably should add her brothers to her "to forgive" list. It was long overdue. Not that forgiving them would magically create a close sibling bond, but she'd be free of that shadow which caused her to stumble each time it appeared.

Take the high road, Sydney. Let it go. Chet and Kevin don't define you and never have. After making a conscious, prayerful effort to let her grievances against her brothers go, she felt lighter, more prepared to believe the best when they arrived the following day for their visit. She'd likely have to make that decision a few more times before it became second nature.

The doorbell rang promptly at one o'clock the following day. Sydney hovered nearby when Carolyn opened the door. "So glad you were able come." Chet and Kevin leaned down to give their mother a hug. They both looked suntanned and wore chino shorts, brand-name polos, and loafers. Chet at fifty-three and Kevin at fifty-one, were pictures of success, entering midlife on a golden wave. At least, that's how it appeared to her.

"Hi, Sydney. Glad you're here. What's it been, a year?" Kevin asked as each brother hugged her in turn.

"Something like that. Life goes by so fast, doesn't it?" She gave them what she hoped was an affable smile. Her goal was to get through the afternoon with a bland mask of pleasant compliance, something she'd never in her life mastered.

"Let's sit in the dining room." Her mother, though weakened, still looked regal as she led them all to the dining room table, which she'd set with China luncheon plates and tall ice-filled glasses. A glass pitcher full of tea sat in the middle of the table, alongside a small bowl of lemon wedges. The air conditioner hummed a layer of white noise from the living room.

Earlier that morning, Sydney had made oatmeal bars, and their roasted sugar aroma still floated through the ground floor. Carolyn served them, along with vanilla ice cream and iced tea. "Have you all had a pleasant visit in Ocean Isle?" She slid the baked treats onto each plate.

"It's been very relaxing. So good to get away from the office and just do what I want." Chet, who had a demanding engineering job, grinned and took a bite of the oatmeal bar. "Mmm. This is great, Sydney. Had no idea you were a baker."

"Thanks. I'm glad you like them. Are the kids enjoying their time?" Silly question. What kids didn't enjoy the beach? Their youngest were teenagers now.

"Are they ever. Sean just discovered surfing, but Keenan is still into body surfing. They each have friends who came, so that's fun for them." Kevin reached for a slice of lemon. The brothers recounted some of their experiences at the beach, as well as their business lives and other projects. Sydney listened courteously and asked questions, half-hoping they wouldn't ask her anything. Her life was messier than theirs, and they might not understand that though she was unemployed and soon to be a housemate with her mother, she was pleased with her direction, if not for the steps that led her there.

"What about you, Sydney? I was surprised you'd decided to stay the whole summer. That's a first, isn't it?" asked Chet.

She was ready for that one. "Yes, it is. Jessie and I hadn't visited for a while and Mom mentioned that we could stay the whole summer if we wanted to." She looked at her mother for confirmation. "After the first week or so, we decided that was a nice idea. Jessie's been saving up for a car, so she got a part-time job. She's at work now but told me to tell you both hello."

They nodded with a smile. "Being a teacher gives you a great opportunity, then, since you have summers off. Glad you took advantage of it."

How much should she say? *Chet and Kevin's opinions don't define you.* "Actually, I decided to quit teaching and do something else. I've been unhappy the last three years."

"Not to mention, unsafe," her mother piped in. Sydney cringed. She hadn't planned to bring that up.

"What do you mean?" Kevin leaned forward.

Sydney sighed. "Last spring, a student physically attacked me, but I had no support from my principal. The whole incident helped me make the decision to resign."

"Oh, that's too bad. Were you hurt?"

"A little bruised. I'm glad the kid didn't have a gun or a knife."

"Yeah, totally. So, what will you be doing instead?" Chet's smooth voice came out as if she'd told him she'd decided to go shopping.

So glad you weren't murdered on the job, but the real question is, do you have another one lined up? Sydney held her tongue. "I got an offer for an analyst job but in view of Mom's cancer, I thought it would be good for us to stay on here so we can help her. Jessie liked the idea, too, so this week I'll enroll her in the high school for the fall."

Both brothers raised their eyebrows and exchanged a glance. "Oh, really? That's a dramatic change, but it'll be a help to Mom, won't it, Mom?" Chet turned his gaze to Carolyn.

"Yes, of course. For now, I'm getting along fine on my own, though it *is* nice to have Sydney and Jessie here."

"So, you'll be *moving* back to Kennessey?" Kevin leaned forward, as if he hadn't fully caught up with the conversation.

"Yes, Jessie and I will be moving here. I'll put my house up for rent and leave everything in storage for the time being." She felt vulnerable to their judgment and couldn't help her flow of thoughts—*you're coming back here after leaving in a cloud of shame when that guy knocked you up—*

That guy, who she loved with all her heart. What would they say to that?

Suddenly, she couldn't care less what they'd say or what they thought. The way they treated her or their current opinions about her didn't define her. "Oh, and another interesting twist in the Sydney story. I've reconnected with Tyler Hoffman. Remember him? He moved back to Kennessey a couple years ago when his dad was sick."

"You mean the guy who—"

"Yes, the very same." She smiled sweetly. "It was a big surprise to run into him again after thirty years. He owns the Silver Lake and Pine Hollow golf courses now."

Kevin's brow furrowed, as if he couldn't keep up with the story. Sydney stifled a chuckle. She wouldn't mention her romance with Tyler and hoped her mother wouldn't, either.

"That's great, Sydney. I guess you guys lost touch after—after college. But I'm especially glad that you'll be here to help Mom out. That's a big relief for me, since I live so far away."

"Yes. I thought it was a good idea for all of us."

The phone rang in the kitchen. Her mother slid her chair back. "I should get this. I'm expecting a call-back from the doctor's office about some tests they ran last week. Excuse me for just a minute. Have some more oatmeal bars, boys." She left the room and went to the kitchen.

An awkward silence ensued. "I don't know what tests those are, so we'll see what she says." Sydney shifted in her chair, tempted to eat another oatmeal bar only to break the tension by doing something with her hands.

"It's nice that you're able to spend more time with Mom. I guess this is a first, the whole summer. And now you're moving here. Just when she's told us about her cancer." Chet linked his fingers across his still-slim midsection, with an expression on his face she couldn't discern.

Sydney's scalp prickled. "Of course, I was in shock and very upset. She hadn't told me before, so it came as a huge surprise."

"I bet it did. So, you came running back."

She furrowed her brows. "No, I told you, she invited us to stay the summer and once we got here, we decided to take her up on her offer. Then a few weeks or so *after* that, she told us—Jessie and me—about her cancer. You both knew about it before, but no one told me. No one in the *family* told me. I was kept in the dark by my whole *family*." She kept her voice level and stared back at her brothers. "So, I don't really know what you're implying."

"Just seemed kind of convenient timing, that's all. Mom's got cancer, you show up and decide to move here, maybe afraid of missing out on something—"

The familiar boiling blood was beginning to bubble just below the surface. Just when she'd had her forgiveness revelation. *Fight my battle, Lord, direct my words.* "Just what do you mean?" She kept her tone icy and controlled, her stare unwavering. "I don't understand, so *do* explain clearly what you're insinuating, Kevin."

She knew her voice had begun to rise then but couldn't stop herself. She held up one hand. "No, on second thought, I think I understand completely. Unfortunately. You two show up here, not to do your minimum 'go see the fam' obligation or even your 'go see mom who has cancer and is going to die' obligation, so you'll feel good about yourselves as you sun on the beach. No, you came to make sure you don't miss out on any abundance that you feel entitled to, though God only knows why you need any *more* of it—"

"I resent that, Sydney." Kevin's steely voice broke through her tirade.

"Oh, I'm sorry, did I offend you, Kevin? Maybe I misjudged you. If I did, I certainly apologize. Or did I rightly interpret your statement? I think you were accusing *me* of being a gold-digger, right? That's ironic since you two showed up here today for that very purpose."

"Now wait one minute!" Chet exploded. "You've turned this whole thing around, Sydney."

"What on earth is going on in here?" Carolyn's voice rang out from the doorway. "I can't leave you all alone for two minutes." She remained standing, a familiar look on her face that told them all they were in big trouble.

"It's nothing, Mom." Sydney made sure she was the first to speak. Sydney the Mouth was out of control again. Or was she? Some things had to be said, things she'd never had the courage to say to her brothers. "Kevin and Chet came today, maybe to inquire after your welfare, but also to make sure I'm not currying favor with you, since you're soon to leave the earth. So you don't give more to me out of gratitude or pity. I want to say, Mom, that it absolutely never crossed my mind for one minute. It's my privilege to help you through the next few months of your ordeal, and I don't expect anything in return. That's the truth."

Chet stared at Sydney, his eyes smoldering like glowing coals while Kevin stared at his own crossed arms, a mutinous set to his jaw. Their mother placed her fists on her hips and stared at her sons. "I believe you, Sydney. It never crossed my mind, either." Her voice was cold. "Is it true, boys?"

When they didn't answer, their mother continued staring at them. "What are you so worried about? This house? Money? Well, I'll tell you something. You both have large houses and wealth and what have you. Though I'm proud of what you've done in your careers, I'm not proud of your behavior toward your sister. You've always been mean-spirited with Sydney. When you were boys, it seemed a common weakness among siblings, but the fact that it has continued grieves my heart. I wanted to raise sons who were kind and looked out for their sister as well as other people, like Christ would want you to do."

Sydney's mouth fell open. Never had her mother said such things. A wave of humble gratitude surged through her chest and tightened her throat.

Carolyn continued. "You're my sons, and even though right now, my anger leads me to want to cut you both out entirely, I won't do that. But this house, I'm giving to Sydney."

A collective gasp filled the room, including from Sydney. "Mom—" she began.

Her mother held up one hand. "I'll divide everything else fairly, but this house is Sydney's." She turned to Sydney and said more quietly, "I owe it to you." For a moment there was silence in the room as Sydney understood, and her brothers sat in shock.

Suddenly, her brothers began to shout. She heard the words, "family home", "our heritage", "house near a beach" but it was just noise to her. Their response confirmed her accusation against them.

Again, Carolyn held up her hand to quiet them. "Heritage or not, that is my decision. You both have plenty of money to rent whatever house on the beach you like, as you are presently doing. Or you can even buy one, and I don't understand why you haven't. Go in together and buy a house by the beach. I don't really care. Now, if you're going to argue about this, you can both just go home."

Silence fell and for a moment, no one moved. Carolyn waited in the doorway for her sons' response. They slid back their chairs. "I think we've had a big misunderstanding here." Chet's voice blustered as he stood.

"I—I'm so sorry about all of this—" began Kevin in an unsteady tone as he also rose.

"I am, too," their mother said quietly. "Very sorry. I hope you'll both think long and hard about this incident. Let it make you better men, not bitter ones. Now, I'm tired and need to rest."

After Chet and Kevin left, Sydney sat still in her chair, unsure of what to say. "Thank you, Mom. For defending me. It means a lot. And the house—I don't know what to say."

Her mother waved at the air dismissively. "They talk about family heritage. If you feel that way, too, you can keep it for posterity. You and Tyler can live here one day, or you can turn it into a bed-and-breakfast. There are good memories here and bad ones. But it's just a house, so you can do what you want with it."

Sydney felt an overwhelming need to hug her mother and weep over her, but Carolyn had already turned and trudged from the room.

Chapter Twenty-Four

"Can you bring out that plate of hamburgers, Sydney? The grill's about ready." Tyler opened the lid to the grill, and a billow of smoke enveloped his head. He stepped back and coughed, waving smoke away.

"Yes, Chef. Coming right up." Sydney pulled herself out of the wicker Papasan chair on Tyler's patio and slipped into her flip flops. She brought out the plate of hamburgers and bratwurst from the kitchen and set it on the side table of the grill.

The summer air was temperate as the sun began its descent, spreading mauve and orange across the sky. Jessie and Zach were hitting a badminton birdie back and forth in the thick grass beyond the patio. Their shrieks of laughter ribboned up into the sky.

"Can I help with anything?" She stood close to Tyler, enjoying his nearness, even if he was distracted with proper placement of each piece of meat on the grill. He finished his task and pulled down the lid, then turned to gather her into an embrace. "Yes, you can help me get more of you." He kissed her lightly, then came back again for a deeper kiss.

"Hey, none of that, you guys," Jessie called out from the yard. Sydney and Tyler turned toward their kids and laughed.

"Thanks for making dessert for Zach's party."

"Oh, it was a pleasure. I've discovered I enjoy baking. I never had time before. And it's a special occasion, even though it's sad for Jessie and happy-sad for Zach." Sydney crossed her arms and cast a glance toward them. Zach made a leap for the birdie, swinging high in the air, and slammed it toward Jessie. Sydney's world felt complete as she panned a gaze over the three of them. "Is Zach ready to leave on Tuesday?"

Tyler shrugged. "He seems to be. His mother has gotten some things he needed, bedding, stuff like that. He'll live in the dorms the first year, and after that maybe get an apartment once he meets some other guys. Seems weird to think of him living in an apartment, cooking for himself. I hope that doesn't happen too soon."

Sydney laughed softly. "I understand. You're a year ahead of me and I dread it already. But the dorms are a good idea to start out."

She'd set the table, prepared the drinks, and gotten the condiments ready. That afternoon after church, she and Jessie had decorated the back deck and part of the fence with helium balloons and streamers. Jessie had made a poster with Zach's name in large letters with the words "Now you're a college dude. Good Luck!"

Sydney returned to her comfy chair to observe, pulling up her legs to lean on them. It had been four days since the debacle with her brothers, which confirmed her feelings about them. Despite their toxic words, no black sheep residue stayed with her. It was as though something had broken inside, and she'd been set free from caring what they thought or if she'd ever have a meaningful relationship with either one of them. They weren't her kind of people, anyway.

Since that day, she'd been busy. She'd registered Jessie at the same high school where she and Tyler had attended, reserved a moving company in Charlotte and a storage unit in Kennessey, and found a rental agency to manage her home for the coming year or until she decided what to do with it. It felt good to have made concrete steps toward moving, even though there was a lot yet to do.

After a festive dinner, everyone helped clear the dishes. Sydney and Tyler cleaned up in the kitchen while Jessie and Zach continued their badminton. Sydney wanted them to spend as much time together as they could.

As night fell, they all went inside. Sydney brought the dessert, a chocolate chip cookie pie, Zach's favorite, and a stack of small plates into the living room. She'd stenciled his name in icing across the top of the pie.

After they ate, Jessie stood and announced, "Ahem! I wrote a going-away song for Zach to remember me by." She looked at Zach, suddenly sheepish, and added, "I'll get my guitar and sing it for you, Zach."

"You did?" Sydney leaned forward in surprise. Jessie took after her mom and grandfather. "Can't wait to hear it."

"Don't expect too much." Jessie disappeared from the room and returned with her guitar. She'd become more self-assured playing in front of people in the last month or so. Sydney, too, was gaining back her confidence with her almost daily practice sessions.

"Here goes." Jessie finished tuning and pulled a sheet of paper in front of her. She cleared her throat. She played a chord to start, then began singing, her voice clear and strong.

"This is a song I wrote just for Zach."
Have fun in college, but please hurry back.
We had such a great summer. Don't ever forget.
Jessie, your best friend ever, I'm willing to bet.
I'm willing to bet.

We talked until late. We laughed at our jokes
We even had fun when we were with our folks.
We like the same movies, we loved the same songs.
Even without that, we'd sure get along.
We'd sure get along.

I'll miss you a lot when you go to school.
You must keep in touch, that is my rule.
You can make other friends, that's okay with me
But your best friend forever is in Kennessey.
Your best friend forever is in Kennessey."

When she finished with a broad grin directed at Zach, everyone applauded. Zach laughed and said, "That's awesome! No one's ever written a song for me. Thanks, Jessie. I won't forget my *bestie*. Isn't that what you girls say?"

They all laughed. Jessie said, "Yeah. Sounds funny coming from you, though."

"That was amazing, Jessie. I'm so proud of my girl!" Sydney clapped her hands.

"Your turn, Mom. Play something." Jessie thrust her guitar into Sydney's hands, catching her off guard.

"Me? I'm not ready to play."

"Sure, you are. I've heard you play. You've improved a lot. I guess it's all your earlier talent coming back to you." Jessie's grin beseeched her.

Sydney made a face. "You think? I've forgotten about seventy-eight percent of it."

At that, Tyler laughed. "Do you remember the one based on Psalm twenty-five?"

"Not sure. Maybe some of the chords, but definitely not all the words." She hummed a few notes and bent her head to find her place on the fingerboard. She started strumming, changing chords, and a few of the lyrics came back. "*Show me the right path, O Lord.*" Though she felt self-conscious at first, her concentration on the newly recalled lyrics took her awareness away from the rapt attention upon her.

"Point out the best plan, O Lord. My trust is in you, without you, oh what would I do, For you hold me tight in your hand."

As she played, she couldn't interpret the expression on Tyler's face, something between admiration and nostalgia. Jessie sat silently listening, and Zach followed her cue. She told them, "Here's the chorus:

All day long, all day long, my trust is in you
Morning, noon, evening too, my trust is in you
And when troubles come and blessings too
As they do for everyone
I'll still praise you for all you have done."

When Sydney finished, a second of silence hung in the air. She nodded a feigned bow, hoping humor would break her discomfort.

"That was amazing, Mom." Jessie's voice was soft. "You sing so pretty. And you *wrote* that song!"

"Your mom is very talented," Tyler said. He stood and went to the hall closet. When he returned, he carried a guitar case. "I'll join you and we'll see if we remember anything else." He briefly tuned his guitar and began a soft strum.

"Wherever you go, I'll be with you. I'll work through your life whatever you do. I'll guide your steps . . . Can't remember what comes next."

Sydney hummed a few more bars and finished his line. *"You can't fall down because I'm around. Always around."*

Sydney's voice blended in with his. As the refrain finished and their voices faded, his eyes locked with hers. This time, along with a warm stirring deep inside, there was a sense that they were building a foundation in the present. The past would bleed through once in a while and for the first time, that was okay. Now they had something greater than failure to build on.

ಃ   ಃ   ಃ

Temperatures early Sunday evening had dropped enough to permit Sydney to sit on the back screened-in porch, the same place where she'd had her encounter with God. She smiled at the memory then took her phone to dial her father's number.

"Hi, Dad, it's Sydney." Time to reach out. Forgive. Stop blaming.

"What a nice surprise." Her father sounded genuinely pleased.

After a few moments of exchanging news, Sydney said, "I have some great news, Dad. Jessie and I are moving to Kennessey."

"Oh, that's wonderful news, Sydney. It'll be so nice to be able to see you and Jessie more often."

"It's my fault we haven't seen each other more, Dad. I'm sorry we haven't visited as often as we should have over the years."

Her father paused. Then, "I'm as much to blame for that, Sweetie. It's easy to get caught up in things and time goes by. We can make up for lost time, can't we?" She heard a smile in his voice. His words hit a thirsty spot and she smiled back. "You're still my girl, you know."

His girl. She closed her eyes for a moment. "I haven't heard you say that in a long time. I'm glad it's still true." A couple tears slid down her cheeks. She'd almost forgotten the sound of those words.

"It's true and don't forget it." Her father chuckled. "Have you already moved?"

"Not yet. I've made a few arrangements."

"What about your job in Charlotte?"

"I quit. I was physically attacked by a student last spring and didn't feel safe anymore. And I'm tired of teaching."

"Oh, my. That's terrible. I'm glad you're okay. Good that you left. Well, you'll find something. You're smart and talented. If I hear of anything, I'll let you know."

Sydney grinned. She appreciated her dad's affirmation, after decades of not hearing it. But she'd been on the verge of making the same suggestion, that he keep his ear open for a job for her. Trying to apply Eden's advice of asking for help.

"Thanks, Dad." So much to say, so many years to recover. But they'd have that chance. Now, they'd have time.

‑ ‑ ‑

Jessie encircled Zach's neck with her arms one last time as her tears began to flow. Sydney's stomach clenched for her. Zach and Jessie had been nearly inseparable all summer, and now he was leaving. Tyler's SUV was packed with everything Zach had brought to Kennessey, minus a few things he planned to keep there for his visits.

Tyler left the car running and stepped toward Sydney as if he were conferring with her. "We'll just give them a minute."

Over his shoulder, he saw Zach kiss Jessie tenderly on the lips and hug her again. Maybe there was something there that would last. Jessie could certainly do worse.

Tyler returned to Zach's side. "Are you ready? We need to get on the road. We have a long drive."

Zach came to Sydney and hugged her. "Bye, Sydney. Good luck with moving."

"Thanks, Zach. I hope you enjoy college. And I hope you'll come back soon to visit."

"I will. I definitely will." This, he said to Jessie. He turned and climbed into the car, followed by Tyler. They both waved. Jessie and Sydney waved back, then watched the car disappear down the road.

Jessie cried softly. Sydney slipped an arm around her shoulders and pulled her close. "I'm sure you'll stay in touch."

"Yeah." Jessie sniffed and pulled tissues from the pocket of her shorts.

"Want to go to lunch somewhere?" Sydney stood back and challenged her with a smile.

Jessie nodded.

"And on our way, we'll drive by to see your new school."

Lunch appeared to cheer Jessie somewhat as she settled into her new reality. Zach had been good for Jessie, and Sydney was thankful. Aside from that, if Zach and Jessie hadn't become friends, Sydney might not have run into Tyler, and her present life would be completely different. She drew in a deep breath of thankfulness.

On the way home, Jessie's phone rang. Sydney couldn't stifle a grin as she heard Jessie say, "Tonight? Sure, I can come. I haven't been there, but I can find out where it is."

She looked to Sydney while she covered the phone with one hand. "Mom, can I go with a couple girls from church to see a movie tonight at six-thirty? It's not a bad one."

Sydney grinned. "Sure."

After Jessie hung up, Sydney said, "Isn't God good?"

"Yup. He knew just what I needed tonight."

That evening after supper, Sydney and her mother read in the living room. It had been a peaceful evening, a sample of many others to come. It felt good and right. Jessie had driven Sydney's SUV by herself for the first time to meet her friends. A clear step of faith for Sydney.

By that time, Tyler would have reached Alpharetta, where Zach's mother lived. Though Tyler and Daphne were divorced, they were amicable and were all going to dinner together, including Zach's stepfather. Tyler was staying in a nearby hotel and planned to head back the next day. He might not have a chance to call or text, since he had obligations. Sydney hadn't checked her phone all evening.

She went to the kitchen, where she'd left her phone on the counter. She scanned the face and saw that Tyler had left a text message. *We got here around four. I miss you already. I should be back tomorrow before five. I'll call between now & then. I love you.*

She smiled and drew one hand to her chest, still be overwhelmed by her relationship with Tyler, by God's grace in bringing them back together.

There was one message in voicemail she hadn't listened to yet. She put in her code and listened as her pulse ratcheted up a notch. "Hello, Sydney. This is Morgan, the social worker from Hanover Adoptions. We met last month. I'm happy to tell you that we got a letter from the Treadwells, Emma's adoptive parents. Let me know if you'd like to come to the office to pick it up or make other arrangements." She left her phone number.

Sydney's hand was moist as she gripped the phone. She set it back on the counter and stood still for a moment, letting the news wash over her. The Treadwells had responded. They hadn't taken very long. Her summer quest, the one she'd planned among others she hadn't, was about to come to fruition. The open circle regarding Emma would finally be closed.

Chapter Twenty-Five

Sydney glanced at Jessie across the breakfast table, nearly bursting with her news about the Treadwells, but she didn't have the heart to distract her from describing her evening with her new church friends. Warmth and gratitude swelled inside Sydney as she listened to the enthusiastic account of the movie and the snacks afterwards.

"So, I'll be meeting them after the service Sunday because the youth group is having a picnic at the Silver Lake Park. It's kind of welcome to fall thing, you know, kicking off the fall youth activities, since school's gonna start soon. Mom, when are we gonna get our stuff from the house in Charlotte? I need more clothes and other stuff to start school."

"Yes, I'm aware of that." Sydney took a final swig of her lukewarm coffee. "We have a moving truck scheduled in a week. I was planning to go supervise that, but you might want to come along to say goodbye to some of your friends. And see your dad, of course." Somehow, consulting with her ex-husband had never entered her mind during the recent tornado of events.

Jessie grew quiet for a moment as her old life collided with the new. She took a deep breath. "Okay. Good idea." She turned back to her cereal bowl.

Once Sydney was sure that Jessie was finished recounting her evening, she said, "Jessie, I have some news for you. We have a letter from the Treadwells."

Jessie's eyes grew round. "We do? That's fantastic, Mom! When can we go get it?"

"What about today? What's your work schedule?"

"I've worked a lot lately, so they said I could be off for a couple days."

On the way to Wilmington, Jessie was wired. Understandable, with her new friends, a letter from the Treadwells, and her imminent goodbyes in Charlotte. She chattered nonstop all the way. And she hadn't mentioned Zach but once that day.

Morgan was waiting for them when they arrived at Hanover Adoptions. Sydney's excitement was replaced by nerves as she waited with Jessie in the small conference room where they'd first talked about the Treadwells.

"Here it is. I haven't opened it, so I can't tell you what's in it, if there are photos, or anything else. You can open it whenever you want." She pulled a legal-size envelope from the file. By its thickness, it looked like there were several sheets of paper inside.

"Jessie, what do you think if we take it back to Kennessey and open it with Gram?"

Jessie nodded. "Yeah, I think she'd like that."

Sydney took the envelope as if it were made of fragile crystal and tucked it into her purse. "If we want to respond to the Treadwells or to Emma, should we bring the letter back here?"

"Yes, that way we can send it to them in our own envelope and that'll maintain confidentiality on both sides."

"Of course."

They thanked Morgan and returned to the car. Sydney pulled away from the curb and glanced at Jessie. "Well, I guess we've accomplished our quest."

They drove mostly in silence on the way home. When they entered the house, Sydney looked around for her mother. There was a note on the table. *Gone to a doctor's appointment. Be home by one.*

"We have to wait for Gram. Do you know if she's even interested in reading it?" Jessie leaned against the kitchen counter.

"No, not sure. I told her this morning we were going to pick up the letter. We'll ask her when she comes home. If you can wait that long."

And what about Tyler? He hadn't been as eager as Sydney to learn about Emma. He'd likely assumed she was in good hands and hadn't dwelt on the fact that somewhere he had a daughter. Or maybe he'd just wanted to forget.

As if reading her mind, her phone rang. It was Tyler. She left the kitchen and slipped into the dining room. "Hi, Sydney. I'm in the car about halfway across South Carolina. Just wanted to touch base and hear your voice."

Sydney smiled. Just hearing *his* voice gave her a stable feeling amidst the new possible turn of events facing her when she opened the letter. "I'm glad to hear yours. Did everything go okay with handing Zach off to Daphne?"

"Yes, we had a nice dinner last night. She's married to a friendly guy named Frank. He's never acted threatened or weird around me, so that's nice. Zach wasn't emotional, of course. Not on the outside, at least. He'll be fine. He'll make friends within about ten minutes."

Sydney laughed. "Yes, I can believe that. I think Jessie may be like that, too. Hey, Tyler. Yesterday I learned that the couple who adopted Emma, the Treadwells, had written us a letter in response to ours. We drove to Wilmington this morning to pick it up."

"And what did it say?"

"We haven't read it yet. Mom's at the doctor's and I wanted to ask her if she'd like to hear it with us. I—I don't know if you're interested in knowing what it says, but we can wait for you if you want. We could do it tonight or tomorrow.”

Tyler paused. “I’m not sure what to say yet, Sydney. Let me think about it, okay? Why don’t you read it with Jessie and your mom and when I see you again, we can talk about it.”

“Sure, that’s fine.” It hadn’t been his quest. It had been hers. But she had to admit she’d hoped he’d want to learn about Emma.

“Will I see you tonight?”

“I’m available, but I’m thinking you’ll be tired after driving seven hours. Do you want to rest, and we can meet tomorrow?”

“I’d love to see you, if you’re up for it. Could you come by at around seven? I’ll be home and refreshed by then, unless you’d rather wait until tomorrow.”

“Yes, I can come by. I won’t stay too late, though.” When they hung up, she felt a pinch of disappointment that he hadn’t been more eager to hear the letter. She decided to respect his choice, whatever it was. They’d had different ways of dealing with the issue from the start. She wouldn’t let it create a barrier.

Sydney had tried unsuccessfully to read, but her thoughts boomeranged all over the place in impatience to know what was in the letter. Thirty minutes later, she heard her mother come in the front door and lock it behind her. She shuffled through the front hallway. Sydney called, “Hey, Mom. How was your appointment?”

Carolyn stuck her head into the doorway of the living room. “Hi, Sydney. Doctor thinks the medication is doing me some good.” She came in and stood near the couch.

“Oh, that’s wonderful. What good news!”

“Hope the trend continues. What did you do today?”

“Jessie and I went to Wilmington to pick up the letter from the Treadwells. Remember, I told you last night?”

“Yes, I remember.”

"I wasn't sure if you wanted to hear it when we did, so we haven't read it yet. We were waiting for you."

"You haven't read it? I would think you would have done that first thing. No reason to wait for me. Well, as long as you did, I'll hear it with you. Let me put my things away first."

Minutes later, Jessie and Carolyn joined Sydney in the living room. Jessie sat next to Carolyn on the couch, and Sydney was near them in the wing-back chair. "Ready or not . . ." She pried the envelope open and pulled out several sheets of paper. Her heart thumped inside her chest. "There are two sheets here and some photos. One of the letters looks like it's from Emma." Her voice faded away as that knowledge swept over her. Her daughter had written her a letter.

She peered at one of the photos in the envelope. A photo of their family. Her breath hitched as she stared at it. In the photo, the Treadwells looked to be about forty years old. Their faces were pleasant. They looked like good people. The knot inside Sydney unwound just a little, yet she felt awed at the same time. Two school-age children, a boy and a girl, sat beside the couple. Sydney thought she could detect some of her features in the girl, like her straight, thick hair. Emma for sure had Tyler's nose and jaw.

"Can I see, Mom?" Jessie's patience reached its limit.

Sydney looked up at them. She handed the photo to Jessie, who shared it with her grandmother. "Oh, wow. That's my sister." Jessie grinned as she stared at the photo. "Gram, that's your granddaughter."

They both stared at the photo for several minutes as Sydney watched them. "Looks like Emma was around ten when that was taken. I'll read the Treadwells' letter first if you're ready."

When they nodded, Sydney began. "Are you both ready?" She moistened her lips.

"Dear Sydney and Jessie,

We were surprised but happy to receive your letter last month. When we first adopted Emma, we did wonder about the circumstances of her birth, and it's so nice that you shared that with us. We were close to thirty years old when we adopted her. We'd been unable to have another child after our son and waited on a list for a couple of years. We were overjoyed to be able to adopt Emma and be her parents. It was wonderful to raise Emma. She's bright and articulate and has always had so many interests.

Emma had a normal childhood, plenty of friends, and she loved to learn—about everything. As she grew up, she became a lovely young woman. I won't give you all the details of her childhood here, but she was active in the youth group at church as well as some sports in school. We live in Michigan, so she went to a small college here and studied horticulture. She always loved plants growing up, so it didn't surprise me that she chose to study them in college. She's now married and lives nearby. The wonderful news is that she's expecting her first child.

I hope that answers some of your questions. I know I haven't been very detailed, but it's a start. I did give your letters to Emma. She was happy to read them. She has written to you herself and enclosed a current photo.

From here, I guess it's between you all what kind of contact you'd like to have. Best wishes to you both. Sincerely, Monica Treadwell."

Sydney looked up at her mother and Jessie to see their reactions. Jessie's eyes were round. "She's gonna have a baby. Did you hear that? Gram, you're gonna be a great grandmother."

Carolyn frowned. "Makes me sound like I'm a hundred years old."

Sydney laughed. "What about me? I'm not ready to be a grandmother yet. Let's see what Emma said in her letter. Here's her photo. Let me look at it first then I'll give it to you."

As Sydney looked at the photo, the direct gaze of her daughter startled her, as though a determined, somewhat feisty personality was shining through. Like her mother. She couldn't suppress a grin. Emma's hair was shoulder-length and thick, like Sydney's. Her resemblance to Sydney was more marked as an adult. In the photo, her pregnancy wasn't showing. Next to her stood a pleasant-looking man dressed conservatively, as if he'd just come from work.

Sydney passed the photo to Jessie. "That's what she looks like now."

"That's my sister," murmured Jessie. "And I'm gonna be an aunt." She passed the photo to her grandmother.

"I'll read Emma's letter now.

Dear Sydney,

It's strange to be writing this letter, but it makes me happy too. After reading your letter, I understood a lot of how I came to be adopted. Being adopted was never a problem for me because I knew I was loved by my parents, and they considered me fully theirs. I wasn't a child who pined to know about her birth parents, so I didn't think much about it, but when your letter came, I was glad to know more about you.

I just turned thirty in July and I'm expecting my first baby. I've been married for two years to Joel, who works as a computer programmer. I was working at a local bureau of agriculture until my second trimester of pregnancy then resigned so I can stay with my child, who is due in December. Joel and I are excited about being parents.

I'm open to occasional contact by letter. That would be a nice way to get to know you better. Again, thank you for reaching out and I hope it was a blessing for you as it was for me. Best regards, Emma."

By the time Sydney finished reading, a painful knot throbbed in her throat. She swallowed. "She sounds really sweet, doesn't she?"

Jessie nodded but looked despondent. "She didn't say anything about me."

"Oh, there's another letter in the envelope. This is for you, Jessie. Want to read it?"

Jessie's face lit up. She took the page from Sydney and straightened up a little taller. "She says,

Hello, Jessie,
Thanks for writing to me and helping me get to know you better. It's nice to have a half-sister! I only grew up with a brother.' Smiley face. 'I was in the church youth group, too. I never played an instrument, but I was in sports at school. Do you play any sports? I gave a lot of that up, but still play tennis. After the baby is born, I'll get back to it. Feel free to write to me if you want to. I would enjoy hearing from you. Take care, Jessie."

Jessie looked up at Sydney. "That's so cool that she wrote to me, my own letter. My sister." She took a breath. "Doesn't sound like she wants to meet me, though."

Sydney leaned forward in her chair. "She *does* sound interested in getting a letter, though. It's a start, Jessie. A month ago, she didn't know she had a sister. You might have a chance to meet her in the future." Or maybe it would drift away, the initial contact having been made. Time would tell.

And they'd both have plenty on their plates in the near future.

ℭ   ℭ   ℭ

Sydney drove toward Tyler's house, nerves and anticipation wrestling for control inside her. Eager to see him, yet unsure of his response to the letter. Would it be something they could share, or had he dismissed Emma long ago?

Ten minutes later, she pulled into his driveway under the canopy of pine trees. It was a peaceful place, and the pine needles on the ground added a layer of silence. A golden light shone out from the living room window and the porch light.

Before she reached the porch steps, Tyler came through the front door and met her on the sidewalk, encasing her in a warm hug. Strength from that hug flowed through her, feeding her thirst. He followed that with a long, searching kiss that left her breathless. "You sure know how to make a gal feel welcome, Tyler Hoffman."

He chuckled and kissed her again. After pulling back, he said, "I missed you, Sydney Davis. What'll I do when you go back to Charlotte to pack up your life there?"

"I know what you'll do." Her hands pressed against his warm chest. His arms still looped around her waist. "You'll thank your lucky stars that the reason I'm gone is to pack up and move back *here*." She grinned at him, then lowered her eyes in a coy glance. "Then we can have lots of time together."

They turned to go into the house, his arm still around her waist. She asked, "How was your drive back from Georgia?"

"Boring and very long. Made tolerable by thoughts of you and a couple podcasts." He smiled down at her as they entered the house. "But I was glad to get Zach settled. He's crossing a threshold, and it feels good to see him at this point. We prepare our kids to get educated and eventually go out and live their adult lives. We miss them but know they're in the right place."

She followed him into the kitchen and waited as he poured them some sparkling water. "You'll have to remind me of that again next year when Jessie goes to college." At least Sydney had one more year before crossing that line. "Right now, I don't think I'd be ready to let her go."

"Have you raised her alone all these years?" Tyler handed her a glass and gestured to the deck in the backyard.

"Mostly. My ex, Cody, and I decided not to do split custody." They sat down, side by side, on the wicker couch. The air was like a warm breath on Sydney's bare arms. She pulled her feet up and crossed them. "That suited him okay because he's remarried. Jessie goes to her dad's every other weekend and some holidays. It's worked out pretty well. I haven't told him yet about the move. It all came about so fast. Guess I have to do that." She frowned. She'd tell Cody the move was what Jessie wanted, which would take some heat off of Sydney.

"I hope he's okay with it."

Silence fell for a moment between them. Sydney wondered if he was thinking about the letter or if he'd forgotten all about it. She didn't want to bring it up if he wasn't open, but he said he'd think about it. Did that mean for days, or only for hours? She'd have to ask but didn't want to.

Tyler let out a long sigh. "I've been thinking about the letter from Emma's adoptive parents, and I—I'd like to hear it." His warm gaze found hers. Relief filled Sydney.

"It's here in my purse. I can let you read it, or I can read it to you. There are photos, too."

"Oh, good. I'll let you read it."

"There's one for me from Emma herself, too. I'll read both. Jessie had written her own letter, and Emma responded to her individually. That made her happy."

Tyler grinned, though his face seemed laced with tension. "I'll bet."

He fell silent as she pulled the sheets of paper from the envelope. "Here goes." She read the letter from the Treadwells, then the one from Emma to Sydney. As she read, she glanced at his face from time to time. The shade of stiffness that had been there when she started reading gradually melted and, in its place, his jaws relaxed into a soft half-smile. When she finished, she folded the papers and glanced up at him. His eyes glistened with unshed tears.

He shook his head and swiped his eyes with the back of his wrist. "Wow. Don't know what else to say." He chucked then blinked. He shook his head and swallowed. "Our daughter. It'll take a minute for all this to sink in. She was theory before. Now, she's not."

"I forgot. We have photos. She'll be less theoretical."

Tyler took the photos from her hand and studied them for several minutes. As he did, the moisture that had begun in his eyes trickled down his cheeks. He gave them back to her. "It's as though that situation has come full circle and it's become something that feels good instead of bad. Know what I mean?"

Sydney nodded vigorously. "I do. Especially now. I don't know why I decided to reach out when I did, but it became like a mission for me to learn about her. I had no expectation that I'd ever hear from her, but I just wanted to learn what happened. But now that she's responded, it's like a link has been closed. We may never meet her, but we know about her and she's a real person. We know what happened, and it's good. She had a good life and seems to be a decent person. That gives me so much satisfaction, Tyler. I can't explain it."

He nodded. "Me, too. Thank you, Sydney, for pursuing this. I'll admit, I wasn't too keen on the idea at first. It was well packed-away for me and had been for years. That may be the wrong attitude, but I confess, that's the way I felt."

Sydney reached for his hand. "I think it's cool the way we were able to see resolution in this issue before going further in our relationship together. But in God's view, maybe it wasn't so much a prerequisite as it was a—" she groped for words, "—a package of grace." Her voice dropped. "A whole package of forgiveness, redemption, and grace that included Emma, my mom, my brothers—and of course, you."

She stopped as the realization flooded over her, each piece of the puzzle and how it had fallen into place. In response to her statement, Tyler leaned forward and took her head gently in his large hands. His eyes met hers, then searched her face before he tipped her chin up to kiss her. His kiss said more than the previous one on the porch had. That kiss had said he'd missed her. This kiss said they'd traveled a long, hard journey together and apart, and God in his grace had healed the broken places and restored them fully.

Instead of being locked in a closet of shame and avoidance, the past was woven into the present where it would take a back seat but add threads of grace to the future. Sydney settled against Tyler's chest as his arms wrapped around her. He kissed the top of her head and leaned his cheek there. Somehow, against all odds and the foibles of their humanity, all those things had worked together for good.

And now, the present and future looked *very* good.

I hope you enjoyed reading *Sydney Rewound*. If you did, please consider leaving a review at the online store where you bought it. It would help other readers discover my books and be encouraged by their inspiring truths. You can also sign up to receive updates about new books at www.Kyle-Hunter.com where you'll receive *Marissa Rewritten* (first book in this series) free just for signing up!

For more romantic stories that take you places . . .

Second Chance Series

In *The Second Chance Series*, you'll meet Marissa, Julia, Sydney, and Eden, four college friends who, twenty-five years later, renew their friendships as they find themselves empty nesters and single again. You'll love getting to know these women and following each one in her own book.

Marissa Rewritten (Book 1) A Novella

Author Marissa Thompson has had a writer's block since her husband died almost two years earlier. Her three closest friends are a comfort. Despite this, things are getting urgent as her career hangs by a thread and repairs on her historic home mount up. Prodded by desperation, Marissa heads to Wilmington, North Carolina for a Civil War research trip. She hopes for inspiration, but receives encouragement from a surprising source, a feisty character from her last novel.

Jarrod Lambert has already lost his wife. He's always been close with his college-age daughter, but she seems to be slipping further away from him. In an effort to reconnect with her, he makes an impulsive trip to see her in Wilmington.

Through an accident, Marissa and Jarrod meet and discover common ground. Will it be enough to overcome the obstacles standing between them?

Julia Redesigned (Book 2)

Can a stack of letters provide clues to an age-old conflict and a doorway to a new family?

For the last three years, Julia De Luca has juggled her successful interior design business with caring for her elderly mother. Following her mother's death, Julia finds old letters from distant relatives in Italy. They remind her of visits she and her mother made when Julia was a child. Could these letters hold the answer to why their trips to Italy ended abruptly when she was ten years old?

These people whose names she's forgotten are the only family Julia has left on earth. How can she reconnect with them after so many years? Would it be crazy to try?

Her compelling desire to locate her distant family leads Julia on an impulsive trip to Florence, Italy. Along with savoring the sights and flavors of Florence, Julia discovers that families can be messy, that it's not too late to fall in love, and that there's more to Julia De Luca than she ever knew.

Romance in Provence Series

The Provence Series takes you with Bree and Lauren, best friends and business partners, to one of the loveliest regions of France. It's not always idyllic in the land of lavender fields and cliffside villages. Join Bree and Lauren as each woman discovers her unique journey—and surprising romance.

Prodigals in Provence (Bree's story) #1

Bree and Lauren own and run Le Bon Voyage, a travel company specializing in tours to charming Provence, France.

Travis is a TV travel critic accustomed to crossing the globe to film documentaries and write books. But he's been in a spiritual desert ever since losing his marriage and ministry five years earlier.

Between film projects, Travis plans to accompany his elderly mother on a tour to Provence, a long-term dream for her. Bree tries unsuccessfully to block him, sure he's coming to spy on the struggling company for an exposé article.

A diverse group of tourists arrives at the rented villa to spend the week and discover the spectacular villages, vineyards, and history of the Luberon mountain region of Provence. Amidst a series of problems and relational tensions, Bree thinks she has all she can handle . . . until she becomes attracted to Travis.

As Bree and Travis are drawn together, will their hidden wounds drive them apart?

A Promise in Provence (Lauren's story) #2

Lauren is at a turning point. If only she knew *where* to turn. Her long-term relationship with Mark is fading fast. Instead, she feels drawn to Jean-Pierre, an attractive Frenchman she'd met the previous summer. When she's laid off from her job as a chef, she decides to go see him in Provence, France.

Mark can't get Lauren out of his heart, even though it's been close to a year since she asked him to give her space. When she goes to France, he's afraid he'll lose her for good. That is, until he decides to go there, too, as a last-ditch effort to win her back.

At first, Lauren is angry that Mark follows her to France. But a joint desire to help a young refugee boy leads them to work together. Lauren finds herself torn between the two men. Worse, she's confronted with obstacles in helping the boy and even greater obstacles within herself.

Stand Alone Novels that take you places . . .

One December

Is there any way to recapture what happened under the moon one December?

Nikki has loved Mike for as long as she can remember. Mike has his own past hurts to resolve, having lost both parents when he was fourteen. He's tried to escape the memories by starting a new life on the West Coast.

At Christmas, he comes back to New York for the first time in three years. He and Nikki rekindle the friendship they had as children and share their newfound faith. Under a Christmas moon, romantic sparks fly...but their mutual attraction takes an unexpected detour.

Nikki is devastated, believing the romance is over. She impulsively takes a one-year teaching opportunity in Paris to face her own fears and to get over Mike.

If they think they can run away from each other, they'd better think again.

"*One December* sizzles with romantic tension, taking the reader on a roller-coaster ride from New York to San Francisco, with a delightful detour in Paris. I couldn't put it down!"

– Elizabeth Musser, author of *The Secrets of the Cross* trilogy and *The Swan House*.

Circle Back Around

Hailey and her father haven't always seen eye to eye, especially in running the failing family textile mill. Frustrated, Hailey leaves the mill and her hometown in North Carolina to start a new life near her sister in Colorado. Only months later her father calls to ask a special favor. He needs heart surgery and asks Hailey to run the mill in his place.

Moving back would devastate Hailey's sister, Hope. Yet Hailey would have an opportunity to possibly save the mill, and at a time when her father needs her most. And maybe he'd even approve of her for the first time in her life.

Filled with self-doubt, Hailey returns to North Carolina and struggles to make a difference at the mill, facing more challenges than she bargained for. Her attractive neighbor, Alex, is almost enough to outweigh the difficulties, but she doesn't know that in the shadows lurks someone who wants to destroy both her *and* the mill.

Read Chapter One of all books at
www.Kyle-Hunter.com

Kyle Hunter writes inspirational romance and women's fiction that sometimes take her characters to faraway places. She lived in France for thirteen years. Currently, she lives in North Carolina where she writes fiction, non-fiction (under the pen name K. B. Oliver) and the travel blog OliversFrance.com and teaches French to adults.